RETURNING TO RAVENS RIDGE

A SECOND CHANCE MOTORCYCLE CLUB ROMANCE

THE RAVENS RIDGE RIDERS
BOOK 1

DJ LAVELY

RAVENS RIDGE
RIDERS

 Formatted with Vellum

It's not what isn't; it's what you wish was that makes unhappiness.
-Janis Joplin

INTRODUCTION

Dear Reader,

Let me start by saying if you're reading this, thank you for being here. I've been waiting a long time to share it with you. Returning To Ravens Ridge is the first book in The Ravens Ridge Riders series. This series touches on topics that may be sensitive to some readers as it deals with issues like addiction, abuse, violence, and grief. Please check your trigger warnings. I understand that some of the characters in this story react and cope with situations in a way that may not be what would be considered "normal." But that's reality, right? I hope you love them anyway. Lastly, I want to remind you that this is a work of complete fiction. Any resemblance to any organization or person is completely coincidental.

Thank you again for being here.
    -DJ

1

ASH

MARCH PRESENT DAY

My entire life, I've longed for someone to make me their priority. I wanted to be chosen, not because they felt obligated, but because they couldn't stand to live without me. When I walked down the aisle the day of my wedding, all I could think was *finally*. He didn't *have* to buy me a ring. He didn't *have* to get down on one knee. He didn't *have* to stick around.

But Casey did.

Now, I sit across from the same man while he tries to explain how he could possibly choose someone else over me. It'd almost be comical if he wasn't blowing up my life with every word.

Almost.

"Ashton, did you hear me?"

I snap out of my daze, looking up from the dark cherry desk to the man I've spent the last five years building a life with. He runs a hand through his perfectly swept, light brown hair.

"I'm not sure? Did you really call me into your office in the middle of the workday to tell me you're leaving me for your receptionist?" Blood rushes to my ears. "*Now* of all times?"

He exhales, adjusting his navy-blue suit jacket. It's the one I picked up from the dry cleaners yesterday.

Because *I* pick up his dry cleaning.

Not her.

No, she's probably busy fucking my husband while I run his errands.

His normally pale skin, now sun-kissed from a recent work trip to the Keys, flushes red. "I just wanted you to know the truth. It's not that I don't love you, I do. I—"

"Love her more?"

"I didn't mean for it to happen." He spins his chair to stare out the floor-to-ceiling windows behind him. The view from the fifth level of this building is breath taking. Puffy white clouds float through the ocean of sky. In the movies, bad days always take place in the middle of a thunderstorm or during overcast at the very least—not in the midst of clear skies and sunshine. What a perfect backdrop for the worst day of my life.

When he turns back, his vacant eyes fall on me. I used to love the way he looked at me—like I was the most captivating person he'd ever seen.

Something flickers in Casey's whiskey-colored irises anytime he catches a glimpse of something he has to have. It happened when we went to the dealership and picked out his brand-new cherry-red Porsche, and it happened when we locked eyes for the first time. It was one of the things that made it so easy to fall for him in the first place.

Who doesn't want to feel like you've changed someone's life just by existing?

He's not looking at me like that now, though. "I'm sorry. I didn't mean for this to happen."

My brows raise. "Well, I guess there's nothing else to say, is there?"

He fidgets with a pen.

"Where's your ring?"

For the first time since we got married, he's not wearing it. Did he take it off this morning? Or was it right before he decided to call me in here? Is it tucked away in his desk drawer? Has he been taking it off every time he has sex with her behind my back?

His eyes snap up, and a crease forms between his brows. "Why would I keep it on?"

He says it like it was a silly question, and I guess maybe it was, but damn... Who takes their ring off before they ask for a divorce? Doesn't that feel like something that should come after?

I spin my gaudy-ass ring around my finger.

When he proposed, I was so in love he could have done it with a zip tie, and I'd have said yes. But the ring he bought me is too big, over the top, and not my style. I never admitted that even to myself until now, but I hate the stupid thing. It feels like it's burning through my flesh.

Sliding it off, I toss it at him like it might bite me.

It plinks off a picture sitting near his open laptop. It's from our daughter Maggie's first birthday. He's holding her with the biggest smile plastered on his face, and I'm behind him, resting my chin on his shoulder.

His eyes are on her, and my eyes are on him.

He sighs. "I don't want you to hate me."

I half laugh, dragging my eyes from the photo to him. "Maybe you should have thought about that before you screwed the receptionist. You *definitely* should have before you fell in love with her."

I wish there was more bite to my voice, more hatred, but

instead it just sounds pathetic. Like how a child might sound when no one chooses them to be on their kickball team in PE. Not mad, just embarrassed and rejected.

I don't hate him. I couldn't. I'm so utterly in love with this man that I might actually throw up. If I thought it'd make a difference, I'd get down on the floor and beg him to change his mind.

But I've begged a man to stay before and all it got me was a big ol' scoop of humiliation to go with my broken heart.

He rests his forearms on the desk. His gold watch taps against the wood.

It feels like I should be crying right about now, but no tears well in my eyes.

I clear my throat. "Maggie will be crushed."

He twists his mouth to bite the inside of his cheek. "I'll be around. It's not like splitting up makes me any less her dad. Whatever we have to do, we'll make it work for her."

Whatever we have to do? How about don't screw women who aren't her mother? That would work.

Oh, too late.

I should yell at him, right? I should stand up and tell him that he's a piece of shit, or say fuck you for doing this to our family and fuck her too. I should pick up the papers on his desk and throw them. Maybe slap him.

But I don't. With a curt nod, I mutter, "Okay."

"I'm gonna stay at my brother's for a while. So, you have time to find a place."

Something cracks, but I don't know if it's my heart or my sanity.

I laugh. Not a little giggle—a full-blown maniacal laugh. He stares at me like I've lost my mind, and maybe I have.

My pulse rages, and I stop. "Thank you *so much* for being *so* considerate after blowing up my life."

"I didn't mean—"

"Shut up! Okay?" My hands fly up. "Stop talking. I'll be out of your house, and you and your little girlfriend can have it all to yourselves."

I storm toward the door, pressure building in my chest. My only thought—*get the hell out of here.*

Before leaving, I add, "Oh, and I quit."

I slam the door behind me, and every head in the office turns in my direction. *Do they know?*

I didn't even have to continue working at his stupid record label after we got married. I only did because I genuinely liked working here. Now it feels like the place is swallowing me whole.

I take a deep breath and glare at the receptionist, who seems to be busy staring at her computer screen to avoid my dirty look. Wouldn't it be fun to run over there and rip every brown hair out of her stupid head? I could get a good fistful of it and slam her face on the desk.

She wouldn't be so pretty with her perfect little button nose smashed in, would she?

Holy shit, Ash. Get a grip.

Since I'm not completely off my rocker yet, I flip her off and stomp to my desk instead.

Let him have her. She's probably terrible.

I groan, flopping down in my chair because I know she's not. I've been working with Rachel for two years. She's fucking delightful—a backstabbing, homewrecking, delightful *bitch.*

Grabbing my purse from the bottom drawer, I shove the pictures scattered across my desk into it. It's strange, for years, this place has been my second home. Now, I'm an outcast.

When I'm done, the only thing left is our wedding picture sitting atop the otherwise empty surface. I zip up my purse and stand, roll my shoulders, and lift my chin. *One foot in front of the other. I can do this.*

My skin crawls as eyes track my departure, but I don't falter.

I can't tell if they're staring at me out of pity or curiosity. It doesn't matter; I'd rather they mind their own business. But that's not how this works.

If they didn't know, they do now. Gossip about how he chose a prettier woman over his wife and child will twist and wind through the office for the next few days, and eventually it'll be like I was never here.

It will be him and her.

One day, no one will remember that I was here first.

When I make it to the elevator, I keep my head held high and my shoulders straight.

If I could fall to the floor and cry, I would. But the last thing I need is for the busy bodies to be talking about how I was dumped, then had a meltdown in front of the whole damn building. Instead, I'm determined to get to the car first.

That, however, feels like quite a feat.

It's not the hurt—I can handle that. It's the upending of my life. It's the complete destruction of the vision I had for my future—for Maggie's future. We'll still be her parents, but she'll be shuffled back and forth, changing her reality. Her dreams will change. Everything will change. That's what feels unbearable.

Having your dreams ripped out of your hands is like having someone dump you in the middle of the desert.

That walk back to civilization sucks. It's hard and lonely. It causes your feet to ache and your mind to wander through everything you could have done differently. And when an occasional man on a Harley rides by, you get your hopes up that someone's come for you. But they never stop.

You just keep walking.

It's not until you finally make it back and have that first sip of water that you begin to see a new life.

Casey was my sip of water last time.

I don't know if I have another long walk in me. The gut-wrenching, toe-curling pain when the person you love no longer wants you is something I never expected to feel again.

I suck air into my lungs in sharp breaths, trying my hardest to gain some semblance of composure before the elevator finishes its descent.

Of course, it's the shortest elevator ride of my life. The doors couldn't have just given me a few more moments. Although there probably aren't enough minutes in a week to make me okay at this point.

What I need is a glass of wine and maybe a good tantrum.

Stepping off the elevator, I race down the hall. At least the people on this floor don't have any idea what's going on upstairs at Jamesview Sound. For all they know, I'm just in a hurry.

Flinging the glass doors open, I rush into the warm North Carolina sun. Normally, I love Raleigh in March—cool mornings and sunny afternoons.

But today it doesn't matter what the temperature is because I'm on fire.

I can't seem to get away fast enough. I'm not sure why,

considering my options are this office and the house I no longer have any desire to call mine.

I meant it when I said, "I do." I figured he'd meant it, too.

Silly me.

Men don't mean anything they say. They choose themselves. Those are facts that I know to be true.

Finally reaching my stuffy black Escalade, I rip open the door and climb inside.

It was a birthday gift from Casey when we first got married. He thought it was an upgrade from my beat-up red Jeep. I never said anything because I didn't want to seem ungrateful, but I loved my Jeep. Letting her go broke my heart.

My head falls back against the leather, and I suck in a deep breath. My chest rises and falls in rapid heaves. My palms sting from clenching my fists so tight my nails dig into the flesh.

Collecting myself, I flip on the air conditioning and pull out of the lot.

I sniff away the tears. I'm supposed to be angry. My fingers tighten around the steering wheel.

I'm not sad, I'm pissed. I'm not sad, I'm pissed. I'm not sad, I'm—

Fuck!

A singular tear breaks free, rolling down my cheek.

2

———

ASH

MARCH PRESENT DAY

When I left my house this morning, it was my home. The hardwood floors in the entryway that I picked out. The eight-person maple farm table in the kitchen that Casey had made after I saw one in a movie. The fireplace he had fixed before we moved in because I'd told him once I love a cozy fire in the fall.

All of it was mine when I headed to work, and now it feels foreign. I don't belong there anymore either.

Isn't that something?

I stood at our gas stove last night making popcorn for Maggie and me before we curled up to watch Dancing with the Stars. When Casey still wasn't home, I washed my face and crawled into her bed. I didn't worry about where he was. I assumed he'd been working late.

Did he even come home last night?

I thought he'd left for work before I got up. He does that sometimes. But he could have stayed with her last night.

He could have been staying with her many nights.

God, I'm an idiot. How did I not notice?

Now, I can't stop running over every time he worked late or was out of town, searching my memory for clues of his affair.

When I got to the house, I knew I couldn't stay. Add it to the list of places I no longer love. So, I grabbed what we'd need and hightailed it out of there. My mom picks Maggie up from preschool on Fridays, so thank God I have the rest of today to get my shit together.

As the doorbell chimes to my stepsister's townhouse, I can't help but chuckle at the familiar feeling of running to her for comfort. She's been that since my mom married her dad, Denny, when we were twelve. We're older now, but misery is misery no matter how much we grow up.

Will Jess and I lie in bed tonight while she wipes my tears and tells me that he wasn't worth it? Will she drag me from the house in a few weeks to do something fun to get my mind off him? Will I sneak away to call him in the middle of the night? Maybe he'll answer.

My stomach churns.

What if he doesn't?

"Ash?" Her brows pinch as she opens the door.

I didn't tell her I was coming because what would I say? Actually, I didn't really decide to come here as much as I just kind of showed up. Like my heart was leading the way because my mind was busy torturing itself with thoughts of my husband's hands on someone else.

When her deep brown eyes take in the mascara streaks on my face, they soften. "What's wrong?"

Oh, you know, the sky's falling, my life's over, men suck, and by the way, can I live with you?

She takes my suitcase and pulls me inside.

"Uh..." I swallow. The words don't want to come out. "I, um—"

"Hey, come here," she coos, wrapping an arm around me. My chin rests on her shoulder, and her lavender scent fills my nose. She's several inches taller than me, but I'm still in my work heels and she's barefoot, making the difference less noticeable.

"Casey's leaving me." As the words leave my mouth, they feel like they're coming from someone else. It's a strange out of body experience. It has to be, right? Because there's no way this is really my life. How can one person be unlucky enough to have their perfect house of cards knocked down twice?

She pulls back, her voice sharpening. "What? Are you kidding?"

"Nope," I say, popping the "P."

"So soon after—"

"Yup..."

The cherry on top? The one person in the world I could call who could make this even a little better, died a couple of weeks ago. Gran was always my safe space, and now...

"What the hell. Are you okay?"

"Uh..." There it is—the burning behind my eyes creeps in, and a lump forms in my throat. "I don't think so."

She sets my suitcase down on the bottom step of the staircase before motioning to the living room.

"Wine?" She pulls a blue scrunchie from her wrist to wrap around her long dark waves.

Nodding, I trail her through the living room into the open kitchen.

I saddle up at the island, ready to drown whatever feelings are trying to bubble up in my stomach.

She pulls a bottle from the fridge. I flinch when she drives the corkscrew into the top, feeling the similarity to what Casey just did to my heart. He might as well have driven his hand into my chest and pulled it out. It's sure as hell not in my body anymore despite the pounding I've been listening to since I left his office.

I'm convinced it's a phantom pulse because it can't possibly be the actual organ.

She slides a glass to me.

The tears finally dried up about halfway here, but it wouldn't take much to turn them back on. I'm not tough. Tears come easily and overstay their welcome. It's anger I struggle with. I want to be mad. I want to hate the people who hurt me. I want to hold a grudge so fierce that you'd fear bursting into flames. But I can't. Forcing those emotions feels like I'm a rubber band being stretched too far.

She leans forward, resting her elbows on the granite. "So, what happened? You guys always seem so happy."

I scoff. "Oh, that's the best part. He's been fucking the receptionist."

"Wait, what?"

"Yep." I laugh even though it's not a bit funny. "I guess he *loves* her."

My eyes stay on the wine swirling in the glass as I bring it to my lips.

"You have to be shitting me."

My brows lift as I suck down as much of the liquid as I can in one gulp.

Setting the glass down, I say, "Oh, and he told me in the office with her right outside the room."

She probably knew he was about to do it. I keep picturing the two of them leaving the office together after I stormed out.

How long had he been telling her he was going to end it with me? God, how long have they even been sleeping together?

I didn't ask enough questions. I just sat there like an idiot. My brain turned to mush, and the only thing I could hear through the fog was *run, get out!* So, that's what I did.

"What a piece of shit! Did you kick her ass on the way out?"

When I don't answer, she huffs. "Of course you didn't. Did you even say anything? Please tell me you at least gave her a big old fuck you as you left."

"I flipped her off."

She groans. "I guess that's better than nothing." With a sharp exhale, she shakes her head. "I wish you'd be a little meaner. I would've trashed the place on my way out."

I smile but it's half-hearted. "I thought about it."

"You should have. You can't let everyone walk all over you." She pulls a package of Oreos from the top cabinet, tossing them down between us. It's a nice gesture, but if I put one of those in my mouth, I'm going to barf. "You put him in his place about one time, and he'll think twice before fucking with you again."

I snort a laugh. "I don't know. It kinda felt like *what's the point*. He made his choice. Why drag it out?"

"Uh, because he hurt you." She rests a hand on the counter and props the other on her hip. "He deserves to suffer."

My chest grows heavy. Tears prick my eyes, and I try to blink them away but fail. One falls, landing on the back of my hand. "I don't want him to suffer. I want him to love me."

And I hate how pathetic that sounds. I'd do anything not to feel like this. I loved him when my eyes opened this morning, and despite his betrayal, I still love him. I don't know that you can ever *un*love someone.

But right now, the only thing that could pull the white-hot knife from my chest is him. If he'd change his mind, the curdling in my stomach would cease. We'd have to work through some shit, but the pain would be over.

My chin quivers, and I growl. I admit, it's not the most attractive noise I've ever made, but fuck it.

"Should we call Nik?" Jess asks.

"Absolutely not!" I wipe my cheeks with the heel of my palm. "She might murder him if she comes to town. Plus, she'll tell Shane, and then I'll have to listen to my big brother explain that he always knew Casey was a piece of shit."

She flicks a brow, muttering from behind her wine glass, "Like he has any room to talk."

"Right. You see why we can't call her then."

She grimaces. "I mean, it might be kind of fun to sic her on Casey. She'll fuck him up better than either of us could."

I cock my head. "I don't want her to fuck him up, Jess. That's the point I'm trying to make."

She throws up her hands defensively. "Alright. I get it. I'm just saying, you know you'd feel better with her here."

She's not wrong. Nik would absolutely make me feel better, but I have enough on my plate without my brother in the mix.

"The last thing I want is to drag anyone from Ravens Ridge into my mess. I'll tell them eventually, but not yet."

With a deep breath, she slaps the counter. "Well, you and Maggie are welcome to stay here as long as you need."

"Thank you."

"What are you gonna tell her?"

"I don't know." She refills my glass when I push it her way. "I can't even fathom breaking her heart like that."

She grimaces. "I mean, he's still her dad. And, as much

as I don't want to give him credit right now, he's always been a really good one. Divorced parents suck, but it's not the end of the world. I mean, look at *me*." She holds her hands out. "My parents did a great job, and they've been divorced the biggest part of my life."

"And what if he walks away?"

"Ash..." She reaches across the island and takes my hand. "He's not your dad."

I nod, rolling my lips under. "I just don't want her to feel like she's not wanted."

"I know. But I don't think she'll ever feel like that. No matter what happens, she has you, and there's no way she could deny how much you love her."

I let out a guttural sound before dropping my head to my hands. "I'm gonna have to tell my mother."

"Hey, maybe she'll promote Shane to the favorite and stay off your case for a while."

A real laugh escapes me. "I don't think even *that* could make him the favorite."

"Yeah. Probably not." Her laugh fades. "When I talked to Nik yesterday, she said he's doing really well."

"She always says that," I mutter.

"So, you don't think it's true?"

I shrug. "Who knows. Even if he is, it never lasts long. I love him, but I really doubt he's completely clean."

She eyes me like I'm going to take it back.

Do I feel bad for thinking that of my own brother? Of course, but hoping he'll turn things around only leaves me with disappointment. I want him to get better, and I'll love him forever. I just don't believe him when he says he's okay.

Jess turns to get another bottle of wine. My phone buzzes on the counter.

Unknown number.

My heart drops.

There's a pretty good chance I know who will be on the other end. If I'm right, that will be the last straw for today. I hit ignore and put my phone face down before she notices.

3

———

ASH

MARCH PRESENT DAY

Casey and I have to be separated a year before we can officially file for divorce, so I'll be his wife while *she* sleeps in his bed for at least that long. Bile rises in my throat every time I think about that fact.

Since moving out, I've spent the last three weeks wallowing on the couch. I've made my way through all the classics: crying myself to sleep, drunk dialing him at midnight, watching *Dirty Dancing* on repeat, and consuming nothing but Doritos.

I've done it all.

When I'm with Maggie is about the only time I feel okay. Something about her sweet face has the ability to make me almost forget the chaos that is my life. The rest of the time, I'm a mess.

Don't worry about him, though. He's wasted no time filling his Facebook with photos of the two of them on dates and at work functions. Not that I've been checking or anything.

Jess's sofa might have a permanent imprint of my butt

now. Every night when I crawl into bed, I tell myself *tomorrow will be the day I finally get up and brush myself off,* and every morning when I wake, the weight of doing that pulls me under, and I find myself right back in this spot on the couch.

Maybe tomorrow.

I don't get it. How can someone vow to spend the rest of their life loving you and then choose someone else?

Gran told me years ago that I deserve a man who wouldn't walk away from me. Her voice repeats through my head all day and night now.

But what if that never happens? What if they always walk away? How many times should I put myself in that position?

It feels like I'm creeping close to the limit.

Anytime I think about Gran, I want to cry. I used to stay with her every summer. She was my favorite person. She didn't want a funeral, so I just got a call that she was gone. That's it. I still don't think I've let it sink in. How could I? I'd barely scratched the surface of grief when Casey turned my life upside down.

We used to talk every morning while I was taking Maggie to school, but aside from the missing calls, everything continued as it was before.

I hate it.

Losing someone so monumental in your life should stop the world from turning, right? At least for a little bit. But that's not how it works. It leaves an aching hole in your chest, but no one can see it. No one else can feel it. The rest of the world goes on while rot spreads in your gut.

When it first happened, I would accidentally forget and call her in the morning only to remember at the sound of her voicemail.

So, maybe my permanent residence on my sister's couch is more than just heartache. It's the culmination of losing the love of my life and the person I'd have run to with my broken heart.

Because make no mistake, I would have called her, and she would have come to Raleigh right away.

My phone rings from where it sits beside me. It's another unknown number. I know answering it will only cause me more pain.

My dad does this. He disappears for long periods of time, then pops up, calling every day for a couple of weeks. I end up accidentally answering one or two, and after a second of stunned panic, I tell him to leave me alone before hanging up. He's the last person I ever want to talk to, especially when I'm in the midst of my life falling apart.

Then again, it would feel good to tell someone to fuck off right about now. And not a soul on earth deserves it more than my father.

Against my better judgement, I pick up the phone with blood rushing in my ears.

"Don't you know how to take a hint? I don't want to talk to you!"

"Uh... is this Mrs. James?"

My cheeks heat. It's not my dad.

Whoops.

Clearing my throat, as my heart rate starts to drift back down to normal, I say, "Um... yes. This is her."

"Hi, my name's Jeff Keller, your grandmother's attorney. Do you have a few moments to talk about Sylvia's estate?"

I sit up straighter. The bag of Doritos falls from my lap, orange crumbs sprinkling across the floor at my feet. Not once in the last few weeks has her estate crossed my mind.

"Yeah. Sure."

"Great. I've sent you a couple of letters in the mail, but you must not have received them. She left you everything, so there's a lot to go through."

He says it so casually, like it shouldn't come as a shock, but I'm not sure I've heard him correctly.

"What?"

"You're her sole beneficiary."

Shaking my head, I rub my temple as a dull ache starts to form behind my eyes. He has to be wrong. I open my mouth to correct him, then shut it before finally saying, "That can't be right. What about my dad, or hell, my brother for that matter?"

"No. All of it is yours. She was very specific about not wanting to leave anything to your father. As for your brother, she did say she knew you'd make sure he was taken care of."

My eyes squeeze closed because I was sure he was wrong until this moment, but that sounds exactly like something she'd say. "I live two hours away. What am I supposed to do with all of it?"

"Well, that's up to you. It's yours."

"No. I know..." Wait. Everything? "By everything, do you mean her house?"

He chuckles softly. "Yes, and everything in it, and her safety deposit box, and her car. Like I said, everything. We will need to set a meeting, and probate may take some time, but she left it all to you."

After setting an appointment and hanging up, I stare at the wall, unable to totally take in what just happened.

I never planned to go back to that town at all. I sure as hell don't need a house there. What's strange is, she never mentioned leaving it to me, and I know for a fact she was team *Ash never sets foot in this hellhole of a town ever again.*

I get why she couldn't leave it to the others, but I'm surprised she didn't talk to me about it. Although, she didn't expect to go to bed and not wake up, I guess.

Eventually, I pull myself from the swirling shitstorm in my own head enough to wrap my head around all of it.

How the hell am I going to deal with a whole house in a town I've refused to step foot in for six years?

I dial Casey when he still hasn't shown up twenty minutes after he was supposed to pick up Maggie. As the line rings, I stare out the window above the kitchen sink, watching a squirrel make its way across the top of the wooden swing set. My fingers grip the cool edge of the white counter harder with every second he doesn't pick up. The warm sun shines through the glass.

"Motherfucker," I mutter under my breath when Casey's phone goes to voicemail for the third time. "Jess!"

I toss my cell onto the counter and run a hand over my throbbing forehead. *I'm going to kill him.* The number of times I've had that very thought over the last couple of weeks is alarming. Isn't it strange how you can love someone so much that you can't imagine spending the rest of your life without them, only to end up wishing you'd never have to see them again? If I could make him disappear, I just might.

That's not entirely true though, is it?

No, because we have Maggie.

Maggie who cries every night at bedtime because she wants her dad to tuck her in like he used to. Maggie, who wanted to call him two days ago when she lost a tooth and was crushed when he didn't answer. Maggie, who's going to be devastated when I tell her he isn't coming today.

And that, folks, is how we circle right back around to: I'm going to kill him.

He was a great dad while we were together, but over the last couple of weeks he's faded into the background, breaking her little heart in the process. I was shocked when he didn't show up the first time. I didn't expect that. However, I'm sure it's hard to find the time when he's with his new girlfriend every fucking minute of every fucking day.

Jess runs into the room with half a face of makeup and a tube of mascara in her hand, her hair still wrapped in a towel.

"Can you watch Maggie today? My meeting's in..." I check the time. "Twenty minutes. Casey was supposed to pick her up, but he's not answering his goddamn phone."

Luckily after getting the call from Gran's attorney last week, my own lawyer was able to get me in quickly.

"I can't. I have a photoshoot this afternoon."

"Shit." I could call him again, but he won't answer. Casey has time for other people when it's convenient for Casey, even if that other person is his own kid.

Dialing my mother, I lean over the island and rest an elbow on the granite. Anything that involves my mother is no doubt painful for everyone involved, but I don't really have a choice.

"Hello?"

"Hey, can you watch Maggie for a bit? Casey didn't show."

"Sure! I'd love to. I'll be right over."

Setting my phone down, I groan. "I guess we're dealing with my mother today."

"Fantastic," she says, sarcastically.

Rubbing my forehead, I sigh.

"You alright?"

I nod. "I'm fine. Just tired."

She eyes me. "Are you having nightmares again?"

"Nope. Just normal tired," I lie.

"I'm ready!" Maggie prances out of her room in a Barbie shirt and an Elsa skirt. Her pink-and-white striped backpack hangs from one shoulder. Her blonde curls bounce as her sock feet shuffle across the carpet. "Is Daddy here yet?"

My ribs squeeze. I flick my attention up to Jess, who raises her brows.

Exhaling, I say, "Maggie—"

Her shoulders slump and her smile fades. "He's not coming, is he?"

A knot forms in my stomach. There's nothing that drives a stake right through my heart quite like that look on her face. I'd do anything if it meant she'd never have to feel this way again.

Kneeling in front of her, I shake my head. "I'm sorry, bug."

Her big blue eyes fill with tears, and the backpack slides to the floor. "We were gonna go to the park today. He promised."

I close my eyes, letting out a sharp breath. I'm sure he did promise. He's just not good at keeping those lately. It's his loss, but she's not going to see it that way. She's going to wonder for the rest of her life why her own parent didn't want her around. She'll probably project that onto every relationship she has, constantly wondering if they actually love her or if she's just another obligation. Maybe she'll spend the rest of her life searching for someone to choose her. And maybe she'll never find that, and she'll be alone forever, second guessing why she'll never be enough.

That thought makes me sick to my stomach. She deserves to feel wanted and loved. She deserves to be her parents' first priority.

I swallow down the lump and the stake, plastering a big fake smile on my face.

"But..." I add, reaching out to hold her hand. "Nana's coming over to spend the day with you. That'll be fun, right?"

She nods, lifting the corner of her mouth, but not really smiling.

When she walks back down the hall to her room, there's a little less pep in her step.

Fuck it. I dial him one more time. I don't know why but there's something about being able to say I called five times that's just a bit more satisfying than saying I called four.

The first time he let my daughter down, a storm began to brew under my skin, and it hasn't settled since. Every time he stands her up—we're at three now—I miss him a little less. My heart hardens toward him with every tear that rolls down her rosy cheeks.

My mother lives right down the road, so by the time Maggie's back to her room, she's already ringing the bell.

When I open the front door, she's on the porch dressed like she's the one with a photoshoot today.

"Hi, sweetheart!" she coos, kissing my cheek as she saunters into the house.

"Hi. Thanks for coming. I don't know what I'd have done without you."

"It's no problem. You know I'll never turn down my baby girl," she says, entering the house without taking her black heels off at the door.

I cringe at her use of *my baby girl*. Her constant need to make up for the lack of parenting she provided Shane and me by overstepping with my child is one of many reasons I keep my distance.

She makes her way farther into the house, making a beeline for the coffee pot I forgot to turn off this morning and flips the switch. It's too late anyway, the smell of burnt coffee already fills the room.

"I'll let Casey know I'm here. I'm sure he'll want to pick her up at some point," she says.

Rolling my eyes, I bite, "If he wanted to see her, he should have shown up when he said he would."

She pours what's left of the brown liquid down the sink before rinsing it out and putting it in the drying rack. "You should cut him some slack."

Here we go.

My mother lives in this delusional 1950's world where if a man puts in even the most minute amount of effort, a woman should be grateful. *Fuck that.*

"I'd cut him some slack if he wasn't such a selfish son of a bitch."

Huh, I guess I've figured out how to be pissed.

She faces me, crossing her arms. "Casey's a good man. You're being petty."

"Petty? He cheated on me!"

"Yes. He made a mistake, but he's been very good to you. You could have it a hell of a lot worse."

"Yeah, and I could have it a hell of a lot better." I grab my purse, slipping it on my shoulder. "Or better yet, how about not at all?"

"Oh boy, here we go. Back to the, *I'm never dating again* act? Ashton, it wasn't cute when you were eighteen, and it's not any cuter now."

I let my arms fall to my sides, and groan. "Can we not do this? I'm already late."

She throws her hands up. "I'm just saying—"

Without turning back, I storm across the living room to put on my shoes. I love my mother, but she has a special way of getting under my skin. I think she might do it on purpose.

My phone buzzes with a text from Casey.

> Sorry. Busy with work.

I roll my eyes. I'm not stupid. He uses work as an excuse because how can you be angry with someone for being at work? But when he says work, it could mean any number of things. Sometimes it's meetings at the office, other times it's a stupid golf trip.

It makes me want to scream.

I like to imagine myself really letting him have it. If I were the version of me from my daydreams, I'd tell him to go fuck himself. I'd tell him, "I'm too good for you, and you were terrible in bed." When I picture it—and I do picture it often—I don't let him get a word in. I just fling insults without a care for how much it might hurt him. Sometimes I even convince myself that I might be able to do it for real one day—but I don't.

I text him back.

> Okay.

Every conversation I have with him, I leave wishing I'd been meaner.

After an emotionally charged visit with my attorney, I say goodbye to my mother without disclosing any of the details before pouring myself a bowl of cereal while Maggie naps on the couch.

My mind reels.

I never needed an attorney until Casey and I separated, but Mallory and I have become well acquainted since I hired her. Especially considering my husband's been a giant pain in the ass every step of the way. He tried to cut me off from all our accounts—she quickly put a stop to that. Thank God because the last thing I need added to my plate right this minute is financial struggles.

He even demanded I give him back the Escalade because it's technically in his name. I threw him the keys. My attorney could have put a stop to that too, but honestly, I don't want the stupid thing anyway. My new Honda Accord gets way better gas mileage and is easier to park.

Jess eyes me suspiciously as she waltzes in the front door. "Hey..."

"Hey," I mutter, not lifting my eyes from the few Froot Loops floating in my bowl.

Dropping her things at the door, she kicks off her shoes and pads toward me with bare feet.

"What did Mallory say?"

I shake my head, blinking a few times. I've cried more than I'd care to admit today. My attorney explained that I could hire someone to clean out the house so I wouldn't have to go back. The more she explained it, the more my stomach churned. I hate that town, but I hate the idea of someone else touching her things more.

Her house was the one place I felt safe and loved as a child, and now it's all I have left of her. Before our parents split, Shane and I used to stay there for the weekend sometimes. It was a reprieve from the fighting. Then they divorced, and we started staying with our dad in Ravens Ridge every summer. Eventually, when he wasn't allowed to have us unsupervised anymore, Gran took us those summers instead.

I was devastated when I left that last time. It felt like I was losing my home, but Gran and my mother insisted that coming back was a bad idea. I still saw her when she'd come to Raleigh to visit, but there were many times I'd wished I could just jump in the car and go to her. Particularly when I was having a tough time with something.

The squeezing in my chest feels a lot like drowning. Jess slowly lowers herself into a chair, watching me closely.

Swallowing, I sit up a little straighter. "She said we could do an estate sale. That everything could be sold that way." My shoulders sag. "I wouldn't have to go back to clean it myself."

She runs a hand down my arm. "That's good! That's what you wanted, right? To not have to go back?"

I shrug. I don't know what I want. That's a lie. I want Gran. For her to wrap me in a hug and tell me everything's going to be okay because I'm not sure anymore. I don't know if I'll ever be okay again. It feels like I'm being pulled apart at the seams, and I don't know how much more I can take. They say what doesn't kill you makes you stronger, but I'm so tired of getting stronger.

Facing her, I clear my throat before saying, "I don't

know. When I think about her house being gone, about not having anywhere to remind me of her..."

Tears spill over, and I wipe them away to no avail because more keep coming. Lifting my eyes to hers, I finish by saying, "I don't want someone else to clear out her things. It's all I have left—"

My shoulders shake, and I drop my face to my hands. She slides closer, wrapping her arms around me, and I sink into her hold.

"I'm so sorry, Ash."

When I speak again, it's broken. "I need to say goodbye."

Her hand runs over my hair as I cry into her shoulder.

My last conversation with Gran wasn't even about anything that mattered. We talked about a stupid book I'd just finished the night before. I thought she'd like it, and I spent the last twenty minutes I spoke to her rambling about something that didn't amount to anything. And now I'll never talk to her again.

She pulls back.

"I need more time with her. I'm not ready to let her go, Jess." I suck in sharp breaths because I might actually suffocate.

I still need her. I know I'm an adult, but I'm not raised— not enough to be without her. My heart aches. It's a dull gnawing that started when Nik called to tell me Gran was gone. It's slashed and ripped at my insides every day since, but the moment I considered letting someone else erase what's left of her from this world, it flayed me open. That house feels like the last piece of her—a piece that should be mine. A final piece that I desperately need.

"You've already made up your mind?"

My chin quivers as I nod. There was no conscious

choice made. I'm not doing what I want. It's what I need. Even if it hurts, even if it gives me no closure and I leave wishing I still had one more piece of her, I need to do this. I need to say goodbye even if it's hard. It's the only way for me to be close to her ever again, and I can't give that away.

"Are you sure?"

"I have to." Blinking, I wipe my face, the tears retreating with my decision. "I need to be with her. Maybe now more than ever."

4

———

ASH

MAY PRESENT DAY

I've talked myself out of going back a dozen times, but I always get caught on the idea that this is the last I have of her.

"Mommy!" Maggie barrels through the living room, launching herself at me.

This is the part I'm sick over. We're a package deal. But Ravens Ridge isn't a safe place for her. Especially when my dad's been calling. I can't risk it. My mom refused to keep her because she doesn't agree with my decision to go back, and Casey says he's going to take her for a few extra days this week, but I'm not holding my breath. So, she's staying with Jess.

I don't know how long it'll take to settle everything, but it's only two hours. I can come back and forth as much as I need. It's not like I won't be able to be here at the drop of a hat if she needs me.

That's what I've been telling myself anyway. It's the only reason I'm even trying to make it work. I need to do this, but I may get there and realize I can't be away from my daughter. I may turn around and come right back. I don't know. But I have to try.

Dropping my suitcase, I kneel in front of her and brush her curls out of her face. "Oh, I'm gonna miss you so much!"

I pull her to me, hugging her tight.

She giggles. "You're smooshing me!"

Letting go, I smile. "You better not have too much fun without me!"

With a big bright grin, she says, "We won't." Her smile falls. "Do you have to go?"

"I'm sorry, bug. I do, but I promise I'll be quick. We'll talk every morning and every night. And if you ever need me, I'll come right home. I'll be back before you know it."

She nods, but it's not convincing.

"One more hug." I pull her to me and kiss her furiously until she starts to giggle. That's my favorite sound. I breathe her in.

Jess pads over, leaning a hip on the back of the couch. "You sure about this?"

I stand. "I'll be alright." My eyes flick down to Maggie.

Jess steps toward her, placing her hands on my daughter's shoulders. "We're gonna be great. I have a week's worth of fun planned. We're not even gonna miss you."

Maggie's eyes light, and I smile.

"Thank you. I'll never be able to repay you for everything you've done for us."

She waves me off. "What are sisters for?"

I wrap my arms around her before hugging and kissing Maggie one more time. With a deep breath, I pick up my bag and make my way to the door.

My hand resting on the knob, I say, "Don't hesitate to call. Anytime. Day or Night. I'll have my phone on all the time."

Jess huffs a laugh. "Yeah, yeah. We'll be fine. I promise."

After opening the door, I step out onto the porch with my heart pulling apart at the seams.

"Pinky promise you'll come back soon?" Maggie asks, holding up her little finger.

A tight-lipped smile on my face, I hook my finger with hers. "Pinky promise. I'll come home tomorrow if you need me to."

She smiles. "Not too soon. Aunt Jess has fun stuff planned, 'member?"

I laugh. "Okay. Deal. I'll come back after the fun stuff."

Standing, I waltz toward the car as my sister and daughter wave at me. They keep waving until long after I've closed the driver's door. I blow her a kiss before pulling away from the curb.

Ravens Ridge is a tiny town, two hours from Raleigh. It's the place Gran was born and raised. Eventually, my mom sent Shane to live there full time because he kept getting in trouble at school.

The first hour of the drive isn't horrible. The sun's shining, and I'm busy pretending I'm not going back to the town that ruined my life six years ago while Bob Dylan serenades me. He was Gran's favorite, and over the years he became a sense of comfort for me. But the closer I get, the more reality eats at my subconscious.

It's not a bad town if you can stay away from the Ravens Ridge Riders. The local motorcycle club is the reason for the growing crime rate and booming drug scene. But staying off their radar is easier said than done, considering my brother's a member—oh, and my jackass ex-boyfriend's their president.

Twenty minutes from Gran's, I'm jolted from my anxious thoughts.

Bang.

My heart plummets as the car lurches, and I pull to the side of the road.

For a moment, I'm transported out of this car into a different time. Nausea rolls through me.

Three things I see: the sun shining in the clear sky, the green grass on the side of the road, a red truck passing me on the other side.

Three things I hear: the air conditioner blowing, my ragged breaths, my heart thumping in my ears.

Three things I feel: the steering wheel—slick from my sweating palms, the leather seat sticking to my bare legs, the dull ache in my thigh that I'm never really sure is real or phantom.

In through your nose, Ash. You're okay.

"Damn it," I mutter, slamming my hands on the wheel.

Climbing out of the driver's seat, I groan at the blown back tire and lift my face to the sky as I fight the urge to cry. I should probably just go back home, right? There is no way this isn't a bad omen. I haven't even made it all the way to the stupid town and things are already falling apart.

"Shit!" My foot collides with the rubber.

Taking a few deep breaths, I try and fail to calm my nerves as I flop into the driver's seat and yank the door closed. My hands tremble as tears stream down my face.

Pulling my phone from my purse, I dial the only person in this godforsaken town I can trust—Shane. Thank goodness he works at the garage in town, but unfortunately, so does Gabe, and steering clear of him is the only shot I have at surviving this trip down memory lane.

"Hello?" My shoulders relax and the tears slow at the sound of his deep voice.

"Hey, Shane," I sniffle.

"What's wrong?" Concern laces his voice.

"I must have hit something. I have a flat tire. I'm fine, just—" I pause for a second, trying to think of the words to describe the clashing emotions I'm currently feeling. "Nervous? I don't know. I don't think I can do this."

"You've got nothing to worry about, I promise. Are you close? I'll come get you."

"I'm like twenty minutes out. Right outside the sawmill." I wipe the tears from my face. "But Shane, you can't tell anyone about this."

"I know. I got you. I'm walking out the door now."

He hangs up, and I drop my head into my hands.

After twenty long minutes, Shane finally shows up.

"You alright?" he asks through my open window.

I nod, and he gets to work changing the tire.

When he's finished, he climbs into the passenger seat. "I put the spare on, but you fucked the rim. I have one back at the shop, but I didn't bring it. Trade me for the day, and I'll bring it to you later tonight."

I meet his stare. He's changed so much in the two years since I last saw him. He still has shaggy dark hair that looks like he just rolled out of bed, but it works. He's always been tall and lean, but he's thinner now—too thin. He has the most beautiful deep brown eyes, but they're hollow and rimmed with dark circles that weren't there before.

He looks a lot like our piece-of-shit father except for his smile. That is all his own. Thank God it hasn't changed a bit. When Shane smiles, so does everyone around him. The second it reaches his eyes, my anxiety starts to melt away.

I open my mouth but quickly shut it. He must see the panic on my face because he says, "I won't tell him it's yours." He grimaces. "I do need to tell you something, though."

"Oh shit." I roll my eyes because I already know what he's about to say. "You told Nik, didn't you?" I glare.

"I'm sorry. You know what she's like. I think she could smell it on me. I had to tell her."

I smack his arm, and he grabs it, rubbing like it hurts.

"I didn't tell her because then she'll rearrange her whole schedule to help me, and she has her own shit going on, dumbass!"

He lifts a brow. "She's actually doing that as we speak."

I scoff. "Damn it, Shane!"

"I'm sorry, okay?"

Taking a deep breath, I rub my temples. "I thought the fewer people who know, the better."

"People? She's your best friend. Hell, your secrets are safer with her than they are with me. She'd jump in front of a bus before she told him anything about you." He quirks an eyebrow. "Actually, I'm pretty sure she's spent the last six years trying to figure out how to murder him and get away with it."

I chuckle because Nik would absolutely do that.

"I know, but I didn't want her to be in that position." With my eyes trained on my hands, a smile spreads across my face because as much as I don't want to cause waves for her, she's my best friend, and I have really missed her. "So, she's gonna come over?"

"Are you kidding? She's waiting for me to tell her you're here so she can meet you there and kick your ass for not telling her." His face falls. "She's pretty pissed at me right now."

"When isn't she?" I scoff. "What did you do this time?"

When he doesn't answer, I add, "Damn it, Shane. When are you gonna wake up? You're gonna lose her one day, or worse... you're gonna kill yourself."

He's a good man, but his addiction has only gotten worse over the years. He goes long stretches convincing everyone he's doing well, but it's always followed by him disappearing for a few days. I think moving out of my mom's house was the beginning of the end for his sobriety.

"You need help—"

"It wasn't that bad. It was one fuck up. I got it, okay? Save your lecture for someone who hasn't heard it already."

It's never just one fuck up.

"I can't lose you. You're the only man I trust." I fight the tears to keep them from falling.

He nods, staring out the window.

"Did Dad call you yesterday?" I ask.

He shrugs.

"Do you ever answer your phone?"

"No. And you shouldn't either. At least not unknown numbers."

I roll my eyes. "I can't ignore every call. Sometimes they're important."

"Sure, you can. If it's important they'll leave a message. That's better than accidentally answering his. What did he say?"

"Nothing. I hung up when I realized who it was."

"You need to be more careful."

Sighing, I say, "I know."

He climbs out of the car, leaning down to say, "I need to get back to work. Take my keys. I'll meet you at Gran's when I get off."

I step out and open the back door to grab my suitcase, shutting it as Shane walks around the car to my side.

"Thanks for always looking out for me." I wrap my arms around his middle and squeeze. "I love you."

"Of course. I'll always be here. I love you too, shithead."

Pulling up to the house, I get an overwhelming urge to cry. I miss her every day. My body refuses to move from the car—every fiber of my being resisting the reality that when I step through that door, she won't be there. French toast won't be cooking on the stove. She won't be humming along to her kitchen radio while she sips her afternoon tea from a cartoon coffee cup at the table. The acceptance and warmth I was showered with in that house, won't be there.

I squeeze my eyes closed, swallowing down the lump in my throat, and step out of the car. Before forcing one foot in front of the other up to the front door, I take one final deep breath, knowing I'm not ready for this, but honestly, I don't know that I'll ever be.

I can see myself swinging on the white wrap-around porch with her smoking a cigarette while I read a Jane Austen book. The yellow siding is like a flashing beacon saying, *welcome home, Ash.* Her ashtray still sits on the glass-top table. It's the same one that Shane tried to stand on to reach a hornet's nest when I was fourteen. He fell, pissing off the hornets, and ended up in the ER.

I'm sure he's been here because there's a mix of her brand cigarettes and his. Her plants are still alive in their hanging pots around the porch, and someone's cut the grass. I smile thinking about Shane coming here to look after things.

He's made a lot of mistakes and drove Gran crazy. But he loved her, and she never stopped believing he could turn things around. She always had a soft spot for him. I think a part of her felt guilty for not intervening sooner with our dad.

Walking through the front door feels like being ripped back in time—apple wallpaper in the kitchen, blue carpet in the living room, an ocean shower curtain in the bathroom. I run my fingers along the worn-out blue couch Shane and I watched movies on when we were hiding out here to avoid our dad. Family pictures decorate the hallway, including one of Gran and me sitting under the magnolia tree out back. The house even still smells like her. Everything's like it was, except she's not here.

When I reach the bedroom that used to be mine, I pause before going in. My heart feels like it might spill out onto the floor. I never got a chance to pack anything up—my pain preserved in this room. Pictures from one of the most excruciating summers of my life hang on a corkboard over my desk. My journal lies covered in doodles of hearts and filled with stupid dreams.

Stepping into the room, I drop my suitcase on the bed before falling to the floor and breaking down. Tears fall from my eyes, soaking into the cream-colored carpet as my shoulders shake.

I don't know how much time passes when my misery is interrupted and the door creaks open.

"Fuck that! If you think you're coming home to visit for the first time in six years just to sit there and cry, you've got another thing coming. Get your little ass off that floor and come here."

My best friend smirks, motioning me toward her, and my heart immediately floods with warmth, a smile spreading across my tear-streaked face.

She leans against the door frame in distressed, wide-leg

jeans and a cropped band T-shirt. Nik has a sharp edge. She's tall and curvy with pale-blonde hair that's currently dyed pink at the ends, but that changes frequently. Her green eyes soften at the pathetic state I'm in.

She grew up in this town, having had to stand on her own her whole life. No one messes with Nik because she has the tongue of a viper. Those might sound like bad qualities, but she loves harder and deeper than anyone I know. Don't think for one second I don't realize how lucky I am to have her as my best friend.

I spring off the floor, wrapping my arms around her. "Oh my god, I'm so sorry I didn't tell you. I don't know what I was thinking."

She laughs, whacking my arm. "I don't know what you were thinking either. You need me to keep you from cracking." She grabs my face. "What the hell, you've been here all of an hour and you're already bawling. Get a grip."

That makes me laugh. No one can help me get up and brush it off quite like Nik. I was pretty shocked when I found out she'd started dating my brother, but honestly, no one else could deal with him like she does.

"So, what's the plan here? Want to get drunk and toss some of this shit?" She gestures to the pictures and other memories scattered around the room.

I grimace. "Maybe we should start with a different room. I'm not sure I'm up for this one just yet."

She grabs my hand and squeezes. "The kitchen? I bet Gran's got some wine stashed away in there somewhere."

I smile, standing and following her out of the room.

We don't make it far before we find ourselves at the table while Nik fills me in on everything I've missed, including the stupid shit my brother's been up to.

Spoiler alert: nothing good.

"God, I don't know how you deal with him. I know he's my brother and I love him, but he's—" I sigh, rolling my eyes. "He's such an idiot."

"That he is." She lifts her glass to her lips. "But deep down, he's still Shane." She shakes her head. "Every time I think, this is it I'm done, I get a glimpse of the boy I fell in love with, and I can't let him go."

I know what she means, but some days it's hard to imagine him ever coming back from his cocaine-induced haze.

"You can't do it for him, you know."

She shrugs. "I know." Moving uncomfortably in her seat, she sits up a little straighter. "Anyway, enough about me. How's Maggie?"

Even as I ramble about my kid and my separation, I can tell her mind's a million miles away. Two bottles of wine later, I've filled her in on every excruciating detail of my life and shown her about a hundred videos of Maggie.

"I have to head out." Putting her glass in the sink, she spins to face me. "Had you told me, I would've made sure to have the night off."

"I know." I sigh, waving her off. "It's okay, though. Shane gets off at six and said he'll bring my car by. He should be here soon."

"Okay, but no more sobbing." She points at me. "It's not a good look on you."

"Hey, are you insinuating I have an ugly cry face?"

"Uh, I'm not insinuating shit, you do, and we've all seen enough of it. You don't deserve any more tears, and we don't deserve to have to look at it." She winks before trotting to the door.

"You're such a bitch." I chuckle.

"Yeah. Well, we all need someone to give us a good kick

in the ass sometimes." She blows me a kiss before stepping out the door and closing it behind her.

I was fifteen when I met Nik. That summer was the first I'd heard of my brother's drug problem—and the year I laid eyes on Gabe Abbott.

5

———

ASH

MAY 9 YEARS AGO

Visiting Ravens Ridge is my favorite thing about summer. For two whole months, I get to hang out with my brother. We're really close, so it's been hard since he moved out of Mom's.

Mom waited around for a while when she dropped me off this afternoon, but Shane never showed up. She blamed his absence on Gran letting him hang out at the Riders' club. My dad was in the club when we were younger, and he'd drag us along sometimes. But I never really understood what they did there.

For the record, it's not Gran's fault. Wherever Shane goes, trouble follows.

He will show up, though. He wouldn't ditch me like this. We always spend our summers together. Once, he took me to the movie theater when they opened, and we stayed all day watching one after another. He's my best friend.

I'm in my room unpacking when the front door opens.

"She waited around all day! Where have you been?" Gran yells, which is weird because she never yells. "Look at me when I'm talking to you!"

I scramble from my room to stand in the doorway but still out of sight.

"Out," Shane mumbles.

"Are you high?" I can't see them, but I imagine she's grabbing his face, squeezing his cheeks together to look into his eyes like she does to decide if we're telling the truth.

"No," he mumbles.

"*Were* you high?"

He doesn't answer. I creep down the hall and peek around the corner. My shoulder bumps one of the hanging pictures, but I catch it before it falls.

"Shane Andrew Michaels, answer me right this—"

"Yes! Jesus, fuck off would you—"

Gran spins on him, waving her finger in his face. Through tight lips, she says, "Don't you dare speak to me like—"

Shane starts to say something, but then his bloodshot eyes meet mine, and he takes a step back from her. He's sweaty and pale. Huffing a breath, he shoves past Gran, then me, barreling to his room and slamming the door behind him.

Gran forces a smile, straightening out her blue button-down blouse. "Hello, sweetheart. I'm gonna go out for a smoke. Why don't you come with me?" she asks, gesturing toward the porch.

She walks toward me, resting a hand on my back.

Gran's small but mighty. She's where I get my short stature from. Her gray hair's pulled away from her face with a sparkly silver clip.

She steps out onto the porch, packing her cigarettes on the way to the swing. I close the door behind me and sit next to her.

"Your brother's a pain in my ass." She shakes her head as she lights one up. "He's just like his damn dad."

Barely more than a whisper, I say, "I don't think he's anything like Dad."

I know Shane—he's brave. He might be the way he is because of our dad, but he's not cruel. He doesn't want to hurt anyone. No one really understands him... they didn't see what he went through.

Well, no one except me.

She exhales, squeezing her eyes shut. Her shoulders slump. "You alright?"

I nod, picking at a string on my denim shorts.

"He's happy you're here. He's just having a hard time. That's all."

"I know," I mutter.

"He'll be better tomorrow. Let him sleep it off. The old Shane'll be back by mornin'."

She finishes her cigarette before going back inside, leaving me on the swing. I don't want Shane to have a hard time. His whole life's been a hard time.

My bare feet sweep back and forth against the carpeted porch as I fight back tears. If Shane was out here with me, he'd probably tell me to quit being a big baby. I sniff them away as a blonde pulls up on a bike.

She stops in front of the house in cut-off shorts, a T-shirt that's too big, and a backward baseball cap.

"Who are you?" she asks, smacking a piece of gum.

I stare at her for a moment, taken aback by her sharp tone.

When I don't answer right away, she snaps, "You can't speak? You know the boy that lives here's weird too."

"No, I just—" I shake my head, pinching my brows together. "Jesus, have you heard of manners?"

She hesitates, dropping her hands to her sides. "It was a joke."

"It wasn't funny, and you shouldn't pop your gum like that. It's tacky."

She chuckles before climbing off her bike and jogging up to the porch. Flopping down on the swing, she holds out a hand. "I'm Nik."

Taking her hand, I say, "Ash."

"How old are you?" she asks.

"I'm almost sixteen."

"Cool! I'm almost seventeen." She rolls her eyes dramatically. "I got held back though, so I'm gonna be in high school until I die."

I laugh again. She is... a lot.

I'm reading on the couch when the doorbell rings.

"I got it!" I shout, darting across the room. Hopefully it's my new friend because my brother still hasn't come out of his room since his fight with Gran yesterday, and I'm bored to death.

Ripping open the front door, I'm stopped dead in my tracks. It's a boy—a really cute boy.

His blond hair is short, and his face is angular in a way that would make him seem like a man if it wasn't for his bright blue eyes and pouty lips. He's tall. Like *really* tall. So tall, in fact, that he looks over my head into the house instead of at me.

"Shane here?" he asks.

I blink, my mouth popping open, unable to pry my eyes from his mouth.

His gaze drops to mine and he lifts a brow. "Speak much?"

God, what is with these people?

Snapping out of it, I say, "Huh?"

His lips press together. "You Shane's kid sister?"

I scowl. "I'm not a kid."

My height makes me look young, but I'm actually only two years younger than my dipshit brother. He just turned eighteen and thinks that makes him a man, but that's because he's like I said before... a dipshit.

"Sure." He grins. "Is he here?"

Shane pushes past me onto the porch. "He's here for me." He nods to the cute boy and says, "Gabe."

I wrinkle my nose. The idiot didn't even bother putting on pants. He's standing on the porch in a shirt and boxers. He looks better than he did yesterday, though.

But he sure as hell doesn't smell better. *Jesus, did he forget how to use deodorant? Or does he just think the cigarette smoke covers the B.O.?*

"Let's go," Gabe says, his eyes dropping. "Uh... maybe put on some pants first."

He glances down, then back to Gabe. "Oh, shit. Alright. I'll be right back."

He squeezes my shoulder as he passes. "I'll be back later, and we can hang out."

I roll my eyes and cross my arms over my chest. "Whatever."

Gabe lifts his brows before jogging off the porch. He climbs through the open window of an old blue sports car—yes, the window—instead of opening the door and climbing in like a normal person. I roll my eyes again.

Boys are so weird.

"Morning, Gran." Stretching my arms, I pad across the kitchen, still in my pink pajamas.

Gran's seated at the kitchen table, the paper in one hand, her Tweety Bird coffee mug in the other. Bob Dylan plays over her outdated CD player on the counter.

"Morning, sweetheart. What's on the agenda for today?"

I shrug. "I might go down to the lake. Where's Shane?"

She puts the paper down, shooting me a sad look. "Who knows? Probably out being a thorn in my damn side."

A familiar scent fills my nose. "French toast?"

She grins. "I'd have let you help me, but you slept half the morning. Your plate's in the microwave."

I turn, eager to get to my favorite breakfast when the front door flies open.

"Look who decided to join us." Gran scoffs, returning her eyes to the newspaper.

"I brought you something," my brother coos, his footsteps growing closer to the kitchen. He sounds more like my brother.

Without glancing up at him, she says, "You can't bribe me, Shane. You owe your sister an apology."

"Oh, come on, Gran. I'm sorry." He appears beside her, laying a few scratch-off tickets on the table.

She gives him an unimpressed look but slides the tickets into the pocket of her gray housecoat before gesturing toward me.

He glances to where I'm standing at the microwave. A mischievous grin brightens his face. "Ash..."

The way he draws out my name, I know what's coming. Pointing my finger at him, I back up until my butt hits the counter. "No. Don't even think about it!"

He keeps grinning that creepy little grin and lunges at me before I can get away, wrapping an arm around my neck and ruffling my curls.

"Goddamn it, Shane! Let go of me!" I flail.

"Are you gonna forgive me?"

"Are you gonna say sorry?"

He sighs but doesn't let me out of the headlock. "I'm sorry. Time got away from me."

"You're such an asshole. Apology not accepted." I jab my finger into his ribs, which are much easier to feel these days, and he lets go, grabbing his side.

"Ow!"

"Serves you right!"

"Come on, how long are you gonna be pissed?"

I shrug. "I don't know. Maybe forever."

A laugh rumbles his chest. "Yeah, okay. What's it gonna take? You want a scratcher too?"

I hate that he knows I'm terrible at holding a grudge. He tries to pull me into a hug.

Shoving off him, I step back. "No, Shane. I want to spend the summer with my brother, but no one seems to know where he went. Instead, we have whoever this loser is in his place."

"Ouch."

"Oh, I'm sorry. Did that hurt your feelings? Good, it was supposed to." I pull my breakfast from the microwave and push past him to sit at the table.

"Ash, I'm sorry. I promise we'll hang out. I just have a lot of shit on my plate right now."

I roll my eyes, and he plops down in the chair between Gran and me.

"Jesus, you're as bad as Gran." He tries to snatch a piece of French toast from my plate.

Gran swats the back of his hand. "No, we just love you. If you want us to be nice to you, grow the hell up."

His playful demeanor dissipates. "I know. I'm working on it."

"You better be." Gran softens before dropping the newspaper and pointing toward the counter. "There's another plate over there if you want it."

His face lights as he jumps up.

6

GABE

MAY PRESENT DAY

"**S**hane!" I shout, nearly tripping over the socket set laying in the middle of the garage.

Silence answers me, and I grind my teeth. I wouldn't say I'm a clean freak, but I pick up my tools when I'm done. Snatching it up, I flip it open before scanning the floor. It's missing the 10mm, and of course it's nowhere in sight. If he thinks he's using mine tomorrow, he has another thing coming. I close the set and toss it on the toolbox with an exaggerated exhale. I'm supposed to be done for the day. My shit's put away, and the last vehicle I had to do is finished and parked in the lot out front. I'm not sticking around to clean up his shit too.

I took over the auto shop and the club when my dad passed almost six years ago. It's not that I don't love it, I'm just here damn near all day, every day.

I make my way through the building to my office that sits at the back of the clubhouse. The place I play both president and shop manager as if one wasn't enough of a headache.

A couple of the members are already perched at the clubhouse bar, having their afterwork beers as I pass.

Once inside my office, I slip out of my coveralls and pull jeans on over my long johns, before shrugging on a sweatshirt and grabbing my shit. I lock my office up before heading back through the clubhouse to the shop.

Before I can open the door to the front office, Dean says from behind me, "Gabe. You got a minute?"

Not really.

"Yeah, what's up?"

Dean was my dad's best friend when they were young. I grew up with his son JT, and we've been inseparable practically from birth.

"Got word today, the missing shipment? It was Pineview."

"You're sure?"

He nods.

Fuck me. We've managed to coexist with the other clubs for the most part over the years, but in the last six months, things have shifted. Now it feels like every week a new club's breathing down our neck.

"I'll take care of it."

"Let me know what I can do." He claps me on the back before walking away.

I take one last deep breath to cool my temper before flinging open the door and waltzing into the front desk area.

Lily sits behind the counter, checking out the last customer. Before he leaves, she smiles wide. "Have a good night."

Coming up behind her, I wrap my arms around her and press my lips to the shell of her ear. "That it?"

Lily's hot. Like *Sports Illustrated* hot. Long red hair, bright green eyes, and an ass that would have any man on his knees. She's been hanging around the club since she graduated high school, and before he passed, Dad gave her the job. We've been sleeping together off and on for years.

We aren't together; it's just physical. The sex is good, and she doesn't ask for much—not that I'd give it to her. Those who get close... get hurt. We both still sleep with whoever we want, but when all else fails, we end up with each other.

"Yep—well, except for the car Shane brought over at lunch." She points to the Honda Accord sitting in the garage.

"Is it done?"

"Yeah, I think it needed a new rim and tire. He ran down the road. Said he'd be back to get it."

Meaning Nik's pissed at him again, and he went down to the bar she works at to smooth things over. Honestly, I love the guy, but I don't know why she stays. I've watched him screw her over more times than I can count, but she always takes him back.

Shane's been my best friend since he moved here. At this point, he's more like my brother, but the kid I met almost twelve years ago is almost unrecognizable.

And I'm the one at fault.

He wouldn't have picked up his little habit if I hadn't brought him around the Ravens Ridge Riders when his dad ran off, but I thought I was doing him a favor by giving him somewhere to belong.

I pick up the plastic sleeve for the Honda. There's no name, but it has a familiar address.

"Whose car is it?"

She shrugs, quirking a brow. "Weird, huh?"

No fucking way. It's weird that she's thinking it too though, right?

"I'm gonna move it out to the lot after I lock up. You can head home. I'll come by later." She nods before grabbing her purse and walking out the front door.

Pulling the keys out of the sleeve, I freeze when my eyes land on a pink jewel "A" keychain.

"Fuck me," I mutter to myself. Blood rushes in my ears, and my heart does a somersault.

I could be wrong. Surely, it's not hers. Why would it be?

I unlock the car and climb in. The moment my ass hits the seat, my suspicions become reality. It smells like her perfume.

Why the fuck is she still wearing that goddamn perfume? Don't girls switch that up or something?

For weeks that sweet vanilla scent clung to my sheets. For months she occupied my every thought. For years I've told myself I would be okay without her. I guess I am technically, but I wasn't for a long time. When she left, I felt like someone had cut off a limb, but I've never regretted it. Not really.

I pull out of the garage, my fingers curled around the steering wheel so tight my knuckles blanch. As I'm about to pull into a spot in the parking lot, my better judgment flings itself right out the driver's side window, and I pull out onto the main road.

7

———

ASH

MAY PRESENT DAY

Shane texted when the shop closed to say he was running down to the bar to talk to Nik, then he'll bring my car back.

That was two hours ago.

Not like it matters. I'm stuck here until I get everything sorted, and seeing as how I don't want anyone to know, I can't very well get out and about anyway.

Luckily, Shane stocked the kitchen for me before I arrived. I pull a bag of popcorn out of the microwave and pour myself a glass of red wine before flopping onto the couch. The soft blue cushions suck me in. As I flip on the TV, my phone rings with a FaceTime call.

"Hello, sweetheart," I sing.

Maggie bounces on the screen, her blonde curls in a wild mess atop of her head.

"Hi, it's 'bout bedtime, so I only have a few minutes," she says like she's heard Jess tell her that a few times.

"Well then, we better make it snappy." I wink. "How was school today?"

"Great! We got a new student, and guess what?"

"What?" I ask, my eyes squinting from the massive smile on my face.

"We have the same backpack! Isn't that crazy?" She dives into a fit of giggles.

"So crazy!"

As her laughter fades, she asks, "Are you coming home tomorrow?"

"Not yet, but soon. I still have a lot of cleaning to do. Would you like to come help?" I tease.

"No way!" Her eyes bug out. "I hate cleaning!"

I knew that'd be her answer. I wish more than anything I could bring her with me, but I'm afraid. I've spent years looking over my shoulder, wondering if my dad will pop out of the bushes. Bringing her here is a risk I'm not willing to take.

"Did Aunt Jess make you pancakes this morning?"

"Yeah, but she knocked over the bowl, and it got the floor all gooey."

"Oh no! Were they as good as my French toast?" I wiggle my brows.

She smiles big and furiously shakes her head.

"I'll make some when I get home, and maybe we can show Aunt Jess how we do it, so she can make it while I'm gone."

"Promise?"

"Pinky promise." I hold my finger up to the phone, and she giggles again.

"Time for bed," Jess says from somewhere out of sight.

"I love you, bug."

"I love you, too, Mommy. Good night."

After she hangs up, I'm settling back into the couch with my snack when the doorbell rings. I drop the bag of popcorn onto the coffee table and dart to the front door with my wine still in my hand.

"Shit, Shane, I still have your key, don't I?"

I undo the deadbolt and fling open the door.

The air whooshes out of my lungs, and I freeze. Everything fades but the pair of blue eyes staring back at me. My heart thunders in my chest. Ghosts don't often ring the doorbell, so the fact that one is standing on my porch has me feeling like I'm on another planet.

I don't even register my glass of wine falling from my hand until the crimson liquid splashes my bare feet. Opening my mouth to say something, no words come out.

"That your car?" The corner of Gabe's mouth lifts as he nods to my Honda sitting in front of the house and leans a shoulder on the doorframe.

My mouth opens and closes. Thoughts rapid fire through my brain, and my knees threaten to buckle.

"How did you know I was here?" I finally manage to ask, my chest rising and falling faster with each breath.

"Your keys." Holding them up, he narrows his eyes at me and smirks. "Did you really think you could have your car in my shop, and I wouldn't know?"

God, he's a smug son of a bitch.

Damn it, he looks good. He's always been attractive, but he's devastating now. His blond hair falls right above his shoulders, and he's put a few pounds of muscle on his lean, six-foot- frame. He's wearing dirty light-wash jeans with a dark gray hoodie. If I had to guess, I'd bet money he's got a handgun tucked in the back of his waistband.

His hand runs across his short facial hair.

"I wasn't thinking about you at all, actually." Crossing my arms over my chest, I ask, "So, what do you want?"

I'm suddenly very aware of how little I'm wearing—a

pair of tiny blue pajama shorts and a matching tank top that's almost too small, leaving everything spilling out of the top. Heat creeps up my neck.

"Just wanted to see for myself." His eyes rake over me, setting my skin on fire. He leans down, picking up the wine glass that—thank God—landed on the doormat and is still in one piece.

"See what?"

"If you were back." He narrows his eyes at me as he stands.

"Well, you've seen. Now you can leave." I reach for my keys he's holding in his other hand.

He pulls them out of reach, and his face softens. "Why now?"

"What?"

"She died months ago. Why are you back now?"

"That's none of your business," I say with my head held high.

His words come out clipped this time when he says, "This town is my business. Why are you here?"

I'm not about to tell *him,* of all people that I couldn't stand the idea of selling this place without seeing it one last time, or that my heart is in pieces and I was hoping maybe a little of Gran's magic could help. I'll never let this man see me broken again. He didn't deserve it when he was my everything, and he sure as hell doesn't deserve it now.

"I'm just ready to sell the place."

He frowns. Not a sad frown, more like a *I'm not buying it* frown. "So, that's it? You just leave for six years and then pop up out of the blue?"

"Yep."

"Hmm." He stares at me for a beat before pushing past into the house.

"What do you think you're doing?" I spin around, following him.

"Coming inside." He whips his head in my direction. "I remember you having better manners the last time I saw you." He quirks a brow with a cocky smile, examining the place. "Not a damn thing has changed here, huh?"

"I have great manners when guests are welcome. You"—I point at him—"however, are not." With an exhale, I collect myself before adding, "Look, I don't know what game you're trying to play, but I don't have the time or energy for it, Gabe."

"Gabe?" He rears back. "I can count on one hand how many times you've called me that." Moseying through the kitchen he says over his shoulder, "And I'm not playing any game. I just wanted to see you."

His eyes sparkle, and his mouth spreads like the Cheshire cat.

That grin is dangerous. It's nothing but false promises. The last time I was in this town I left with my heart broken and my sanity hanging by a thread all because of this asshole. But I'm not that girl anymore, and I'm not taking his shit.

I play innocent, batting my lashes. "Yeah, isn't that what you go by?"

His eyes never leave mine as he sits at the kitchen island. "Not to you."

He tilts his head back slightly and shoots me a look that probably works on every woman in the world—except me.

I cock my head. "Well, you don't really know me anymore."

"I can see that." He grabs the bottle of wine, filling the glass before bringing it to his lips.

Crimson liquid sloshes onto the counter as I snatch it away. "What do you think you're doing?"

Still grinning, he throws his hands up. "Catching up with an old friend. What's it look like I'm doing?"

I slam a hand down. "This isn't funny, and I'm not your friend."

"You used to be."

For a moment my breath hitches because somewhere deep in my subconscious I wish that were true. I wish we could take it all back and things could be different.

But they aren't.

"You know, I've had a long time to think about that, and I don't think I was."

I'd like to explode, but I'm trying not to be so emotional as my mother likes to point out. So instead, I calmly say, "Please, just tell me what I owe you and leave." Throwing a hand in the air, I add, "Forget I was even here."

"Don't worry about it." He stands from the stool, dropping the keys to the counter. "It's on me."

As he swaggers toward the door, I try to keep my eyes on anything but him. Shouldn't there be a rule against looking like that after you break someone's heart? Shouldn't you inevitably get uglier just on principle?

He grips the doorknob, turning over his shoulder. "I'm sorry about Gran."

I nod as my already cracked heart throbs.

Then he leaves.

And I stand in the middle of the living room staring at the front door, feeling like someone's sucked all the air from the room.

8

———

GABE

MAY PRESENT DAY

I barrel out of Gran's house with my fists clenched at my sides, stomping off the porch before jumping in JT's truck. I texted him to pick me up when I got here.

He smirks.

"What?" I bark.

"Nope, I know better than to say anything to you with that look on your face." He starts the truck.

"And what look is that?"

"The one that says you're gonna rip my head off if I say the wrong thing."

"I'm fine, just get back to the garage. I have shit to do." I turn up the radio before staring out the window.

But he's not wrong. I'm pissed. Why am I pissed? Fuck if I know. Like I give a shit what she does.

Except I knew the moment she opened the door in those goddamned pajamas that I was fucked. How was I supposed to act like I had any damn sense with her looking like that. She needs to go.

I don't know what I expected charging over there, but it

wasn't that. She looks just like she did six years ago—maybe better. Hell, her gray eyes were even swollen and red just like they were the last time I saw her. When she opened the door tonight, her blonde curls were pulled up, leaving more of her fair skin on display than I of all people should have been seeing.

The night sky passes by my window to the sound of my teeth grinding all the way back to the shop.

Shane's pacing in the parking lot when we pull up. I take it they were hoping I wouldn't know she was here, but I don't give a shit. Like he has the right to be mad at anyone after everything he's done the last couple years.

"What the hell did you do?" he yells, charging toward the truck. His jaw tics, and for just a moment I think he might hit me as he balls his fists at his sides.

I walk right past him, brushing his shoulder on the way and not bothering to respond. I'm not doing this.

"Hey!" He grabs me by the shirt, pulling me back to face him.

I shove him off. "What?"

"Where have you been?" he growls.

"Where do you think I've been, Shane? Cut the shit."

"Why would you go over there? Haven't you messed with her enough?" His eyes darken. Shane's my best friend, but this is where things get muddy because he's her brother first.

"If you didn't want me to know, you shouldn't have left her keys on the desk."

He takes a step forward, getting in my face. "You know I love you like a brother, but that is my actual fucking sister!"

Every time we've come to blows it's been over her. He struggles to get anything else right but protecting her he does well.

"She shouldn't be here!"

I don't know where that even came from. Ever since I saw those keys, my skin has been on fire. I need her to go.

He stares me down. "Yeah, well she is."

"She wasn't supposed to come back." My nostrils flare. "That's how this works. She stays away, and we pretend none of that shit happened!"

I never explained myself to Shane. Didn't need to. We just agreed that I wouldn't ask about her and we'd all move on.

"Yeah, I know. But she got the house." He runs a hand over his mouth, taking a deep breath and stepping back. "When it's sold, she'll be gone."

"Make sure that she is."

A car door slams, and the daughter of Satan charges straight toward us.

"Oh fuck," I grumble, turning my back to her. "Here we go."

"What the hell is wrong with you two? Huh?" Nik storms across the parking lot. "You just can't leave her alone, can you?"

I like the girl, but she doesn't hide her disdain for me. I hurt her best friend, and she's spent the last six years making sure I know what she thinks of that. I've come close to catching a right hook from her a couple of times too.

"Yeah, save your breath. Big brother already gave me the lecture."

She stops in front of us, smacking my arm before smacking Shane's.

Pointing a finger at him, she shouts, "She trusted you to not mess this up, Shane. What the hell."

"Hey!" I shout, stepping between the two of them. "This wasn't his fault. I just had a feeling, okay?"

She rolls her eyes, crossing her arms.

I throw my hands up, walking backward toward the shop. "I'm just saying, he gives you plenty of reasons to be mad at him. Don't blame him for my shit too."

They're right. I had no reason to go over there. I haven't seen Ash in six years, and it was my choice to end things in the first place.

Her expression softens, and her shoulders relax. "I'm heading over there. I don't want her to spend her first night here alone."

"I'm gonna finish up here, then I'm right behind you." Shane kisses her.

As she makes her way back to her car, Shane shoots me a look, mumbling, "Don't fuck with her."

He brushes past me.

Running a hand over my face, I exhale. My plate's full enough without dredging up the past. I love my club, but some days it feels like it's swallowing me whole.

JT quirks a brow.

"Don't start," I warn, on my way to my bike. "I'm going to Lily's."

My grandpa and his friends opened Ravens Ridge Auto when they were young because the only thing they loved more than fast cars and loud bikes was working on them. When money got tight, they started dealing in stolen cars and parts. It was simple enough, and no harm really came from it. Then someone got the brilliant idea to get in the drug game, and it all went to shit from there.

It's overwhelming to say the least.

My mom's the one who grounded my dad. He'd get sucked into the bullshit with the club, and she'd bring him back to earth. I don't do relationships, but that's what Lily does for me in a way. She can pull me out of my head and set me straight. She tells me what I need to hear—even when I don't want to hear it.

She lives in a small one-bedroom house down the road from the garage. It's not much from the outside—a white fence and a little yellow house. There's not even a porch, just a stoop. The inside's nice though. She's spent a lot of time remodeling —hardwood floors and gray walls. When I hop off my bike and jog up the stairs, she's already holding the door open.

"Hey, asshole," she coos in a Southern drawl.

She steps out of the way and shuts the door behind me. "I thought maybe you decided not to come tonight."

Kicking off my shoes, I say, "It was just a long day."

She wraps her arms around me and tilts her head back, her fiery ponytail sways to one side. "I can fix that."

Yes, please.

My eyes drop to the tiny white top that her tits are straining to spill out of. "That's not what you wore to work..."

With a sly laugh, she pulls away from me and walks to the kitchen.

Fucking tease.

"You hungry?" she asks.

"Always."

Following her, I throw my shit down on the white countertop in the tiny eat-in kitchen. She insisted on white because she watches all those home renovation shows where they put white countertops in every house. I know because she turns them on when she's trying to hint at me to go home.

"Want a beer?" She pulls two from the fridge without waiting for my response.

After handing them to me, she pulls two plates from a cabinet, scoops lasagna on each, and takes them to the table.

"What'd Shane do this time? I heard Nik yelling at him earlier."

I shrug, taking my place as she slides into the chair across from me. "Who knows? He's a pain in the ass."

Lily's one hell of a cook, and I think she's convinced I'm a manchild that can't take care of myself, so she insists on feeding me a few nights a week. It's a weird arrangement, but it works for us. It keeps us both from being alone, and she's one of the only people I can actually relax around.

We eat in silence, but she keeps eyeing me like she wants to say something.

When I'm almost done, I ask, "What?"

Smirking, she lifts a brow. "Is she back?"

"Who?"

She narrows her eyes and points her fork at me. "You know who. Don't play dumb with me."

With an exasperated exhale, I grumble, "Yeah. I think she's here to sell their gran's house."

She makes that face. The one I fucking hate. The one that says, *I know where this is going* or *I know what you're thinking* or *I know you're about to do something stupid.*

I already did the last one by showing up at Ash's house.

I cross my arms over my chest and lean my chair back on two legs. "Don't do that."

Her brows lift. "Do what?"

"You know what. That was forever ago. I don't give a shit if she's back or not."

"If you say so." She shoves a bite of food into her mouth, her teeth scraping against the fork when she pulls it out.

As I put the other two legs back on the ground, I shake my head. "You're a pain in the ass."

She grins like she's proud of herself.

After cleaning up the dinner mess, we head for her room.

On the way here, all I could think about was getting lost in her. Letting the rest of the world melt away when I sink into her.

But when Lily's fingers graze over my shoulders, my chest, and down to the hem of my shirt, my mind's a million miles away.

Or—ten miles down the road.

With a shake of my head, I pull her hands back, grip her ass, and lift her.

She squeals as I drop her to the bed.

I can't do sweet tonight, and Lily picks up on that. When I lean over, she rakes her fingers through my hair, pulling it at the root. Instead of kissing her neck, I sink my teeth into her shoulder and grind against her, causing her to hiss.

"Someone's in a mood."

Pulling back to stand over her, I tear my shirt over my head, and her gray eyes meet mine.

No.

Green. Not gray.

After undoing her skin-tight jeans, I tug them down with a single pull and throw them to the side. She licks her lips, climbing off the bed. This is a dance she knows well, no stranger to waltzing me right out of my head. She drops to her knees and undoes my belt before tugging my pants down.

Batting her lashes, she wastes no time, wrapping her lips around my cock.

I groan, letting my head fall back. "Fuuuuck."

She hums as she descends, her hot, slick mouth stroking up and down my length. I shudder when she pauses to swirl her tongue around the tip.

"More," I whisper.

As she swallows me down again, I thread my fingers in her blonde—*RED* hair.

Lily has red hair.

My grip tightens and I push her deeper until she gags. Her nails dig into my thighs, and she moans.

She comes off with a pop when I pull her head back and pants through her full pink lips. I yank her up from the floor, and she wraps her legs around my waist. Her nails scrape across my scalp.

She grips my hair and pulls my head back before catching my bottom lip between her teeth.

I toss her back onto the bed.

When I rip her panties off, she sucks in a sharp breath. "Hey, I love those—"

I'm inside her before she can finish that thought, my lips crashing into hers. My thrusts quicken, and she writhes under me. I bury my face in her neck. Without missing a beat, she pushes at me, and I let her climb on top.

But instead of watching her tits, I'm staring at the ceiling as she grinds and bounces.

I shut my eyes, but that only makes it worse. So, I open them again, only now realizing she's stopped moving and is staring down at me.

"Gabe..."

Gabe.

"You good?" she asks.

No. I think I'm losing my goddamn mind.

"Yeah." I squeeze her hips. "Keep going."

She purses her lips, then climbs off me. "Are you shitting me? It's been six years, and Ashton's *still* cockblocking me!"

"What?" I ask, sitting up to watch as she climbs out of bed and starts putting her clothes on.

"Oh, come on! Don't give me that bullshit! We both know you're not into this tonight, and there's a blonde with a spectacular rack to blame."

"You're insane, you know that? I'm just tired. This has nothing to do with Ash."

She stops, holding her pants and cocks her head to the side. "And you're full of shit. Look, you wanna talk about your feelings? Great, I'll listen. You wanna finish what we started? Perfect. But if you wanna spend the evening lying to yourself, get out. I'll finish my damn self."

I glare at her. She has no idea what she's talking about. Sure, I don't like that Ash's back. I don't want her here. But my issues are way bigger than some girl I dated a million years ago. I'm almost twenty-seven years old, not some teenager pining over a girl I can't have.

She lifts a brow. "That's what I thought."

I scoff. I'm not doing this. Not tonight. Lily knows damn well what she's doing. She's pushing my buttons on purpose.

"You don't know what you're talking about."

Grinning like she won, she flings herself back onto the bed. "I know everything."

Without another word, I grab my clothes from the floor,

then yank open her bedroom door. "You can be a real bitch, you know that?"

"Love you too. Toodles!"

My skin crawls as I bolt. Maybe I'm more bothered by Ash than I'm willing to admit, but what good does it do me to sit and talk about it. What I needed was to forget about it. But I can't even seem to do that right tonight.

This shit doesn't happen with Lily. We're the perfect match for that reason. She doesn't want anything from me, and I'm not capable of giving more than this anyway.

She's safe. A way to blow off steam that my club can't take from me.

The club is the only thing I can have that I won't break, and it's the reason I can't have anything or anyone else.

9

GABE

MAY 8 YEARS AGO

This year was supposed to be about freedom. Being our senior year, we should be doing whatever the fuck we want, but I might as well be chained to the clubhouse table. Freedom's an illusion. You're tied to the school system until they spit you out, then you're just another pawn in the government's game. I guess if I have to choose the club or being another cog in the wheel, I'd choose the club, but I'm never going to get that choice anyway.

My dad's proud to have something to hand down to me, and don't get me wrong, I do love it. It's been my life, but these days he seems to want to talk about my future with the club rather than normal shit.

Nothing this year has been how I expected it to be.

JT's up Katie's ass these days. Barely eighteen and he acts like they're married or some stupid shit. Shane's secret —I say that lightly because honestly, he's the only one that still thinks it's a secret—drug problem is so far out of control he spends most of his time so high he might as well be in outer space.

I keep my head down as I strut into school a whopping ten minutes late. Shouldn't be a big deal, but it will be. Thank God we only have another couple weeks of this shit.

"Mr. Abbott," the principal, Mr. Wallace, shouts down the hall. "My office."

Groaning, I spin on my heel. "Fuck me."

"Watch your mouth," he says, heading for his office.

Surprise! He called my mother. Want to know who wasn't surprised? My mother. I swear that fucker calls her once a week.

I couldn't get away from him fast enough after he told me I was getting detention for the rest of the week—again. The bell rings as I make it to my locker.

"Where were you?" Shane asks, coming out of our first period class as I put my stuff away and slam the door.

"Office." I take off toward second period with Shane.

"Damn, again?"

I shoot him a dirty look. "Yeah. Not all of us get a fucking pity pass."

Shit.

I shouldn't have said that. Ever since his dad put him in the hospital, everyone gives him a free pass. And they should. The kid deserves a break, but damn, I wish they'd get off my ass for a while.

"Jeez, somebody's got his panties in a twist," he bites, shoving me sideways.

"Sorry." I shake my head. "It's not your fault. I think that motherfucker has it out for me."

"Wallace?"

"Yeah."

"Maybe he just wants an excuse to talk to your mom," JT teases, coming up beside me. *Eavesdropping prick.*

"Fuck off with that shit!" I spit.

"Hey, don't blame me just cause your mom's a babe." He throws up one of his lanky-ass arms. He looks like Gumby. After puberty, he just kept getting taller but the rest of him stayed the same. Like someone stretched him out too far.

My jaw tics. "Shut the fuck up, JT."

"Why do you do this?" Shane asks.

"Because he wants his ass beat." I glare at the dumbshit.

"Gabe, you couldn't beat my ass if Shane held me down first."

We file into Social Studies. "Want to find out?" I toss my books down on the desk, and they land with a crack. "Shane, get his arms!"

"Fuck no." He throws his hands up, lifting his books above his head in one hand. "I'm not getting in the middle of your little lover's quarrel."

Sliding into my seat, I wink at Cassie Lowe, the cute brunette that works at the Ice Hut. She sits in the desk closest to the windows which means here in a minute when the sun gets a little too hot, she'll take off that jacket, and every jackass in the room will spend the hour struggling to keep their eyes on the whiteboard instead of her rack.

She grins. "Hey, Gabe."

Shane rolls his eyes. "Are you gonna sleep with the entire school before graduation?"

"I don't know. I hadn't planned on it, but now that you mention it..." I smirk, quirking a brow. "Maybe."

As Katie slides into the seat in front of JT, she narrows her feline green eyes at me. "You're disgusting."

I wink at the little she-devil.

She scoffs, flipping her shoulder-length brown hair as she turns around.

"Is there even anyone left?" JT bites, turning around in his seat.

I chuckle. "A few. I guess I'll have to get my ass in gear, huh?"

"Abbott, Michaels, Taylor!" Mrs. Baron shouts. "Do I need to call your parents?"

"No need." JT throws up a hand, leaning back in his seat. "Mr. Wallace already called his mom this morning."

I jab him hard in the side with my pencil, and the two knuckleheads I call friends laugh hysterically.

After school, JT drops Shane and I off at my house. I'd be driving my badass vintage Corvette, but thanks to Mr. Wallace, my dad took it away last week.

The second my foot crosses the threshold my mother's on me. "Gabriel Jonathan Abbott, were you late this morning?" Half her blonde hair is pulled back off her face as she barrels toward the front door.

I pretend to think about it for a minute, dropping my backpack to the floor. "I don't know. That was a long time ago."

"Do not play with me." She snaps me with a kitchen towel. "All I ask is that you show up. I don't even care if you pass, although that would be a bonus."

"Well, good news. I showed up." I trot down the hall toward the kitchen, Shane trailing behind.

"Late!" She spins, hot on my tail.

I finish my trek backwards. "Right, but that's not what you said."

Spinning when I hit the kitchen, I'm met with my dad's stern stare.

"Gabe, please tell me I didn't just hear that Mr. Wallace called your mother again." He's doing the classic Jon Abbott stance: feet apart, arms crossed, shoulders back. Pair that with his huge stature and dark features and he's one intimidating motherfucker.

"Hmm... you should do something about that. I think that guy has a thing for her."

Shane chuckles as we both slide into the barstools at the island.

"Gabriel!" he barks. "Half this town already thinks you're a punk. Don't give them more reasons."

My laughter comes to a screeching halt. "Yes, sir."

"Oh, and the rumor I heard about you at fight night better be just that." He glares at me for a minute before stalking out of the room.

Shane winces because he knows as well as I do, it wasn't a rumor.

10

ASH

JULY 8 YEARS AGO

"What happened between you and Jordan last night? Someone said you broke up," Nik asks as we pull into the field behind her friend Akers's house in the new red Jeep my mom got me this year for my birthday.

"No. My brother's asshole guard dog caught us at the sawmill and scared him off," I grumble. I met Jordan at a party a few weeks ago with Nik and he's practically lived at Gran's since.

That is until last night.

"Who? Gabe?"

"Yep." We jump out of the Jeep.

"The party's back here." She gestures toward the woods, and I follow. "Why's he care anyway?"

"No clue." Shrugging, I whine, "I can't even breathe this summer without one of his friends tattling on me."

Leaves and sticks crunch under my Converse sneakers. The further into the woods we walk, the more I'm starting to think I should have worn something other than a T-shirt and denim shorts. With my luck, I'll wake up covered in poison ivy tomorrow.

"Were you guys... you know?" she wiggles her brows.

"No, thank God we were just about to leave. You should have seen it, though. He literally threatened to cut his eyeballs out and send them to his mom if he ever looked at me again!"

"Jesus! Can you imagine if your brother found out you two were hooking up?"

I shoot her a stern look. "Nik."

"Sorry." She winces, looking around. "But seriously, he'd murder him."

"Yeah, which is why he's not gonna find out."

Not that it matters now. My dating days are over for the summer because Shane's made sure every guy in town knows his little sister is off limits.

Which is really annoying because I'm already invisible to the guys back home. Until this summer, I'd only kissed two boys. I thought Jordan really liked me. We had fun together, and he never pushed me to do anything I wasn't ready to do even when hours of making out led nowhere.

Well, until last weekend. I don't know what I was expecting, but a couple of thrusts while he grunted in my ear wasn't it. I was kind of surprised; sex always seemed like such a big deal, but now that I've done it a handful of times with him, I don't get the hype.

When Gabe showed up, Jordan backed down immediately. He drove me home in complete silence, and I haven't heard from him since.

A fire is the only light aside from the moon illuminating the swarm of teenagers drinking and laughing. Music blares from an old black truck that's parked backwards on a gravel path between the trees.

A cute guy parts through the crowd, making a beeline for us. "Nik!"

He flips his wavy blond hair that's just shy of being in his eyes and flashes a big bright smile. He's got one of the kindest faces I've ever seen.

She wraps her arms around his waist. "Hey!"

With his chin resting on the top of her head, his light eyes meet mine. "Who's your friend?"

"I'm Ash." I hold out a hand.

"Ash?" His brows shoot up. "Like Shane's sister?"

"Uh... yeah?"

"In that case"—he finally shakes my hand—"I'm Theo."

Nik shoves him, laughing. "Shut up!" Hooking her arm with mine, she tells me, "He's joking. This is Akers."

"Theo's my brother." He chuckles. "But if Shane finds out you were here, he'll kick my ass."

Here we go. My brother's going to ruin my *whole* summer. I don't know why he's so hellbent on putting his nose in my business. Any other time, he barely acts like I exist. Actually, between him and Gabe, I've wondered if I'm invisible at times. They come and go from Gran's without saying a word to me.

If Gabe weren't such a douchebag, I might have a teeny, tiny crush. I mean, he's one of the cutest guys I've ever seen. But luckily his rotten personality keeps me from thinking about those perfect lips on mine. And I definitely don't daydream about what his calloused fingers would feel like on my skin.

I grin. "Don't worry about Shane. I'll deal with him."

"Yeah..." He narrows his eyes. "You know what? Maybe just don't tell him you came. He can't cut my dick off if he doesn't know."

Nik rolls her eyes. "You're such a wuss."

Grinning, I say, "I swear not a word about this to my brother." I pretend to zip my mouth and throw away the imaginary key. "My lips are sealed."

"Deal." With a stern look to Nik, he says, "That means you too, blabber mouth."

She scowls. "Like you have any room to talk."

"What's that supposed to mean?" He rears back. "I know how to keep a secret."

"Bullshit! You told everyone about Gabe and that girl in the bathroom!"

"No, everyone already knew about that. You could hear her from the hallway!"

Nik scowls. "He's disgusting."

"I think you're just jealous it wasn't you."

She huffs. "I wouldn't let him near me if he was the last man on Earth! He's already slept with half my class. No thanks."

I watch the whole interaction with the biggest grin. They're funny. Back home, my class is so big, there are kids I've been in school with since kindergarten that I've never spoken to, but here, they all know each other's whole life story.

He shrugs. "Let's get you a drink. Might as well have fun before your brother murders me."

He jogs over to a truck, climbs into the bed, and pulls a few beers out of a cooler.

A boy who looks just like him, but with darker hair, sits on a toolbox in the bed. He nudges Akers's shoulder. "Go easy tonight. I'm not cleaning puke out of Mom's carpet again."

"Fuck off! Why are you even out here? Don't you have friends of your own?"

"Yeah, but then who would look after you?" The older boy leans back against the truck and tips his drink.

Akers gives him a dirty look before hopping out of the bed.

After handing one to me, he holds the other just out of Nik's reach. "Are you gonna play nice tonight? I'm not feeding the bear alcohol if she's just gonna maul me later."

Nik scowls. "In your fucking dreams, loser. I bet there isn't a girl in a thirty-mile radius that'd maul you."

"Alright. No beer for you."

11

GABE

JULY 8 YEARS AGO

"Remind me why we're going to a high school party?" Shane asks from the passenger seat of my car.

I shoot him a dirty look. "We just graduated. Settle down. Plenty of people from our class will be there."

He rolls his eyes.

As we pull up at Akers's, there are already cars parked everywhere. Shane jumps out of the car, lighting a cigarette before his feet hit the grass.

I flick my eyebrows. "Jonesing?"

"Shut up," he grumbles as I head into the woods.

"Gabe!" Theo shouts from the bed of his truck.

He holds out a beer, and I take it, hopping up on the open tailgate. "What's up?"

He shakes his head. "Playing babysitter, I guess. My dad said I'm supposed to be keeping an eye on Akers tonight." He grins, holding out his arms to the party. "My eyes are on him."

I chuckle. Theo's a year older than me and his little

brother Akers is a year younger. I've known them my whole life.

He leans forward resting his elbows on his knees. "I heard your dad's giving you and Shane the apartment above the shop."

"Yep. Handed us the keys this morning."

"Badass! No more riding home with Daddy when I drink too much. I'm crashing at your place from now on."

His dad, Phil, is in the club. He's a fucking prick.

Shane appears, sliding onto the tailgate next to me.

"Feel better?" I ask.

He doesn't answer but gives me a shitty look.

When my phone dings, he asks, "Who's that?"

"Lily," I mutter, texting her back.

"Who?"

"The redhead that hangs out at the club." My tone's clipped because I know he knows who I'm talking about. She was in Theo's class, and she's been hanging out at the clubhouse since she graduated.

His face scrunches. "Why's she texting you?"

"I don't know. Maybe because I have this face and am a great lay."

He scoffs. "More like she thinks it's gonna get her keys to the castle. You're so fucking stupid."

In all honesty, he's probably right. I don't think Lily has any sort of feelings for me, but I'm sure she thinks if she hangs around long enough, she'll end up my old lady.

Never going to happen. I'm not settling down with anyone for a long time, if ever. I like Lily, but I don't do drama, and she has her share of it.

"Also isn't she kind of..." He wrinkles his nose and curls his lip.

"Maybe." I grin. "But she gives great head."

He furrows his brows. "You're a dirtbag, you know that?"

"Is your dad gonna let you prospect this year?" Theo asks, sitting on my other side.

"Yep. Shane too."

He nods. "No shit."

JT should be too, but the dipshit went and got himself arrested. Since he's been in trouble a few times before, he may be sitting there for a while.

A wave of blonde curls catches my eye next to the fire. I nudge Shane. "Isn't that your sister?"

"Fuck! What the hell is she doing here?"

I shake my head. She notices us and glares. Then the little shit flips me off.

"Woah! What the hell did you do to her?" Theo asks.

Shane huffs, hopping off the tailgate. "She thinks it's his fault none of the guys in town will talk to her." He shrugs. "Said you threatened one of them or some shit."

"I mean I did, but the kid's a douche. Who cares?"

He takes off toward her, and I hop down to follow.

His shoulders tense the closer he gets. "What the fuck do you think you're doing?"

She spins around with a scowl. "Excuse me?"

"Does Gran know you're here?"

"Uh... that's none of your business, Shane. Go away."

Akers stands behind her with his head down. He knows damn well that Shane's going to kick his ass for this.

"You invited my sister?" he shouts.

Ash puts a hand on Shane's chest as he steps toward Akers.

"*Nik* invited me. I just met him. Can you take your bad attitude and cigarette breath somewhere else? We're trying to have fun, and you're ruining it."

He rears back, scoffing. "You're sixteen, Ashton! You shouldn't be drinking in the fucking woods with this punk!"

"Yeah, and you're nineteen, jackass! What's it matter?"

"Your brother's kind of a dick," her pink-haired friend whispers.

Ash glances at her. "You have no idea." When she turns back to Shane she adds, "Are you done?"

"No, I'm not done. You're going home! Get your shit!"

She puts a hand on her hip. "I drove."

"Well, too damn bad. You forfeited that Jeep when you drank this." He pulls the beer from her other hand and dumps it on the ground.

The irony of this situation isn't lost on me. Like Shane has any right to lecture anyone.

"Will you drive my shithead sister home?"

When I realize he's talking to me, I rear back, pinching my brows. "Uh... no. You take her home."

He blows a sharp breath through his nose and leans in closer to whisper through gritted teeth, "Please, I just texted Marcus to meet me here."

I roll my eyes. Marcus is his dealer. He's a dirtbag.

Sucking my teeth I nod, reluctantly. I don't want to play chauffeur, but I know Shane. He'll get fucked up and forget all about the issue with his sister. Then he'll wake up tomorrow feeling like a piece of shit.

It doesn't matter to me if she goes to a party, but it matters to him, and I don't want him to beat himself up in the morning.

Turning to her, I say, "Let's go."

She scoffs. "Are you kidding me? Shane, I am not leaving with this asshole!"

He grins at her. "You are, or I'll call Gran, and she can come get you."

"What about Nik?"

"No, that's where I draw the line. I'm not a fucking taxi driver," I say.

Nik grabs her arm. "It's fine. I don't really want to leave. I'll have Akers take me home."

Ten minutes later, she drops into my car, pouting. I start the engine and pull out. Maybe she'll be mad enough to stay quiet the whole drive.

"Why don't you get a new car? What is this, like forty years old?"

I whip my head in her direction, my eyes bugging out of my head. "Are you fucking kidding me? This is a 1970 Corvette LT-1!"

She scowls. "Okay?"

"Okay, well they only made one thousand two hundred and eighty-seven of them. It's a classic."

"Sheesh." She throws her hands up. "I didn't know it was a..." She waves one of her hands around. "Whatever you said."

I exhale, loudly, glancing back to the road. "Yeah. Well, it's a badass car. So... yeah."

Why am I losing my cool with a sixteen-year-old girl? I shake my head and crack my neck.

"God, you're just as pissy as my brother. Do the two of you twist each other's panties or just your own?"

I glare at her. This is the last time I'll ever agree to help Shane out. His sister is an annoying little shit. And I do mean little because she only stands like five-feet tall.

She crosses her arms over her chest. "You had no right to put your nose in my business. I can handle myself."

"Noted."

"Who I hang out with is none of my brother's business."

I quirk a brow. "Maybe not, but if he caught wind that

you were fucking some kid in the back seat of a car at the sawmill, you'd have a dead boyfriend and a brother behind bars. So, if you think about it, I did you a favor."

She whips her head toward me. "What is wrong with you?"

"You know, I can see the resemblance. Shane asks me that same question all the time."

She glares, before forcefully blowing air out of her nose and slamming back into the seat. "Great. Well, you can pat yourself on the back. Now no one in town will even look at me." She shakes her head and stares out the window.

That catches me off guard because there's no malice in her voice this time. I look over at her.

Shit. She's kind of pretty.

Nope. Absolutely not. I can't think of my best friend's little sister as pretty. No matter how true that may be. No matter that her blonde curls look like morning sunlight, or that her gray eyes are almost silver with the moon reflecting off them. Or that her bottom lip is just a little fuller than the top, and she's wearing this berry color that I can't seem to peel my gaze away from as she bites the top one. And it especially doesn't matter that the moment she climbed into my car, the space filled with the most pleasant warm vanilla smell. None of that makes it okay for me to see her as anything but my best friend's sister.

I don't know what to say, but that sad look on her face has my stomach tying itself in a knot.

So, I hit the gas. She straightens, grabbing the seat with both hands.

"Are you insane?" she shouts over the roar of the engine.

I glance over at her, grinning. "Now whose panties are in a twist?"

"I don't know." She cocks her head, blinking. "How about I tell my brother you asked about my panties?"

Fuck me. Why did she say that? Not only will he absolutely kick my ass if she tells him that, but now I have to resist the urge to think about her goddamn panties, which is definitely over the line.

My jaw tics, and I speed up.

"Or that you tried to kill me!" she shouts.

"Oh, don't be a wuss. We're fine."

"You're going like a million miles an hour, Gabe!"

"Nah. Just ninety."

She stares at me for a minute before cracking a smile and rolling down her window. The night air blows in, flinging her hair around, and I grin, rolling mine down too.

A full, warm sound leaves her mouth, and I wish I didn't like it so much.

Her laugh is like summer.

12

ASH

MAY PRESENT DAY

Nik barrels through the front door and throws herself on the couch, half on top of me.

"Are you okay? I will kill him if you're not."

"I'm fine. God, get off me, you psycho," I say, pushing her off my lap.

"I cannot believe he did that. What the hell is wrong with him?" She swipes a handful of the popcorn that's still sitting on the table.

I wasn't lying. I am fine. But I have been staring at the wall since he left an hour ago.

"I don't know. I think there's a lot wrong with that man. I still don't know what he wanted."

She rolls her eyes, throwing a piece of popcorn at my chest. "Is that what you were wearing?"

"What?" I laugh.

"I can tell you exactly what he wanted if so."

"Oh my god. Shut up," I squeal, plucking the popcorn from my cleavage before tossing it in my mouth. "I'm exhausted. I've accomplished absolutely nothing today."

"You just got here. Plus, I'm off tomorrow. I'll help you with whatever you need."

"Thank you." I lay back on the couch and throw my legs over her.

"So, what's the deal with *Casey* anyway? I thought he was perfect." I don't miss the way she says his name.

She was pretty skeptical of him from the beginning. It's weird. Nik has this sixth sense for reading people; she can see straight through their bullshit.

He started his own record label, when he was nineteen, and it took off immediately. After deciding to skip college, I was in need of a job, and it seemed like a sign when an opening popped up at one of his offices. He shouldn't have even been there the day of my interview—it was scheduled with the office manager—but he was.

He walked in that day in an expensive navy-blue suit and short dark hair swept back, not a piece out of place. His caramel eyes met mine, and I was totally done for. We were married within a year.

I shrug, picking at a string on my pajamas. "He fell in love with someone else."

"What a fucker."

"I know. I think I attract assholes."

"Oh, babe, you definitely attract assholes."

Laughing, I cover my face with my hands. "I feel so stupid. How many times do I have to let a man run me over before I learn? I should've known he was gonna do this." I shake my head. "I should've known, Gabe—"

"Look, I don't know about Casey, but I was here for the Gabe shit, and I'm telling you right now, no one knew. I still don't understand what happened, but it wasn't your fault, and you can't keep beating yourself up for it."

"I know. I just feel like I keep letting myself be blinded by the wrong men."

"Well, that might be true, but at least you keep getting back up. You may have the worst luck at picking men, but you are the toughest bitch I know."

I pin her with a look. "I have a severely tear-stained pillow that would disagree with you there, but thanks." I give her a half-hearted smile, my mind drifting to the gnawing in my chest. "I miss her."

"Gran?"

"Yeah. Being in this house..." I shake my head. "It's hard. I keep expecting her to waltz in and tell me everything will be fine or turn on Bob Dylan and make me dance until I stop crying."

"Well, I won't make you dance, but you are gonna be okay." She squeezes my arm. "She'd be so proud of you."

"I'm just ready to get this house dealt with and start over."

"That's the spirit!" She pats my leg before leaning back at the other end of the couch. "Now, what are we watching tonight because Shane's an asshole, so I'm sleeping over."

After two bottles of wine and a bag of popcorn, we're giggling on the couch when the front door flies open.

Nik shoots up. "What the fuck, Shane. Go home. It's girls' night." Her words come out a little slurred.

"Yeah, and you are *my* girl. No way you're sleeping in my Grans' house without me." He walks over and wraps his arms around her.

"I'm still mad at you, fucker. Get off me," she snaps, pushing at his limbs to get free.

He drops his hand to her waist and whispers, "Come on, baby. I want to go to bed. It's been a shit day."

"Yeah, well your sister's had a shit day too, no thanks to you, so she needs me more."

"Um, for the record, I don't. I'm headed to bed." I stand from the couch, balancing our glasses in one hand and the popcorn bag in the other. "I really don't give a shit if you sleep on this couch or in his bed so long as you're not in mine. You're a blanket hog." I make my way to the kitchen.

"I am not!" she snaps.

"See, she doesn't need you, and you kind of are," Shane pleads, wincing.

She smacks his arm before glaring at him and pointing her finger. "Fine, but you are still in deep shit."

"I promise I'll make it up to you," he whispers, but the house is silent.

"Gross! If I hear even a peep of what you two are doing in there, I will throw you both out of this house."

Nik and I have managed to get the majority of the kitchen and living room done. Now, against my better judgement, she's convinced me to take a break from our week-long cleaning binge to have a girls' night.

While I wait for Nik to pick me up, I dial Jess.

She picks up on the second ring. "Hello?"

"Hey, how'd it go this evening?"

"Fine. Casey picked Maggie up about an hour ago. How's *Ravens Ridge*?"

"It's fine." I laugh. "Gabe showed up."

"What! When?"

I kick my feet up on the coffee table and grin to myself

thinking about Gran swatting them down. "When I got here Monday night."

"How am I just now hearing about this?"

"I haven't had a chance to tell you. You've had Maggie every time we've talked." I'm not about to have this conversation in front of my kid. "It was horrible. He acted so strange and then stormed out."

"Wait. You let him in the house?"

"No! He just barged in." Because Gabe Abbott is a brute, who doesn't understand when he's not welcome apparently. "Anyway, Shane says he talked to him. So hopefully that's the end of that."

"Was he an ass?"

"He's always an ass, but Jess..." I groan. "He looks good. Like, really good." I think I could actually melt right off the couch thinking about it. Shouldn't it be illegal to be that damn sexy if you're a complete and utter jackass?

"I'm not surprised. He was a smokeshow before, but that doesn't make up for him being a piece of shit."

"I know. I wasn't saying I'm gonna hook up with him or anything. I just..." I trail off for a second, trying to collect what it is exactly that I'm saying. "It was just harder to see him than I imagined."

"Oh, before I forget, did you order something for Maggie?"

"I don't think so, why?"

"You didn't order a..." Plastic crinkles in the background. "Bratz doll?"

I exhale. "Goddamn it. No, it's probably from my dad."

Hesitantly, she says, "Why would he be sending her a doll?"

"The hell if I know. He does that from time to time when he's not busy calling me from unknown numbers."

"What the fuck, Ash! Why haven't you said anything?"

"I don't know. He'll get the memo and piss off eventually. I don't think it's anything to worry about."

"Have you seen him?"

"God, no. Last I heard, he was still in Florida."

She sighs. "Alright, but be careful."

"I will. Just take it to Goodwill or something. She doesn't need gifts from someone she doesn't even know."

After hanging up, I take to finding something to wear. I settle on a black miniskirt, a dark red satin camisole, and tall, high-heeled boots. I refresh my blonde curls and put on a basic face of makeup with a berry lip.

When Nik shows up, she's wearing low-rise black cargo pants and a handkerchief top with her hair pulled back in a clip. This bitch looks like a million bucks even with very little makeup.

Walking in, it's a typical bar—dark and smoky. There's a band playing and a decent crowd. Tables frame the outside of the room, leaving space in the middle for the dance floor.

"Come on. First one's on me," Nik throws over her shoulder, grabbing my hand, and pulling me toward the bar.

After getting drinks, we find a small table in the corner.

"Suck it down so we can dance," she yells over the music.

I do as she says, taking a big gulp.

"Come on. I don't need to be drunk to dance," I yell, dragging her to the dance floor.

One drink turns into three, and suddenly, I realize just how badly I needed a night of freedom.

"That guy keeps looking at you." She gestures behind me to a guy leaning back on the bar with a beer in one hand. He's cute. His dark curly hair stops right above his shoulders. He nods toward us, smiling, and I smile back before turning to Nik.

"I'm not in the market for any of that tonight," I say, shaking my head.

"Maybe not, but a little fun never hurt anyone," she shouts right as a hand comes down on my shoulder.

The man from the bar stands behind me, smiling. "I'm Collin. Can I buy you a drink?"

"Oh, um, I don't know..." I grimace.

Nik nudges me.

"Uh, sure. Why not? I'm Ash."

Leading me to the bar, he asks, "Are you new here? I haven't seen you around town."

"Sort of. I used to visit my grandma here in the summer. I inherited her house, so I'm back until I get that sorted out. You?"

"Not originally. I moved to town a few years ago."

He places his hand on the small of my back.

"Are you seeing anyone?" he asks.

"No." I shake my head. "You?"

"No." He laughs. "It'd be pretty shitty for me to hit on you if I were, wouldn't it?"

Shitty, indeed.

The bartender hands me another drink, and we head back out to the dance floor. The more I drink, the more I loosen up.

After a couple of shots, Collin slides into a chair, pulling me onto his lap before handing me another drink. His hands find my waist, and it all feels easy. Like maybe I could be a girl who casually meets a guy at a bar and loses herself for a while. I've had enough feelings and emotions for a lifetime. I only want his attention. He can keep everything else.

Nik grabs my arm. "Hey, unless you're planning on

going home with that guy, you might want to slow down, babe."

He leans in, kissing my neck, and I break out in goosebumps.

"It's just fun. I'm fine!"

I throw back a shot, but as I lay it back on the table, I knock over a glass and then burst into laughter. The room spins while I regain my balance.

"Okay. I have to pee. Will you be okay for a minute?"

I nod, brushing her off.

Collin grabs my face, and his lips crash into mine. There are no sparks, and my stomach doesn't flip, doesn't even flinch. It's not like it was with the others; there's no feeling behind it, but it's nice to feel like someone wants me.

His tongue meets mine, and suddenly, it's six years ago, and I'm not broken. This isn't me and some random guy in a bar; it's me and the first boy I ever truly loved, sitting by the lake, his hands in my hair. I get lost in it, and for the first time in what feels like forever, I'm free. Like I've been plucked right out of my life and placed somewhere sweeter.

But then I open my eyes, the spell's broken. This is a bar, and he's not the boy I loved so much it ruined me.

He rakes his eyes over me. "Fuck, you're really pretty."

My stomach drops.

Pretty.

I hate that word.

Pushing it from my mind, I close my eyes and lean in for more, hoping to go back to the world that only exists in the mind of a broken, drunk girl.

13

———

GABE

MAY PRESENT DAY

I was drinking at the clubhouse when JT talked me into ditching to go to the bar.

It's packed. We order a couple beers before settling into two stools with our backs to the bar. It's not often that we step away from the club and go out, but it's nice to be able to relax. I don't have to worry about Shane doing something stupid, or a fight breaking out. This place isn't my responsibility the way the club bar is.

That is, until I scan the room.

My eyes spot a blonde straddling some guy in the corner. His hands are in her curls, and the hair on the back of my neck stands up. I grind my molars.

Fuck me. There goes my stress-free night.

"Yeah, I'm not staying long." I lean toward JT.

His eyes find the exact spot mine seem to be glued to. "Is that Shane's sister?"

"Sure looks like it." My nostrils flare.

"Who's the loser with his tongue down her throat?"

I glare at him. He spins in his stool with his eyebrows raised, propping his elbows on the bar.

I return my eyes to her. My blood is boiling, and I think I might actually be vibrating.

He hands her another shot when they finally come up for air, and she stands, stumbling in the process. After taking the shot, Ash lazily falls back onto his lap.

She's trashed.

Throwing her head back onto his shoulder, a warm laugh leaves her lips, and I swear, I can almost hear it even over the loud bar. I grip the beer can so hard it crackles. Then, he pulls down one side of her jacket and kisses her shoulder.

Fuck—I can't watch this. If I sit here, I'm going to explode. "Listen, man, I'm sorry, but I gotta go."

JT nods as I start toward the door, trying not to stare, but I can't help it. She's a magnet. When I glance back one last time, my eyes catch the guy sliding his hand across her stomach. She doesn't flinch. As she tries to lift her head from his shoulder, it rolls to the side.

Goddamn it.

No! She is not your problem. This is not your fucking drama. You're no one to her.

Then his hand moves a little lower, and I'm moving. A familiar feeling washes over me. One that I felt a long time ago in a situation not dissimilar to this one. My feet are racing in her direction without my mind telling them to.

The thing is, I'd probably step in no matter who it was. I don't like guys like that. But it's not just anyone, is it? It's Ash, and I'm on fire. I rip her from his arms, flinging her toward Nik, who's racing in our direction.

"Are you blind or just stupid?" I yell as the guy stands.

"What's your problem, man?" He throws up his hands.

I grab the front of his shirt and grind my teeth. "You

can't see she's too drunk to hold her head up? Or you think it's cool to grope her anyway?"

"Is she your girlfriend or something? What the fuck!" he yells back, trying to shove me away.

"Put your fucking hands on her again, and I'll cut the goddamn things off. You hear me?" I shove him back.

"Hey—" JT barrels across the bar in our direction, but I don't stop until he steps between us. "Enough! They will call the cops. Walk away." He grabs my shoulders, pulling me back.

I can't think. I want to rip this fucker apart. My chest rises in short, sharp bursts. "I don't give a shit. They better call more than the cops because I'm about to kill this piece of shit!"

"Yeah, we're not doing that." He turns to the weasel. "Now would be a good time for you to get the hell out of here."

"I didn't do anything. She was all over me!"

That's what does it. Those words set something off in me, and I lunge for him.

"Now, or I'll let him go!" JT shouts, his grip tightening on me.

The guy damn near takes out a table as he scrambles away. The room around us comes back into focus, and I realize Nik's yelling. I whip my head around to see a pair of gray tear-filled eyes.

"What are you doing here, you fucking caveman?" Nik shouts.

"What are you doing? You just leave your friends with creeps at a bar?" I shout back at her.

I don't even know who I'm mad at anymore. I'm just pissed. I'm a pretty reasonable guy. I don't lose control of my temper often because once I do, I can't focus. I'm ready to burn the damn building down.

"I was in the bathroom!"

I groan. "Your bathroom breaks are really becoming a problem for me."

"What's it have to do with you anyway?" Nik yells as Ash sways, glaring at me.

"I'm not gonna just let *that* happen!" I grab Ash.

"What are you doing? Get off her!" She tries to pull Ash away from me.

"I'm taking her home."

"I'm not going anywhere with you," Ash slurs, trying to shove me off.

"Well, you sure as hell aren't staying here," I growl, dragging her toward the door by her arm.

"You're not supposed to go near her." Nik chases after her. "I'll call Shane."

I spin on her. "Go for it. He's probably too fucked up to pick up the phone by now, so good luck."

I shouldn't have said that considering his reason for getting high tonight probably has something to do with the fact that his best friend fucked over his little sister and now he's stuck in the middle for all of eternity.

Nik rolls her eyes. "You're a son of a bitch. You know that?"

"Yeah. I know." I turn my attention to Ash, who's got tears running down her face. Grabbing her shoulders, I bend down to eye level. "Look, I won't even talk to you, but please let me give you a ride home."

She gives a slight nod, dropping her eyes to the ground. Nik glares at me.

"Do you need a ride too, demon?"

"No, my cousin Kara's here. I'll ride with her." She

points her finger at me, stepping closer. "Do not lay a finger on her, or I swear I will kick your ass, and then watch while Shane murders you."

"Got it." I grab Ash by the hand, leading her out the door. Throwing my bike keys to JT, I say, "Let me borrow your truck. Her drunk ass will fall off the back of the bike."

He nods, tossing me his.

"Come on." I pull her by the hand toward the truck while she stumbles over her own feet. With the passenger door open, I pick her up and put her in before leaning over to buckle her.

When I climb into the driver's seat, she's tucked her feet under her with her arms wrapped around her knees, and her head down. She's older now, but she looks like the fifteen-year-old that opened the door all those years ago.

As we pull out of the parking lot, she lifts her head to stare out the window and says, "How pathetic. Ash is back and needs saving again."

"Not pathetic." I swallow, trying to calm the rage still brewing. "It's not wise to drink that much in a bar full of strangers, but this wasn't your fault."

She sits in silence before finally saying, "Why are you doing this?"

"Why am I doing what?"

"This. Taking me home. Bailing me out again."

I glance at her and then back to the road. "There's no world where I'd let anyone do that to you."

She lets out a deep breath, closing her eyes. "What? You're the only one allowed to hurt me?"

I grip the wheel.

"Nothing to say to that?"

"Ash, don't."

"No. What happened?"

"Let's not do this." I shake my head. "Not now, anyway."

"Why? It's been six years, Gabe. Don't you think I deserve answers after everything? Don't I deserve a little more than a fucking text message?"

My eyes stay trained on the road and my jaw clenches.

"Whatever," she scoffs. "You're worse than that guy at the bar. Do you know that? What you did is worse than anything he could have done."

My knuckles are turning white.

"You owe me answers, but by all means, keep acting like you didn't do anything wrong." Her words come out slurred.

I finally snap. "Yeah, Ash. You deserve answers, but I can't give them to you. Especially not while you're shit-faced, so let it go."

She rolls her eyes and drops her feet off the seat, crossing her arms over her chest, not saying a word the rest of the drive.

When we pull up at the house, she's passed out. I round the truck and dig through her purse for her keys. Her driver's license falls out. I pause, staring at it.

It doesn't say Ashton Michaels, it says Ashton James.

She's fucking married. Or she was. Her left hand has a tan line where a wedding ring used to be.

I can't explain why, but that feels like someone's run a stake through my chest.

I grab her keys and pull her from the truck, cradling her in my arms. After carrying her up the steps, I traipse through the house to her room and lay her down, covering her up before taking in the room.

It's all exactly the same.

My eyes catch on the corkboard above her desk. Our

memories are still splayed out across the wall. My mouth goes dry, and I think that stake in my chest turns. They look like different people—just a couple stupid kids, too in love to see how bad things could get.

Plucking one down, I stare at a picture of us outside the club the day before it all went to hell. She's wrapped around my waist and smiling from ear to ear.

Fuck me. I glance at her, fast asleep on her bed. This girl might actually kill me if she doesn't go home soon.

I fold the picture and put it in my pocket before leaving her room and closing the door. It's been years and I still can't manage to stay out of her goddamn drama.

14

GABE

JUNE 7 YEARS AGO

I'm not going to lie, the parties that come along with this club might be the best part. They throw parties every Friday and Saturday night. There's always a big crowd, lots of beer, and the hottest girls in this town. Sure, they sleep with members or in my case, prospects, because they think it'll get them a foot in the door, but what guy my age wouldn't love that? I don't think I'll ever settle down. Why would I?

Currently, I'm leaning up against the bar, a beer in hand, and Lily wrapped around me.

I take a swig as her lips meet my skin. She runs her tongue up my neck to my ear before whispering, "Take me upstairs?"

I pull away. It's barely midnight. Plus, Shane's here somewhere, and the last time I saw him he was well on his way to Mars. I know he isn't my responsibility, but I feel obligated to make sure he makes it upstairs before he's arrested—or dead.

"I gotta wait for Shane. Seen him?"

She shakes her head, and instead of being disappointed,

she smirks and slides her hand under the waistband of my pants. I'm rethinking my previous statement, when a blonde with the tips of her hair dyed pink comes charging at me like her ass is on fire.

"You're Shane's friend, right?"

I've seen this girl before but can't quite place her. I pull Lily's hand from my pants and stand.

"Uh, yeah."

"I'm here with his sister, and I can't find her. Do you know where he is?"

"Like his little sister, Ash?"

"Yeah. Duh."

That's it. It was dark at Akers's party, but this is definitely the girl that brought Ash. Shane's going to have a fit when he hears what they've done now. "Why is Ash here?"

She releases an exasperated sigh, rolling her eyes. "We snuck in. Not the point. She was sitting over there." She points to a chair near the pool table. "With some creep named Max, and now she's gone."

Shit. Dread coats my stomach. Max is one of the newer members, and something about him gives me a bad vibe. He always gets a little too rough with the girls, and there have been rumors about him being kind of pushy but nothing solid. I don't like the idea of him anywhere with Ash.

"As soon as we find your friend, the two of you are leaving. Got it?" I snap, pushing past her to make my way through the crowd. She follows.

"I'll help." Lily trails close behind.

My pulse pounds in my ears, and my steps quicken. When I get to a closed door in the hallway and find it locked, all the blood drains from my face. If that fucker is in there with her, I might actually kill him.

Taking a step back, I drive my heel into the wood beside

the knob. It splinters as the door flies inward, slamming into the wall inside.

What I find has my breaths turning shallow and the muscles in my jaw tensing as I clench my teeth. Shane's sister is lying on the couch, black tears streaking her face.

Max, who was trying to undo her pants when I came in, has now shot back with both hands in the air like he doesn't know what's happening. *What. The. Fuck.*

"Are you fucking kidding me!" I charge toward him.

"Shit," Lily mutters, moving to Ash and kneeling in front of her. "You're okay."

He mutters some bullshit, but I don't care to hear anything he has to say. My fist connects with his face. Blood trickles from his busted lip. Pinning him to the wall with my forearm, I pull my handgun from behind my back and point it directly at him.

"What the hell do you think you're doing, huh?" Spit flies from my mouth.

"I-I," he stutters. Blood coats his teeth, collecting in the spaces between them.

"Do you have any fucking idea who that is?"

"She's just some chick. What's your problem!"

I press into his throat harder with my arm, cutting off his oxygen. With gritted teeth, I lean my face so close, our noses almost touch, and I say, "That's Shane's sister, you dumbfuck!"

His eyes widen, and he drains of color. "What? No! She said she was eighteen."

I pull my head back, pursing my lips, and pinching my brows. "So, this is fine as long as she's eighteen?" I demand, still pointing my gun at him.

It's taking everything in me not to blow him to pieces.

"I wasn't doing anything! She was all over me."

Nik snaps her attention to us. "No, she wasn't!"

"I'm also pretty sure you don't have to drug someone willing to fuck you, idiot." I smack him upside the head with the gun. "She can't even hold her head up. What the hell did you give her?"

"Look, she seemed like she was into me. I was just trying to help her relax." He must see how close I am to ending him because he adds, "Please, put the gun away."

I take a step closer to him, pressing it under his chin. The sound of Ashton sobbing pulls me from my murderous rage.

"You're damn lucky she still had her pants on when I got here, or you'd already be dead." I pull it away, shoving him toward the door. "Get the fuck out of here and pray Shane doesn't find you."

With a quick nod, he shuffles for the door, holding his bloody face. When I turn around, Ash is in Lily's lap, sobbing and gripping her for dear life. Nik sits beside them with tears in her eyes. I squat in front of the couch.

"You okay? Did he hurt you?" I ask in the kindest voice I can muster with the amount of rage pulsing through my veins.

She shakes her head, still crying. It keeps rolling to the side as the drugs threaten to take over.

"Give her to me." I pull Ash from Lily's hold and press her to my chest. Her nails dig into my arm. "I've got you. You're safe now, I promise." I turn to her friend. "You need to go home. I'll have Shane come get her."

"I'm not just gonna leave her!" she demands.

"Yes, you are. I promise she'll be fine, but I can't babysit you both. So go home."

She stares at me for a moment, obstinance in her eyes.

"I'll take you home. She'll be fine, I swear." Lily stands, running a hand across Nik's back.

Eventually Nik nods, stalking out of the room with Lily.

I sit on the couch and hold onto the girl as she grows increasingly relaxed in my arms. Pulling out my phone, I dial Shane. Of course, it goes to voicemail.

"Fuck!" I shout, and she grips me harder. "Shh. Everything is fine. You're gonna be fine."

Brushing a hair out of her face, I notice the blood under her nails and smirk.

Good girl.

After trying to call Shane a dozen more times and getting his voicemail, I stand and carry the now passed-out girl upstairs. On the way, she whimpers a little before cracking open her eyes.

"Wow. You're beautiful." She giggles, and I can't help but smile.

Once inside my apartment, I try to lay her on the couch, but she holds onto me for dear life. So instead, I sit with her still in my arms and drift to sleep.

I'm startled awake when Ash shoots up from where she was passed out in my lap. "Hey. Morning."

"Morning?" Her brows pinch.

I close my eyes and exhale. "Do you remember anything from last night?"

She shakes her head. "I remember sneaking in here with Nik. Then some guys came over." Her eyes widen. "Oh, no. Did I do something? Oh, God! Did we?"

"What? No! I think... I think someone slipped you something in a drink, but Nik and I found you before anything happened."

She nods, but her brows don't relax.

"I couldn't get a hold of your brother, and you were out by the time we got up here, so I let you sleep it off. I texted him, but he still hasn't responded. I can take you home when you're ready."

She starts to nod again, but then her face turns a unique shade of green, and her hands fly to cover her mouth as she vomits into them.

"Oh, shit. Are you okay?" I jump up to grab a waste basket.

"I'm so sorry," she cries, her face crumpling.

"Hey, it's fine. It's not your fault." I scoop up her hair to hold it back as she starts to heave again, careful not to get a handful of puke.

"Listen, why don't you shower, and I'll get you something to replace what you just ejected from your stomach. Then I'll take you home, yeah?" I rub my hand in circles on her back.

"Why are you being so nice to me?" she asks, lifting her head from the trash can.

"You're Shane's sister. It'd make me a pretty shitty friend if I let something happen to you."

"You don't have to feed me. I'll just rinse out my hair, and we can go."

"It's fine, really. Plus, maybe your brother will finally show up."

"Please don't tell him," she begs quietly, grabbing my arm.

"Ash, I have to. None of this is your fault, at all." I crouch beside her. "Yeah, you shouldn't have been here, but that doesn't give Max the right to do that to you." I grab her chin, lifting her eyes to mine. "You didn't deserve this." Tears roll down her makeup-streaked face. "But I need you to promise me something."

Her chin quivers. "What?"

"I need you to promise you will never take a drink from someone you don't know. Hell, don't take them from guys you do know. You get your drinks yourself from now on. Got it?"

She nods. "I'm so sorry." A sob breaks from her throat, and I pull her to my chest, running a hand down her hair before remembering the vomit and pulling it away. I feel bad for the girl, but that's where I draw the line.

"It's okay. Come with me. I'll show you to the bathroom, and then we'll get you out of here."

After getting her everything she needs, I return to my bedroom to get her some clothes. She was terrified when she woke up, and I hate that. Her normal quick-witted, smartass comments have been stifled by whatever emotions threaten to pull her under.

I pull out a T-shirt and a pair of sweats from my closet. I'm a big guy, so they'll probably swallow her, but it will have to work.

I'm laying them out on the bed when I hear crying from the bathroom. *What the hell?*

"Fuck me," I mutter under my breath.

This is exactly the sort of thing I try to avoid. I don't do drama or tears. I could leave and let her figure it out, but for some reason my heart hasn't let me in on quite yet, I can't. I knock, opening the door enough that she can hear me.

"You okay?"

At first, there's no response, but then she lets out a cracked sob. "No. Not really."

There's only a little over a year between us, but I'm not about to open that can of worms. Driving her home last summer was one thing, but her naked in my bathroom is another.

"Take a couple breaths. I'm right here. You're safe, okay?"

"O-okay." She keeps sobbing.

Shit.

I wish her fucking brother would answer his phone. Making a mental note to beat the shit out of him, I ask, "Do you need anything?"

"N-no. I just—" She gasps a few more times.

I open the door more, covering my eyes with one hand even though it's too foggy to see anything.

"Hey, I'm right here. You're fine. Can I help you?"

What the hell am I doing?

"Yeah."

"Shit. Okay, I'll close my eyes, but can you stand and turn around? Here." I hand her a towel while still covering my face with the other. "Wrap this around you. I'll help you get the puke out of your hair, at least."

She takes the towel from me, and I cover my eyes.

After a few seconds, she says, "I'm ready," in a small voice that guts me.

She's standing with her back to the foggy glass door, her face in her hands. Every gasp has her shoulders jerking. Her hair's wet, weighing down her curls. I grab the shampoo from the ledge, pouring some into my hand.

"Okay, I'm just gonna wash your hair. That's all. Can you lean forward?"

It feels like trying to approach a baby deer. She flips her hair over, holding the towel with both hands in front of her. I run my shampoo-covered hands through her hair, making sure to get all the vomit out. She makes these little gasping noises every so often that feel like a sucker punch to my gut. I should have just killed the motherfucker last night. I'm certain after watching her break down like this that letting him go was a mistake. Pulling the showerhead down, I rinse out the shampoo.

"You might want to shower again later, but at least you don't have puke in your hair." I wring it out, and she stands up straight.

"You okay now?"

"There's blood on my fingers," she whispers.

"Yeah, I think you're pretty scrappy."

She lets out a half-laugh with big round eyes, and my heart clenches. I just want to fix it so she'll stop making that face. Nothing has ever bothered me the way that crease in her brow does, or the way the corners of her mouth turn down just slightly. But the worst of it are the tears pooling in her eyes. I really hate that.

Her voice comes out small when she asks, "Do you promise nothing happened?"

"Yeah." I nod. "I swear. Nothing happened."

Leaving her to get dressed, I get started making breakfast and curse myself under my breath. How in the hell did I end up in this situation? This is what I get for being nice. If I'd minded my own business—

No, if I'd minded my own business, something would have happened.

A few minutes pass before she appears in the doorway, wearing my clothes, with her hair a wild mess around her. My breath hitches. It's not even a sexual thing; she's just so pretty. I'm not into art, but I could understand wanting to stare at something for hours if it were as perfect as her.

Her eyes move to the floor as she tries to blink away tears.

"I hope you don't mind French toast. That's all I've got."

A smile spreads across her lips. "It's my favorite."

She pads across the floor, pulling out a barstool. "Thank you. I'm so sorry for everything." Her gray eyes stay trained on the counter.

"Hey." I wait for her to look up at me before continuing. "Don't worry about it. I'm just glad you're okay."

She nods, her eyes glistening as she tries to sniff away the tears.

"Do you want a drink? Water, milk, coffee?" I ask.

"Water's fine."

Too late, I realize I'm missing a very important ingredient as I slide the glass of water and plate of food to her. "Shit. I don't think I have syrup."

She waves a hand in front of her face. "That's okay. I don't like syrup anyway."

"What? Who eats French toast without syrup?"

"Me, I guess." She shrugs.

I slide a fork over to her. "Okay, weirdo."

15

———

ASH

JUNE 7 YEARS AGO

I have yet to leave my bed since Gabe brought me home. I've been lectured about not taking drinks from people, but in that moment, I didn't think about it. I feel stupid and embarrassed.

Speaking of embarrassment, I can't even think about Gabe without my cheeks catching fire. If I ever see him again, it will be too soon. He had to damn near climb in the shower with me.

How long do you think I'd have to stay in this room for him to forget I exist?

"Are you planning to come out of here anytime today?" Gran asks from the doorway.

I shrug, rolling over onto my side to face her.

"Do you want to talk about it?" she asks, padding over to sit on the edge of the bed.

I debate what to say, feeling ashamed that I put myself in that position in the first place. "I went to the clubhouse with Nik last night."

Her eyes widen, pinning me with a *you did what* look.

"I know it was stupid. I learned my lesson."

She exhales. I'm bracing for her to reprimand me, but instead she says, "Lord knows I did my fair share of dumb shit when I was your age, so I won't lecture you about doing the things teenagers do, but I've lived in this town a long time, and that club has brought nothing but tragedy to the people who get involved in it."

I sit up and nod, grateful she's not mad.

"Your grandfather was a member at one time."

My brows shoot up because I've never heard this before. He passed away when I was a baby, so I don't remember him.

She smiles briefly. "He loved it, and I know firsthand how good some of those men can be." Her smile fades. "He stepped away when his best friend was killed in a disagreement with another club. We decided our family was more important. It scares the shit out of me that your brother has been sucked into that world." Exhaling, she shakes her head. "I don't think I could handle watching you go down that path too."

"I'm sorry, Gran."

"I know, sweetheart." She tucks a curl behind my ear. "Just be smart, okay?"

I nod.

She places a hand on my cheek, the smell of Marlboro still on her fingers. "I'll tell you what, why don't you go sit by the lake? You can just as easily mope out there as you can in here, and there's not a damn thing a little sunshine can't fix."

She's probably right. Getting outside might help. If nothing else, maybe I can get a bit of color this summer.

I head out the back door with a Diet Coke in one hand and a Jane Austen novel in the other. It's a beautiful day, and I take several deep breaths, enjoying the fresh air as I mosey across the backyard to the water. Kicking off my shoes, my muscles relax when my body makes contact with the ground. The blades of grass between my toes are weirdly soothing. Before opening my book, I lay staring up at the magnolia tree branches swaying in the breeze.

A few chapters in, a familiar rumble filters in behind me before Gabe appears in my periphery.

Well, shit.

"Are you trying to steal my secret hiding spot?" Gabe asks, staring off at the lake.

"It's not a secret if I know about it, is it?"

"I guess not." He flops down next to me. "I've never seen anyone else back here until today."

I throw my arm over my eyes to block the sun after putting my book down on my belly.

"Well, it's basically in my backyard. Don't worry; you can have it back in a couple weeks. We can share custody of it."

He laughs, lying back in the grass beside me and rolling his head in my direction.

"You okay?"

I nod.

"Really?"

I think for a minute. Physically, I'm fine, and I guess I should be because nothing happened, but the feeling of being completely out of control has me frozen. I don't know how to be around other people anymore. Like I'm still wandering around somewhere in the memories I don't have from that night.

"Actually, I don't know."

The corner of his mouth quirks up. "You don't have to be okay."

I nod, holding back tears. I'm so tired of crying, especially crying in front of him. "My brother's really lucky to have you."

With his face to the sky, he says, "Want to see my other hiding spot?"

"How many do you have?"

"Two, but I'll show you if you promise not to tell anyone."

I stick out my finger. "Pinky promise."

He laughs, hooking his with mine before standing and leaning down to drag me up with him. "Come on."

We walk across the yard and he helps me onto the back of his motorcycle, wrapping my arms around his waist.

I thought the first time I saw him again would be weird, but it's not. Actually, I'm more at ease with him than I have been with anyone since that night. Maybe because he's the only one who knows the truth. I don't know.

When we pull up at the garage, my pulse speeds up. "Is it really a secret hideout if it's just your apartment?"

He laughs, hopping off the bike before holding out his hand to help me. "Ha ha. I'm not taking you to my apartment, smartass. Follow me."

He leads me down the alley beside the garage to a fire escape, and we climb up the ladder, stepping up onto the roof. He sits, letting his legs hang over the edge.

"Kind of dangerous, don't you think?"

"Not if you don't fall." He winks.

"So, what? You sit up here and contemplate jumping?"

"No! I come up here to think!" He laughs.

I sit next to him. "Think about what?"

"I don't know." He shrugs. "Everything."

"Hmm." The town sprawls out before me—rows of buildings, neighborhoods that look half their size from up here, and green fields that fade into the blue sky. When I turn back to him, he's watching me.

I ask, "Do you like being in the club?"

"Yeah. For the most part. I mean, I'm not actually a member yet. Just a prospect." He nods. "Sometimes I wish we could do things differently, but most of the time I love it. I love the guys and the garage."

"What would you change?"

"Well," he sighs before continuing, "the drugs are obviously an issue. It's not a secret considering your brother walks around like a fucking coke advertisement."

I wince at the mention of Shane.

"Shit." He grimaces. "Sorry, I didn't mean it like that. I shouldn't have said that to you."

"No. It's fine. I get it. He's kind of a mess these days."

"Anyway, I don't really have a choice. It's my dad's club, so one day it'll be mine."

"You can't do something else if you wanted to?"

"No." He laughs, shaking his head. "He's been prepping me to take it over my whole life. That's my purpose."

I feel a little bad for him. It must suck to have your future planned out for you like that.

I turn my attention to the view. "This is kind of nice. Looking out over the town, I mean. It kind of makes it all seem so small. So much more manageable."

"I thought you might feel that way." He reaches for my hand and squeezes it.

I exhale. "I'm so embarrassed about last night. You must think I'm such an idiot."

"Not at all. No one deserves what he did to you."

I give him a small smile, shaking my head. "Well, I'll never be able to thank you enough. I guess I owe you one."

"You don't owe me shit." He nudges my arm. "Want to know a secret?"

"Isn't this place a secret?"

"Well, yeah, but I mean a different one."

I nod. "Okay."

"I don't like many people, not really. But for some reason you've grown on me."

16

———

GABE

JULY 7 YEARS AGO

"Jesus, do you work here now or something?" Akers teases on his way out for the night.

Ash smirks, flipping him off. It took a few evenings of sitting on the roof, but Ash seems to be back to her usual self. She has, however, taken up shop at the garage. After dropping something off to Shane one day last week, she's decided sitting on a workbench and yammering on about whatever's on her mind is how she'd like to spend her summer.

Honestly, I don't mind. I like it when she rambles.

When he leaves, she asks, "How late are you working tonight?"

The clock hanging above her head reads 8 pm. I guess I lost track of time.

I close the hood of my Corvette. It belonged to my grandpa, and then my dad, and now me. It's broken down more than it's not, but I love it.

"You do realize you don't work here, right? You don't have to sit here until I'm done."

"I know." She shrugs. "But I don't have anything else to do. I'll go if it bothers you."

Shit. She took that the wrong way.

"No. It's fine." *More than fine. Please stay.*

"Do you think this is what you want to do for the rest of your life? Like, do you want to work here every day until you die?"

"I don't know. Maybe?" Wiping my hands on a rag, I lean against the car. "I mean, I love the garage. It's all the other shit I could do without."

"I don't know what I want. I don't think I really care about a career, you know? Like, sure, it would be nice to do something you enjoy and get paid for it, but I just want to be happy. I want to spend time with people who care about me and want to be around me and go on trips and go to concerts and just live. You know?" She stares into the distance like she can see it all playing out.

"Yeah. I mean, I get that, but it all takes money."

She shakes out of her daydream, focusing back on me. "Yeah, I know. I just mean I don't want to spend my life being miserable. I spent the majority of my childhood with people who didn't really want to deal with me. I don't want to spend my adult life like that." She says it like it's a fact, like she's not even sad about it.

"What's the deal with your mom anyway?"

"Nothing really." She shrugs. "She loves us. She's not a bad person. I don't think she was cut out to be a mom. She's just kind of biding her time until we're all grown and she doesn't have to be responsible for us."

"That's bullshit."

"Yeah. She tries, I guess. She's pretty well off, so we have everything we could want. I just—I don't know, I feel like I'm more of a burden. That's part of why we never told her about our dad. It felt like we'd be inconveniencing her more."

"Damn, do you think she actually didn't know?"

"At first, no. I don't think she did. She knew what kind of guy he was, but I think she hoped he'd be different with his kids. After a while, though… I mean, she saw what we were like when we came back after the summer with him." She picks at a string on her shorts.

"That sucks. Does she know now?"

"Yeah, we had to go to court, so she heard it all, but it was Shane's case, so I didn't have as much to do with it. I just confirmed his story, mostly."

"Was he like that to you, too, or just Shane?" I almost don't want to know. I've heard rumors, but Shane doesn't talk about it.

"Not as bad." She shakes her head. "I'm pretty lucky. I was always good at staying out of his way. Also, Shane would step in anytime he turned on me. The worst I ever got was a hand across the face a few times."

My heart drops, and I rest my hand on her leg. "Fuck, Ash. I'm so sorry."

"It's fine. I was only here in the summer. Shane had to deal with him all the time. That's the part that pisses me off. My mom didn't want to deal with him, so she shipped him off to that house."

"Yeah, what Shane went through was awful, but you matter too."

The faintest smile spreads across her face. "I'm fine."

When she lifts her eyes back to mine. I say, "I know, but if you ever aren't, I'm here."

She smiles, nodding.

Taking a step back, I start putting tools away. "Anyway, want a ride home?"

"I drove." She jumps down. "Want to go to Dee's?"

"Dee's? Like the diner?"

"Yeah, duh, we've both been here all evening. I'm starving."

"Uh, yeah, I guess. I just have to lock up first."

When we slide into the cracked leather of the red-and-white booth, she beams at me. "This is my favorite place. Shane and I used to hide out here sometimes if we knew Dad was in a mood. It kind of became my comfort place. Dad never came looking for us, so I knew we were safe here."

She plays with a straw wrapper.

An old country song plays over the jukebox. The waitress is topping off the only other customer's coffee when she sees us and smiles. The old man in a flannel shirt and a baseball cap nods to her before she walks away, heading toward us.

She's about my mom's age. She has dark hair pulled up and is in a blue-and-white dress with a white apron. The name on her tag says Lorraine.

"What can I get you, kiddo? Your usual?" the waitress asks.

Ash nods, smiling. "Thank you."

"And you?"

"Uh... same." I hand her my menu. I've been here a few times but obviously not as much as Ash. I don't have a usual.

Ash stifles a giggle. Covering her mouth with her hands.

"What?"

"Nothing." She shakes her head, her curls bouncing around her.

I can't help but smile. Actually, I don't think I've ever smiled as much as I do when I'm with this girl. Which I know is a red flag. I should definitely be pumping the brakes on whatever is going on here, but I can't. When she's not around, she occupies most of my thoughts. "No, what's that face for?"

"Well, I hope you weren't planning on a well-balanced meal." She grins, biting her lip.

"What?" I squint, tilting my head. "Why, what did we order?"

"Well, I ordered fries and a strawberry shake. You ordered '*same.*'" She uses air quotes as she says it.

I laugh. "I can't think of anything better, actually."

Her smile widens.

I could sit in this booth with her for a lifetime. Come to think of it, I haven't felt this relaxed since my dad made me a prospect. That's the problem. I can't force myself away because being near her is the best I've ever felt.

She's the sun, and I'm stuck in her orbit.

17

ASH

MAY PRESENT DAY

You are quite pretty, sweetheart.

I wake with a gasp. Glancing around the room, my shoulders finally relax. *Just a nightmare.* For a moment, I don't remember last night, but all at once, everything comes flooding back.

I'm still in my clothes. Rubbing my eyes, black mascara smudges onto my fingers. How did I end up in my bed? I remember Gabe dragging me out of the bar, but that's about it.

Damn it, he must have carried me inside. Of all the men in the world, why did it have to be him? It's not enough that he broke my heart, but it seems I'm destined to embarrass myself in front of him for eternity.

I slide out of bed, move to the dresser, and strip off my smoke-infused clothes before throwing on a T-shirt and wiping the leftover makeup from my face.

I get all of two steps out of my room before almost falling over my own feet when I see what's on the couch. The man who haunts every one of my dreams is stretched out, fully clothed, with an arm tucked under his head. I walk over to where his sweatshirt's draped over the back of the couch and throw it at him.

"Get the fuck out," I bark.

Startling awake, he sits up, rubs his eyes, and squints at me.

"Good morning to you too, sunshine." Noticing my bare legs, he lifts a brow.

"No. It's not a good morning. A man I hate is on my couch. Get out," I repeat, trotting to the kitchen. If I have any chance of surviving today, I need coffee immediately.

"You know, a thank you would be nice," he yells from the living room.

"Thanks for the ride. You're welcome for the accommodation. Get. Out."

He appears in the doorway, leaning on his shoulder. "We could have coffee."

"Or we could not. I'd prefer it if I never saw you again," I bite, avoiding his eyes. I don't want to see if it hurts him. I just want him to disappear.

"Ouch. Okay. Well, I'll go then," he says, but he doesn't move.

"You do that. I need to get busy on the house, and I can't do that if I'm occupied throwing you out."

When I glance back, he's gone. I move to the doorway of the kitchen, watching as he grabs his shit.

Before reaching the door, his eyes meet mine for the first time this morning. "Are you okay?"

"I'm fine." Throwing up a hand with a fake smile plastered to my face, I add, "I always am."

I retreat to the kitchen.

Fuck him. I appreciate that he didn't let me do something I'd regret last night, but I don't owe him shit. He's an asshole and a liar, and I want him as far away from me as possible. The door closes, and I let out a deep breath.

I need something in my stomach and a shower before I can do anything else today.

Just as I finish drying my hair, Nik calls to ask if I could give her a ride to the shop. As we drive through town, I can feel the stress evaporate from my body. It's crazy how one day can take a place you loved and turn it into a nightmare. As I pass places that hold some of the most joyful times of my life, I can only think about the last few moments I spent here.

That day broke my heart in a way it could never be repaired. Of all the horrible things I've experienced, it was that one day that changed me irrevocably. Even the heartbreak with Casey can't compare to the damage the beautiful boy from Ravens Ridge did to me. He dropped my heart off a cliff, and I can never get it back.

We pull up outside the garage, and I park in a spot facing the building. My heart plummets. A familiar redhead stands out front with the guys. Wrapped around her waist are the arms of the man who ruined my life.

"Is he still fucking her?"

Nik follows my line of sight.

"No, you know how they are. I don't know why they don't just get married and get it over with. She's the only one that can put up with his dumbass." The second the words leave her mouth, she winces. "Shit. I'm sorry. I don't know why I said that."

"It's fine. I don't give a shit what he does," I say, but I can't pull my eyes off them.

Her mouth twists into a sad smile. "Are you okay?"

I finally snap out of it. "Yeah. Totally fine. Just tired."

The nightmares had all but stopped before I came back. I guess it's just being here, but they've been keeping me up more nights than not.

"Okay. Thanks for the ride." She climbs out of the car.

When I lift my gaze again to the couple, his eyes meet mine. The bright smile instantly fades, his arms dropping from her waist. I avert my eyes as my phone rings.

"Shit," I mutter under my breath. Casey has called half a dozen times over the last week, but I always ignore him. He's supposed to talk to Jess if he needs something pertaining to Maggie, and she'll get ahold of me. Something about all of this shit with Gran has my pending divorce weighing on me less and less. It all still sucks, but I have my own shit to deal with.

"Hello?"

"Ashton, I've been calling all week. Where are you?"

"I told you, I'm out of town. Is Maggie okay?"

"Yeah, she's fine. I called because I wanted to talk to you."

My brows crease. In the weeks since we split, he's not once asked to talk. "Talk about what?"

"About us." He says it like it was silly of me to ask. Like I should already know.

"Uh... Casey, we're separated. There is no us."

He exhales loudly. "I know. That's what I wanted to talk about. Baby, I screwed up."

I almost choke on my own saliva.

He continues by saying, "I got caught up in the moment. It was a mistake."

"A mistake?"

"Yeah. I don't know what I was thinking. I thought this is what I wanted, but I miss you."

"And what about Rachel?"

"We broke up."

Something nags at the back of my mind.

"Did she break up with you, or did you break up with her?"

He doesn't answer right away, and my stomach sinks.

"Why's it matter?"

I scoff, rolling my eyes. I've spent weeks dreaming about this call, but not like this. I don't want to be his second choice. I don't want to spend the rest of my life wondering if he really wants to be with me or if I'm just the one he falls back on. Maybe a few weeks ago this would have been enough, but not now.

"I'm sorry, Casey. I'm not interested in being your back up plan."

"That's not what this is."

"Is it not? You chose her. The only reason you think it's a mistake now is because she dumped you. I can't do that to myself. And frankly, I have enough shit on my plate without this drama."

"You're not hearing me. It was a mistake. It doesn't matter who broke up with who. I want my wife back."

"Well, I'm sorry. I don't want to be your wife anymore."

"Where are you? Can we sit down and talk?" He's getting aggravated, but I don't care. If anything, this conversation is making me see just how much I don't want to work things out with him.

"No. I don't want to talk. And I told you I'm out of town dealing with some family shit."

"Okay, but where?" His tone's sharper this time.

"If you have to know, I'm in Ravens Ridge. I'm selling Gran's house."

"Huh," he says like he's figured out the answer to a riddle.

"What?"

"That's it, isn't it? You're finally getting your big chance to win him back. Is that your plan? To run off into the sunset with him?"

My mouth pops open because I cannot believe we're having this conversation. I laugh. "Have you lost your mind? I told you what happened with him. How can you even say that?"

"I mean, it looks suspicious."

"No, it doesn't. Gran died just before you dumped me. Great timing, by the way. Now, I have to clean out her house. That's all it is."

"You're really gonna do this to me, and to Mag—"

"No, Casey. You did this. You cheated, and you chose her over us. You made this bed."

"Yeah, and who suffers for it?"

"Why don't you let me worry about Maggie," I spit.

"I'm her father!" he shouts.

I stop, closing my eyes and sucking in a sharp breath before I say something I don't mean. "If you cared about us, you wouldn't have cheated in the first place. So, please for fuck's sake, let it be." Every word leaves me feeling more exasperated.

"I'm sorry. I didn't think—"

"No. It seems you don't think about anyone but you. Do you know how devastated she is every time you don't show up when you say you will?" I shake my head as a few stray tears sneak their way out of my lashes. I'm so sick of crying.

"Ashton, baby, please let me fix this."

With that, my heart cracks open. "I don't think it's something you can fix. I need time. I need to figure out my own shit, and I can't do that and fix our marriage at the same time. If you want to fix things, fix them with Maggie. She's the one that matters."

"So, you're giving up on us?"

I exhale, letting my head fall back on the headrest. "Sure. If that's what you want to call it."

The line goes dead, and I look up to see Gabe still staring at me before I pull out of the parking lot.

18

ASH

MAY PRESENT DAY

When I enter Gran's house, Shane's lounging on the couch, flipping through channels.

"What are you doing here?" I ask, closing the door behind me.

Being away from Maggie was eating me alive, so I took the weekend off and went home to Raleigh to be with her.

"Nik's pissed at me again. I stayed here last night. Probably be staying here again tonight," he says without looking back at me.

"You do realize I'm selling this place. You can't use it as your oasis from reality anymore."

"Well, you haven't sold it yet, have ya?"

That's when I notice the credit card and straw sitting on the coffee table. "Are you kidding me?" I smack the back of his head from behind the couch.

"Ow! What?" He grabs his head.

"Please tell me you didn't come here to do drugs. What the hell is wrong with you?" I point at the evidence on the table.

"What?" He suddenly realizes he's left his shit out.

"No. It's not like that. I—" He cuts off as I stare at him with crossed arms.

"You what? Knew Nik would have your ass if she knew you were high, so you came here to do it instead?" I flop down next to him. "Shane, this shit has to stop. When I talked to Nik a couple days ago, she said you were really trying this time. What happened?"

"I was! I mean, I am. I fucked up. But I swear, everything's fine."

I shake my head. "You can't keep doing this. We love you, but this is hurting everyone, including you."

He hangs his head. "Yeah. I know."

I stare at him for a moment, wishing I could will him into staying clean before standing from the couch and clapping my hands together. "Okay, well, I'm not gonna pretend I'm capable of kicking you out, so let me make you some dinner, and maybe we'll try again tomorrow. Yeah?"

He nods without making eye contact.

"Shane, you can do this. I know you can." I briefly place my hand on his knee before heading to the kitchen.

The rest of the evening we watch movies and eat spaghetti on the couch in front of the TV. It's like it was when we were little and we'd spend the summer with Dad, but this time, I'm the one taking care of Shane.

"Are you gonna at least call and tell her you're here?"

He shakes his head. "She knows." He flips through the options on Netflix.

"I know she worries, though. She might appreciate knowing that you're okay."

He shakes his head again.

"God! Do you even give a rat's ass about her?"

"Don't start, Ash."

"No, really? It doesn't seem like it. She's wasting her life on you. You do realize that, don't you?"

"Yeah! I know! I tried to end it, but she won't fucking give up! Okay? I know I'm a piece of shit! Is that what you want to hear?"

"No. You aren't. You just have your head so far up your own ass you can't see what you're doing to her."

"I know what it does to her, and I'm trying, okay? I'm fucking trying!" His voice cracks, and he shoots up off the couch. "Fuck this. If I wanted to be bitched at, I would've stayed at home."

I dart across the room, blocking the door. "Don't you dare storm out of here. I'll leave it alone. Okay? No more bitching, but you don't leave. I'll stay up all night worrying if you do, and I need to get some sleep so I can finish this shit. So please, please do not leave," I plead as tears start to well.

He steps back, thinking hard before lifting his face to the ceiling and exhaling loudly. Finally, he nods and stomps off to his room, slamming the door behind him. I know he's pissed, but I don't care.

I head to my room, change, and slip into bed.

I wake early to make a quick trip to the grocery store for the ingredients to make French toast for him.

When I pull back up at the house, the front door is open.

"What the hell," I mutter.

With a plastic sack in each hand, I jog up the steps and enter the house, kicking the door closed behind me.

"Shane!" I bark, my breaths growing sharper as I contemplate how I'm going to murder him for leaving the damn door open.

No response.

"Hey! I'm back!" Sweeping the house, I notice his room's empty, and my heart sinks.

He left.

"Goddamn it, Shane," I mutter under my breath. This is the shit that pisses me off. Everyone talks about how flaky he is, and I defend him every time. But then he does stupid shit like this, and I feel like a fool for having his back.

I pull out my phone and text him on my way back to the kitchen. Stopping in front of the table, I blindly lay the grocery bags down, sighing. This is the last straw. After his little stunt last night, I'm going to put my foot down. I can't keep making excuses for shit. I love him, but enough is enough.

"Hello, Ashton." The familiar voice sends a chill down my spine.

My fingers stop typing, and every muscle in my body freezes at the sound. I lift my eyes slowly, without moving my head.

Nothing comes out at first when I open my mouth. Swallowing, I say, "Hi, Dad."

He looks the same as he did the day I watched him beat my brother to within an inch of his life. He's a little older, but his eyes are just as vacant, and his smile's just as vicious. I can't process the fact that he's here, standing in front of me. Like, I've somehow convinced myself he wasn't real. I'm instantly thirteen again and not sure how to react.

I realize I'm holding my breath and inhale sharply. "What are you doing here?"

"Can't a guy visit his daughter?" he asks.

I guess a guy could, but not this one. If he's here, it's because he wants something. I don't know what, but the danger that lurks if I don't give it to him has my stomach churning.

When I don't answer, he says, "Sit down."

My hands shake, and I jump before scrambling to place my butt in the chair.

"I'm disappointed you won't take my calls. Your grandmother was always a master manipulator. Now that she's gone, you and I can have the father-daughter relationship we deserve." He flashes his teeth. If it was anyone else, it might be considered a smile, but I know what this is. He's a predator, and I am, once again, his prey.

I blink, trying not to move a muscle. You never know what will set him off. That's a lesson I learned long before our parents divorced.

"Okay."

"But first, I want what's mine. The old bitch left everything to you." He scoffs, moving toward me, his beady eyes burning into mine. "I understand why she'd leave your brother out of the will. Although, she's the reason he's the worthless piece of shit he is. If he'd stayed with me, he'd have learned his lesson eventually."

I practically have to bite my tongue to keep from saying something. This is a good time to stop defending my brother.

"But I digress, I came for her jewelry box." He braces his hands on the table, leaning toward me. His eyes narrow and he shouts, "Where is it?"

I jump, shaking my head. "I don't know."

"What do you mean, you don't know? Have you not been cleaning the place out?"

"I have, but I haven't seen it."

He slams a hand on the table. "Liar!"

My hands tremble, and I squeeze my eyes shut as a tear rolls down my cheek.

He takes a step back, collecting himself. "Has your brother been here?"

"Y-yes."

He nods, scowling. "Fucking figures." He gets in my face again and lowers his voice. "You let that little fucker in here—"

I flinch as he reaches out a hand. His fingers run through my hair, and my stomach churns.

When he speaks again it's in an unnaturally sweet tone. "I need you to get it back."

Holding my breath, I nod.

He forces a smile before grabbing a bag of things off the table and walking toward the door.

When it slams, I gasp, opening and closing my mouth like a fish out of water as tears stream down my face.

19

————

GABE

MAY PRESENT DAY

I was fine before I knew she was back. Then, as usual, the first sign of drama, and I fall back into the same old pattern. Ash has a problem, so I run in to fix it. She is not my responsibility anymore, but my stupid brain never got that memo for some reason.

I could have gone to Lily's after the bar, but I didn't. Instead, I stayed there. Now, I can't seem to get Ash out of my head. Every time I close my eyes, I see nothing but her. I keep waking up in a panic at night after dreaming about that piece of shit with his hands on her. I need to forget about Ashton fucking Michaels—or I guess, James.

Shane never mentioned that she got married because of our "don't talk about his sister" agreement. I don't know why that stings so bad. Yeah, there was a time I thought it would be us, but I quickly learned I'm not cut out for real. I can't keep myself out of harm's way, let alone someone else. Saving her from some creep at the bar is easy, but I can't save her from me.

I'm finishing an oil change when Nik, who was talking

on the phone to someone in the waiting area, barrels into the shop. "You fucking asshole!"

I wipe my hands on a rag as she launches at Shane.

"What the fuck!" he shouts, stumbling back.

He throws his hands up to block his face, when she smacks his arm, yelling, "You left the house unlocked!"

"What?"

JT yanks her back as she says, "Gran's house! You left it unlocked! Ash came home, and Adam was there!"

JT's eyes flick to me, and I grind my molars.

Shane's mouth pops open as he drops his hands. "What? Is he still there?"

He's already moving toward the door before she answers.

I'm seconds from rushing out behind him when Nik says, "No, he's gone."

Before reaching the door, he asks, "Is she okay?"

Nik shakes her head and rushes out of the garage behind him.

"You good?" JT asks.

My hands grip the rag so tight my knuckles blanch, and I clench my teeth. "Find Adam."

The next couple hours, I pace in the garage, wishing I could go over there. Turns out my new mantra is *she's not my problem* because I've repeated that about two hundred times.

JT appears in the doorway of my office, and I stop before perching on the edge of my desk. "Did you find him?"

He shakes his head, plopping down in the chair in front of me. "He's gone."

"Where?"

"No clue, but we've looked everywhere. Phil searched Adam's old house. He's fled."

I lift my head to the ceiling and run my hands over my face. "When we find him, he's dead."

"Have you heard from Shane?"

"No."

JT exhales, pulling out his phone to tap out a text before slipping it back in his pocket, then sighs. "What the fuck, man."

"Are you gonna go over there?"

He shakes his head again. "You?"

I glare at him.

"What? You gonna act like you didn't do the same shit with her a week ago? We're still pretending you don't care?"

Sucking my top teeth, I stand, round the desk, and collapse into my chair. "Shut up."

His phone dings and he mutters, "She's okay."

"You asked him?"

He grins, nodding. "Not that you give a shit or anything."

I roll my eyes. "Thank you."

No one's heard from Shane since Adam's ambush, and he didn't show up for work today.

If I had to bet, I'd guess he's with Marcus. He doesn't get his supply from us. We only handle weed, coke, and occasionally pills, but he can get anything he wants over there.

Everyone wants to know what I know and what I'm

going to do. Shane's an adult, and I'm not his babysitter. I could go over there and drag Shane out of the dilapidated house, but it'd cause one hell of a turf war, and in the end, he'd go crawling right back. So, my hands are tied.

But he's been MIA for a week this time which has me worried. When he's hiding out from everyone else, he usually at least lets me know he's alive.

I slip into my office and flop down in my chair, rubbing my hands over my face. Someone knocks on the door.

"Hey, you okay?" Lily coos, cracking it open.

"Yeah. I'm fine." I run a hand through my hair.

"Need a little pick-me-up?" She slithers across the room to perch on the side of the desk. Her jasmine perfume fills the room.

I grin as she slides a hand through the back of my hair, bringing her mouth to mine. My hands find her hips, slipping under her spaghetti-strap top to rest on her bare back.

Then, the door opens.

"Jesus, Gabriel. Can you act like you've got some damn sense for once?" My mother stands in the doorway with her hands on her hips. Her blonde waves rest at her shoulders as she glares at me with blue eyes.

I groan, letting my head rest on the back of the chair.

Lily stands, pulling her shirt down and dropping her eyes to the floor. "Hi, Colette."

"Hello, Lily. Honey, can I have a moment with my son?"

Lily nods, hugging my mother briefly before exiting my office. As the door closes behind her, my mom sits in the chair across from my desk.

"Do you need something? I'm kind of busy."

She laughs. "Yeah, I could see how busy you were."

As the smile falls from her face, she doesn't say anything.

"What?" I bite.

"Have you heard Ash is back in town?"

"I have."

"And?"

"And what, Mom? What she does is none of my business."

She pins me with that specific look only moms know how to do—the one that says *do I look that stupid, I'm your mother, you can't lie to me.*

"Seriously, don't make this a thing."

"I'm not making it anything. I'm worried it's already a thing. You can lie to your friends, hell you can lie to yourself, but you can't lie to me. I know what that girl meant to you."

"Yeah, 'meant,' past tense. She's basically a stranger. So, like I said, she is none of my business."

My mother stares at me for a moment, obviously not believing me, but eventually she gives in and pushes off the chair. I stand, letting her pull me into a hug.

"I love you, Gabriel. I just wanted to make sure you're okay."

"I love you too, Mom, and I'm always okay."

I desperately need to clear my head. Nothing does that better than the wind on my face. Grabbing my cut from the back of my chair, I head for the door.

"I'm taking the rest of the day. I need a ride," I tell Lily on my way out. Maybe I'll run into Shane and kill two birds with one stone.

I've been on edge since my dad showed up, feeling like he might pop up at any moment. Gran used to send me out to the lake when something was bothering me, and I swear today it's calling my name.

Grabbing my book, I practically float out the backdoor. The weather-worn wood deck creaks under my steps as I prance across it and down the three steps. The summer breeze whips through my hair and freshly cut grass sticks to my sandals on my jog to the edge of her open backyard.

I cross the gravel road that wraps around the lake before barreling toward my little slice of paradise. It's mostly flat green grass, but there are a few trees surrounding the water and a long dock that we used to fish off of when I was a kid. A few feet from the water stands the most beautiful magnolia tree.

After kicking off my sandals, I flop down in the grass under it. The second my body hits the ground, I groan. God, I've missed this. Gran used to say the lake was magic. I don't know if it's fixing anything, but it's definitely what I needed.

Staring up at the blooms floating across the bright blue

sky, I inhale the smell of the water and lean up on my elbows to take it all in. The trees are probably a little taller, and I'm sure there are new fish in the lake, but it all seems the same from here. My heart sinks. This will be my last summer here. My conflicting emotions about Ravens Ridge don't negate the fact that I have beautiful memories here, and I'm going to miss this place—I'm going to miss Gran.

I pull out a Jane Austen novel and lie back, using it to block the sun. When I was a teenager, I used to spend hours out here, reading and staring up at the clouds. The sounds of the water rippling in the background with the occasional plunk of a fish jumping is the perfect soundtrack for laying in the summer sun. It's like everything else disappears, and it's just me and Mr. Darcy—or in today's case, Emma.

I can feel Gran out here. Like she's all around me. Maybe she's the wind that blows a stray curl across my face or the magnolia blossom that falls and lands on my forehead. I've been so caught up in the grief of her not being here, but what I wasn't seeing is that she is.

Just as Harriet realizes her love for Mr. Knightley, a rumbling from behind me has my heart taking off. I sit up, turning to look at the road. My chest grows tight when I see him.

Gabe hops off his bike, taking off his helmet and shaking out his hair before placing it on the seat. The sun hits the blond strands, lighting him up to look almost ethereal. It's cruel really. Then he slips off his leather cut, draping it next to the helmet. I've seen him do exactly that a dozen times, but this time it fills me with apprehension instead of anticipation.

Finally, he notices me and stops. For a second, we stare at each other. An invisible wave of pain and unspoken words—and words I *wish* had been left unspoken—cascade between us. My scalp prickles under his gaze.

Just when I think he's going to jump back on his bike, he waves and takes the first step toward me. His boots leave the grass pressed into the earth with each stride.

"Sorry. I didn't even think about you coming out here. I'll leave. It just didn't feel right to not at least say hello," he says.

"It's okay. I believe I told you we'd share custody, though." I offer him a smile. "Technically, this is my time."

He lets out a half-laugh. "Yeah. Well, I've been using your shares for a while now." Sitting beside me, he takes a deep breath. "How's it going with the house?"

"Fine." I shrug. "There's a lot of stuff."

I don't know if it's the magic of the lake or the exhaustion of the last few months finally kicking in, but I don't have the energy to fight with him.

"I bet. People tend to accumulate a lot of shit over a lifetime."

"Yeah..." I look down at my hands not saying anything for a beat. There's something I've been wishing I could say but haven't because we've been at each other's throats every time I've seen him.

Finally, I just say it. "For what it's worth, I'm sorry about your dad. He was a really great guy."

"He was. Thanks. It's kind of weird now. You think you'll get used to life without someone eventually, but I don't know if I ever will. Things weren't great between us before he passed. I was going through my own shit, and..." He shakes his head. "I just wish I could go back, I guess."

My eyes take in his profile. Nik called and told me when Jon died. I wanted to reach out, but I knew he wouldn't answer.

He sighs. "Anyway, I'm alright. I still have my mom, and lord knows she's up my ass enough for the both of them."

Knowing Colette, I'm sure she is.

I nudge him with my elbow. "I'm sorry for being such a bitch before. I'm just having a hard time right now, I guess."

"It's okay. You haven't given me anything I don't deserve."

"That's probably true, but I'm still sorry. And for the record, I do appreciate you getting me out of that bar the other night. I don't know what I was thinking."

He lifts a shoulder and matter-of-factly says, "No problem. I'll always have your back."

When our eyes meet, my words get stuck behind my teeth. For a moment, I recognize the man sitting beside me. But that's not right. That man doesn't exist, and pretending he does will just end with disappointment.

"That's not true," I whisper.

He rolls his lips under, holding back whatever he wants to say. A second ticks by, then two before he says, "Ash—"

I clear my throat and stand. "Anyway, I guess I need to get back in there. I have a lot to do."

Whatever he's about to say, I don't want to hear it. If it's an apology he wants to give, I don't want it. And if he's just going to repeat what he said back then, I don't need to hear that either.

"Yeah, you better." He turns back to the water. "I'm sure your husband's ready for you to come home."

His words have my legs turning to Jell-O, and my heart begins to pound against my chest. It's not like I was trying to hide that. I mean, Nik and Shane were at my wedding, I knew he'd probably heard, but something about that comment doesn't sit right.

"Don't do that."

"Do what?" he asks, not bothering to look away from the water.

"Act like you know anything about me."

He finally turns back to look at me, and something shifts. Whatever he was feeling before is gone. He quirks a brow. "Don't I?"

"No. You don't. I'm not the girl I was when I left. You made sure of that, didn't you?"

His face falls before his nostrils flair and he stands, moving closer.

"What's he think of that tattoo on your ass?" he asks with a cocky smirk.

There he is. The man underneath the façade. The one who says things just to cut me.

I lift my chin, trying to conceal just how much he's still able to get under my skin. "I had it removed."

He scoffs. "Yeah, I bet you did."

Shrugging, I say, "It'd be pretty pathetic to keep it since it was just a stupid summer fling, don't you think?"

Bullseye.

Pain flashes in his eyes. Good. I hope it hurts like a bitch. No one deserves it more than him.

Spinning on my heel, I keep my shoulders straight all the way back to the house, not reacting until I slam the door to my bedroom.

I'm still stewing long past dinner time. I flop down on Gran's couch, flipping on the TV. He has a lot of nerve showing up here to play that Jekyll and Hyde shit. You'd think he'd get tired of messing with my head after a while.

A thud comes from outside the front door.

"What the hell," I mutter under my breath, sitting straight up.

When I hear it again, my heart lurches. Before I can

spiral into a panic, I recognize Shane's voice through the door.

"Motherfucker," he mumbles.

Relief washes over me, and my shoulders relax. I jog over and rip it open. "What are you—"

Everything stops.

He's stumbling around on the porch with dirty clothes, greasy hair, and pronounced dark circles.

"Oh my god. Are you okay?"

He shakes his head, shuffling inside.

Reaching up, I grab his face. "Shane, what the—You're burning up."

He heaves, and I race to the kitchen, dumping the groceries I bought earlier on the counter. I shove the bag at him just in time for his stomach to empty.

"It's okay. Get it out," I soothe, running a hand in circles on his warm back.

When I'm pretty sure the vomiting has paused long enough to move, I grab his arm and guide him to the couch. "Come on. Sit down."

As he does, his eyelids get heavy and his head bobs.

Tapping the side of his face, I shout, "Shane. Hey!"

"Hmm." He cracks an eye.

"Hey. Are you okay? What should I do? Should I take you somewhere?"

I've seen him high before, but not like this. He shakes his head, heaving again.

"Shit." Grabbing the bag, I lean him forward, but most of it lands on the floor before he flops back on the couch. His eyes close one last time, and his breathing slows.

"Shane. Open your eyes. Tell me you're okay!"

He doesn't respond this time, and my heart thumps wildly in my chest.

I need to do something.

Think, Ash. Think.

I guide him down to his side and run my fingers through his hair.

What the hell.

Grabbing my phone, I squeeze my eyes shut. Shane lays lifeless as fear plows into me. I need help or I'm going to lose my brother.

Nik—No.

He'll kill me if I let her see him like this.

JT.

Pulling his phone from his right pocket, I try turning it on, but when the screen lights up, it says two percent.

Shit.

Racing to my room, I rip my charger from the wall before returning to the living room. With shaky hands, I plug it in and scroll through his contacts before hitting the call button with my heart in my throat.

His voicemail picks up. *Hey, it's JT. You can leave a message, but I probably won't listen to it. Beep.*

"Goddamn it," I mutter under my breath, knowing what I need to do.

I scroll through his contacts until I get to him, then press call.

"What the fuck, man. Where are you?" The gravelly voice shouts from the other end.

"Gabriel? I—"

My voice cracks, a sob breaking free before I finish the sentence. His name rolls off my tongue like a prayer.

Despite what's happened, I knew he'd answer. He wouldn't let anything happen to Shane, and if anyone can handle a crisis, it's Gabriel Abbott.

"Ash? Hey, what's wrong? Where's Shane?" The concern lacing his voice has me trembling.

"He's here. He just showed up, and I—I don't know what to do. It's bad. Please help me." My words become more panicked as tears race down my cheeks.

"Okay. I'm on my way. Is he conscious?"

"He was, but he's not now."

This is the nightmare I've been dreading for years, and I'm not ready to lose him. He's been there for me when every other man in my life has let me down. He's my partner in crime, my sounding board, my shoulder to cry on, and my best friend.

"Yeah. I'll be there in a minute. Get him on his side in case he pukes."

Too late for that.

"O-okay."

I turn the phone on speaker, stretching the charger across the room to lay it on the coffee table, so I can crawl over to the couch and grab Shane's hand.

"Gabriel?"

"Yeah?"

"Please don't hang up."

I press a kiss to Shane's forehead and brush the hair from his face. "Please be okay. Please. I need you," I whisper so only Shane can hear me.

"I won't. I'm pulling out now. Everything's gonna be fine. Is he on his side?" The turn signal clicks in the background.

"Yeah." I sniff.

"Okay, good. That's good. You've got this."

"I can't lose him," I sob, dropping my forehead to his arm.

"I know. I'm so sorry, Ash. When's the last time you heard from him?"

"Um..."

He was here a week ago, when everything happened with my dad. Nik called this weekend asking if I'd seen him, but I figured he was just avoiding me because he felt guilty.

"I guess a week ago. God, where's he been this whole time? He looks terrible."

"A week-long binge will do that to you," he mumbles.

21

GABE

MAY PRESENT DAY

I'm going to be responsible for the death of my best friend.

I brought him into this world, and it's going to kill him.

Her voice was a shock after that conversation we had this afternoon. Things got a little too real, and all I could think was *make it stop*. So, I acted like an asshole. I'm good at that these days.

Now, her sobs over the line are about enough to make my heart stop beating in my chest. I know how much he means to her, and I'm not sure she can handle losing him. Until they went to live with their Gran, Shane was the one who watched out for her. He was more like a parent than a brother for a long time.

Jumping out of the truck, I race to the front door. It's unlocked, so I barge in.

"Is he breathing?" I ask, tearing through the house to where Ash sits, looking every bit the broken girl I saw leaving town six years ago. She's beside the couch, holding Shane's hand.

"Yeah. I think so." She sits back onto her butt.

I kneel and tap his face. "Hey. Wake up, fucker. We've gotta go."

He groans, rolling his head to the side. At least he's still alive. I've seen him every which way but sober over the years, but I've never seen him this bad.

"Alright. I need you to help me out here," I groan, hoisting him to his feet. He doesn't really help, but he is at least trying.

His eyes open a bit and his brows pinch. "Gabe?"

"Yeah. I'm here. What the fuck are you doing to yourself, man?" I grunt, trying to keep us both standing. "I need you to help me get your big ass to the truck, okay?"

He nods, trying to shuffle to the door.

It's not pretty, but we get there. Ash grabs her shit and runs out behind us.

"I'll sit in the back with him," she yells.

After shoving him into the back seat, I wait until she slides in before shutting the door and racing around the truck.

"If you puke in this truck, you're cleaning it up the second you're discharged," I snap back at Shane as I climb in the driver's seat, but he's already out again.

On the way to the hospital, I call JT. He's going to pick up Nik and meet us there. The whole drive, Ash sits in the back running her hands through his hair and whispering as tears stream down her face.

I hate it when she cries. It feels like a shirt that just doesn't fit quite right.

Within seconds of arriving at the ER, we're surrounded by doctors and nurses who rush him inside. Ash stands next to the truck, tears spilling down her face.

So, out of something that feels an awful lot like habit, I pull her to me.

"He'll be okay." Her floral shampoo fills my nose, and I resist the urge to press my lips to the top of her head.

Her shoulders shake as she wraps her arms around me. It's familiar, and something stirs in my chest that I know is going to hurt later, but right now all I can think about is her.

Eventually, she pulls away with blotchy cheeks and bloodshot eyes.

"I need to be with him," she says.

She's wearing nothing but tiny pajama shorts and a matching tank top. I reach back into the truck, grabbing my gray hoodie before pulling it over her. Because she's so short, it covers more than the shorts did.

"Thank you," she mutters, not making eye contact with me.

"I'll wait for Nik. We'll be in when she gets here."

She nods, disappearing inside.

When JT and Nik show up, Nik flings open the door and shoots out of the passenger seat. "Is he okay?"

"I don't know. They took him inside."

She doesn't stop to listen.

JT smacks my back, pulling me into a hug. I wouldn't say I'm an emotional guy. I can count on one hand the number of times I've really lost my shit, but this is testing my ability to hold it together.

"He'll be fine," JT says.

We've been inseparable since birth, except for the few years he did in jail. He's had my back more times than I can count, and now is no exception.

I nod, and we head into the building to find out if we lose a brother tonight.

Pacing as half the club fills the waiting room, I'm surprised I haven't worn down the white flooring.

The clock ticks—ten minutes, twenty, an hour. Still no news.

Ash sits by the window with her legs curled under her. She's been staring out at the night since I came inside. It's hard to watch.

Against my better judgement, I walk over and place a hand on her shoulder, sitting in the chair beside her. Her eyes are puffy and glistening. I don't know what I'm doing exactly, but I can't sit across the room and do nothing. Not when she's like this. Her face scrunches as tears roll down her cheeks. She collapses to my chest, her shoulders shaking, and I wrap my arms around her. This is probably a bad idea. She's supposed to hate me. That's how this works, but she needs someone. And as much as I hate to admit this, I think that someone is me.

"How are you feeling?" I ask.

"Like I've had my heart ripped out and then shoved back in upside down."

I snort a laugh. "I'm so sorry."

When she pulls back again and speaks, her voice is softer. "Thank you for answering."

The way she's looking at me makes me feel raw and exposed. Like she can see straight through the mask I've been hiding behind.

"Always." I tuck a piece of hair behind her ear. "I'm sorry I ever made you feel like I wouldn't be there if you needed me."

She swallows, blinking as she collects herself. "I appreciate this, but it changes nothing."

"I know." I nod. "It's fine."

With a finger under her chin, I tilt her head. "Let me be

what you need tonight, and tomorrow you can go back to hating me."

And that's a bad move. I know. She's not mine.

But I can't sit back and watch her go through this alone.

A nurse appears from around the corner, glancing around the packed room. "Are you the family of Mr. Michaels?"

Ash lifts her head. "Is he okay?"

"Yes, we're just waiting for a room, then he'll be moved. He's very lucky. If he hadn't been brought in when he was, he probably wouldn't be here."

A cracked sob leaves her throat, and she covers her mouth with a hand, muffling her words when she says, "Can I see him?"

The nurse nods. "We had to give him something. He was very agitated when he came to. He's tired, but he's awake. I'll take you back." She smiles as Ash jumps up, scurrying after her.

No one says a word for long minutes as we wait for Ash to come back.

"I'm his fucking father!" someone shouts from the front desk. I grind my molars. *I know that voice.*

JT throws his arm out. "I got it. Stay here."

A few of the other guys follow him out of the waiting room.

When he comes back and plops down beside me, there's a deep crease between his brows. "He left. I sent one of the guys to trail him."

I run a hand down my face and groan. "What the fuck did he want?"

"To see Shane, I guess. They told him Shane didn't want to see him."

"No shit. What made him think he would to begin with?"

JT shakes his head.

"This fucking night."

"I know what you mean." He snorts, going silent for a moment before adding, "I get why you're doing all this, but you should take a step back. I can take Ash home later."

He's probably right, but not a fucking chance.

"It's fine. It's not like that."

He nods, but I can tell by the look on his face he's not buying it.

I'm still stewing over Adam when Ash finally comes back. He's the reason my best friend can't check his demons, and he's the reason the love of my life can't trust anyone. Well—one of the reasons.

Fuck.

I knew it the moment she leaned into me. What was locked up tight is slowly slipping through the cracks, and I've spent the whole night trying to keep it at bay, knowing it will crush me if I don't. She's the only thing I've ever wanted, and the only thing I can't have. The one thing that's been just out of reach, and her in my arms feels like dangling a fucking carrot in my face.

The years of convincing myself I don't still want her are useless because yes, the fuck I do. I can feel the mudslide happening, but it would seem I'm completely useless in stopping it. Sometimes it feels like there's two different people trapped in my head. The one who can't imagine living a life that she isn't in, and the one who knows that's not an option. These days, they don't seem to be coexisting very well.

The nurse leads Nik and I to his room next.

"I need a minute with him if that's okay," Nik says, grabbing my hand.

I nod, and she slips into his room.

Leaning against the wall outside, the night soaks in. I'm sure the last person Ash wanted to call was me, but I couldn't let her go through this alone, so I swooped in like I always have, and I'll be damned if she didn't fucking let me.

I've never stopped loving her, and I definitely never stopped wanting her. I just stopped letting myself have her. Right now, it's hard to remember why that is. I've always been sure I made the right choice, but watching her break tonight and lean into me... I don't know.

This was the least I could do for Ash. I might not be able to love her like she deserves, but I'll never pass up an opportunity to ease her pain. Deep down, I'm still me despite everything. And she's still Ash. That means more to me than I wish it did.

Nik peeks out and taps my shoulder. I follow her back into the room. My best friend lies in the bed, a monitor beeping above him and an IV running in his right arm. He still looks like shit but not quite as bad as earlier.

"What the fuck, man." I squeeze his arm.

"Can I have a minute, baby?" he asks Nik.

She nods before shuffling out of the room.

"Listen, I'm so sorry."

"I know. It's all good. I'm just glad you're okay." I release him and sit in the chair by his bed.

"Nik told me Ash called you. Thank you for showing up like that. I—" He chokes on a sob. "I forgot she was there. The last thing I wanted was for her to see me... to have to—"

"I know. I would do anything for her." I pause before adding, "And you."

He sighs, wiping away tears. "I gotta get some help."

"Yeah. I know."

"The doctor said they can set me up with a rehab. I can go straight there when I'm discharged."

"That's great, man."

"Yeah." He takes a deep breath. "Except it's a shit ton of money I don't have."

I scoff. He would have it if he didn't snort it all. But then I guess he wouldn't need rehab then, would he?

The club brings in a small fortune, so I don't hesitate to say, "Don't worry about it. I'll cover it."

"Gabe, I can't ask you to do that."

"You're not. Honestly, at this point, I'm not even offering. I'm demanding. You have to go."

He drops his chin to his chest. "Yeah. Alright."

I stand. "Look, your sister's knocked out in the waiting room. I'm gonna get her home. I'll come back tomorrow."

When I return to the waiting room, Ash is sitting in the same chair, watching cars pass on the street out front like she's been doing most of the night.

"I'll take you home. You ready?" I ask.

She nods, and I grab her hand, leading her to the parking lot. I open the passenger door and watch as she climbs in.

It all seems so familiar—like in a different universe, we do this all the time. Maybe there weren't so many obstacles, and those kids figured it out.

We drive in silence. I'm not sure she's paying attention because she's been staring blankly out the window, but she perks up when I make a right in the opposite direction of Gran's house.

"Where are we going?" she asks.

"Dee's. You have to be starving."

Nothing else would be open this late anyway, but for

what it's worth, Dee's was always her favorite. There's little that fries and a strawberry shake can't fix for Ash. The hint of a smile graces her lips.

I park in an empty spot and jump out.

When I come back with a bag and two cups in my arms, she turns in the seat to face me.

I hold out a shake. "You okay?"

"Uh-huh," she says, her gray eyes looking through me instead of at me.

I wish there were more I could do than buy her a goddamn milkshake.

She sips on the shake and picks at the fries on the way home but doesn't say another word even as we pull up at Gran's.

Halfway up the porch, Ash freezes, eyes fixed on the front door. I take her keys from her and unlock the door.

She emotionlessly stares into the living room but doesn't budge from the porch. "I thought I was gonna watch my brother die in this house tonight."

Those words slice a hole straight through my gut, but I swallow it down. "I know, but he didn't. Thanks to you."

She finally walks into the house, leaving me to stand in the doorway unsure what to do. I don't want to leave her here like this, but she's not mine, and staying with her feels like crossing the thin line we've been walking all night.

Like stepping into a role that isn't mine and hasn't been in a long time.

Except maybe this *is* my purpose in her life. To be here when she needs me and then fade into the background when it's over.

I step back out to the porch to leave when she whispers, "We can still go back to hating each other tomorrow, but please don't leave tonight."

I could never hate you.

My feet turn around, my hands shutting the door behind me of their own accord. If she wants me here, that's exactly where I'll be.

She starts to sit on the couch when her eyes catch on the vomit still splattered on the floor.

"I got it." Getting a towel from the kitchen, I quickly clean up the mess.

When I finish and wash my hands, I find her curled up in a blanket on the far end of the couch like she can't bring herself to sit where he was at. She pats the cushion, so I drop next to her, and she lies on my chest like it's where she belongs, and I can't stop myself from thinking maybe it is.

Or maybe I'm just a masochist, who desperately wants it to be because I know this is going to hurt, and yet, here I am anyway.

22

ASH

MAY PRESENT DAY

I haven't seen or heard from Gabe since the night of Shane's overdose. I was a little disappointed when I woke the day after and he was gone. I just wanted to live in that delusion a little longer. My heart felt like it was cracking in half all over again.

This makes no sense, but he didn't feel like the Gabe who broke my heart. He felt like my friend, who would sit on the roof and listen to me ramble. Gabriel, who doesn't tell anyone his feelings, but shared little tidbits with me. Gabriel, who I know will be there when I call.

I needed that version of him, and I think he knew it because he slipped on that mask for the night, and God, I've missed him. His sweet and smoky scent wrapped around me as he cradled my body to his chest.

The more I think about it, the more I struggle to reconcile the differences between the man who broke my heart and the man who bulldozed in when I needed him. I don't understand how those two can be the same person. Maybe I never will.

If I had doubts before, I don't anymore. The boy I loved

is in there. I didn't imagine him, and he wasn't made up. He was real, and he's still there somewhere. He might not be for me anymore, but he existed, and there's something validating about that even if my heart bleeds a little for what could have been.

With Shane at rehab for ninety days, I'm determined to finish the house, so I can list it when he gets home. Today, I'm working on Gran's room. I've put it off until last because it feels like closing the book on this part of my life, and I'm not sure I'm ready for that. I've cleaned out her closet and vanity, packaging up anything I remember her wearing to take home with me.

Kneeling on the floor, I look under her bed. Behind an old suitcase, there's a shoebox. The edge tears off as I pull it toward me. My name's scribbled across the top in sharpie.

When I lift the lid, I recognize exactly what's in here. My heart sinks at the sight. Gabriel and I got close the summer before my senior year. When I went home at the beginning of August, he sent me a letter. I was surprised at first. He hadn't texted or called at all since I'd gotten home. I kind of figured he was busy with his own life. With each letter, the more I started to wonder if we could be more than friends. Eventually, we started texting some, but the letters were different. Like how he was different when it was just us. When I came home the next summer, I brought the letters with me. I was a lovesick teenager and couldn't imagine leaving them behind, I guess. Then he broke my heart. I threw them in the trash before heading home to Raleigh, but here they are.

I open the box and pull out the letters.

August 15

Ash,

Holy shit, it's quiet without you here. I didn't realize how much you talked until I woke up today, and you're gone. I'm sitting here on the roof and it's just so fucking quiet. Anyway, I figured if I'm going to sit in silence, I might as well write to you to pass the time. I don't know when you go back to school, but I hope you have a good first day. Don't get caught up with any shitheads this year. I've got enough on my plate right now and don't have time to drive 2 hours to kick some fucker's ass. You left your jacket in my truck last week. I saw it when I ran to town this morning. I'll hold on to it until you come back. We found out JT might get out early, so that's pretty cool. I could use another friend since my favorite one left yesterday.

Anyway, you don't have to write back if you think it's stupid.

Gabriel

August 30

Ash,

I never said I missed you; I said it was quiet. Don't flatter yourself. I have a life. I wouldn't be mad if you came back early, though. No one else is as entertaining as you. The club is fine, I guess. I don't know what I'm doing to tell the truth. I'm still not sure I want it anymore. Everything feels so fucked. Happy late birthday, by the way. I hope you had a great day.

Love,
Gabriel

December 24

Ash,

Does your family do a big Christmas thing? We usually do, but things are weird this year. My dad seems to treat me more like a club member than his son. I should be happy about that I guess, but I'm not. Don't tell anyone, but I don't think I'm okay. I'm not sure I have been since you left. I know that's cheesy, but I need my best friend to talk to, I guess. I know I

said before I don't miss you, but I think
I do.
    Love,
    Gabriel

April 10
Ash,
    I'm sorry about your breakup. I told
you he was a dick. Before you say it, I
know, I think they're all dicks, but that's
because you only pick assholes who don't
deserve you. You really need to have someone
look at your picker because it's clearly
broken. On a brighter note, at least you
only have a little over a month left of
high school. Do you know what you're going to
do next? If you move across the country,
don't think that gets you out of coming to
visit. You're obligated to come once a year
at least.
    Love,
    Gabriel

I haven't moved for hours. I've been sitting on the floor reading dozens of letters from a time when I was falling in love with a boy two hours away. A boy I didn't think would ever love me back.

My phone rings from where it sits on Gran's dresser. After stuffing the letters back into the box, I push off the floor and pick it up.

"Hello?"

"Hi, sweetheart. How's it going?" my mom coos, in her fake, sweet voice.

"It's fine. I'm about done here. I think I'll be back tomorrow." I drop to sit on the edge of the bed.

"Oh, wonderful. Maggie's really missing her mom."

She knows how guilty I feel for being away from her. I don't know why she feels the need to say shit like that. If she knows you're insecure about something, she just can't help poking it.

"I miss her too. I'm ready to be home."

"I never did like that town. Why your grandmother stayed in that dump all these years is beyond me."

"It's not that bad."

"Either way I'm glad you'll be done with it. You know, I'm so proud of you for walking away from that Ravens Ridge boy and finding something better."

I scrunch up my nose. "Casey *cheated*. I wouldn't say that's better."

She exhales. "You and Casey are in a rough patch. Every married couple goes through stuff like this."

Rolling my eyes, I say, "Are you hearing yourself? It's not a rough patch. It's over."

She sighs. "You're always so dramatic."

"No. I'm not. You just never listen to me!" I shout.

"Do not raise your voice at me. I'm just trying to help."

And with that, I can't take it anymore. She's always *just trying to help,* but I'm not the one who needed it. But she's never once attempted to do anything for her kid that actually needed help—has been screaming for it for years.

"Help? What about Shane? You're his mother too. Why don't you ever try to help *him*?"

She groans. "I've tried to help him plenty."

"Have you? Because I've never seen it."

"Where is this coming from?"

"I don't know, Mom." I shake my head. "Maybe I'm finally tired of trying to please you."

"Please me? Give me a break. When have you ever done what I wanted you to do?"

"My whole life! You didn't want me to go out with my friends, so I stayed home. You didn't want me to stay in Ravens Ridge, so I left. You didn't want Shane around, so my relationship with him suffered. You didn't want me to go to visit Gran after everything happened, so I didn't. Hell, you didn't want me to tell—"

"Do not blame me for everything that's gone wrong in your life. You came home because that boy threw you away like trash! That is not my fault!"

"Right, but you weren't gonna let me stay anyway, so what's it matter?" I shout.

"We're not doing this. I've given you everything. I've supported you and helped when you needed it."

"Right." I nod, laughing. "As long as I followed your rules."

"I've only tried to help you make the right choices. You're twisting things around."

"Yeah? And what makes you such an expert? Your first husband was a real peach after all."

"That's not fair! I was a victim in that situation too!"

"Yeah, and then you sent your own child away to be his next victim," I bite out through gritted teeth. "You have no idea what Shane went through. You put him in Dad's hands. You let it happen!"

"I didn't know!"

"How could you not? He did it to you first!"

The next words out of her mouth come out broken. "Because I never thought he'd do that to his own kid."

My chest heaves as I try to calm down. "And what about now? Why can't you do the right thing for Shane *now?*"

"I'm well aware of the mistakes I've made, but I don't know what to do for him now!"

For the first time maybe in my life, my mother sounds human—broken. Like she regrets what's happened too.

"You could at least try."

She sniffles. "I have to go. I'll see you tomorrow."

And like that, her emotions are tucked back away out of sight. But now at least I know they're there.

It only takes about a week for me to finish cleaning out the rest of the house. My ship feels like it's sinking, and every day that passes I'm inching closer to drowning. It doesn't feel right to sell the house without Shane, though. I want him to have a chance to say goodbye if he wants to.

Until then, I'm going home. I need a break, and Maggie needs her mom.

23

———

GABE

AUGUST PRESENT DAY

After work, I head to the clubhouse to meet Nik. I promised her I'd help set up for Shane's coming home party tomorrow.

"Hey," I greet her, strolling in, not looking up from my phone. When she doesn't answer, I glance up and freeze.

Nik stands next to a fold-out table, grimacing as someone else fiddles with a floral centerpiece.

Shit. Ash is here.

Her hair's tied up on top of her head, and she's in an oversized band T-shirt with the shortest black skirt I've ever seen.

She offers an apologetic smile. "Hey, Gabe. I hope you don't mind; I tagged along."

Waving a hand, I say, "You're good."

Fuck me, I can't stop staring at her mouth. She's got that berry color on her lips, and it has me in a trance. I slowly pull my eyes from her and rub my palms down my jeans. "What do you need me to do?"

Nik says, "I have a few boxes out in my car. Can you grab them?"

I nod, heading toward the door. This is bad.

I grab the boxes from Nik's car before heading back in.

"What did you bring?" I ask, walking in to see the two of them standing near the bar, shots in hand. "You realize it's just dinner, right?"

"We're starting with Tequila," Nik announces, holding out a shot glass. "I need all the liquor I can get to make it through tonight. God, I don't know why I'm so nervous. I keep thinking what if something happens and he doesn't get to come home or what if he comes home tomorrow and goes right back to his old shit."

"He's coming home," I say, placing a hand on her shoulder. "Don't worry, he's got this."

I lift my glass before throwing it back.

After a couple of drinks, Ash goes to the bathroom.

Nik nudges my shoulder. "I know what you did for Shane. Thank you."

My brows pinch.

"We'll pay you back. I'm just so grateful. He wouldn't have gone if you hadn't paid for it."

"Don't worry about it." My mouth turns down, and I shrug. "I just want him to get better."

She smiles, running a hand down my arm.

Then I add, "But uh... do me a favor? Don't tell Ash. It's easier if she keeps hating me."

She nods.

When Ash returns, she asks, "Want to play pool?"

"Nah, I'm terrible." Nik gestures toward me.

Absolutely not. Playing pool, a little drunk, with Ash is a terrible fucking idea. She turns those gray eyes in my direction and my stomach bottoms out.

"I'll play if you want." Apparently, I'm in the mood to play with fire.

Ash doesn't seem sure either but nods anyway.

Midway through the game, I can't hold back my amusement anymore.

"Well, you haven't gotten any better in the last six years." I cover my grin by taking a swig of beer before setting it back down.

"Ha ha." She rolls her eyes, leaning over the table. "It's not like I've had time to play pool. I have a life."

"I'm just saying, I think you've actually gotten worse, if that's even possible."

She hits the cue ball straight into the corner pocket, and I cover my mouth to stifle a laugh.

"Shit!" She spins to point at me. "Watch it. I'll kick your ass."

"Damn!" Taking a step back, I throw my hands up. "At least you're not still a sore loser."

That gets a real laugh from her—bright and warm. "Fuck off, would ya?"

Nik stands from the table she's been sitting at watching. "Okay. I need to get out of here. I have to pick Shane up bright and early." She wraps her arms around Ash. "Want me to drive you home? I've pretty well sobered up."

Ash appears to be thinking about it.

Then she says, "Nah. I'm gonna turn this game around before I head home."

Then she sticks her fucking tongue out. Literally, sticks it out like a child. I have to turn around to keep from cracking up.

She's such a shit. One would think she'd grow out of it, but she hasn't.

Thank God.

She has a way of making you want to strangle her and bury yourself in her all at the same time.

Nik nods, but her eyes flick to Ash one last time before she leaves.

"Okay." Ash picks up her stick and laughs. "Ready to get smoked?"

"Yeah. I would love to see how you plan on coming back from this mess."

"Oh, I have my ways." She quirks an eyebrow.

"I remember your ways all too well. When I turn my back, you're gonna bat a few of your own into the pocket, right?" I mirror her facial expression, remembering how she used to cheat. I'd let her because let's be honest, I never gave a shit about the game when I was with her.

"Are you accusing me of cheating?" She holds a hand to her chest, trying not to smile. "I'm offended."

"Uh-huh," I say, pointing my stick at her. "Be offended with your hands where I can see them."

The smile she was holding back breaks into a full-on laugh.

We finish our game, and she walks to the bar, flopping down on a stool.

"Well, I may have to walk home because I think I've had one too many shots." She hiccups as I sit on the stool next to her.

"I think you've had more than one too many. Maybe about three too many," I tease. "JT's still around here some- where; I can get him to give you a ride."

"Hmm. That would be nice." She wiggles her brows and bites her lip. "Man, he grew up, didn't he?"

I can't tell if she's fucking with me. He spends the majority of his spare time in the gym working out the pent- up aggression he's had since getting out of jail.

He's huge.

Between that, his dark wavy hair, and tattoos, women

throw themselves at him, but he doesn't sleep around much. He's single, but his baby mama, Katie, keeps him on a pretty tight leash. I don't get it. She doesn't want him, but every time she catches wind that some other girl might be in his life, she swoops in and puts a stop to it. He loves his two kids, so he puts up with it for them, I guess.

The thought of Ash and JT like that makes my blood boil.

"Jesus. Chill. A girl might think you're jealous if you keep glaring like that," she chuckles. "No need to worry. I won't jump JT on the way home."

That does it. I'm no longer allowing him to drive her home. An image of him railing her in the back seat of his truck has my head literally spinning. No fucking way. She starts laughing and reaches over the bar to grab the Tequila bottle, but I stop her with a hand on her wrist.

"I think you've had plenty, Ash. You're gonna fucking barf, and I'll be pissed if I have to clean up after you."

She rolls her eyes, letting me take the bottle, her ass plopping back on the leather seat. "Whatever you say, Dad. So, where is JT? I should probably get out of here soon."

"Oh, no fucking way he's taking you home. You're walking. I can't trust you not to take advantage of him."

She throws her head back, laughing again.

"Oh, come on. I swear to keep my pants on. Please don't make me walk," she begs, clasping her hands and batting her lashes.

Fuck, her bottom lip shoots out, and I can't stop staring. She must notice because she pulls it back in and straightens.

"I'm kidding." She clears her throat. "I think I've had my fill of the boys in this club."

Ouch.

I pull out my phone and text JT.

"So, tell me what's new with you. What have you been up to all this time?" she asks, startling me for a second.

She's been so standoffish since coming back, and now she's making small talk. It's weird, but I have the familiar urge to spill every detail of my life to her. Of course I can't. She's not the same girl anymore.

"Nothing, really." I shrug. "Just club shit. You know basically the same shit I was doing six years ago."

She nods, avoiding my eyes. "I'm separated."

"Oh, shit. I didn't know. Are you happy about it or—"

I assumed, but I never knew for sure.

"Yeah, I mean it sucks. No one gets married thinking they're gonna end up divorced, but I'll be glad when it's final and I can put it behind me." She takes a deep breath before continuing. "Before you ask, he cheated," she says, shaking her head as her face falls. "I just keep falling in love with men who can't love me back."

"Ash—"

"Don't. I was there, remember? I know exactly what you said to me that night. You can play the nice-guy role all you want now, but it doesn't change what happened."

She's right. Nothing I do now can make up for the pain I caused her. The longer she's around though, the harder it is to keep telling myself I made the right choice.

"You're right. Nothing I say will make up for it." I thread my hand in hers. "But what I did and what he did, it's not on you. It's not because you're not worthy. It's because we're idiots, okay?"

She stares at our hands before pulling hers away.

"Right. Well, he was shit in bed anyway. At least maybe this way the next one will be better in bed."

It's such a change from her previous attitude that it

takes me a minute to process the words before bursting out laughing.

"Jesus. Ash, what the fuck?"

"What? It's true. I tried to give him pointers, but it was like talking to a brick wall."

I shake my head, rubbing a hand over my eyes. "Okay. Well, good to know, I guess."

Her eyes graze over me before landing on mine, and our laughter fades. We sit staring for a moment before I pull mine away.

"Look, I know you don't want to hear it, and that's fine, but I am sorry. There hasn't been a day in six years that I haven't wished things were different. Ash, I—"

That's true, I do wish things had been different, but I can't go back, so telling her anything else will only hurt both of us. "I'm just fucking sorry."

Nodding with her eyes not leaving the bar top, she's silent for a beat before saying, "Thank you."

She starts to say something before JT walks in.

"Did somebody call an Uber?"

She lets out a fake laugh, hopping off the stool. "Wow, if I knew I'd get such a hot driver, I'd have worn something else." She walks toward him.

I scowl, and she sticks her tongue out.

"Baby girl, you know you could make a garbage bag look good," JT says, throwing an arm around her shoulders.

I point my finger at him. "Hands off. The last thing we need is for Shane to come home to that shit show."

24

———

ASH

AUGUST PRESENT DAY

Shane stopped by this afternoon when they got home. After catching up with my brother, Nik dressed me in a blue-and-white floral sundress with tan woven heels before we all headed to the clubhouse.

As we stroll in, JT shouts, "Wow. Forget the garbage bag, baby girl. You should only wear that dress from now on."

A smile spreads across my face, and my cheeks heat.

"Hell, no. Another one of you fuckers hits on my sister, and I'll kill you. I'm not going down this road again," Shane says.

I keep finding myself staring at my brother. It's been years since I've seen him this healthy. The dark circles are gone, and he's already put on some weight. He looks like my brother again.

"I'm teasing. You look beautiful, Ash," JT says, pulling me in for a hug.

"Thank you."

JT turns his attention to Shane, pulling him into a hug next. "It's so good to see you, man."

Gabe stands, making his way over to us.

Holy shit.

He's wearing black dress pants and a gray dress shirt. The top couple buttons are open, and he has the sleeves rolled up showing his tattooed forearms. The intricate sleeve of winding snakes and flowers on his right arm is the same as I remember, but the grayscale, hyper-realistic skull on the other is new.

His eyes latch onto mine before scanning the dress. When they make it back to my gaze, his eyebrow hitches, and it's like I've been lit on fire.

There's always been a physical energy between us, even when we were strictly friends.

Dipping my head, I dart across the room to an empty table and take a seat. God, what I wouldn't give for this to not be a sober party. I just have to get through tonight.

"You okay?" Colette asks from behind me.

"Oh, hey!" I stand, throwing my arms around her. "I'm great!" My smile is big and genuine as I pull away from her. "I hoped I'd get to see you while I was in town."

"I wondered if you were planning to avoid me the whole time you were here or if you'd eventually come around."

I love Colette, but I've heard enough stories to know I don't want to be on her bad side. I don't think she's been as involved in the club since losing her husband, but she's no saint.

"Oh. No. I wasn't—I mean I didn't mean to avoid you. It was more—"

"It was my son you were ignoring?" She quirks a brow. "Yeah. I know. Listen, I love him dearly, but I'll always want what's best for you. You know that, right?"

I nod.

"Anyway. You look beautiful tonight, sweetheart. Don't be a stranger, okay?"

I nod again as she turns, walking toward Shane before wrapping her arms around him. A hand lands on my lower back before I sit.

"You really are stunning tonight," a deep voice whispers in my ear. I can feel his breath on my neck, and his scent fills my nose.

I spin to find Gabe standing so close I forget how to breathe.

"Thank you. You look nice yourself."

His eyes are focused solely on mine, and it almost burns. "Have a good night, Ash."

The second his hand leaves my back, it's like a part of my body has detached itself. I still crave his hands on me like I did when we were together.

He is not yours anymore, Ash.

Dinner goes off without a hitch, but I can tell Shane's nervous. His knee bounces under the table the entire time.

When everyone finishes eating, Nik leans over and whispers something in his ear.

She touches my arm. "I think we're gonna head home. I can come back later and get you if you want me to."

"No, that's okay. I'll go with you now."

"Fuck that." JT leans back in his chair, putting it on two legs. "You'll miss all the fun. We're about to get this party started. I'll take you home later."

The guys were trying to keep it reined in until Shane left. I should leave, but it's been nice seeing everyone again, and I'll be headed home for good soon. One last night won't hurt anyone.

Nik gives me a questioning glare. "You good?"

"Yeah. I'll catch a ride from JT."

This might be a terrible idea, but I don't care. I'm tired of being worried about everything all the time. I want to have fun for one night.

It doesn't take much for dinner to turn into a drunken mess.

As I find a spot at the bar, my world is flipped upside down as the door swings open. He stands out like a sore thumb in his expensive blue suit and pristine dress shoes. I slide off the stool and waltz over to my soon-to-be ex-husband in sheer horror. His lip curls as he scans the place before his eyes land on me.

"Casey, what are you doing here?" I ask.

"I told you. I want to talk."

"Okay? I was just home for a few months. We could have talked any of that time. Why are you here now?"

"I had work shit while you were home."

"How did you even know where to find me?"

He looks at me like *duh*. "I called your mom."

Of course, my mother would tell him.

"Well, I'm kind of in the middle of something. We can talk some other time." I start for the bar, and he grabs my arm.

"I drove two hours to see you. The least you can do is give me ten fucking minutes."

I yank out of his grip. It'll be a cold day in hell when I let him manhandle me.

Stepping closer, I whisper, "Casey, I'm not doing this here. You need to go."

"Are you kidding me?"

As I'm about to say something, the hair on the back of my neck stands up.

The looming presence behind me says, "I think she said no."

Casey grins like a hyena, narrowing his eyes.

"You must be Gabe." His eyes flick between me and the man who just can't seem to stay out of my damn business. He huffs, "I'll leave when I've talked to *my wife*."

Gabe moves past me. "You'll leave when I tell you to leave, or you can be carried out in a fucking body bag."

I zip around him to stand between the two.

With a hand on Gabe's chest, I say, "Enough. This is none of your business. Go!" Pointing my finger toward the table he was sitting at, I stare him down.

He glances between me and Casey for a beat too long before letting out a forceful exhale and stomping away.

I grab Casey by the arm, dragging him out the door. "We can talk outside. Let's go."

As we hit the parking lot, he pulls away from me. "What the fuck was that?" His brows lift, and he gestures to the clubhouse with an open palm. "That's who you'd rather be with?"

"I'm not with anyone, Casey. God, you don't listen at all, do you?"

"No. I heard it all loud and clear. Your criminal boyfriend threatened to murder me."

"He's not my boyfriend!" I shout, stomping my foot because it doesn't seem to be getting through his thick skull. "Listen to me. I don't want to be with you because you're self-ish, and demanding, and a cheater! It has nothing to do with anyone else. I don't want to be with you because of you!"

He stares at me, gritting his teeth. "This is a bad idea! Hanging around here?" He shakes his head. "It's a bad move and you know it."

"I'm not hanging around here. I'm here for my brother. That's it."

He lifts a brow. "Is your brother in there right now? Is he partying with everyone to celebrate his discharge from rehab?"

My cheeks heat. "He just left. I was catching up with old friends, and then I was heading home too."

"Yeah." His mouth turns down, and he scoffs. "It looks like you were just leaving."

He stomps across the parking lot.

"Casey, it's not like that."

Why am I chasing after him? I don't owe him an explanation; he's the one who betrayed my trust.

"It's not like what, Ashton? You're not fucking your ex-boyfriend behind my back?"

I rear back and laugh. "One, I'm not fucking anyone. And two, you have a lot of room to talk."

"It was a mistake! I keep telling you that!" he shouts before throwing his hands up defensively. "You know what? Forget it! Have a great life."

He barrels toward his car. This time I don't chase after him. He blew up our marriage, not me. I don't have anything to feel guilty about. As I stand in the middle of the lot and watch as he pulls away, not a single regret for refusing to take him back crosses my mind.

I make my way back inside and order a shot.

After a few drinks, I'm holding up the bar with JT for an hour, when he asks, "So, tell me, how did this Casey guy manage to let you slip out of his hands?"

"Well." I pause, laughing. "He let more than his hands slip into someone else."

I don't know if it's because I'm drunk or because I truly don't care anymore, but it doesn't sting as much to say it out loud.

"Oh, damn. How do you keep managing to pick the world's biggest dumbasses?"

I burst out laughing. "Um, one of those dumbasses is your best friend."

"Oh, I know, and don't think I haven't told him exactly how stupid I think he is."

I elbow him, taking another swig of my beer.

"Are you trying to move in on my girl?" A tattooed arm wraps around my shoulder, and I glance back to find Gabriel and JT having a silent conversation.

"Oh. Now she's your girl?" JT asks, glaring at Gabriel in a way that doesn't seem like he's joking. "I thought it wasn't like that."

Gabriel rears back. "That doesn't mean you can have her," he snaps, voice laced with venom.

I put my hands up between the two of them.

"Okay, I think I'll decide who gets to have me." I turn to Gabriel. "Might I remind you; I am not your girl. I haven't been in a very long time."

Removing his arm from my shoulders, I recognize what's happening.

He's trashed.

Gabriel doesn't get drunk. He likes to be in control, but he's completely wasted right now.

He leans down with his mouth to my ear and whispers, "You've always been *my* girl."

The way he emphasizes the word, sends a shiver down my spine. I tilt my head up so I'm face to face with him.

"No."

He fucking smirks.

"Yes, Ash," he replies before walking away.

JT stares at me with his eyebrows raised.

"What?"

"Nothing." He shakes his head. "Just... maybe stay away from him tonight. I don't know what his deal is, but that can't be good."

"The fact that he's drunk?"

"Yeah. He's not been this drunk since—" He sucks his teeth, shaking his head.

All of the shots have gone straight to my bladder, so I get up and head for the bathroom. Gabe being drunk puts me on edge. I don't know why he's decided tonight of all nights to get wasted, but nothing good can come from it. I should've left when I had the chance.

When I come out of the bathroom, guess who's leaning up against the wall right outside the door?

"What the hell. Stalker?"

Gabe laughs, and it's a bright warm sound. It reminds me of our days on the roof. He steps toward me until we're so close I can smell his cologne.

"What are you doing, Gabe?"

"Did you love him?"

"What?" I take a step back until I'm met with the brick wall behind me. He closes the space, bracing a hand above my head.

"That fucker in the suit. Did you love him?"

"Of course I did. Why would I marry him if I didn't?"

His jaw clenches, and he eyes me closely.

"It wasn't like us, though." He bites his lip, his eyes flicking down to my mouth and back up. "Was it?"

"Gabe, get a grip." When I try to sidestep him, he moves, blocking me. "I moved on, and so did you. Let's not play this game."

"And what game would that be? You know as well as I do that, we"—he gestures between us—"will never move on from this."

"I don't know shit. You never loved me anyway. Remember, or did you get amnesia?"

He scoffs. "You don't really think that, do you?"

"It's literally what you said. So, yeah, I do think that."

He nods a few times, running his tongue over his top teeth. "I know what I said." His throat bobs, and his eyes burn into mine. With each inhale, my chest brushes his.

Before I can say anything, his hand moves to my neck and slides up the back of my head into my hair.

My breath hitches. "What are you doing?"

My eyes snag on his mouth. His tongue darts out over his bottom lip, and his face moves closer to mine. He stops just shy of our lips touching.

"Tell me to stop," he whispers.

I open my mouth to say it, but nothing comes out.

This is a bad idea, but there's nothing I want more than to kiss him. I close my mouth and bring my eyes up to meet his. He doesn't look any surer than I feel, but there's a buzzing between us. Something that I can't ignore. I could pretend to put up a fight, but that's all it would be—pretend. Because I've never not wanted to kiss Gabriel Abbott since I saw him on Gran's porch when I was fifteen.

When he doesn't move, I launch toward him, our mouths colliding. It's electric. His tongue parts my lips, and I sink into him like I've done a hundred times before.

Suddenly, it's like we're kissing for the first time again in this very hallway. I wrap an arm around his neck, and he lifts me slightly off the floor before I hook my legs around his waist. When a small moan escapes my throat, he presses me back into the wall. It's easily one of the best kisses I've ever had.

It feels like being swept away at sea. It's intoxicating, but it also feels like drowning. Or like drinking saltwater.

You're so desperate for something to quench your thirst, but the more you drink, the thirstier you become. No matter how much I kiss him, I'm never satiated. The second we part, I always want more.

When I tangle my fingers in his hair, he goes completely still. I pull back from him, searching his face. His eyes are closed, and his brows are pinched.

He puts me back on my feet before letting out an aggravated exhale.

"Fuck!" His chest heaves as he tries to catch his breath.

"What's wrong?"

"I can't do this. I'm sorry. I—" He takes a step back from me, putting a hand on his hip and running the other down his face. "We shouldn't have done that."

"What do you mean?"

He cannot be doing this again.

"We can't do this! You're you and I'm—" He turns his back to me. "This was a bad idea."

My stomach sinks.

I didn't think about it before kissing him. Bile rises in my throat. Swallowing, I run my thumb across my bottom lip, and stare at him for a few seconds.

When I can't think of anything else to say, I mutter, "I'm gonna go."

My eyes stay trained on him as I slowly back up before turning to dart across the room. He calls my name, but I'm not doing this.

Reaching JT at the bar, I say, "Can you take me home now? I'm not feeling so well."

He searches my face. "Are you okay?"

Trying my damnedest to keep tears from falling, I nod. "I'm fine. I just want to go home."

Grabbing my things off the bar I add, "Now!"

He stands, and I follow him out to his truck. Once we're on the road, the dam breaks and I start to cry.

Turning down the radio, JT asks, "Ash, really, are you okay?"

I shake my head.

"What happened?"

"Nothing. I—" What do I say? I let him mess with my head once again. "I don't know why I let him do this to me."

"Who? Gabe?"

I nod. "The sad thing is, after everything, I still want to believe he felt the same way. I want to believe that a part of him is miserable without me, too."

"Ash, I know this won't make things better, but he did. Hell, I think he still does. I don't know why he does this shit, but it's not because he doesn't fucking love you."

25

———

ASH

MAY 6 YEARS AGO

Y ou'd *think* graduating high school would earn me a little bit of my brother's attention, but when I hit town, he's missing.

Ruder still, so is my *supposed* best friend who should be celebrating *with* me.

"Hey, stranger," I say, tipping my invisible cowboy hat from her doorway.

Then I notice she's not alone. "Oh shit! Sorry!"

Right as the words come out, a head of familiar dark hair pops up from her pillow. "Oh my god! Shane?" Whipping my head to Nik, I bark, "What the fuck? Are you sleeping with my brother?"

"Shit. Ash. I'm so sorry. What are you doing here?" she asks, scrambling out of bed, attempting to shield him, like I haven't already seen that my brother is in her bed.

"You've been avoiding me!" I point my finger at Shane. "What's he doing here?"

The whole time his eyes are trained on the ceiling.

"Uh. Well, he's my boyfriend." She winces. "I'd tell you

exactly what he's doing here, but I really doubt you want to know since—you know, he's your brother."

"Ew, Nik!"

"I'm sorry. I'm really sorry. Go wait for me outside. I'll be out in a minute."

I head out to the porch and sit in one of the white rocking chairs. Nik's house is tiny, but it's charming.

The front door swings open. "Okay, hear me out. I never meant to fall for your brother." She moves across the porch and hikes herself up on the railing in front of me. "It just kind of happened. I swear I was gonna tell you."

"Nik, I don't care. I just can't believe you hid it from me?"

"Really? I was so worried you'd hate me when you found out."

"I mean, it's weird, but I love you both. It might take some getting used to, but if you're happy, I'm happy."

"Oh my god! I'm so happy. I think I might love him."

"Shit! Wait, how long have you been dating?"

"Since the end of last summer. After you left, I ran into him and we've kind of been together since."

I smile. "I'm happy for you."

"I've been such a shitty friend, Ash. I'm so sorry."

Narrowing my eyes, I say, "I'll forgive you if you promise to ditch him tonight to hang out with me."

She grins. "Deal."

The door swings open again, and my brother, now fully clothed, steps out.

"Good morning, sunshine." I beam up at him as he pops a cigarette between his lips and lights it. "Ew. You're so gross."

He flips me off, sitting in the chair next to mine. "So, what are we talking about?"

"I'm stealing your girlfriend tonight." I stick my tongue out.

"Great. Finally, I can get a minute away from her. Your friend's real clingy, you know." He pretends to whisper, pointing at her.

Nik slips off her shoe and throws it at his big dumb head. "I'll remember that the next time you climb through my window in the middle of the night."

He laughs, leaning back in his chair and taking a drag. "Oh yeah? What are you gonna do?"

She quirks a brow, and the weirdest thing happens.

My brother, the smartass, pain in my side that's a prick to literally everyone, says, "I was teasing. I'm sorry."

And winks at her, actually winks. I about fall out of my chair.

Nik lifts her chin. "You're gonna have to do better than that."

A dimple appears on Shane's face, and his lips purse to hold back a smile. "I take it back. You aren't clingy."

"And?"

"And I am in fact not excited to have a minute away."

"And?" she asks, lifting a brow and crossing her arms.

"What the fuck? I don't know?" He leans forward, resting his elbows on his knees. "What else do you want from me?"

Pointing a finger at him, she says, "Admit that *you're* the clingy one."

Gabe pulls up in his *classic car* and honks. His eyes meet mine and linger for a beat too long.

Shane's brows crease, and his lip curls as he stands. "Oh, fuck right off!"

Nik howls with laughter.

Putting out the cigarette, he jogs down the porch to jump in the car.

"See you later, loser!" she shouts after him, waving a hand in the air. He flips her off with the biggest smile I've ever seen on his face. The whole thing is equal parts confusing, nauseating, and adorable.

He smacks Gabe upside the head before saying, "Stop staring at my sister, dumbass."

Nik convinces me to spend our girls' night at the clubhouse. I'm not sure you can still call it girls' night if Shane's there, but I'm just happy to spend the evening with her.

When we pull into the parking lot, there are people everywhere. We get out and walk up to the door, finding Gabriel standing outside with a group of people. He glances in my direction, giving me a tight-lipped smile, but doesn't say anything.

I don't know what I was expecting. After digging through my closet for thirty minutes, I decided on a white floral-embroidered dress. I put my hair up and took it back down a dozen times until finally throwing it into a bun and saying forget it. The whole time I pictured Gabriel getting one glance and whisking me into his arms.

Stupid, right?

I smile back, pretending I'm not disappointed and walk into the building.

Inside, the music is deafening, and it smells like alcohol. It's just like I remember it the night I was drugged. My stomach clenches. I hadn't really thought about how I'd feel coming back here for the first time.

"Hey, baby," Shane says, grabbing Nik around the waist and pulling her to him. When he releases her, he pulls me into a hug next.

"Hey, shithead."

"Hi." I wave awkwardly.

"I'm in the middle of a game, but I'll come find you when I'm done," he says to Nik before heading back to the pool table.

"I'm gonna get a drink. Want one?" she asks.

"No. I think I'll drink water tonight."

We find two seats at the bar. A red neon sign that reads Ravens Ridge Riders hangs above a wall of liquor bottles.

After a while, a man sits next to me, smiling, and says, "Well, hello."

He has dark wavy hair and deep brown eyes. Tattoos snake up both arms.

"I'm JT." He holds out his hand, and I shake it.

"Ash."

"Oh." His eyes widen. "Shane's baby sister."

I nod.

"He threatened all of us before you got here."

"What?" I ask.

"Yep, if anyone touches you"—he makes a slicing motion across his neck—"he'll kill 'em."

My eyes bulge, and my mouth pops open.

"Unfortunately for Shane, I can take him," he laughs.

If you didn't know he was in a motorcycle club, you could mistake him for a GQ model. He's taller than Shane, and his shirt clings to his lean body.

"Well, unfortunately for you, I'm not interested in anyone from this club."

Well, no one who's interested in me.

He nods. "Well, if that changes, you know where to find me. With that being said, I'm a *great* friend."

"Good to know." I grin.

"So, who're you looking for?" At my pinched expression, he huffs. "Oh, come on. That door is *not* interesting enough to earn this much of your attention." He darts his eyes over, then back, and over again dramatically.

"I uh—"

Have I been doing that?

"No, I'm just paranoid. My last time here was, well... not great."

"I heard." He gives me a sad smile. "Nothing like that will happen tonight. Anyone even looks at you wrong I'll snap their neck." He smiles for real this time.

"What? Why?"

"We're friends now." He nudges me with his elbow.

"We are?" I giggle. "I don't remember agreeing to that."

"Yeah, well." He shrugs. "I decided we are."

Squinting, I bite my bottom lip before saying, "You're trouble, aren't you?"

"Oh, fuck yeah. I'm the most trouble, but I've got your back." He winks. "Always."

I don't know why, but I want to be his friend. Have you ever met someone and you just instantly know that you can trust them? That's what it's like meeting JT. There's something so warm about him that I feel like we could talk all night.

"Okay, deal. We can be friends."

I glance at the door again as Gabriel walks in. A tall redhead strolls over, wrapping herself around him.

Well, shit.

My heart drops to my stomach, and I wish I had better control of my face because I'm pretty sure it's fallen.

JT clocks my disappointment. "Oh... shit. You were looking for Gabe?"

"No? No. I—"

"It's okay. I won't tell anyone. But for the record, that's Lily. I don't think he's interested these days, but that doesn't stop her."

"These days?"

"Yeah, I mean he used to screw around with her, but I don't think he has in a while."

"I don't care." Obviously, I'm lying, but who wants to be the little sister pining over her brother's best friend who won't ever give her the time of day?

"Okay." As if he doesn't believe me, he adds, "If you say so."

"I do," I bite.

He throws his hands up defensively. "Want to play pool?"

"Uh..." I shake my head. "I don't really know how."

"That's okay, I'll teach you." He stands. I thought he was tall before but, holy shit. He towers over me. "Maybe it'll distract you from staring at that dipshit." He nods toward Gabriel.

Turns out JT *is* a really good friend. He's spent the last hour trying to teach me to play pool. I'm horrible at it, but I'm having so much fun I don't care. My cheeks burn from laughing so much.

"Okay, new plan. You're naturally terrible, so maybe just cheat."

"What?!" I whip my head around.

"I mean, I think you're a lost cause. Knock a few in

when no one's looking." He laughs. "That's the only chance you've got."

I shove his shoulder. "You're terrible!"

"No, my dear, you are terrible. I'm trying to help you." He places a hand on my lower back and guides me toward the bar. "Let's let someone else have the table so they don't have to be subjected to watching this anymore."

I'm stopped by a hand around my upper arm.

"Can I talk to you?" a familiar voice says.

Gabriel stands slightly behind me, glaring daggers at JT who grins like a child.

"I guess." I let him lead me back to the hallway by the bathroom.

He's pissed.

I yank my arm away from him. "What the hell is your problem?"

"What do you think you're doing?"

"What do you mean?"

"With JT."

"Uh, playing pool? What's it look like?"

My brows pinch, trying to puzzle out what he thinks he saw.

"It looked like more than pool, Ash. What the fuck? Do you have some kind of crush on him or something?"

"No? He's my friend." Crossing my arms, I say, "Kind of like how I thought *you* were my friend."

"Friend?" He scoffs. "You don't even know him."

"Right. I just met him, but he's already a better friend than you."

He rears back. "What's that supposed to mean?"

"He doesn't ignore me. News flash. I got here a week ago, and you've barely acknowledged my presence. You haven't even spoken to me tonight until now. You've been too busy with that redhead."

He rolls his eyes. "I wasn't trying to ignore you, Ash."

"Well, you did." I feel like a child throwing a tantrum, but I don't care. My feelings are hurt. "I thought—I mean, all those letters, I—" Pressing my fingers into my lips, I sigh and look away.

He steps in closer. "What?"

I blink a few times, trying to keep the tears at bay before quietly saying, "I thought you liked me."

His jaw tics.

"Look, I should go. This was a bad idea."

As I start to walk away, he grabs my wrist, spinning me to face him. He stares down at me. His throat bobs, but he still doesn't say anything. My eyes sting, and it's like someone's laid a brick on my chest.

"Fuck—" he mutters and bites his bottom lip. "I *was* trying to ignore you. I've *been* trying to ignore you."

He lets go, and my skin feels bare without his warmth. Giving me his back, he lifts his face to the ceiling with his hands on his hips. His shoulders rise with a deep inhale.

I'm not sure if he's talking to me or himself when he says, "This is wrong. You're Shane's little sister. I'm not supposed to—"

When he turns back to me, there's something different in his eyes. They burn into me for a moment too long before he mutters, "Fuck it."

"What—"

He cuts me off when his mouth slams into mine.

Holy shit. I was right!

He guides me until my back is against the wall. His lips are soft, and he smells faintly like the cigarette he smoked earlier. Normally I wouldn't find that so attractive, but it is on him. One of his hands slides up the back of my neck into my hair, and the other squeezes my hip. His tongue darts out, and I open to him, wrapping my arms around his neck. I don't want this moment to ever end.

I'm completely lost in him when he breaks the kiss, staring at me for a moment before squeezing his eyes closed.

"Shit," he whispers, taking a step back.

"What?"

His face scrunches, and he runs his hands over it. "I shouldn't have done that."

Before I can ask what he means, he adds, "We can't do this."

I shake my head, searching his face for answers. My neck heats, and my heart pounds against my sternum. "I don't understand."

He exhales, tilting his head to the side. "Ash, I don't want to hurt your feelings, but—"

He regrets kissing me.

My heart sinks because I know he just blew up our friendship.

Pressing my fingers into my mouth that's still craving his, I murmur, "Oh my god."

"I'm sorry, I didn't mean to—"

Still shaking my head, I cut him off. "No."

What the hell is happening. My vision blurs as tears well in my eyes. "That was cruel."

He opens his mouth, but I don't let him speak. "How dare you play with my head like that? I thought you were my friend!"

I admitted that I have feelings for him, and he kissed me only to take it back immediately. I feel betrayed and humiliated.

With his lips pressed tightly together, he stares at me.

My bottom lip trembles. "Don't ever speak to me again!"

When I start to leave, a crowd has formed. JT gives me puppy-dog eyes, and I feel like a fool. My cheeks are on fire, making the tears feel cool.

"What's wrong?" Shane grabs my shoulders. Then he glares at Gabriel. "What the fuck did you do?"

Gabriel storms off.

"Come on. I'll take you home." JT grabs my hand, guiding me out of the building as Shane takes off after Gabriel.

Once we're in the truck, I break down. I just want to get out of here. I don't want to stay in this stupid town this summer. I hate it here, and I hate Gabe. I convinced myself he was someone else with me, but he isn't.

"You okay?"

"No, not really?"

"He didn't mean that."

"It sure sounded like he did."

"Listen, I know this isn't gonna make you feel better, but I'm gonna say it anyway. Gabe's a great friend, but emotionally, he's a child."

"Well, he wasn't a great friend to me," I mutter, wiping the tears away with the back of my hand.

"True, but I don't think he really wants to be your friend."

"Obviously." I roll my eyes.

He doesn't want to be anything to me.

"No. I mean, he obviously wants more than that."

Snapping my head toward him, I bite, "Is that why he humiliated me?"

"Well, no. He did that because he's an idiot. You don't

have to forgive him, but mark my words, he didn't mean any of that."

When I don't respond, he says, "I'm sorry, though."

"I just want out of this stupid town."

26

___

GABE

MAY 6 YEARS AGO

I didn't mean to hurt Ash. I just don't know what I'm doing. Shane's my best friend. His sister should be off-limits. But I can't stop thinking about her. She took up shop in my brain when she took up shop in the garage last summer. I'd made peace with keeping my distance until JT decided to play buddy-buddy with her last night.

I'm sitting on the couch when JT lets himself into my apartment without knocking. He acts like he lives here too. Although, he might as well. Shane's never here anymore.

"Don't you know how to knock?"

"I do." He plops down beside me. "But what fun is that?"

I scoff.

"What's up? And don't blow smoke up my ass."

With my gaze glued to my coffee table, I say, "I'm fine. Just don't care for drama from little girls with crushes."

His brows raise. "So that's how you're playing it? You're gonna act like you didn't drag her away like a caveman last night?"

I shrug.

"You can pretend there's nothing going on if you want, but if there *is*, you're blowing it."

"It was a mistake," I mutter, peeling the label off a Mountain Dew bottle.

"Good. 'Cause she's leaving."

My heart thunders against my chest that feels a lot like an elephant is sitting on it.

She's leaving? Because of last night?

Good. We'll both be better off.

It's too complicated. She's Shane's little sister. My best friend. I can't do that to him.

"*You* know you'll be good to her," JT adds, standing. "The next asshole might just hit it 'n' quit it."

He grins at my scowl but puts his hands in the air. "Just saying."

The asshole doesn't shut the door behind him, like he thinks I'm going to follow.

I'm not. She's none of my business. She's Shane's business.

He should be the one making guys stay around.

But he's never around...

And fuck JT, because I'm out the door before I can stop myself again.

I don't notice Gran sitting on her front porch swing until she speaks. "I assume you're here for that grand-daughter of mine?"

"Um, yeah. Is she here?"

"Packed all her shit last night. Says she's going home."

She takes a drag, glaring at me. "You wouldn't know anything about that, would you?"

"Uh, yeah, I might."

"Thought so. The only reason I'm not running you off right now is because I think deep down you're a good man. I want you to earn a second chance. But that's it. She's been through enough, and she doesn't need you adding to it."

"Yes, ma'am."

With pursed lips, she puts her cigarette out before saying, "She's out back."

With that, I race around the house.

Ash sits on the grass, leaning back on her hands and looking out over the lake. When I get close, she turns her head.

Her gray eyes are a little bluer and swollen from crying, and she has a pink petal from the magnolia tree stuck in her hair.

After shooting me a dirty look, she gives me the cold shoulder. "Go away."

I sit next to her. "I fucked up."

"Yeah, well, I don't care." She picks a piece of grass and spins it in her fingers. "I thought you liked me, but don't worry. I'm all clear now."

I wince.

She needs to know I meant every second of that kiss— that it was the bullshit I spewed after that was a lie.

"Ash, I'm sorry. I regret it so fucking much. I wish I could take it back."

She scoffs. "Wow, that's every girl's dream. To know a man regrets kissing them."

"No, not the kiss. Fuck! Everything else. I just panicked."

She wipes her face. "I feel stupid for liking someone who'd humiliate me like that in front of all of those people."

"I don't know what to say. I'm an asshole, and I shouldn't have done that." I reach for her, but she pulls away before standing, brushing her hands off on her pink sundress.

When she heads for the house, she says, "I don't care."

Scrambling to my feet, I follow after her. "Ash, please don't leave."

She stops but doesn't turn around. Her voice is thick when she says, "I have to. I hate this town."

There isn't a lick of venom in her words.

"No, you don't." I take a step toward her. "You hate me... Or you're trying to, at least." Reaching for her arm, I say, "The problem is, you can't."

When she finally faces me, she asks, "Oh, yeah? Why is that?"

"Because deep down you know I didn't mean it." My fingers brush her arms and she tilts her face up to me. "And you know how I feel about you. Even without me saying it."

She swallows hard, blinking away the emotion in her eyes.

My arm snakes around her waist. "And *I* know how you feel about *me*."

She doesn't move away, so I pull her to me. Her breath hitches. I can't keep my distance. If Ash is in Ravens Ridge, then I'm with Ash. That's how this works. There's an invisible force dragging me toward her.

Placing a hand on her face, I brush away a tear as it falls from her eye. I kiss her softer this time, and she lets me. Her lip gloss tastes like strawberries, just like last night. After a second, she reaches up to wrap her arms around my neck. When I lift her, she locks her legs around my waist.

Barely taking my lips from hers, I say, "I'm so fucking sorry, Ash."

She shakes her head. "Please don't hurt me like that again," she whispers against my mouth.

"I won't." After inhaling her one more time, I lower her to the ground. "Come over tonight."

I want to stay here with her forever, but I have to get back to the shop. She nods, and I grab her hand, leading her back to the house.

"I knew you liked me," she says under her breath.

"Yeah, something like that." I chuckle because I more than like this girl. I'm pretty sure I've loved her since last summer.

All day at the shop, my thoughts stay on her. The smell of her hair and the way her soft skin feels on my fingertips. I brutally count the minutes until I'm finished.

I finally clock out and impatiently wait for her outside. When she arrives, we head up to my apartment.

Standing inside the doorway, she rocks back on her heels. "So..."

"Alright." I grab her hand and drag her to the couch. "Don't be fucking weird now."

She giggles, plopping down next to me.

"What're we watching?" I ask, my gaze drifting to her bare thighs in those tiny denim shorts.

I jerk my eyes away.

Stop being a creep.

She shrugs. "Whatever you want."

"Hmmm, what about something scary?"

"Sure!" She grins.

Ash has the cutest fucking smile. It's wide and bright, and her teeth are just a little crowded. Like just imperfect enough to convince you she's real.

"It won't give you nightmares?"

Rolling her eyes, she shoves my shoulder. "Oh, fuck off."

I click on a movie and grab her legs, pulling them across my lap. She relaxes into the couch and turns her head, attempting to cover a grin.

The first jump scare, she about leaps on top of me.

I laugh, throw an arm around her, and pull her to my chest. "You okay? I thought you weren't gonna be scared?"

"Shut up!" She swats me.

I catch her hand, pinning it against my chest, right over my heart. Our eyes lock. The air goes still, and the TV fades into the background as my heart pounds against her palm.

I'm drowning in her gray-blue eyes.

My eyes slip to her pink lips that shine with that fucking strawberry lip gloss. They part.

Fuck me.

I think strawberry's my new favorite flavor.

I've already done this. Twice actually. So, why does it feel like crossing a line to kiss her right now. One very fine line.

"Gabriel..."

I cross that line with a leap and press my lips to hers. It's soft and brief, a question.

Is this okay?

She draws her hand out from where I clasped it to my chest, and my heart sinks.

Way to go, Gabe. You fucked it up again.

Pulling away, I open my mouth to apologize, but she laces her fingers behind my neck.

The next word from her lips is a whisper. "Again."

The world falls away as I'm consumed by all things Ash. Her lips. Her taste. Her smell. Her touch. This time, I kiss her hard, wrapping an arm around her back. I never want to come up for air.

We don't separate until the movie ends. Only noticing because what replaces it is a bright infomercial.

She jolts, and I'm forced to release her. When she doesn't say anything, I smile. "Well, there's that."

She laughs, dropping her head to my shoulder, but not before I catch a glimpse of the pink blooming over her cheeks.

Goddamn, she's cute.

Lifting her head, she gives me a tight-lipped grin before standing. "Thanks for tonight."

Mid-stretch, I whip my head in her direction.

"Oh, you think you're leaving?" The corner of my mouth lifts, and I shake my head as I stand. "No fucking way. I've been waiting a year for you to come back, now I may never let you leave again."

She giggles as I pull her into me.

"I mean, it's pretty late already. Don't you have to open the shop tomorrow?"

I kiss the top of her head and say, "If you really want to go back to Gran's, I'll let you, I guess, but wouldn't it be so much easier if you stayed here?"

Her brows pinch when she pulls back. "You want me to stay here?"

"If you want. If it's too soon, it's fine. I just—"

She shakes her head. "No, it's not that. I'm just surprised. Last night I went home thinking you didn't like me, and now you're asking me to stay. I think I might have whiplash."

I laugh, wrapping my arms around her and lifting her off the ground. "Ash, I'm fucking crazy about you."

27

ASH

MAY 6 YEARS AGO

"I can find you a T-shirt to sleep in if you want," Gabriel says as we step into his bedroom. His apartment's about what you'd expect from a twenty-year-old guy. There's no decor, and everything's a little messy. But it's not as bad as Shane's room used to be.

He's clearly the tidier of the two. I was here last summer, but with everything that'd happened with Max, I didn't pay that much attention. This time, I take in every detail.

His bed sits on the right side of the room with blue flannel sheets. Posters of cars and motorcycles are tacked up on the walls. I'm a little surprised there aren't clothes strung across the floor.

He pulls a shirt from the dresser in the corner and tosses it to me, nodding to the door that I know leads to a bathroom.

I smile, moving across the room and closing myself inside to change. Even his bathroom's cleaner than I'd expect. His mother must be very proud. I slip out of my clothes and into his black T-shirt as a wave of butterflies flutter across my chest.

I've not dated much. And my lack of experience in this department makes my hands sweat. Jordan's the only guy I've had sex with. I don't know what Gabe expects.

If I stay, is he going to expect me to have sex with him?

My stomach clenches.

Coming out of the bathroom, I'm stopped dead in my tracks by a shirtless Gabe standing beside his bed. A black raven tattoo that matches his leather cut covers the majority of his back with the words *The Ravens Ridge Riders* arching above and below the bird. Every muscle is visible under his skin, causing my cheeks to heat.

I must have a look on my face because when he glances at me, he says, "What's wrong?"

I shake my head, faking a smile. "Nothing."

He narrows his eyes, taking three long strides to me before resting his hands on my hips. "Try again."

I sigh. What do I say? *I'm freaking out because I'm afraid you're going to try to have sex with me and I don't know if I'm ready for that?*

"I—"

He leans closer. "You what?"

"I've only ever had sex once."

Good job, Ash. Blurt out the most awkward shit you can think of. If I could smack myself upside the head, I would.

He cocks his head to the side. "Okay...?"

"I don't know what I'm doing. Not that we're having sex. But if you wanted to, I don't want you to be disappointed. I don't really know how any of this works." *Shut up, Ash.* "Not that I think you're just trying to sleep with me or anything."

He grins.

"I don't know what I'm saying. I'm just not good at this sort of thing. Shit." I press my fingers into my lips. "I'm so sorry. I'm rambling." As embarrassing as it is, tears prick my eyes.

"Hey." He bends down to eye level. "I don't expect anything. I just wasn't ready for you to leave. Don't freak out."

I swallow, nodding. "I'm just nervous."

"You don't say?" He chuckles. "Look, I don't ever want to do something you aren't ready for. You don't have to be nervous with me."

My shoulders relax as he pulls me into a hug. My cheek presses against his hard chest when he wraps his arms around me, lifting my feet from the floor and putting me in his bed.

He stares down at me. "We can take this slow, but I'm all in." His thumb brushes my cheek. "I've been all in."

My heart leaps, and I roll my lips under, holding back a smile.

"I don't plan on seeing anyone else, but I also don't think it's fair for me to ask that of you on the first date, so I don't expect that in return. I just have no interest in anyone else."

"This is a date?"

"I mean, yeah, sort of." He brushes a stray curl from my face. "Obviously, I'll take you out on a real date sometime. I just figured it might be nice to chill after the fiasco of last night."

Nothing can conceal my wide grin this time.

He quirks a brow. "Is that a yes? You'll go on more dates with me?"

I nod, eagerly. "Yeah. I'll go on all the dates with you, Gabriel."

He slips into bed beside me, pulling my body to his. His skin pressed against mine ignites something in my core. One corner of his mouth lifts. His full lashes flutter as he takes in every inch of my face like he's trying to commit it to memory.

"You're so fucking pretty," he says.

It's funny because being called pretty shouldn't be so heart stopping. But when he says it, it is. It's in the way the words leave his lips, sounding like I'm the prettiest girl he's ever seen.

My lips tingle from wanting him to kiss me again, and my chest rises and falls heavier than before. His blue eyes meet mine, and his tongue makes a pass over his full bottom lip.

He snorts a laugh, rolling to his back to stare up at the ceiling.

I deflate a little, I want him over here, tangled up with me—staring at me.

"This is wild." Rolling his head in my direction, he says, "I almost can't believe you're here."

Blushing, I ask, "What do you mean?"

"I haven't stopped thinking about you for a single minute since you left last summer."

My eyes roll. "You're so full of shit."

"No. I'm dead serious." His brows raise. "I really don't think I'm ever gonna let you leave again."

I bite my lip. "Deal."

The backs of his fingers ghost across my cheek.

I like the way his bed smells. And I know that's a weird thing to think, but it's true. There's a layer of his cologne, but it doesn't smell exactly like it does on his skin because it swirls with the clean notes of his shampoo on his pillow, and a hint of laundry soap, all mixed with what I can only describe as *him*. I imagine it's that pheromone thing they say you only like if you're attracted to someone—or is it you're only attracted to someone when they have the right pheromones. I don't know, but I feel like I might drown in it if I don't kiss him.

I bring my lips to his softly. My heart thunders in my chest. When I pull back, he slides his hand into my hair, bringing our mouths together again. He shifts to his side, his hand finding its way to my lower back, pressing my body to his.

Every inch of my skin feels like it's on fire. When his tongue parts my lips and sweeps my mouth, I slide my leg up to drape over him. His fingers dig into my hip. I might actually melt right into the blankets. Something shifts—soft waves growing hungry as they crash into the shore. I can't get enough.

His leg shifts forward just enough to press between mine, sending a wave of heat coiling up every vertebra. Lost in the moment, I roll my hips and sweep my tongue across his in time with the ribbons of molten lava twirling in my abdomen.

He takes his mouth from mine and opens his eyes. My breath hitches. I want more. Our heavy breaths rise and fall simultaneously before he pulls me on top of him as he rolls to his back. I straddle his hips, lowering my chest to his and bringing my lips to his neck. The panic from earlier a forgotten echo now. I just want to touch him. His hands roam up my bare legs, causing goosebumps to erupt over my skin.

He groans, and I sit up to stare at him.

I've never been so attracted to someone in my whole life. I just want to look at him, commit every inch of his body to my memory. I never want to forget a single minute with this man.

He grimaces, rolls me off him, and says, "Shit. Sorry. I swear, I'm not trying to pressure you into anything. I kind of got caught up in the moment."

I shake my head. "I don't feel pressured. I just wanted to look at you."

He swallows, blinking at me like he doesn't know what to do. Without saying a word, I climb back on top of him, letting my hands rest on his chest. He doesn't move.

I lean forward, placing my lips back on his. He gives me the moment, letting me explore his mouth while my hands wander over his skin. Grinding against him. His fingers trail over my legs until stopping to grab my ass.

When I break the kiss this time, I whisper, "I don't know what I'm doing."

"Ash, we don't have to—"

"I know. Just tell me what to do."

He doesn't say anything at first, just lies under me staring into my eyes like he's trying to decide. Then, he flips me to my back, sliding his hand under the T-shirt. His fingers run over my lower stomach, causing me to shudder. They skate over my skin, running laps on my body. When he slides them between my legs, my eyes grow heavy. It's light at first, but when he presses his palm against me, I rock my hips. My mouth pops open, and he covers it with a kiss.

Heat races up my neck. Pulling his lips from mine, he moves to my jaw then my neck, sucking and nipping at my skin as I practically ride his hand. His mouth covers my nipple through his shirt, and he sucks.

He slides his fingers into my panties and my back arches when they touch my bare skin. I grip his soft sheets. When he slides one finger in me, I gasp.

"I don't know." He smirks. "You seem to know what you're doing."

My eyes open, and I realize he's staring at me. Breathless, I say, "I'm not doing anything."

"You are." The smirk fades, and his eyes turn hungry. "And no one has ever looked so beautiful doing it."

His fingers curl, and his thumb finds my clit. I grind against him before breaking apart, whimpering as I clamp my thighs around his arm.

He kisses me through it—first firm and desperate, before turning soft. He takes me in, and the corner of his mouth lifts as he pulls his hand away and lies on his back.

My brows furrow when he tucks an arm behind his head.

Is that it?

It was great, but I kind of thought we were just getting started.

Sitting up, I ask. "What are you doing?"

"I told you this wasn't about sex." He shrugs.

My heart sinks. I didn't think he meant he didn't want to. I just thought he was trying to be respectful. Now I feel silly.

"Why are you making that face?" he asks.

"I uh... I think I misunderstood. I..." I half laugh to keep from crying. "I thought you were just saying we didn't have to if I wasn't ready. Not that you didn't want to."

His eyes narrow, and he takes my hand. I'm about to shut down when he places it over his sweatpants and lifts a brow. My hand wraps around his very hard cock, and I didn't know it was even possible for my heart to pound harder, but it does.

"I fucking want to. I just don't want to screw this up. I don't want you to do something you'll regret tomorrow. But make no mistake, if I knew for sure you were ready, I'd have buried this in you ten minutes ago."

I stare at him with wide eyes, my hand still on his dick. His words have me feeling like he didn't just get me off two minutes ago.

Shifting onto my knees, I lift my chin and take a deep breath. "I won't regret it."

"Ash—"

My grip tightens, and I rub my hand over him through the fabric. "I won't. I'm not caught in the moment. I'm not even a little unsure. I want this." My words catch in my throat. "Please—"

Before I can finish my thought, he flips me onto my back again, kicking off his pants and tearing my panties off. His nostrils flare, and he stops for a moment. "If you change your mind, we'll stop."

"I won't change my mind."

He grabs my thigh, hiking it up before sinking into me. His movements are slow, letting me adjust an inch or so at a time, but it still stings a little.

I can see the question even before it leaves his lips, so I nod. "I'm okay."

He moves in a slow, gentle rhythm, staring down at me and bracing himself on his forearms above my head. His lips meet my neck, and I writhe under him, balling my fists in his plaid sheets.

A noise I don't think I've ever made before leaves my throat. It's part groan, part purr, part whimper—all feral. His eyes light. "You look so pretty when you do that."

There he goes again, calling me pretty. And I have to say, it has just as fierce of an effect the second time. Placing a hand on the back of his head, I bring his mouth down to mine. This time, I consume him.

I roll my hips trying to get closer—to get more—and lock my legs around him, my heels digging into his ass.

His lids grow heavy, and a crease appears between his eyes as he groans, *"Fuck."*

I love that face.

He's always so in control. Every expression and word is deliberate and thought out. But not right now. This is Gabriel unraveled. Just like he was last night when he kissed me.

"You're so fucking perfect, baby," he mutters, flipping us over so I'm on top of him again. He doesn't wait for me to ask before he says, "You can't do it wrong. Just move."

His hands guide my hips, and any thoughts I was having disappear at the feeling. My head falls back.

He sits up, sliding in the bed until his back is against the wall and tangling his fingers into my hair before guiding my face to his.

As I move, his eyes burn into me, and he says, "Just like that. You're doing so well."

My forehead falls to his as his hands run over my skin under the shirt. Then he yanks it over my head, tossing it to the floor. He rests his palms on my hips before sliding them up my body in an excruciatingly slow trail to my ribs. His thumbs brush the edge of my breasts, and I quicken my pace. The moment they graze my nipples, I shudder.

He's watching me so closely, but I don't feel afraid. I'm not questioning what he's thinking or what he's feeling. I can almost see every thought as it moves across his eyes.

Instead, I feel beautiful. I'm the one doing this to him. Just me.

With one final roll, I collapse into him with a moan. He palms the back of my head, resting the other on my ass, and swells inside me before groaning, *"Fuck, Ash."*

My cheek lies against his warm shoulder, our breaths heaving as I relax into him. Not a single regret in my mind.

The moment it was over with Jordan, my chest squeezed as panic tried to strangle me. This time, it's just peace. My mind is clear of every thought except how much I like him.

His hand kneads the back of my head as he lets out a deep breath, kissing my hair. "You okay?"

I nod against him. "I am fantastic."

He wraps an arm around the middle of my back, squeezing. "You really are."

The corner of my mouth lifts. I could stay like this forever.

He shifts us until we're curled up under the blanket with his chest pressed against my back. A muscular arm wraps around my shoulders.

He's quiet for a minute before saying, "What's going on in that pretty little head?"

I half laugh. "Nothing. I'm just happy to be here with you. I'm so happy, Gabriel."

He presses a kiss to the side of my head. "Why do you keep calling me that?"

"That's what you signed your letters as." I shrug. "It feels like that's what this version of you is called."

"And what version is that?"

"The one that's mine."

I wake to the sound of a woman's voice in the other room. When I toss my arm back, it lands in the empty sheets, and my eyes pop open. Climbing from the bed, I grab his T-shirt off the floor and pull it on.

As I open the door to his room, the unfamiliar female voice fills the room. "Jesus, you'd think you'd warn your mother before she walks in on you half naked."

"You could knock. That'd fix that problem," Gabriel grumbles, slipping his sweatpants on over his black briefs in the middle of the living room. His voice is husky and rough like he too just woke up. God, everything he does is hot. The pants ride low on his hips as he ties the drawstring.

Stop eye fucking him in front of his mother.

"I've been showing up every Sunday morning for two years, and it's never been a problem." The floor creaks, and they notice me in the doorway.

The tall blonde woman turns her bright blue eyes to me.

She smiles warmly. "Well, hello."

She's wearing a pair of low-rise boot-cut jeans and a black V-neck shirt and doesn't look even remotely old enough to be his mom.

"Hi." I lift a hand to wave awkwardly.

"You must be the Michaels girl I've heard so much about." Her voice is bright and welcoming, and her amber-and-saffron perfume fills the space.

What does she mean she's heard about me? Probably from Shane, right? Is it naive to think Gabriel told his mom about me?

"Mom," Gabriel warns, and I think I have my answer. My cheeks heat.

She waves him off, moving to put the groceries in Gabriel's fridge.

"Your dad's going up to Durham this morning to meet

with their new president. Your Aunt Corrine wanted me to come help with the store today. I was gonna tell her I had plans with my son but"—she glances between Gabriel and me before winking—"something tells me you'll let me off the hook this time."

He puts a gallon of milk in the fridge and says, "Dad didn't say anything. Did everyone else go with him?"

"No." She shakes her head. "Just Dean and Mike."

He nods and she moves to wrap him in a hug. "I love you, sweetheart."

"Love you too, Mom."

When she pulls back, she flicks her attention to me. "Nice to meet you, honey. I hope to see you around." She narrows her eyes at her son. "Maybe next time with more clothes."

He rolls his eyes as she leaves, closing the door behind her.

Then he flashes me the most devastating smile. "Morning."

28

—

GABE

JUNE 6 YEARS AGO

For the first time maybe ever, someone sees me for me, instead of Jon's kid, or the future president. To Ash, I'm just Gabriel.

And God, do I love that.

I never realized how lonely I was until Ash. She's the most intoxicating person I've ever met. When I'm with her, I can go from feeling the weight of the world to feeling completely at ease. I think I love her, but that seems crazy.

It's been three weeks, and I've yet to break the news to Shane. Luckily, he lives on another planet most days, so he hasn't noticed. But it's only a matter of time. And I'm certain that's going to go over like a lead balloon. I don't give a shit, though. She's mine. There's nothing he can do about that now.

When I left for work this morning, she headed to Gran's. She's supposed to meet me here when I'm done at work to hang out in the clubhouse. I'm finishing up in the shop when I catch a glimpse of men standing outside the door talking to my dad and a few of the other guys.

Shit.

The closer I get, I realize it's Tony. He's been the president of the Iron Angels since before my dad took over this club. After a long history of beef, they finally came to an agreement on turf a few years ago, and that's worked for the most part. But he's a shady bastard. Anytime his club's involved, it puts my dad and everyone else on edge.

"Don't push me, Tony," my dad barks through his teeth.

Tony's eyes flick to me. "We'll talk again soon, Abbott." Then, he strolls out.

"What was that?" I ask, following my dad into his office.

"Nothing," he replies curtly.

"Obviously, it's not nothing."

He sighs, mulling over what to say. This is the frustrating part of being his kid. He wants me in the club, but then when shit gets sticky, he wants to leave me out of it.

"He thinks we sold on his side."

"And did we?"

"Not that I know of, but if someone did…" He shakes his head.

Jon Abbott "the president" fades and the man that raised me rises to the surface. His eyes soften but his brows furrow. He opens his mouth to say something but stops and swallows hard. "Shane's sister upstairs?"

"No. She'll be back later."

He nods. "Having her here is a bad idea."

I blink a few times. "What?"

"This isn't a place for a girl like that." He brings his eyes back to mine. "If you care about her, you need to keep her away from this club. Especially with Tony sniffing around."

I don't say anything at first, trying to process what he's saying. "She's my girlfriend?"

"Yeah. And that right there could be the thing that gets her hurt—or worse."

"Are you suggesting I don't date?"

"No, but—" He sighs. "This world is ugly. If you bring her into it, you risk something happening to her."

"What about Mom? How's that different?"

"Because your mother can handle it."

"And how do you know Ash can't?"

He doesn't answer. Instead, he stands there, staring at me like I should know. Then he adds, "Even as strong as your mother is, there have been times over the years I've questioned if I made the wrong choice by dragging her into this mess. I don't want you to do the same."

"I wouldn't let anything happen to her."

Glancing away, he clenches his jaw, then walks away without another word.

Ash's tough, and it'd be a cold day in hell before I ever let something happen to her. She's safe with me.

As I waltz through the door between the garage and the clubhouse, Lily barrels toward me, draping her arms over my shoulders.

"Hey, stud."

"Hey, Lil. What's up?"

After Ash left last summer my occasional hookups with Lily became less and less satisfying. It didn't feel right. Eventually, I stopped taking her home with me at all.

She pushes her tits out, tilting her head to the side. "You're liable to hurt a girl's feelings ignoring my texts like this."

"Sorry." Pulling her arms off me, I take a step back. "I'm kind of seeing someone."

Her brows lift. "For real? Like you have a girlfriend?"

I nod.

"Damn." She laughs. "Is she here?"

Scanning the room, my eyes find the head of blonde

curls perched on a barstool. She lifts her head to the ceiling and laughs at something JT said. I gesture toward her. "At the bar."

Lily looks her over. "Cute. Wanna share?"

I pin her with a look. "Not a fucking chance."

"I never thought I'd see the day." She smiles. "Good for you."

I make a beeline for her, leaving Lily behind. She's got her back to me, her shoulders bare in a blue sundress.

Wrapping my arms around her waist, I whisper into her hair, "Did you think you could slip in, and I wouldn't notice?"

"I figured you were busy with your friend. I didn't want to interrupt," she bites, not turning toward me.

What the hell? Ash is never cold, and my brain almost can't comprehend what's happening at first.

"What?" Rearing back, my brows furrow. "Lily's just like that. There's nothing going on with her."

Her eyes stay trained on the bottles behind the bar. In a bored tone she says, "I don't care. It's not like we're together. You can do what you want."

Did she fucking bump her perfect little head?

The fuck we aren't.

I spin her around on the stool, crouching to eye level. "I don't know what planet you're living on, but we"—I gesture between us—"are absolutely together."

Then she rolls her fucking eyes, lighting me on fire.

"No, Ash. Don't fucking roll your eyes. You're mine." I lean forward, bracing myself on the bar behind her.

Her breath hitches.

"No one else. You."

She looks away from me, and I grab her chin bringing her back.

When her eyes finally meet mine, she mutters, "Can we not do this here?"

I nod, standing up straight and running a hand over my mouth as I take a step back.

She doesn't want to do this here? Alright.

I wrap an arm around her legs, pinning her sundress down, and throw her over my shoulder.

She squeals. "Put me down!"

JT raises a brow, not saying a word as he turns his attention to his whiskey.

Storming through the crowd, people stare. Good. I hope everyone sees so they know exactly what we are since she apparently doesn't get it.

She's about to, though.

I pack her across the parking lot, rip open the door, and drop her into the passenger seat of my car. After slamming the door, I round the car and climb into the driver seat.

"What the hell is wrong with you?" she shouts. "Where are we going?"

"Not here," I say through gritted teeth.

She flops back into the seat, crossing her arms over her chest.

I don't say a word or even look at her until we pull into an empty parking lot down the road. After putting it in park, I turn in my seat and say, "Okay. Would you like to tell me why you're throwing a damn hissy fit?"

Her mouth pops open, and she scoffs. "Me? You hauled me out of there like a maniac!"

"No. I hauled you out of there like the brat you are, Ash."

"Brat? I'm a brat because I don't want another girl throwing herself at my boyfriend—" Her cheeks flush, and she looks away. "Or whatever you are."

"One, she wasn't throwing herself at me. And two, I told her I was seeing someone, but you must've already been pouting at the bar when that happened."

She stares out the window. It's annoying we're even having this conversation because she's all I fucking think about. I couldn't give anyone an ounce of my attention because she bleeds me of every drop I have to give. And I wouldn't want it any other way.

She sucks her teeth, but I see her eyes soften in her reflection in the window. "You told her that?"

"Yeah, obviously! Do you really think I do that? Right in front of you, nonetheless?"

She shrugs.

"I would never do that to you." I grab her chin, making her look at me. "Never. In case you were confused, when I said I don't want to see other people, I meant it. I only want you."

She stares at me not saying anything for a moment before she exhales, closing her eyes. "I'm sorry. I panicked. I saw her hanging on you, and I saw red."

"Jealous, huh?" I chuckle. "That's kind of hot."

She rolls her eyes, and I lean over to kiss her, only breaking it long enough to add, "It's only you. It will only ever be you."

I kiss her harder, letting my hand slide from her hair, down her body until I reach her bare leg. Her thighs part when I squeeze, and I slide my hand under her dress to run my knuckles over her panties. When she rocks into me, I break the kiss to say, "Ditch the panties."

"Gabriel—"

I lift a brow. "Ditch them, or I'll tear them off, and you can go back to the party with nothing under that dress."

She looks at me wide-eyed. I don't think I've ever had

sex this much, but every time I'm around her, we seem to find ourselves naked. Since the first time, Ash has become more confident. She doesn't need me to tell her a damn thing anymore.

A grin pulls at her lips as she reaches under her dress and slides them down her legs before tossing them to the floorboard. Her teeth find her bottom lip, and I yank her across the car onto my lap and devour her mouth. She wraps her arms around my neck, grinding into my cock that strains against my jeans so hard it aches. The strap of her dress falls off her shoulder.

She's a dream illuminated in the moonlight. With a hand on the back of her neck, I pull her toward me to kiss her neck, then her chest before pulling down the front of the dress and covering her breast with my mouth. She arches before frantically unbuckling my belt. I take over, undoing my pants and sliding them down just enough that my cock springs free.

She grins, moving to position herself over it before sinking onto me, and we groan in unison.

I fist her hair and drag her mouth to mine.

It's wild and desperate, like I can't quite get close enough. Probably because I can't. Every minute away from her, I'm counting down the minutes before I can get back to her.

"The moment I saw you in this dress, I wanted to bend you over that bar so everyone would know you are mine."

She swallows. "Even the redhead."

I tighten my grip on her hair. "Especially the redhead. If you want we can take this party back to the clubhouse and let her watch, but I don't think it'll get the reaction you want. She's kind of got a crush on you too."

She stops, staring at me like she can't tell if I'm serious.

Grinding into her, I nip at her collar bone. "Can't say I blame her."

She grins, pressing her lips to mine and twisting her fingers in my hair. "And what if I decide I like her more than you." She giggles as she says it.

I pull her back by her hair and narrow my eyes. "Not fucking funny."

The giggle turns to a full-blown cackle, and my chest warms.

Shit. It's not even been a month, but I definitely love this girl.

She finishes and I follow close behind before we put our clothes back on and head back.

When we walk into the clubhouse hand in hand, I think she's feeling better, but in case she needs more convincing, I'll drive it home.

I stroll through the crowd, dragging her behind me. When Theo tries to flag me down, I ignore him. I'm on a mission. As we make it across the room, I step onto a stool and jump up on the bar with a shit-eating grin.

She pulls at my jeans, her eyes widening. "What are you doing?"

I smile at the crowd, none of which are paying any attention to me, so I shout, "Hey, fuckers!" Everyone turns in my direction. "This"—I point down at her—"is Ash. You probably know her as Shane's sister."

My dad glares at me, shaking his head.

"But if you didn't know, she's also my girlfriend." Still grinning, I add, "So, fuck off."

I finish by flipping the bird and jumping down. Grabbing her face, I crash my lips into hers. Her back hits the edge of the bar.

She giggles uncontrollably.

To be sure I made my point, I ask, "Are you still confused about where we stand?"

She shakes her head, continuing to laugh. "You're crazy."

"Yeah, maybe," I say, burying my face in her neck to conceal my grin. There's nowhere I want to be more than wherever she is. I'm officially one of those guys that other guys make fun of, and I don't give a shit in the slightest.

Then the hurricane I've been bracing for, barrels toward me. "Absolutely not! Have you lost your goddamn mind?" Shane yanks me away from his sister.

I stumble back.

Here we go.

"Shane! Stop!" Ash yells, trying to step in front of him.

It's no use, Shane shrugs her off, pointing a finger in my face. "You're not dating my sister!"

I fake frown, then grin. "Weird. I think I am."

"I will fucking kill you!"

"That's unfortunate." I chuckle. "It'll have been worth it, though." Looking over his shoulder to the girl I'd gladly take this beating for, I say, "It was so nice knowing you, baby."

And I wink.

Just like I knew it would, that sets him off. "You're a fucking psychopath. She's my sister!"

"And my girlfriend."

His eyes bulge, and he lunges for me. "You're dead!"

Too far, Gabe.

Grimacing, I shuffle back with my hands up to avoid his swing. "Okay. Okay. Listen, man. I'm sorry. I really am. I wish she wasn't your sister. But I can't help it. I'm crazy about her."

The smile that pulls on my lips is purely subconscious because I am wholly fucking obsessed with her.

"Shane. Stop." She puts a hand on his shoulder.

He flicks his attention between us, trying to figure out how the fuck to process it. Just when I think he's about to hit me, he takes a step back and scoffs.

"I can't believe this shit." Turning his back to me, he puts his hands on his hips and tilts his face to the ceiling. When he finally addresses me again, he says, "If you hurt her..."

"I know."

"I'm so fucking serious."

"I got it." My eyes flick to her. She takes a couple of steps toward me, and I wrap an arm around her neck, pulling her to my chest.

"Fuck," he groans. "Goddamn it. This is gonna end badly."

Then, he exhales and stomps away.

Ash chuckles against my chest.

"He took that better than I expected," I say with my lips pressed to the top of her head.

She throws her head back to look at me. "What? That was terrible!"

"I fully expected him to hit me."

She shakes her head, and I kiss her nose. I'd let him hit me a hundred times if it means I get to have her.

"**F**uuuck, Ash." My head drops forward, and I brace

myself on the shower wall in front of me. "Eyes up here, love."

Ash lifts gray eyes to me as she kneels at my feet with her mouth wrapped around my cock. Her fingers dig into my thighs as I rock into her perfect mouth. I may never be able to fuck anyone again because nothing has ever compared to this. She hums around me as I push all the way to the back of her throat. I'm right at the edge when the bathroom door flies open.

Ash's eyes widen, and she slides off me.

"What the fuck, Shane?" I shout.

Ash's eyes fill with horror as she clamps a hand over her mouth. The shower door has frosted glass except for the space at the top, giving me the ability to glare at the motherfucker.

He stops in the doorway. "Shit. Sorry, do you have my clippers?"

"What?" I ask as he starts digging through drawers.

"My clippers. Nik said she'd cut my hair, but I can't find my clippers."

"I don't have them. You barely even live here anymore! Get out of my bathroom!"

Something in my tone has him freezing before slowly turning around. "Please tell me my sister's not in there with you."

It's taken a couple of weeks and one very awkward camping trip, but I think Shane's finally settled down about me dating his sister. Don't get me wrong, he doesn't like it, but he doesn't look like he's going to explode every time he sees her with me—or he didn't until now. Now he looks like he might actually throttle me.

I glance down to see her roll her lips under and squeeze her eyes shut.

Shrugging, I say, "Your sister's not in here with me."

"You're a goddamn liar."

I throw my hands up. "You didn't ask if she was, you said tell you she wasn't, so that's what I did!"

He grimaces, turning around. "Uh! Fuck you!"

"Don't barge into my bathroom if you don't want to know what I'm doing!"

He shuffles from the room, muttering, "I hate you both."

As the door slams, Ash giggles. "He's gonna kill you."

I quirk a brow, grabbing her head to guide her right back to my cock. "This is so worth it."

After our shower, Ash gets ready, and we grab dinner before heading to the clubhouse.

Nik drags Ash to the dance floor the second we walk in the door.

JT slaps me on the back. "Hey, man."

"Hey," I reply, never taking my eyes off her. "What's up with you? I haven't seen you much lately."

I've only seen him at work or club meetings the last couple weeks.

He takes a deep breath and bites the inside of his cheek. "Well, I haven't told anyone yet, but Katie's pregnant. I've been trying to move her into my place, but as usual, she's being a pain in my ass."

I'd never say this to him, but she's kind of a bitch. She treats him like shit, and he lets her. They break up all the time, but she knows he'll come running back when she calls. Now, she's got him for eighteen years.

"Congratulations?"

"Yeah. I mean, I always wanted kids one day, but it's definitely a surprise. It wouldn't be so bad if she'd stop fighting me on everything. I'm trying to do the right thing, but damn."

I let out a half-laugh, feeling kind of bad for the guy.

"You seem happy." He's not looking at me anymore. Instead, he's staring straight at the blonde bouncing around the dance floor. It's funny, it doesn't matter what song plays, she seems to know all the words, singing along at the top of her lungs.

A smile spreads across my face. "Yeah. I am."

"I'm glad it worked out. I gotta tell you, I like her. You better not fuck it up." He laughs, but I don't think he's joking.

When she spins around, the lights reflect off her blonde curls. She's glowing, and a laugh breaks free, filling the room.

"Oh, shit." JT's brows shoot up. "You're in love with her, huh?"

I glare at him. "Don't do that mushy shit with me. Fuck off."

He laughs as I walk away.

A while later, I'm sitting at a table when Ash stumbles toward me, singing along to some girly song she's playing. This is what she does. She waits until everyone's had too much, then she convinces some drunk bastard to give her the aux cord. Then we all have to suffer through her shit for the rest of the night. She leans against the table in front of me, swaying and singing a love song at me before grabbing my face and putting her lips on mine. She lifts her arms in the air, throws her head back, and belts out the chorus.

"You're drunk." I laugh.

Hooking her arms around my neck, she shakes her head. "Nope."

I wrap mine around her back and pull her onto my lap. "Yes, you are. Who'd you con into giving you the cord tonight?"

"Akers." She grins. "He's an easy target."

Anytime Ash wants something, Akers damn near trips over himself to make sure she gets it.

These days, I think she's got us all wrapped around her finger.

As if he knew we were talking about him, Akers pops out of nowhere. "You going to fight night tomorrow?"

"Eh... I don't know. I'll probably hang out with Drunk the Skunk here instead."

Her mouth pops open. "That's rude." Grinning at Akers, she says, "What's fight night?"

Akers lifts his brows. "Just a bunch of grown manchildren beating the hell out of each other. It's stupid, but we've all been going since like freshman year."

Her eyes light. "Ooo. Sounds fun! I wanna go!"

I don't know why that catches me off guard. I shouldn't be surprised. Ash is always down to do something fun, but I was more than willing to blow it off just to be with her.

"You wanna go?" I ask.

"Why? You don't want me to?"

I shake my head, leaning in and just before I kiss her, I say, "I want you everywhere I go."

29

———

ASH

JUNE 6 YEARS AGO

Fight night's exactly what you'd expect. It's mostly men, standing around in an old, abandoned building. The floors are concrete and some of the windows are busted out. The crowd's rambunctious to say the least, gathered in a circle where two men beat the hell out of each other in the middle.

I clutch Gabriel's arm until we find JT and the other guys.

"Damn, did you get prettier overnight?" JT shouts, wrapping an arm around me.

"You're asking to get your ass kicked with that shit, you know that?"

"Ha. You're not as smart as you look if you think he could kick my ass."

He pulls away from me before Gabe shoves him playfully, saying, "You won't be laughing when I put my foot up your ass."

They all do that weird guy hug. You know, the one where they start with a handshake that turns into an embrace.

Boys are so strange.

"Want to make a bet?" Gabriel smirks.

We're close to the front. A bigger bald guy punches a still large but slightly smaller guy with dark hair, and he topples over. The crowd explodes.

"On what?" I bite my bottom lip.

He grins proudly, puffing out his chest. "On me. If I win my fight, you get my initials tattooed on your ass. If I lose, I'll get yours."

As he finishes, he pulls back to read my face.

"Your fight? What do you mean? You're fighting someone tonight?"

This crazy motherfucker grins from ear to ear when he nods. My hands start to sweat. I don't know that I want to watch him fight someone. What if he gets hurt?

Although, what if he doesn't? I should not find the idea of him winning as hot as I do.

"Gabriel! What the hell!" I squeal, swatting his arm. "I'm not getting your initials on my ass!"

"Oh! Come on!" He chuckles, beaming down at me.

I cross my arms over my chest. "You're crazy!"

He laughs, shrugging. "Maybe. Is that a yes?"

"No!" I shriek. "Absolutely not!"

He cocks his head, raising a brow. And I can tell by the look on his face that he's up to something. He doesn't at all look like I said no, instead he looks like I asked him to duel.

"Well, there goes my motivation to win. Guess I'll have to get my ass kicked."

Walking backwards, he pulls his shirt off revealing his smooth muscular abdomen and the intricate snake tattoo that starts on the right side of his chest and wraps around his shoulder, twisting down his arm. The crowd erupts when he steps into the circle of people.

"What? No!"

He's still staring at me with that grin before he winks, and a man announces the start of the fight. I hadn't even noticed the last one was over. I was busy being shell-shocked by his idea of me getting a tattoo on my ass. He's standing across from a guy who's slightly bigger than him with dark hair and tattoos covering every inch of visible skin except his face.

At the last minute, Gabriel tears his gaze from me. He jumps around a few times, still smiling like he's not about to actually fight someone. The guy cocks his fist, and like Gabriel said, he takes a hit. Blood trickles from his lip.

"Gabriel!" I gasp, covering my mouth.

He bends at the waist, wiping his mouth. My body lurches forward and JT throws out an arm to stop me. As Gabriel stands, he laughs like a lunatic. Licking the gash in his lip, he moves in front of the man, quirking a brow like *come on.*

The guy swings again but barely makes contact with Gabriel's jaw. He rears back, obviously not impressed before lifting his brows at me this time, but I don't budge.

Let the idiot get the shit kicked out of him. That's what he gets for being stupid.

The second the other guy's fist barrels into his abdomen, I regret that thought.

Please, don't let him get his ass beat.

He clutches his stomach and coughs.

In a raspy voice he shouts, "Make the bet, baby."

He takes another hit to the face, harder this time; blood sprays, speckling the concrete.

"Oh my god!" I shriek, my chest clenching and my stomach churning. I feel like I can't breathe.

JT rolls his eyes. "Fucking dumbass," he mutters under

his breath before shouting, "Jesus, Gabe! Enough fucking around!"

He dodges a punch, jumping sideways and wiping the blood that's trickling from his brow. "Come on, Ash, I'm losing here!"

And I know it's insane, but I can't help it. There's no way I can stand here and watch this guy beat the hell out of him. Also, maybe there's a little part of me that wants to get his name tattooed on my body. Maybe there's a part of me that would have done it without the coaxing at all. I belong with him.

"Fine! Okay, yes!" I yell over the screaming crowd. "Just quit letting him hit you!"

He chuckles, winks, and then it's on.

He spits blood to the side and proceeds to royally kick the guy's ass. I know it's messed up, but it's so hot. His muscles strain with every punch and sweat beads on his skin. I think I might be salivating watching him.

JT fights after Gabriel, if you can even call it that. The other guy didn't stand a chance. JT's like a machine. It's honestly a little scary to watch.

"Where have you been?" Gabriel asks, guy hugging Shane as he and Nik walk up. The fights ended a few minutes ago and everyone's leaving.

"We had shit to do." He wraps an arm around Nik's shoulders and gestures to Gabriel. "What happened to your face?"

"It's your sister's fault. Don't ask." He smirks.

Shane examines me, confused, but doesn't ask.

Once we've all returned to the clubhouse for the night, Gabriel comes up behind me, wrapping his arms around my middle and bringing his lips to the shell of my ear. "Time to pay up, baby."

"For what?"

"The bet, remember?" He wiggles his brows.

My eyes go wide. "Now?"

"Yeah, Leroy can do it in the back."

I don't know who the hell Leroy is but why am I not surprised that they all let someone put ink in their skin in the back of the club.

I stare at him, and his face softens.

"You don't have to. I was just messing with you, but I'm glad you'd do it to keep me from getting my ass beat."

I think about it for a second, and honestly, I don't know why I'm kind of disappointed he's letting me off the hook. Until tonight had I thought about wanting his initials on my body? No. But now... I don't know.

I blurt out, "No, fuck it. Let's do it."

He grins, cocking his head back. "You're serious?"

"Yep, take me to him."

It's entirely out of character for me, but I can't help it; I'm reckless for Gabriel Abbott.

He drops the cocky smile, and his eyes examine mine. "I really was joking. You don't have to do this."

"I want to."

A grin spreads across his face.

Gabriel gets mine first. I told him he didn't have to because he didn't lose, but he said he planned on it either way.

He's nuts.

Now I'm lying on a table getting my very first tattoo... on my ass. He's almost done when Shane and Nik walk in.

"Oh my god! Put your clothes on! Jesus!" Shane yells.

"Shut up," I snap as the guy says I'm done, and I move to stand.

"GA?" Nik asks, confused. I'm beaming, about to tell

her they're Gabriel's initials when she finishes, "Like, general admission?"

All the amusement leaves my face, and my mouth pops open. I hadn't thought of that. I spin to Gabriel with wide eyes and my mouth open. He rolls his lips under, sucking in a deep breath, and staring at me like a deer in headlights.

That is, until he cracks up, cackling like a maniac.

"Oh, baby. I'm so sorry," he laughs with pinched brows as he moves toward me, wrapping his arms around my shoulders.

"What the hell!" I jab him in the side, my face pressed to his chest. "Gabriel, it's not funny!"

He pulls back, still hooting and hollering. "I know. I'm sorry."

He doesn't sound sorry.

As much as I try to hold onto the horror, I start laughing too because I mean, it is kind of funny, and his laughter is infectious.

"Don't worry. No one but me will see it anyway."

I bury my face in his chest, half laughing, half groaning.

"Gabe!" a voice booms, causing everyone to whip in the direction of the large dark-haired man it belongs to. I've seen Gabriel's dad a few times, but I haven't really met him. He's intimidating to say the least.

He jerks his head, gesturing for his son to come here.

"Be right back," Gabriel mutters, kissing the top of my head.

"What the fuck happened to your face?" his dad says. I think he's trying to be quiet, but his voice travels.

"It's not a big deal."

"No? You're about to inherit an entire club one day. Do you think these guys want their president getting his ass kicked at a fight club?"

Gabe's brows shoot up, and I know he's about to say something smart. "Well, technically I'm not president yet, and... I didn't get my ass kicked."

His dad grinds his teeth. "That's not the point."

Gabriel's face falls. "I know, sorry."

"No more."

Gabriel nods before turning back to me. He slings an arm around my shoulder and says, "Come on, General."

I groan, burying my face in him. "Don't call me that."

30

———

ASH

JULY 6 YEARS AGO

I'm lying on the couch in Gabe's apartment waiting for him to finish up at the shop. He should be closing up right now. I sound needy, counting the minutes until he's back with me. It's just that I've never been around someone who makes me feel like Gabriel does. Like I'm important and he genuinely wants me around. I've spent the night with him damn near every night for the last eight weeks, and every night he still asks me if I'll stay with him. Like he wants to make sure I know that he wants me here.

Pop!

I sit straight up at the sharp crack coming from downstairs and pause the TV.

Silence.

I settle back onto the couch, chalking it up to someone dropping something.

Pop!

This time I recognize the noise as a gunshot.

I stand, scrambling across the room to slip on my shoes as my heart pounds against my sternum. I rip open the door and race out of the apartment, shooting down the stairs.

My pulse speeds up, matching my feet. After I make it to the last step, I barrel down the hall in the direction of the shop.

Pop!

I jump and quicken my pace.

As I round the corner, a large arm wraps around my shoulders, his forearm pressing on my throat. Cold metal presses into the side of my head.

"Don't fucking move, bitch," an unfamiliar voice demands. He smells like cigarettes, and his hot breath on my face reeks of whiskey. "If you say a word, I'll shoot you."

I look out of the corner of my eye. His deep brown gaze narrows, and he smirks. When he opens his mouth again to speak, his words snake out between crooked yellow teeth. "Do you understand?"

I nod, feeling all the blood rush from my face.

He pushes me forward. My feet shuffle, and my hands tremble at my sides.

As we get through the doorway and around a car, my heart sinks.

"Oh my god," I mutter under my breath. The man's grip tightens, and I swallow the sob building in my throat.

A few feet from us, Rider's kneel on the concrete floor with their hands up. A dozen men I've never seen litter the shop with guns drawn. I frantically rake my eyes over every face, taking inventory of the men I've spent my summer getting close to. At the front of the pack are Gabriel, my brother, and JT.

My chin quivers, but I don't make a peep. JT's eyes full of pain flick to the side before closing, a deep crease forming between his brows. I follow his line of sight and bile churns in my stomach.

No.

My legs start to buckle, but the arm around me tightens, holding me up.

Blood pools, slowly inching away from the body lying face down. His blue work jumpsuit is darker in the places where the blood soaks into it. Crimson paints a chunk of his light hair in the back. His head's turned so I can't see his face, but I know him. I'd know him anywhere because he's my friend.

Akers.

I don't have to see that his chest isn't rising to know he's gone. There's too much blood for him not to be, and I can't hold back the whimper that bubbles up from my core.

"Look what I found," the man says from behind me, pulling my racing thoughts out of the tundra of pain I'm paralyzed by.

I have to peel my eyes away from Akers, my chest burning.

Shane sees me first, flinching as his eyes bulge. His hands clench and release as his chest rises and falls faster with each ragged breath.

I drag my eyes down the row of Riders until they land on Gabriel. He shakes his head, his whole body tensing—frozen for a moment with his eyes glued to me. The terror clears from his stare, replaced by something darker. His nostrils flair, and he grinds his teeth.

"If you don't get your fucking hands off her, I will kill every fucking one of you." He's not yelling, just cold. He looks every bit the criminal he is.

A man my dad's age steps forward, running a tattooed hand through his slicked-back dark hair and snorts a laugh. "Now, I don't think you're in any position to be making threats, boy."

He's in a leather cut, but he's not a Rider.

"No?" Gabriel glares at him. "I'm telling you right now, Tony, if you want any chance at an agreement with us, you will let her go." He trembles, sweat beading on his forehead.

"Now!" Gabriel shouts.

I jump. Everything feels too loud, too bright.

"I don't know." Tony paces in front of him, his boots clomping on the ground like the steady rhythm of a leaky faucet. "Your piece-of-shit dad can't even control his own guys. Why would I want to do business with Rider scum? I think I'd rather rid myself of the problem altogether."

His eyes flick to me. When they return to the boys, he smirks.

He chuckles, taking a couple of steps in my direction, his eyes only landing on me when he stops.

"Or..." He pauses, pretending to think about something, tapping a finger against his salt-and-pepper beard. His mouth spreads into a wide grin, sending a chill up my spine. "I could take the pretty one with me. She seems like an efficient leash for a couple of you." He spins to face the boys again. "Who would you choose, Gabe? President daddy or the pretty one?"

I squeeze my eyes closed, warm tears rolling down my cheeks.

Gabriel stares at me, the muscles in his jaw flexing. When I open my mouth to say something, the brute shoves the gun against my temple harder, making my lips clamp shut.

My breath hitches, and I can't get my hands to stop shaking. The compulsion to look back at Akers, brushes against my subconscious, but I keep my eyes trained on the boys, moving from Gabriel to JT.

Tears glisten in his eyes as he mouths, "You're okay," with a nod, trying to blink them away.

"If you take her, it'll be a war," Shane spits.

I want to tell him, *it's okay* like he used to when I watched him get brutalized by our father.

Don't worry. Don't cry. Everything's okay. I'm gonna be okay.

We're gonna be okay.

Run. Don't worry about me.

Just run.

Tony's lip curls. "It would seem it already is, gentlemen." He takes a final step toward me, until his clove cologne overwhelms my senses. "You are quite pretty, sweetheart. No wonder these boys are in such a tizzy over you."

Bile rises in my stomach. Pretty coming off his tongue feels like battery acid.

He runs the backs of his stubby fingers down my face, and I jerk away, my lip curling.

"Don't fucking touch her," Gabriel yells while JT shouts, "Get your hands off her."

He scoffs, glancing back at them. "Put her in the truck."

The man lifts me off the ground. I scream and thrash, but he's got an arm wrapped around my middle. No matter how I flail, I can't break loose. The feral sounds coming from my throat don't even sound like mine. If he gets me in that truck, that's it.

"Fucking bitch," he grumbles, when my elbow catches his cheek. It does nothing to help my escape.

"Get the fuck off my sister!" Shane jumps up and surges toward us.

He collides with the man holding me.

Pop!

The air whooshes from my lungs as we hit the ground.

Pain erupts through my leg. My gut churns.

Someone screams.

No. That's me. I'm screaming.

"Shane!" My voice is drowned out by shouting and gunfire.

Flat on my back, I stare up at the ceiling and try to breathe through it, but it's closer to a pant. The cold concrete nips at my back. I turn my head, watching as feet run by under the truck that blocks my view of the chaos.

"Gabriel!" This time my voice is no more than a broken sob.

Trying to roll onto my side, my leg screams in agony. I manage, but when I try to sit up, my hand slides across the floor.

My fingers are painted scarlet with blood.

My blood.

The room sways. My head feels heavy. I melt into the floor, my muscles giving in to the gravitational pull.

I'm going to die.

Sirens wail in the distance.

Thump. Thump. Thump.

My vision blurs, and I close my eyes.

Thump. Thump. Thump.

Warm amber fills my nose. *Hmmm.* I love that smell.

"You're okay. Ash, you're fine," a voice filters through the fog, and fingers run through my hair. "Ashton, can you hear me?" When I pry my eyes open, JT's kneeling in front of me. His brows are furrowed and a tear snakes down his cheek.

I smile.

He grabs my hand, squeezing it tight. It's nice—warm.

Then he's gone, replaced by black.

"Ashton, baby girl. Open your eyes."

It's hard, but I do.

"You're okay." His voice cracks as he says it.

Big brown eyes bore into me.

JT, a great friend.

His mouth moves, but a soft pitter patter fills my ears, drowning him out.

Rain. I love rain.

Except I can see the sun still shining in through the windows behind him.

Blue eyes appear in my line of sight. They fill with tears when they lock onto mine.

Gabriel. That's love. A song plays in my head, or maybe I'm singing it—I don't know. Something about a butterfly. Gran.

I'm in my bed. She's sitting on the edge humming the Dolly Parton song. Her hand runs through my curls. The scent of Marlboro fills the room mixed with the night cream she puts on just before bed. I'm so happy.

I smile.

"Ashton, baby! Come on! Open your eyes! Please!"

When I open my eyes, his face crumples, and his chin quivers.

Why's he crying?

When I try to move, I'm ripped back to reality by fire tearing through my leg.

Shit. My chest squeezes. That look. He looks—

No.

My eyes close.

31

ASH

JULY 6 YEARS AGO

Beep. Beep. Beep.

My eyes are heavy when I try to open them.

"Ashton," a soft voice says from beside me. For a moment, I think she's my old piano teacher. I must have zoned out during a lesson again. Damn it. She's going to make me practice the hard one again for not paying attention.

"My name's Brooke."

Brooke? My piano teacher's name's Sherry.

"I'm your nurse."

Nurse?

"You just had surgery. It went great. You're gonna be just fine, okay?"

Is this real? A dream? She's so far away. Or maybe her voice is in my head. I can't tell.

"Can you open your eyes?"

I try. They're so heavy. The bright lights sting. I squint but eventually get them open.

"Great. Are you in pain?"

I shake my head. It feels fuzzy, and I'm so tired. She says something else, I think, but she's getting farther away.

When I open them again, I'm in a different room.

Someone shifts beside me, grabbing my hand.

"Shhh. It's okay. You're okay," Gran soothes.

The stiff pillow crinkles under my head as I turn to glance at her. She gives me a warm smile, but it doesn't reach her eyes.

I open my mouth but can't speak.

"Here," she says, grabbing a white cup from the bedside table. She holds up a spoon with one nugget of ice.

Immediate relief washes over me the moment it hits my tongue.

"Better?" Gran asks.

I nod.

"Are you in pain?"

I hadn't noticed at first, but now that she's asked, the dull ache in my thigh starts to pulse.

My voice is gravelly, and my throat feels like I've swallowed a razor blade when I say, "My leg."

"I'll get the nurse." She stands, quickly exiting the room.

A minute later, she comes back with a nurse.

"Hello, Ashton. How are you feeling?"

"Tired."

"That will wear off with time. Are you nauseous at all?"

I shake my head.

She gives me a medication in my IV before leaving. My thoughts feel like sludge. Like I have questions, but I'm trudging through mud to get to them.

My mother suddenly appears in the doorway, holding a coffee in each hand.

"Oh, honey, how are you feeling?" Her voice is sweeter than I've ever heard.

"Um..."

"She just woke up." Gran shoots my mother a look.

Mom hands a coffee to Gran before sitting in the chair on the other side of my bed.

"Thank God, you're okay. We were scared half to death."

"Brenda!" Gran bites. "I just told you; she just woke up."

My eyes flick between the two. I don't know what's happening. They never get along, but they're tenser than normal.

"What—"

Gran clears her throat, sliding to the edge of her seat. "Do you remember anything?"

It's fuzzy. I was in Gabriel's apartment, waiting for him.

I was afraid.

Not of him—

No, it was something else. I ran down the stairs.

And then...

And then, he grabbed me—

It floods back all at once—gunshots, the garage... Gabriel. Tears fill my eyes, and my chest squeezes.

"What happened?"

Gran runs her hand through my hair. "You were shot, honey. They had to remove the bullet. You lost a lot of blood, but you're okay. You're going to be okay."

I scan the room. *How long was I out?*

"Where's Shane? Gabriel?"

Gran's gaze flicks to my mother, then back to me.

"You're brother's fine. He came by after he was bailed out."

"Of jail?"

My mother rolls her eyes. "He almost got you killed, Ashton."

"No." I whip my head in her direction, shocked by the bite in her tone. "No, he's the reason I'm alive."

She scoffs. "You wouldn't have even been at that place if it weren't for him and that piece-of-shit kid he hangs out with."

"Gabriel? Mom, he's not a piece of shit! He's my boyfriend."

She laughs. "No. You're done with them. When you get out of here, I'm taking you home."

"The hell I am." I try to sit up, but my muscles feel like Jell-O.

Gran places a hand on my shoulder. "Okay, enough. She's been through *enough*, Brenda."

Mom crosses her arms over her chest and leans back in the chair. "I'm not losing another child to this godforsaken town."

I sleep most of the day, slowly coming out of the fog a little more each time I wake. The next morning, my thoughts are clearer.

Where is everyone? I know my brother can be unreliable, but I can't believe he hasn't come back. And Gabriel? Where the hell is he?

Gran said Nik was here yesterday, but I was asleep. She's texted a dozen times to tell me I better be okay.

"Have you talked to Shane?" I ask.

Gran nods. "He called this morning."

"Is he coming to visit?"

She sighs. "No. I don't think so."

My shoulders slump.

"It's not you, honey."

I know what that means. It's because of my mom, but

I'd rather have my brother with me than her. I wish she'd just go away. She doesn't even know me, but she thinks she knows what's right for me.

"Ashton, your mother means well. She's just scared. We didn't know if you'd make it through surgery. She thought she was going to lose you. Give her some time to process."

Three days I sit in the hospital stewing and waiting for one of the guys to show up. No one does. On day four I wake to a text Gabriel sent in the middle of the night.

This isn't working, sorry.

Nik called shortly after I got home from the hospital to tell me they're doing Akers's memorial today.

I immediately got ready. I'm sore and tired, but I don't care. I need to be there.

Dressed in all black, I limp from my room. I'm not going to lie, this sucks. They gave me pain medicine, but it still hurts. I can walk, but it's not pretty or quick. They said I may get lucky and make a full recovery, but we won't know if I have any residual nerve damage until it's completely healed.

"Where are you going?" my mother asks. "And where are your crutches?"

"To the memorial." I grab the stupid things from where I'd leaned them against the couch earlier and prop them under my arms. They're a pain in the ass.

"Absolutely not! You aren't going anywhere near that place."

Ignoring her, I keep moving toward the front door.

"Ashton!"

"He was my friend! I know you think everyone here is trouble, but Akers was good to me! He was nice and funny, and I cared about him. He cared about me! Now, he's gone, and I'm going!"

Gran grabs her keys from the counter. "I'll take her with me."

"No—"

Gran throws up a hand. "Brenda, let the girl grieve for one day. Tomorrow, you can take her home and never come back. But give her this."

She frowns but doesn't object.

Gran and I head to the car without a word.

I hate this. A week ago, I felt like I'd finally found the place I belong. I had friends—Gabriel. I finally had my brother back even if he is a mess. Now, Akers is gone, and I guess Gabriel is too. I'm alone.

Halfway to the church, I mutter, "Thank you for bringing me."

She exhales, not taking her eyes from the room. "I don't think it's a good idea, but I'm not gonna be the reason you don't get to say goodbye."

"Do you think Gabriel will be there?" I ask, knowing that's the reason she's saying it's not a good idea but not caring.

"I would assume."

I nod, not saying anything else the rest of the drive. He owes me an explanation. You can't just break up with someone like that, then never speak to them again. Especially after everything that happened.

Gran waves at people as we pass them on the way into the building. Thunder rolls through the overcast sky. We sit in a pew near the back. It's packed. Kids our age, probably people he went to school with, and men in leather cuts filter in with tears in their eyes. The air's heavy. A picture of him sits near the front. My chest feels like there's a cinderblock resting on it.

Why am I the one still sitting here and not him?

JT turns around from the second row. His eyes meet mine, and he lifts a hand with a sad smile. I return the gesture. Colette sits in the front, her arm wrapped around Akers's mother, rubbing circles on her back.

Just as the service starts, Gabriel sneaks in. His eyes flick in my direction as he makes his way up to where JT is and slides in beside him not giving me a second glance. Jon turns back to Gabriel from the front row. For the first time, I see him shift to nothing more than a father. His eyes silently saying, *Are you okay? I'm here.*

He reaches over the back of the pew and squeezes his son's shoulder.

Akers's brother speaks. His mother wails. Everyone mourns a life taken too soon and a light ripped from our hearts.

There's a lot of talk of God and Heaven. That feels strange. How could this be what God wants? How can all of these broken hearts, cracking like glass, be the work of God? Akers wasn't even part of the club yet. He was barely a prospect, and only because it's the world he was raised in. What would he have been if his dad wasn't part of this club?

When it's over, everyone stands. Gabriel hugs Akers's family before making a beeline for the door.

"I'll be right back," I whisper.

"Ashton—" Gran tries to stop me, but I'm already out of the pew and hobbling after him without my crutches. It hurts, but I push through.

I *need* to talk to him.

When the doors swing open, he's already down the stairs. He doesn't even look back. It's started to rain. Of course it has because even Mother Nature knows the loss we've suffered.

"Gabriel!" I shout, struggling down the steps.

He keeps charging forward as if the rain's drowned out my voice. A knife twists in my stomach as my mind catches on a memory of my screams being drowned out by the downpour of gunshots.

"Gabriel! Please, stop!"

Finally, he freezes as I step onto flat ground.

He glances over his shoulder, exhaling.

What do I say? I don't even know what the hell is happening between us.

"What are you doing?" I ask.

He spins. "Leaving."

"No, not right this minute. With me."

His eyes flick away for a moment. "I don't know what you're talking about. We broke up."

My heart thumps with the rhythm of the rain. "No. You dumped me in a text while I was lying in a hospital bed. Don't you think we should talk about that?"

He flinches but immediately covers it, leaving me wondering if I even saw it at all. My hair's soaked, a few strands sticking to my face.

"None of it matters."

It matters to me. All of it matters to me.

"Why?"

He lets out an exasperated exhale. "I'm just not feeling it, alright?"

What the hell does that even mean?

"You were feeling it just fine before I was shot."

He shrugs and shoves his hands in his pockets. "Yeah, and now I'm not, okay? Just go home."

When he finally meets my gaze, his expression's cold. Gone is the boy I knew. No sign of the kindness I've gotten used to this summer. Only indifference. He's not my Gabriel; I don't know this man.

"So what? We're just done?"

"Ash—"

"No. Fuck that! I love you." I step forward.

He can't just decide when we're done. I know what we felt this summer. It can't just be over like this.

I try grabbing him again, but he pushes me away.

"I don't know what you want me to say; I don't want you here."

I rear back like he's slapped me. Shaking my head, my words come out choked. "You don't mean that."

"Yeah, Ash. I do."

The world stops spinning around me, or maybe it speeds up. I'm not sure. All I know is, I can't breathe. Or think, for that matter.

"No. No! You're lying."

This isn't happening. Now I'm sure this is a dream—no, a nightmare, because my Gabriel wouldn't do this. He loves me.

"It's done." He scoffs, starting to walk away.

Grabbing his arm, my voice cracks as I say, "Please don't do this."

He sighs, bringing his eyes back to me. "I'm not doing anything. Summer's almost over, anyways."

"So?" My brows pinch. "What, this was just some fling for you?"

I know it wasn't.

He's mine. I don't know why he's doing this, but I know we weren't just a fling!

"Yeah." His eyes drop to the ground, and for a second, I think he's going to change his mind. The man I know flickers under the surface for a moment.

"No, it wasn't," I snarl, my lip curling.

Then he's gone again. Back to that damn indifference. "I'm sorry if you thought it was more than that."

I stare blankly at him for a second before shouting, "I didn't think it was more than that. It *was* more! And you know it!"

"I'm not dealing with this fucking drama. Just go home."

When he starts to walk away again, I chase after him, gritting my teeth from the pain. My heart pounds against my ribs like it's trying to get out, and maybe it is because it belongs with him.

"Gabriel!" I grab his arm, then slap his chest with a wet *smack* before shoving him backward.

He stumbles back a few steps, before continuing toward his truck, his jaw ticing. "Ash, stop."

The sound of the rain hitting the pavement is so loud. Why is it so loud! I can't even hear myself think. It's just the goddamn rain and my thundering heart.

As he reaches his truck, I let out a scream, bending at the waist. Am I losing my mind? I can hear how out of control I sound, but it's like I can't stop it. It's all happening too fast.

I charge toward him, ripping him back by the arm until his back is against the truck.

"Don't you dare leave. Say you love me!" I choke as I say, "Tell me you fucking love me!"

His face is cold when he speaks, words rolling off his

tongue without a trace of emotion. "It wasn't real. I don't love you. I never loved you, Ash."

"No!" Raising a hand, I try to slap him.

"Stop!" He grabs my wrist. "Just fucking stop. It's pathetic."

Everything crashes down around me as anger rages in my veins, but it can't exceed the crippling pain. My skin pulses like there's something under the surface about to explode. I'm a tea kettle, and if he walks away from me, I'm going to blow.

Tearing my wrist from him, I say, "Pathetic? You know what's pathetic? That you can't admit you love me too. I don't know why you're pretending you don't!"

"Because I don't! Why don't you fucking get it? You were a great fuck. That's it. Just go!"

I stumble back a step, pointing at him. "Fuck you! You're a liar!"

"Yeah, and you're a fucking child." He climbs into his truck.

No.

No.

I didn't mean it. I didn't mean any of it. Please come back.

I race to stop him, wishing I hadn't let my anger get the better of me. Wishing I'd been able to reason with him. "Please, don't go! Gabriel! Please!"

But he slams the door and pulls away before I reach him. My hand smacks into the side of his truck as it passes. The pain erupts over my skin and down my leg. My chest caves in. It's like I'm burning alive. Dropping to my knees, the hard concrete grounding my pain. Gravel crunches under his truck tires as he gets farther and farther away, and

I bury my face in my hands and let the weight of his words drown me.

Gentle arms wrap around me as my shoulders shake, and Gran's soft voice filters through my cries. "You're gonna be alright."

"I love him," I choke out.

"I know, but you deserve so much more than this."

I sob harder. I don't care what I deserve. I don't even care about the horrible things he said. I want him to come back.

I feel like I've been stranded in the middle of a desert. He was the only person who's ever truly seen me. Truly loved me. He made me feel special and worthy. Now, I feel empty, and abandoned, and alone. His last words slowly soak in, and I feel like every bone in my body is cracking open. I'm raw, equally exposed and invisible, if that makes any sense.

I sit in the parking lot for what feels like an eternity, sobbing and secretly hoping he'll come back for me.

But he never does.

32

———

GABE

AUGUST PRESENT DAY

Finding Shane waiting for me in my office this morning is the last thing I need.

She walked in wearing that damn sundress last night, and I was screwed. Then her husband showed up. I don't like him. To be fair, I wouldn't have liked him anyway because he got her, but I especially didn't like how he was talking to her. I kept drinking, hoping after a few shots I'd be able to brush it off or pass out. All it did was make how much I want her very fucking clear.

I knew I was pushing things by bombarding her in the hallway, but I didn't plan to kiss her. When she said she loved him, it did something to me, and I couldn't stop myself.

"What are you doing here?" I ask.

"I needed a break from Nik asking if I'm okay. I know she means well, but the constant worry is driving me up a wall."

"I'm sure she'll chill once you've been home for a bit," I say, sitting at my desk.

He leans back in his chair. "Heard you were pretty

fucked up last night." There's a hint of a question in his tone, and I grit my teeth.

"I'm just stressed with this club shit. It's fine."

He quirks a brow.

"What?"

"I'm just not buying it."

"Well, it's the truth so drop it, okay?"

"Look..." He leans forward. "I know I have no room to talk after everything I've done. But I'm begging you, please don't fuck with her. I appreciate you being there when she needed you. Especially since it saved my life. But she'll let you back in if you ask. So, I'm begging you... don't. Just leave her be."

"I came because you needed me. That's all it was."

He nods, sitting back in his chair.

JT knocks, poking his head in the door.

What the hell. We're not even open yet and these fuckers are already up my ass.

"What?" I ask.

"My guy lost Adam."

"What do you mean lost him?"

We've been trailing him since he showed up at the hospital. That's the best I could do to keep Ash safe, aside from killing the motherfucker.

"I don't know. I'm gonna head over there and see what happened."

I nod.

"Fuck," Shane mutters, standing to follow JT from the room. "I gotta check on Ash."

My mind stays on the girl I'm not supposed to think about all day while I work. I'm finishing up the last vehicle of the day when I hear, "Did you kiss Shane's sister at the party?"

I roll out from under the minivan I'm working on and sit up, resting my arms on my knees. Lily stands beside me, smirking.

"It sounds like you already know the answer to that."

"Word travels fast."

"Alright... Out with it."

She throws up her hands. "I'm not saying a word. You wouldn't listen to me anyway." Crossing her arms over her chest, she continues, "However, if I were talking to someone who *does* listen to sound advice, I'd say he should pull his head out of his ass. I'd tell him it's clear to literally everyone but him how much that girl means to him, and he deserves to be happy. I'd also tell him not to fuck it up because what he did last time was fucked up."

I run my hands through my hair, sighing. "None of that matters. She almost—" Shaking my head, I run my tongue over my teeth and try to collect my thoughts. "I was doing the right thing. If I go back on that now, it'd all be for nothing."

"Would it?"

I scoff. She's not fucking getting it. "Yeah."

She places her hands on my shoulders. "You're so very clueless, my dear Gabe. You aren't the guy you were six years ago, and she's not the kid she was. Maybe an honest conversation would do you both some good."

"Yeah. That's the part that sucks."

I think that's what's been eating me alive since she came back. Because no matter how different we are, my feelings are the same, and I'm pretty sure hers are too. The magnet that pulled me to her back then is just as strong. Nothing about my love for her changed or dulled. I doubt it ever will.

I'm going to spend the rest of my life missing her.

33

ASH

AUGUST PRESENT DAY

All I have left at Gran's is to meet the realtor to take pictures. Once I'm done, I can put this whole place behind me. So, I'm sitting at the table, looking through a photo album and soaking in the last moments of my time here.

I'm halfway through a bottle of wine, when someone knocks on the door.

"One second," I shout, wiping my hands on my overalls and jogging to the door.

When I open it, Gabriel stands on the porch with his hands in his pockets. The hard expression I've come to expect over the last few weeks is entirely gone. The tight line of his mouth has softened and the crease that lives between his brows has smoothed. There's a boyishness there that reminds me of the kid that stood on Gran's porch all those summers ago. I haven't seen him since Shane's party a week ago, and I've shed a fair number of tears over the whole damn thing.

"Gabriel—" My brows pinch. "What are you doing here?"

He sucks in a deep breath like he's preparing to dive underwater. "I... uh—fuck. I don't know where to even start really. I replayed this in my head the whole way over here, but now..." He shifts his weight, pausing to collect his thoughts. "Listen, I know I should keep my distance and let you go back to your life. But..."

I've never seen him like this. If it's fear or sorrow, I can't tell, but his breaths are ragged, and his eyes glisten.

"I can't watch you leave again without saying this. So, here it goes."

Leaning a hip on the doorframe, I watch him square his shoulders and lift his chin.

"I know what I said before you left—" He swallows. "And you have every right to hate me. I hate myself for that night."

The air grows thick. My chest heavy, every inhale feeling like an impossible task.

"I was afraid. What happened... it scared the shit out of me. You almost died because of me and I—" His words catch in his throat. He swallows them down before continuing. "I couldn't be *the reason* something happened to you again. I couldn't stop seeing you at the shop... You were... I thought you..."

He presses his fingers into his eyes. "I sat in that cell, not knowing what happened, and I wanted to die. I've never felt that way, but I didn't want to live to see the day that you weren't there."

My chin quivers. I've spent six years waiting for this. Dreaming of these words. *Am I dreaming now?* Our past swirls around us, creating a cyclone of my pain, his fatal words, our destruction. His voice is the only thing keeping my feet on the ground.

"It ate me alive. And when you were okay, the only

thing I could think was how can I keep you safe. The only answer I could come up with was to get you out of here."

He clears his throat and sniffs. "And I've missed you like hell, and it's fucking hurt like a bitch, but if it kept you from ever living through that again... I don't regret it. Not a bit. I'd live the rest of my life with my heart ripped from my chest to keep you out of this shit. But I hate that you've spent all these years believing I didn't fucking love you." He takes a step toward me, his eyes burning right through me. "That I don't, still love you." Another step. "Ash, I've never loved anyone or anything the way I love you."

I tip my head up. He's so close I can smell his cologne, and as he presses my hand to his chest, his heart thumps wildly under his palm.

"We can't undo it, and I can't take back the shitty things I said to you, but I need you to know it was real." His voice shakes when he continues, "It was as real to me as it was to you."

He searches my eyes, and my mouth goes dry. My mind screams for me to turn him away. Tell him it's too late, that I never loved him. To hurt him like he hurt me. But my heart can't. It craves his words. All I ever wanted was to know it was real. I needed to know that he's walked around with a gaping hole in his chest for the last six goddamn years too.

"I've spent every day trying not to think about you. Every day convincing myself not to jump on my bike and ride straight to you. I fell in love with you when I was barely a man, and I've loved you every goddamn day since."

I swallow as a tear breaks free from my lashes. "You're a liar."

"I was. I lied through my damn teeth that day." His hand slips into the back of my hair to cradle my head. "But I'm done lying. I'm done pretending."

I sniff, trying not to completely fall apart. His tongue swipes over his bottom lip as we stare at each other. I'm surprised he can't hear my heart screaming in my chest. It's always belonged to him. *The backstabbing bitch.*

More than anything I want to jump into his arms. I want to pretend that we could just start over, erase that horrible ending and move on. But he's right. We can't take any of it back. I'd do anything to go back and change how things played out, but we can't. And there's no way to make this work now. I have Maggie. And he has his club.

A cracked sob breaks from my chest. "You sent me a fucking text."

He pulls me to him, pinning my head to his body with a palm on my head. "I know. I'm sorry. I wish I could take that back. I just didn't think I could do it if I saw you. I'd have backed out."

"I didn't want to leave."

"I didn't want you to leave either. But you had to."

I nod because he's right. If I'd stayed, who knows what would have happened. His final act of love was sending me away, and he sacrificed what he wanted to make sure I was okay. That reality soaks into my bones.

"I wish there had been another choice."

I nod. "Me too."

He pulls back and rests his forehead on mine. "I hope you're so fucking happy, Ash."

"You too." I sob harder, resting my hands on his face.

When we finally part, he watches me as he steps off the porch and flashes me a sad smile.

Then, like flipping a switch, he turns back into the president of the Ravens Ridge Riders, squaring his shoulders, stuffing his hands in his pockets.

"It was good to see you, Ash."

Then he turns and strolls back to his bike.

Finishing the house is a bittersweet feeling. As much as I can't wait to get home, I have so many memories here. Maybe there's a part of me that will always long for a little of the magic that used to live within these walls, but it's time to move on.

After meeting with the realtor, I make my way through the house with what little I'm taking with me in hand.

This is it. Taking one final look back at the only place I've ever felt at home, I soak it in—the mornings with Gran, all the days watching movies and fishing on the dock with Shane, the nights I stayed up writing in my journal about the boy I thought was the love of my life.

As much as I didn't want to come back, I think saying goodbye to my past could be really good for me. It's time. It's time to put all of that to bed and really move on. It hurts, but there's a part of me that's being set free when I walk out that door today.

I miss Gran, but no matter how much I still feel her in this house, she's not here. She'll never be here and holding onto this piece of my past won't change that.

When I first came back, Nik said Gran would be so proud of me, and I wasn't sure I believed it then, but I do now. She would be proud of me for closing this chapter and making it to the other side. Because make no mistake, when I walk out that door, I will be on the other side of Ravens Ridge. I will have survived it. Then I'll just live to tell the tale.

As a tear rolls down my face, I hear, "Did you think you could leave without saying bye?"

I spin to find Nik standing right inside the door.

Dropping my shit, I wrap my arms around her. "Never, I knew your ass would show up." I chuckle.

"I'm gonna miss you. It's been kind of nice having you around."

I pull back. "I know, but Shane says he's gonna come visit so you can hold him to that."

"Oh, definitely. It's been too long since I've seen Maggie. I bet she's getting so big."

"She is." I give her a sad smile.

On my way out of town, I pass the garage, feeling like someone has stolen the breath from my lungs. He's given me more than he'll ever know, and I'll always be glad to have loved him, but there is no room for us in this life.

I make one more stop at the bank before hitting the highway. I'm surprised to find the jewelry box my dad was looking for in her safety deposit box. He was wrong. Shane never took it. I stash it in my purse before finally heading home.

34

———

GABE

JULY 6 YEARS AGO

he night of the shooting.

"Abbot, Micheals, Taylor." The guard unlocks the holding cell.

Shane jumps up, storming out like his ass is on fire. He hasn't said a word to me the whole time we've been here. His sister was in my apartment, and now she may be dead. I've spent my share of time in jail, but this has by far felt like the longest. Part of me dreads leaving, though. What if when we get out, they tell us she's gone. At least in here, I can still hold out hope.

After getting our shit, we head to the parking lot. Shane puts a few yards between us before pulling out his phone. JT goes to him.

My mother wraps her arms around my neck, sniffling. "Oh, honey! God, I'm glad you're okay."

"Ash?" The voice that comes out of me doesn't sound like my own.

She pulls back. I don't like that look on her face. "Last I heard, she was still in surgery."

Relief and dread swirl and tangle in my gut. She's alive, but for how long?

"Is she gonna be okay?"

She shakes her head, like she doesn't want to answer. "I don't know."

My vision blurs. "Akers?"

She blinks. Her chin quivers. I don't need her to shake her head again to know.

"Fuck." Turning my back to her, I wipe my face with my shirt.

My dad approaches and squeezes my shoulder. When I spin around, he pulls me to him. "I'm sorry. I'm so fucking sorry."

We've lost club members before, but this is different. I've known Akers damn near my whole life. I was there when he finally learned to ride his bike because Theo told him he couldn't come with us to the corner store until he could. When we snuck him into our grad night because even though he was a year younger than us, he spent most of his time with our class instead of his own. The night we thought we were going to jail for egging our teacher's house, Akers was the first to get caught because he panicked instead of running. Luckily, one of the other kids had a dad on the police force and got us off the hook.

Now I'll never see him again. Eighteen years of memories over in one moment. And I did nothing to stop it.

Maybe if I'd—

JT's voice breaks through my spiral. "She's still in surgery. Shane's heading over there now."

My mother rushes over to Shane. When she reaches for him, he brushes her off, putting up his walls. She says something to him, crossing her hands over her heart. Throwing his hands up, he responds, then stops, watches her as she speaks. After a few moments, he puts his hands on his head.

His chest heaves once.

Twice.

He collapses into her.

"Take me to the hospital," I demand.

"Gabe—"

"Dad! I'll walk if I have to, but you'll have to put me in the fucking ground to keep me from going."

He thinks about it for a beat before nodding.

"You coming?" I ask JT.

"Yeah. Let's go."

My mom drives Shane separately.

When we walk into the waiting room, he spots me, his eyes widen, and he charges. "What are *you* doing here?"

"Fuck, Shane! I'm sorry." Tears pool in my eyes.

He pins me to the wall, getting right in my face. "Be glad she's still breathing because if she wasn't, you wouldn't be either."

"I didn't want this to happen." I shove him off. "I love her!"

Pointing in my face, he shouts, "I told you this was a bad idea! I told you to leave her the fuck alone!"

My voice cracks when I speak again. "I didn't mean for her to get hurt."

"Yeah. Well, she wouldn't have almost bled to death if she hadn't been in your fucking apartment, would she?"

My chest feels like it's on fire.

"Hey!" My dad steps between us. "Enough. This isn't about either of you right now. You can fight this out later."

"There's nothing to fight out. He's dead to me," Shane spits, walking away.

I can see it on my dad's face. He doesn't think Shane's wrong. This is my fault. I loved her, and it almost got her killed... it still might.

Pressing my thumb and index finger into my eyes, my words leave my lips through a sob. "I thought I could keep her out of it."

"I know." I've never seen my dad cry. Not one time. But he has tears in his eyes.

"I fuck—" Groaning, I swipe my hand over my face as it crumples. "I fucked up."

He presses his lips together and claps my back before walking away and leaving me to stand in the waiting room with tears in my eyes and my heart in my throat.

Eventually, I settle into a chair on the farthest corner of the room away from Shane.

We sit in the waiting room for what feels like an eternity before Ash's mom comes out to get Shane, glaring daggers at me the entire time.

He's gone for all of about twenty minutes before he reappears, grabs his things, and storms off. Over the next few hours, the crowd dwindles until it's just me.

Eventually, Gran comes out.

I stand. "Is she okay?"

She nods. "She'll be fine. You should go home. Get some rest."

"No. I want to see her first."

She sighs, a sad smile gracing her lips. "You can't."

My brows pinch. "What?"

"Her mother's not gonna let you see her. You might as well go home. You two can talk when they let her go."

"No. I need to see her." I try to push past her. "I have to know she's okay."

She puts a hand on my chest. "I'm sorry. Not tonight."

A pat to my chest, then she walks away, leaving me standing there desperate to put my eyes on the only person I give a shit about right now.

I don't know how much time passes when her mother finds me passed out in a chair. She kicks my boot with her black heel, startling me awake.

I lean forward and rest my elbows on my knees, rubbing my eyes.

"Go home."

"No."

"You've done enough. She's done here. Hanging around like this is only making things worse."

"That's not up to you. If Ash wants me to leave, let her tell me that herself."

"What is wrong with you? She almost died because of your stupid club. Is that what you want for her?"

"No. I—"

"This town is a death trap. You can't protect her from that. If you love her at all, you should be able to see that. The best thing you can do for her is let her go."

She doesn't say another word before walking away.

At first, I'm pissed. I imagine myself barreling past the desk and barging into her room. I'd wrap my arms around her, kiss her lips, and tell her I'm so in love with her. In love with every single thing about her. But security would try to stop me, and another night in jail might push me over the edge. Then, I think I'll wait her out. I'll stand at the door until they discharge her, and I can finally get my eyes on her.

It doesn't happen all at once, but over the next couple of hours, her mom's words chip away at my false confidence. She's right. I can't keep Ash safe. My dad tried to warn me about what would happen, but I didn't listen.

Everyone else saw it. They tried to tell me I was going to hurt her, and I was too selfish and in love to believe it, but they were right. I did this. I might as well have been the one to pull the trigger, and if I don't end things, that's exactly what I'll be doing.

Sealing her fate.

I stand and leave the hospital.

After driving around for hours, trying to make sense of what just happened with Ash at Aker's memorial, I finally head to the garage.

Since I can't go back for her, maybe I can drink her out of my system.

My dad stops me as I storm through the parking lot. "Gabe—"

"Don't!"

"Gabe, listen to me."

I whip toward him. "No! Fuck off! You're the whole reason any of this happened. You and your goddamn club!"

"Gabriel!" he shouts. "I'm trying to be understanding because you lost a friend, but watch your mouth."

Stopping, I lift my face to the sky, running my tongue over my teeth.

"I lost more than a friend."

I lost the love of my life because I dumped her while she laid in a hospital bed.

Because of me.

I typed out that text and deleted it a dozen times before finally hitting send. I knew if I saw her, I'd cave. If she'd looked at me with those gray eyes full of tears, I'd have taken her right back. Which is exactly what I wanted to do at the memorial. I saw her the moment I set foot in the church and my heart squeezed, ripping and tearing inside my chest, but I walked straight ahead. I grieved the boy who could have been a brother if not by blood. Then, there was no more oxygen left in the room.

I had to get the fuck out of there because being that close and knowing I'd have to walk away was eating me alive.

He sighs. "Son, I'm sorry."

"Save it." I start toward the club. "I don't want to hear it."

He stops me with a hand on my shoulder. "Too bad. I *am* sorry. I hate what happened, but if you're gonna be in this club, ending things was for the best. You saved her from a lifetime of hurt."

"Great! And what if I don't want to be in this club anymore?"

He rears back, his brows pinching. "You don't mean that."

"Oh, I very much do." I stomp away from him before I can say something I regret.

"Where have you been?" JT asks as I march through the door.

I grunt, walking past him until I get to the bar. Grabbing a fifth of whiskey, I find a corner to sulk in.

The last image I'll have of Ash is her in my rearview mirror, tears soaking her cheeks as I tore her heart out and stomped on it at the memorial.

At least, I hope that's the last I ever see of her, because I'm not sure I could turn her away a second time. As the amber liquid burns my throat, I decide I'll never bring another into this mess again, and I won't ever allow myself to become attached to someone that I can't keep.

It hurts too fucking much.

35

———

GABE

AUGUST PRESENT DAY

Ash left, *again*.

My heart feels like it's been ripped open from the inside, *again*.

And I don't know that I can handle it this time.

I'm struggling to keep myself from regretting everything.

I've spent the last two days trying to convince myself I could let her go.

The problem is, I still haven't fully accomplished it. On one hand, maybe she finally got the closure she needed, and she'll never think of this town again.

I should be able to live with that. It's what's best for her.

On the other hand, I don't know what I want without her. Scratch that. I know exactly what I want.

Only her.

I don't think I ever got past what happened, but I found a way to convince myself that I did the right thing and learned to live with it. Maybe I would've if Ash hadn't come back. But I knew the second I found her keys in the garage, it'd break me to let her go a second time.

I've gotten as far as the truck a handful of times since she left, only to talk myself out of going after her. Then I saw that picture I took from her room.

I can't live like this.

For the first time in years, my mind is crystal clear.

I know exactly what I want. I want the girl I've spent afternoons with under the magnolia tree and shared secrets with on the roof. I want a life where we're safe and happy and she tells me when I'm being an asshole and I get to listen to her ramble about whatever pops into her head.

I want years with her, not just summers. With my heart thumping wildly in my chest, I put on my shoes and walk out of the apartment. Pulling out my phone, I call JT.

"Hey, man."

"Hey, can you open the shop tomorrow? I'm gonna be out of town."

"Sure. Where you going?"

"To Ash's."

"You're going after her?" he asks excitedly.

"Yeah. Enough fucking around. I love her."

"Yeah, I know." I can hear him smiling through the phone. "Good for you. You deserve to be happy, man. So does she."

"Oh, one more thing, can you get her address from Shane?

"Uh, sure. I'll try"

"Don't tell him it's for me. He'll freak out, and I'm not ready to deal with that shit," I say.

"I've got you."

This time, I make it all the way to my truck and climb in. Turning the key, there's no voice talking me out of it this time.

I have to try.

My hands sweat and my knees bounce the entire two hours to Raleigh. This is what I should've done six years ago.

My dad was wrong. Brenda was wrong.

I was wrong.

Nothing matters without Ash.

She's the sun. It's cold and dark outside her orbit, and I don't want to live there anymore. I miss her warmth and her laugh.

She's mine, and I'm not letting her get away again.

I find Ash's car parked by the curb in a picture-perfect neighborhood. Nice houses line the street. There are kids riding bikes on the sidewalk. This is the life I was trying to give her when I sent her away, but it didn't keep her from hurting right along with me, did it?

Walking up to the porch, there's a swing and a tiny Minnie Mouse folding chair. A half-empty cup of coffee sits on a glass-top table. My eyes meet the storm door in front of me, and I ring the doorbell before hearing the chimes from inside the house. I suck in a breath as the moment comes into focus. The wait is finally over.

Hopefully.

I guess she could send me away, but I don't think so.

We aren't over. We never were.

Footsteps thunder on the other side before I finally hear the click of the lock.

This is it. I'm about to get my girl back. Warmth spreads across my chest, and electricity surges through my veins.

As the dark wood door swings open, a little girl wearing a princess dress, a pink sock on one tiny foot, and a purple sock on the other stares up at me.

Whose kid is that?

I look at the number on the house again before taking in

the wild blonde curls, half pulled up on top of her head with frizzy ringlets falling around her face like she's been rolling around on the floor.

Her wide grin falls, and her big blue eyes lose a bit of their shine.

"It's not him, Mommy!"

Mommy?

Clattering rings out from deep within the house, and Ash shouts, "Who is it, then?"

Her lips twist, and her shoulders slump as she looks back at me with those eyes.

What color were her ex's eyes?

My heart thumps in my ears, and my chest squeezes.

This isn't real.

"How old are you?" I manage to croak out.

Her brows pinch, but then she grins big and holds up an open hand. "Five."

All the air whooshes from my lungs.

His eyes weren't blue.

I step back, sweat collecting on my brow. It didn't feel this hot before.

"I think he's sick! He looks green!"

"What? Close the door, Mag—"

I can see Ash out of the corner of my eye, but I can't tear them away from the little girl.

"Gabriel..."

She's staring back at me with those eyes.

My fucking eyes.

Ash steps in front of her.

"What'reyoudoinghere?" It comes out as one long word, and it's all the confirmation I need.

That's my daughter.

36

GABE

AUGUST PRESENT DAY

Why is all the Jack gone? I toss the empty bottle in the trash before picking up the Jim Beam beside the kitchen sink.

Also, empty.

There's no way I drank that much.

I open all the cabinets, scanning the contents before slamming them shut when I come up short. Groaning, I rub my hands down my face, then slide to the floor.

Fuck me.

I sniff, then wrinkle my nose.

More booze, or a shower?

Really, it should probably be both. I don't know how many days it's been since I did. I've just been locked up here, drinking my rage away. No shower needed for that.

But the crushing pain that wracks my sober body is unbearable, so more booze is a necessity.

After a quick shower, I grab my keys and head out for task number two.

I'm coming out of the gas station when I run smack into Ash.

"Oh," she says, stumbling back, her phone still in her hand. Her wide eyes lift to mine. "Gabriel—"

Fuck me. Why is she here? The universe must really have it out for me because I'm nowhere near ready for this shit.

She's looking at me with puppy-dog eyes, and I hate it.

I'm not doing this today.

With my head down, I brush past her, moving as quickly as I can to my truck.

"Gabriel, please."

Keep going.

"Please, stop!"

Those words bring me to a halt. We've done this before. I walk away; she chases me down. It all ends the same, doesn't it?

A few days ago, I thought we were meant to be. But I had it all wrong. All we're good at is hurting each other.

She grabs my arm. I don't turn, just look down at her fingers on my bare forearm.

"Gabriel. I'm sorry—"

"So, it's true?" I ask, clenching my jaw.

"What?"

"The kid, Ash." Spinning on her, I yank my arm away. "She's mine, right?" It comes out sharper than I'd like.

Her eyes soften. Pity. Not regret.

"Why?" My voice cracks.

She takes a step back. "I—"

"You what? You just hid my own kid from me for six years, then forgot to mention it all goddamn summer?"

"It's not like that."

"No?"

She shakes her head, tears forming in her eyes. "I tried

to tell you, but you ignored all my calls, and then I thought—"

"She's my fucking kid!" I ball my fists.

She rears back, the tears retreating and her brows furrowing. "I was trying to keep her safe."

"You can't possibly think I'd—"

"What was I supposed to think! You broke up with me in a fucking text message! You made me think I was crazy for believing you loved me! You called me pathetic! Even then, I tried!" Her voice comes out shrill and her neck flushes. "You fucking blocked me!"

"Could've called Shane. You took years from me! Years! *And* you let someone else raise her!"

"No." She shakes her head. "*You* made your choice the day you left us."

Has she lost her goddamn mind?

"Us? I didn't know!"

A crowd starts to form, watching this tiny woman scream at the big bad wolf.

"Ugh!" she shrieks, stomping her foot. "Are you even listening to me at all!"

"Enough!" Lily barrels toward me.

Where the hell'd she come from?

Ash rolls her eyes. Hard. "Don't worry, you can have him back when I'm done."

Lily blinks, her brows lifting. "Ash, that's—"

She turns her ire back on me.

"You're done talking. Now you get to shut up and listen. You did this to yourself! Do you really think just because you showed up at my house and said sorry, you're suddenly the good guy here?" she shouts, her fists clenched at her sides.

Fuck.

Her face turns a bright red, her eyes steel.

"I loved you!" she shouts, stepping toward me with that finger raised again. "I never *once* blamed you for what happened! But how dare you act like this is all my fault!"

Lily steps between us, pulling her phone from her pocket. "I'm calling Shane! Stop it!"

"Good. Call him! I've got some shit to say to that motherfucker too! Might as well air it all out!" Holding out my arms, I step back from her.

"You don't get to blame him. You did this!" She lunges, but Lily catches her by the arm. "You have no fucking clue what I've been through! How horrible it was! How bad I wished I'd just died that night!" Her voice breaks and she shoves Lily off her and clumsily bats her hair from her face. "Don't fucking touch me!"

She gets right in my face. "You had your whole fucking club to get you through it. Hell, you even still have my brother. I had no one! I grieved alone! I healed alone! And I made my fucking decision alone!"

My chest heaves, but I can't find the words to say. Every nerve in my body feels exposed, and the eyes watching us feel like they're burning my flesh from my bones.

There's no air left. My throat tightens.

"I can't do this," I mutter, tearing open the door and climbing in my truck before looking at Lily. "Tell Shane he knows where he can find me."

I need to get the hell out of here. I can't do this. Not right now and definitely not in front of half the damn town at a gas station.

I've not felt whole since the day Ash left, but this is a brand-new type of empty because there's no solution that fixes this.

I'm silent on the way back to the shop, not exploding

until I finally put it in park. Then a guttural scream leaves my throat, and I slam my hands on the steering wheel. Over and over and over.

Letting my head fall back on the seat when I'm done, I grip the wheel until my knuckles blanch, and my chest heaves as I catch my breath.

I'd give anything to talk to my dad right now. That might sound strange considering he was one of the people telling me to send her away in the first place, but he'd know what I'm supposed to do now. He'd tell me how to make this right. He wasn't perfect, and I had mixed emotions about him when he died, but he tried to be a good dad. And in a lot of ways, he was.

Once I've half-ass collected myself, I go inside and find a spot at the clubhouse bar to throw myself a pity party.

I open the top of a cheap bottle of whiskey and pour a glass. *Fuck her for doing this.*

I pour another. *Fuck this club for taking her from me in the first goddamn place.*

And another. *Fuck me for letting her go.*

Another.

The door swings open and blood roars in my ears.

And fuck Shane for not telling me.

"Gabe—"

Charging toward him, I shove his shoulders. "Did you know?"

"Gabe, listen." He throws his hands up.

Pinning him to the wall, all I see is red. "Did you fucking know!"

My hands shake. I'm ready to rip his head from his body. The look on his face says it all, but I want to hear him say it.

"Yeah, I knew," he says softly, looking down.

Scoffing, I shove him before running my hands through my hair.

"You have to understand—"

"Understand? You want me to understand that I have a fucking kid no one told me about?" Spit flies from my mouth as I shove him back again. "You're supposed to be my best friend!"

I don't know what's worse, the fact that the life I dreamt of with Ash was happening all this time without me knowing. Or the fact that now I know and can't have it.

"I know." He closes his eyes tightly.

"Yeah, you know." I shake my head, trying to collect my thoughts. "Six years, Shane. Six fucking years you've all been lying to me."

"She was broken, man. Like, really fucking broken because of you." He points his finger at me, and I swear to God it takes everything I have not to reach out and break it.

"Yeah, and why is that, huh?" Answering my own question, I shout, "It's because no one fucking told me!"

"Okay." He nods. "And why do you think we didn't tell you?"

"I don't know!"

Am I losing my mind? Because it feels like he's not hearing himself. After all the shit he's done, he's really going to act like my actions were so unforgivable. I have a kid! No excuses can justify him hiding that from me.

"Because we were all trying to look out for that little girl! All any of us wanted was to keep her safe!"

"Yeah? You don't think I would've felt the same way?"

That's all anyone keeps saying. Like that wouldn't have been my number one priority. I was petrified after what happened to Ash. I wouldn't put my kid in a position to be hurt, but what's it say about me that they all think I would've?

He shakes his head.

I add, "I didn't ask about her because you told me not to. Meanwhile, you lied to my face every goddamn day!"

My hands tremble, and I think if it was possible, smoke would be billowing from my ears. I stomp toward the bar before throwing over my shoulder, "You're fired, and you're done with the club. Get out."

"She's my fucking sister!" he screams, his voice coming out strangled this time. "Gabe! My baby sister! You can't expect me to choose you. I'm supposed to protect her! That's my job, and I let her get hurt! None of this would have happened if you'd just stayed away from her!" He deflates, his arms dropping to his sides. "Why couldn't you just stay away from her?"

"Because I loved her!"

"Yeah, and that almost got her killed!" he says, approaching me. "Is that what you want for Maggie too?"

I swing.

He stumbles back, covering his mouth as blood trickles down his chin. I close in on him, my fist landing on his cheek this time, knocking him to the floor.

I climb on top of him and rear back again.

JT grabs my wrist and yanks me backward.

I flail. "You're a fucking piece of shit."

"Yeah, I am, but I think you need to look in a mirror because so are you," he snarls, wiping blood from his mouth as he stands.

"Well, if I wasn't before, you all made sure I was when you made me a fucking deadbeat, didn't you?" I try to lunge, but JT doesn't let me free.

"Yeah, blame us all you want, man, but you played your part in this shit storm too," he says.

"Fuck you!" I scream.

"Enough!" JT booms, flinging me away from Shane.

I shrug him off, storming toward the bar.

"Get him the fuck out of my club," I growl over my shoulder.

Pulling another bottle from behind the bar, I pour one more glass of whiskey. Shane walks behind me as I glare at him until he's out the door.

I lay my head down on the bar, sucking in breath after ragged breath. Nothing has ever come close to making me feel this much fucking rage. Not the night I found Max with Ash or the night I took her home from the bar. This is a different level entirely.

A hand falls on my shoulder, and I lift my head ready to fight. When my gaze lands on JT, I say, "Get the fuck away from me."

I yank my arm away. Fuck him too. He should have let me beat Shane to a pulp.

"No," he says firmly, leaning closer and sitting in the stool next to mine. "You're my best friend. I know this sucks. But you can let me help you and be there for you, or you can deal with it alone. Either way the situation is the same. You don't have to push everyone away."

I grind my teeth, letting his words sink in. Staring down at the bar, I try to get a handle on my emotions, but it doesn't work.

"I don't need help."

He scoffs. "Yeah, you do. You've been drowning since the day she left, then your dad died, and now you find out you have a kid. That'd be a tough road for anyone. But you don't have to do any of this alone, so stop being a dick and talk to me."

I push my index finger and thumb into my eyes and exhale. The cracks in my walls are slowly widening and everything's spilling over. Pressure builds in the middle of my chest.

My hands shake.

I can't be here.

I can't do this.

I fucking hate this place.

Standing, the stool knocks over, hitting the ground with a clatter. I storm across the room and pick up a chair before tossing it at the glass door to the shop. Fuck this place. I never even wanted it to begin with. I rip a pool stick from the stand and head back to the bar. My heaving breaths turn to screams as I smash it into the wall of liquor bottles. Amber liquid splashes as glass explodes with each swing. She should have been mine. But this goddamn club took her from me.

It's taken everything from me.

I wouldn't have had to send her away if it weren't for it.

I could have—

Standing in front of the mess I made, the pool stick falls from my hand.

Ash couldn't stay here.

I couldn't let her.

But I stayed.

Damn near choking on my words, I mutter, "I chose this club over her."

When he doesn't say anything, I look back at him with tears pricking my eyes.

"I chose this fucking club over her," I shout, slamming

my hand down on the wet bar with a smack. My nostrils flare.

"I know."

Shaking my head, I bite my top lip before saying, "And it cost me my kid."

As a tear rolls down my cheek, the last of my control slips. Grabbing the bottle of whiskey in front of me, I chuck it at the wall of broken liquor bottles.

"I loved her!" I shout, pounding a hand on my chest. "I would have chosen her if I'd known! I wanted to choose her! I wanted her!"

I could have kept her safe without making a mess of everything in the process. I broke her heart. I ended us. I turned my back on her.

And she fucking survived.

My voice comes out smaller when I say, "I still love her."

"I know." JT's somber this time.

It all hurts twice as much because she's not just some girl I used to have feelings for. She's the girl I've loved my entire adult life. The girl I've thought about every night before I fall asleep. And I left her out in the cold. I abandoned her when she needed me.

"She did it alone," I say, sucking in a sharp breath. "She was alone because I wasn't there!" My voice cracks, and I brace myself on the bar, letting my head fall forward. "I wasn't fucking there for—"

I can't even get the rest of my words out before I feel like I'm being squeezed to death. I'm burning from the inside out, and I want to climb out of my own skin. He nods.

Shrugging away tears with my shoulder, I regain a hair of my composure and clear my throat, resting one hand on my hip and wiping my upper lip with the other. "I fucking hate this club."

And with that, the floodgates open. I slide to the floor and drop my head to the cool mahogany cabinets, completely losing myself. My shoulders shake with the weight of my own choices. I've never fallen apart like this before, but it's like something's detonated in my chest.

I don't know why it took me this long to realize it. I made the wrong choice six years ago, and I'll have to live with that for the rest of my life.

"Listen to me." JT kneels beside me and places a hand on my shoulder. "It'll probably take time for you to figure out what to do from here. It might take Ash some time too. But you have another chance. It might not feel like it right now because it's still fresh, but this is your opportunity. Fuck the past six years. Fuck the mistakes. You have a kid. I won't pretend to be father of the year, but I wouldn't give mine up for the world. I know you just found out about her, but I think that's what you're saying. So, don't. Don't give her up. Figure out your shit, man up, and be her fucking dad. She's five. There's still plenty of time."

That feels like a punch straight to the gut.

I don't know what I'm doing.

Feeling the weight of everything that happened today crash down on me, I let out a long breath.

How bad I wished I'd just died that night!

Her words keep ringing in my ears, making me feel like I might throw up.

In trying to protect her, I did more damage than that bullet did. I'm the reason she got to that place, not the club, not Tony.

Me.

"How the hell am I supposed to fix this?"

37

———

ASH

AUGUST 6 YEARS AGO

oday's my follow-up appointment with my family doctor. I'm just ready for all of this to be over. My leg still hurts, but it's not so bad if I'm not standing. Since I've barely left my room, that's not a problem.

I'm so tired, and when I'm not tired, I'm crying. I cry so hard I make myself sick. For the most part, my mom leaves me be with the exception of the therapy appointments she insisted on. I hate therapy. The lady just makes me talk about everything that happened over and over again like I don't relive it every night when I fall asleep.

Like I don't see Akers every time I close my eyes.

So now I'm sitting in a packed waiting room, looking like I just rolled out of bed because I actually did just roll out of bed. My eyes are red and puffy, and my head is pounding.

"Ashton Michaels," the Nurse says.

Standing, I adjust my crutches and hobble away from where my mom sits to follow the nurse into the office.

"How are you feeling?" she asks.

"Fine," I murmur, as she puts me in a room and asks me

a bunch of questions before leaving me to wait on the exam table for the doctor.

A few minutes later, the doctor knocks on the door before entering. "Ashton? Hello, dear, how are you?" She takes a seat on the stool.

She's a middle-aged woman with dark hair, wearing a white coat. Her red-rimmed glasses sit on top of her head.

"I'm fine."

"Good. How's your pain?"

I shrug. "It's fine."

Her lips pinch into a tight smile. "You've been through so much, are you talking to someone?"

Nodding, I say, "I have a therapist."

"Great. That's really good. So, I do want to go over some of your test results." She glances at the computer hanging from the wall before adding, "Would you like your mother to come back?"

That strikes me as a little odd. My mom stopped coming with me to the doctor when I turned eighteen. She probably wouldn't have come today if I were able to drive.

"Um... no. That's okay."

She flashes a small smile. "Okay. Well... I don't know if you were aware of this, but we ran a pregnancy test with your labs earlier, and it did come back positive."

"No. That's not possible. They did that at the hospital. It was negative, and I've not been with anyone since."

"They did, but you may have just been too early in your pregnancy for it to be detected."

Your pregnancy.

The words leave her mouth, but when they hit my ears, it feels like she's saying it in slow motion.

No.

There's no way.

My head spins, and I feel like I might actually throw up.

"Ashton? Are you sure you don't want us to have your mother come back?"

"No! No, I'm okay."

"Okay, you'll need an ultrasound in a couple weeks. I'm not an OBGYN so we'll get you a list of doctors to choose from to get that set up."

I swallow again, nodding.

"Are you sure you're okay?"

"Uh-huh." Tears prick my eyes.

She reaches for a box of tissues and holds it out to me. "I know this can be scary, but you have options."

She continues to talk, but I'm no longer listening. Instead, my mind wanders to Gabriel—all the nights I spent with him, where he is now, what he'll say when he finds out I'm pregnant.

After getting lots of information and picking an OBGYN, the doctor leaves the room.

When I stand, my legs feel like they've forgotten how to carry me. I walk silently out of the office.

Luckily, my mom had to take a work call and spends the entire drive home on the phone, not noticing me wiping away tears.

There's no way I can tell her. I don't want to tell anyone. I want to go to bed, and maybe I'll wake up, and all of this will be a terrible dream.

Pulling out my phone, I send him a text.

I need to talk to you. Call me

I try to call Gabriel every day, but he never picks up.

Every night, I lie in bed and imagine him answering. He'd say he made a mistake and wants us to come home. Then I imagine what our lives would be like because I don't think he'd abandon me if he knew.

But I guess he already has, hasn't he?

"Jesus, are you ever gonna move on with your life?" Jess moans as she walks into my room before flopping down beside me. It's been a couple of weeks since I found out I'm pregnant, and I still haven't told anyone. Well—except my therapist. I guess she's come in handy after all because now she's the only person I can talk to.

We lay side by side, facing each other. I sniffle and take a deep breath, closing my eyes tightly.

"Come on, Ash. You can talk to me. I'm your sister. I'm always on your side."

"I'm pregnant," I whisper.

"What?" She sucks in a sharp breath, sitting straight up off the bed. "Are you serious?"

I nod, crying harder.

"Holy shit. Does your mom know?"

"No. No one does."

"What about Gabriel? You told him, right?"

I shake my head.

"Ash, you have to tell him. You shouldn't have to do this alone."

"I've called a bunch of times, but he won't answer."

"Shit. I'm so sorry." She lies back down and throws her

arms around me. "He's such an asshole. You're probably better off without him anyway."

"I don't wanna do it alone."

She squeezes me tighter. "You won't. You have me. We'll do it together."

Choking on my tears, I say, "I have an ultrasound today."

"Do you want me to go with you?"

I nod.

Jess never leaves my side. She sits on my bed while I get ready for the appointment. She drives us there and holds my hand while I lay on the table. Then, something changes. I guess it hadn't completely sunk in yet, but everything shifts when the tech turns the sound on and I hear that tiny heartbeat. All the events from the last few months flash through my head, and I'm hit with overwhelming clarity.

That's a real baby. My baby. I've always assumed I'd be a mom one day. Never this young, but one day. And the last few months of my life have been nothing but loss and heartache. I'm alone. My future's been ripped from my hands, and for some reason, this feels like a flashing beacon.

I'm afraid, but this baby's my new future.

Jess squeezes my hand, and when I roll my head toward her, she's smiling.

I've been so stuck on contacting Gabriel that I haven't stopped to consider what would happen if he did answer.

Protecting this baby is the only thing that matters.

I think about that man holding a gun to my head. That's the world my child would be a part of if Gabriel were around.

I finally get why my mother wanted me out of that town because at this very moment, I would do anything to keep my child away from Ravens Ridge.

Eventually, I break the news to my mom, and after several long conversations, we decide not to tell Gabriel.

I'm going to be a mother all alone.

I get why they call it labor. Holy shit. I thought I was going to literally split in half. The nurses said she came pretty fast for my first baby, but eight hours seemed like forever. We've been patiently waiting for her to come for a week, but it seems she wasn't ready.

This morning, a week overdue, my water broke. There were times over the last several months that I wasn't sure I could do it. And today has been a whirlwind of emotions, but the moment they placed her in my arms, I knew it was worth it.

The first thing I noticed when they handed her to me was how much she looks like him. It's a bittersweet feeling. Part of me loves that I have a little piece of him, the other part feels like this reminder might turn the knife from now until eternity.

"Oh, sweetheart! You did so well," Gran coos as she walks into the room.

I beam up at her. For the first time in my life, I'm proud of myself. Gran came to stay with us last week so she could be with me the whole time. My mom's been better lately, but she's not Gran.

"Did you pick a name yet?" Jess sits on the couch in the corner of the room.

I've had a name picked out since I found out I was having a girl, but I haven't been ready to tell anyone.

"Yeah." I nod, grinning. "Magnolia June."

There are "awe's" from everyone in the room except Gran. She gives a tight-lipped smile, and I know she sees right through me.

After passing her around for what feels like an hour, the room finally clears to just Gran and me. She sits on the edge of the bed, smiling down at Magnolia in my arms.

"Magnolia, huh?"

I can't meet her gaze.

I've never met anyone who can read every thought in my head like she can.

"Uh-huh."

"Ashton, I'm so proud of you." She squeezes my arm. "He's missing out on two very special girls."

Tears prick my eyes, and I finally lift them to hers.

"You know, your grandpa and I used to sit under that tree." She gives me a sad smile. "The first time I saw you two out there, it reminded me of us."

I wipe a stray tear with my shoulder.

"Heartache is so painful, my dear, but what a gift it is to experience a love so deep." She takes a breath. "When I lost him, it felt like a great injustice, but as time has passed, I've realized I was so lucky. Even if I didn't get fifty years with him, I got a love that most never experience. I know you only got one summer with that boy, but what a special summer you had."

I let the tears flow as Gran wraps her arms around me. It *was* a special summer, and looking down at the perfect child in my arms, I have no regrets.

38

ASH

AUGUST PRESENT DAY

I tried to call Gabriel a dozen times after he left Jess's house, but he wouldn't pick up the phone. Isn't that ironic? So, I packed an overnight bag before heading back to Ravens Ridge.

I'd just pulled into town when I ran into him at the gas station.

My heart caved in. He looked... I don't know. Broken? Lost? I've never seen Gabriel like that. Normally, he's the strong one. But then, there he was dark circles, messy hair, and eyes full of thunder.

I didn't plan on yelling at him like that. Honestly, I'm not entirely sure where it came from. All that has had too much time to stew, I guess. When he pushed the right buttons, it just boiled over.

I could have gone home after that. I only came to town to talk to him, and I think we both said about all there is to say. But it felt like Gran's was calling to me. Since it hasn't sold yet, I couldn't come up with a reason not to take a detour before I head home.

Sitting by the lake, I kick off my shoes and stretch out

my legs. I wonder what Gran would say about this mess. She'd definitely know about it by now. Talk about airing out your dirty laundry.

It needed to happen, though. He needed to hear me out. I did what I did for Maggie. It wasn't about hurting him. Once I found out about her, the shit between Gabriel and I took the back burner. It was only about Maggie.

I did the right thing.

Gravel crunches, and I turn to find JT's black truck coming down the road. He parks several yards from where I'm sitting. With a warm smile, he lifts a hand, and I return the gesture. As the passenger door opens, my heart clenches.

Gabriel appears from around the truck.

It's only been a few hours, and I'm not sure I'm ready to go another round with him. He's in fresh jeans and a black T-shirt and has pulled his hair back.

He stops in front of me with red puffy eyes and puts his hands in his pockets.

Shifting onto my knees, I say, "Gabriel—"

"I screwed up. Ash, I should've—I missed out on my own damn—" His voice breaks, and he pulls a hand from his pocket, pressing his fingers to his eyelids. "I know where you were coming from, keeping her from this place. I get it, really. But you could have told me. I would've been there."

"I didn't know," I whisper. With a deep breath, I continue, "After everything that happened, I felt like I didn't even know you. What was real—" Biting my top lip, I drop my gaze to the grass.

He crouches in front of me and places a hand on either side of my face. He smells like him but also like alcohol and cigarettes. This close, every bloodshot vessel in the whites of his eyes is visible.

As tears begin to well, his blue eyes darken. "I fucked up. I royally fucked up, and I'm so sorry. You were never a fling. You weren't pathetic. You were everything. My whole fucking world."

The fist squeezing me from the inside twists.

Wrapping my hands around his wrists, I stare up at the man I loved so much it almost killed me. I don't know where we stand anymore, but I don't want to hate him. And I'm so tired of hurting each other.

A single tear rolls down his cheek as he says, "I owe you a hell of a lot more than an apology, but there aren't enough words in the world to make up for this shit. So, I'll just keep telling you how fucking sorry I am."

My heart cracks open and I sob. How can I not? This is an impossible situation. Neither of us are wholly at fault, but it's fucked all the same.

There are years of wear etched into his forehead that weren't there before. That mask he wears to keep everyone out has been in place for far too long.

Like a white flag, I pull him to me, wrapping my arms around his shoulders as they shake and his chest heaves. I think all these years, I assumed he'd been out living his life while I was trapped in the dark corners of my mind that were created that day, but he has his own demons.

I don't know how long we stay like that, but eventually I pull back, taking in his tear-streaked face.

He's broken, and I hate it. I'll always choose my daughter over anyone else, but I wish choosing her didn't mean hurting him. The problem is, I don't know where we go from here.

Ravens Ridge isn't a place I can bring her. He was right before. He lost years with her. Years that, no matter how this turns out, he'll never get back. But there will be more years, and my stance on things hasn't changed. The only difference is, he'll feel every one of those years without her now.

Maybe not telling him before was actually the kinder choice.

He eventually shifts to his butt and rests his elbows on his knees. "This is a mess."

"Yeah..." I sit beside him.

A long silence stretches between us.

Finally, with his eyes trained on the water, he says, "Did you mean it before when you said that you wished you'd died that night?"

I knew he'd take that hard. It's not really something I've talked about outside of therapy because she says that's a pretty common feeling with people who experience that type of trauma.

"I did. Especially before I found out I was pregnant. Things changed after that, but before I felt like it was pointless for me to have survived instead of him. He had a church full of people who were devastated that he was gone. And I —" I swallow, trying to get the words out. "I kept getting thrown away by people I loved."

His brows pinch. "Ash—"

I put up a hand. "You let me go because you loved me, I get it. But I didn't then."

He looks at me dead in the face and says, "I don't care what's happened over the last six years, I'm glad it wasn't you. I miss Akers every day, but I wouldn't have survived it if it'd been you."

I have to blink back tears. *Jesus, how much am I gonna cry today!*

"I'm okay now. Therapy helped—well, and Maggie. She made everything worth it."

He's quiet for a long time before finally asking, "Can I meet her? Just once?"

He must think I'm going to say no because before I can respond, he adds, "I can come there. Everyone heard us today, so it's not like they don't already know she's mine."

My chest squeezes. It feels cruel to say no.

"Please?"

Goddamn it.

"Yeah. You can meet her."

He closes his eyes, taking a deep breath and turning back to the lake. "Does she know about me?"

I don't want to hurt him more than I already have, but there's no changing what's happened over the last six years. Maggie and I have had a whole life outside of Ravens Ridge.

Shaking my head, I tell him, "I met Casey a couple of months after I had Maggie, and he just kind of jumped right in." I shrug. "I mean, she's five. I couldn't very well tell her all this shit."

God, I hate this. I wouldn't want to do this to anyone, but this is Gabriel.

My Gabriel.

"You don't have to tell her who I am. If it's easier for her, I mean."

Placing a hand on his back, I angle my body to face him. "Look, I don't expect anything from you. I made an impossible choice, and in doing so, I knew what I was signing up for. This changes nothing."

He rears back with furrowed brows. "No. This changes everything. She's mine even if she never knows it. I'll respect whatever you decide, but I'm not that guy."

I tilt my head as my chin quivers. "I don't want her to get hurt."

He peers straight into my eyes and clears his throat. "I

would never let anything happen to her. I just want to meet her."

"Okay."

A smile spreads across his face, and for the first time since he showed up, the storm retreats a little from his eyes. "Her name's Maggie?"

"Yeah." I grin. "Well—Magnolia, but we call her Maggie."

I couldn't help it. I wanted him to be a part of her even if he never knew. We fell in love under the magnolia tree, and the most beautiful thing came from it. Her name felt like the obvious choice.

His eyes turn glossy.

There's a nagging part of my brain that just wants to make this better. I just want this aching we're both feeling to stop. So, I ask, "Do you want to see pictures?"

He nods, and I scroll through my phone until I find a picture from the day she was born.

"She was kind of stubborn. I went a week past my due date."

I hold out my phone.

"She's perfect," he chokes out.

"Yeah, she is."

After finding a more recent photo, I hold it out to him next. "That's from the first day of school." She's in a pink dress with little black Converse sneakers. "Ignore her hair. It's always a mess." She's got my curls, and for the life of me, I can't seem to keep them from looking like she's been rolling on the floor.

"Her teachers adore her. But they always comment on how much she talks in class." I chuckle because the kid gets it honest.

He smiles for a moment before rolling his lips under, blinking.

When the gnawing in my chest still doesn't cease, I add, "I can send them to you if you want."

"Thanks." He leans back on his palms and lifts his face to the sky. "I'm sorry you had to do it alone."

"I wasn't alone. I mean, it felt that way at first, but I had Jess and Gran. My mom's been really great with her. She's a way better grandma than she was a mom. Eventually, we had Casey, and sure he's been shitty lately, but he was good while we were together."

"I'm still sorry." He runs his tongue over his teeth. "I'm sorry it wasn't me."

My shoulders sag, and I whisper, "Yeah, me too."

Over the years, sometimes I'd wish he were there or wonder what our life would've been like if he had been. Sometimes I'd break down and convince myself to call him again, but I couldn't.

He wipes a tear from my cheek. "I'm so proud of you, Ashton."

39

GABE

AUGUST PRESENT DAY

I'm on my way to officially meet my daughter.

The majority of the last two weeks have involved me reliving the poor choices I made six years ago, beating myself up over them, and wallowing. But JT's right. I can't change any of it. If I don't get my shit together, I might miss out on more. That might actually kill me. Now that I know, she's all I think about.

I pull up outside Jess's house and hop off my bike. Casey's standing at the bottom of the stairs in a gray suit talking to Ash and smiling.

When she notices me, she pops up off the step she was sitting on. She's in a T-shirt and denim shorts. It's funny, she doesn't look all that different from the girl that opened the front door that first summer I met her.

"Hey, you're early. Casey was just dropping Maggie off."

I nod at Casey and hold out a hand, trying not to grind my teeth. Obviously, part of me is grateful he was here for them, but I'd be lying if I said I wasn't jealous.

"Hey, man," he says, his jaw ticking as he takes my hand.

I'm not the one who got to raise your kid. Chill the fuck out.

He wraps an arm around Ash. "I'll call you later."

Placing a hand in his suit pocket, he trots across the yard to his fancy-ass car.

Yeah, I still don't fucking like him.

"He seems like a douche," I joke, watching him leave.

Ash laughs, swatting my arm. "Be nice. He's trying."

"Trying what? To get back in your pants? I can see that."

She cocks her head and smirks. "No. He's trying to do the right thing."

My brows shoot up.

He thinks she'll eventually give in and take him back. But I could tell by the way she looked at *him,* that will never happen. She didn't look at him the way she's looking at *me* right now.

The way she always looks at me.

"Anyway, you ready?" she asks.

I hold up a pink gift bag. "As ready as I'll ever be."

I figured a gift wouldn't hurt in this situation. She deserves more than a stupid doll, but that's the best I could do with twenty-four hours' notice.

"Maggie, we have company!" she shouts into the house.

Footsteps thunder down the stairs into the living room before a head of blonde curls appears and leaps into her mom's arms.

Ash laughs, picking her up before turning to me. "Maggie, this is Gabriel."

Ash has slipped up and called me that a few times, and every time she does it, my heart lurches in my chest. It's probably just a habit, but I sort of hope she's doing it on purpose.

Maggie has on a different princess dress, and her hair might be wilder than it was the first time.

Rubbing my sweaty hands on my jeans, I try to muster a warm smile. I don't want to screw this up.

She narrows her eyes at me. "You were here before. You 'bout barfed on the porch."

I snort a laugh. "Yeah. That was me." Holding up the gift bag, I add, "I brought you something."

"What is it?" she squeals.

Ash puts her down and her eyes go wide. "Open it and find out."

Maggie takes the bag before racing to sit on the couch and ripping the paper out.

"I love Barbies!" she shrieks, pulling the doll from the bag. "Mommy, look! I don't have this one!"

"Wow, that's awesome." Ash sits next to her. "What do you say?"

"Thank you," she says, eyeing me as I sit on the other side of the couch.

"So, you're in kindergarten this year?"

She nods. "I'm five and when you're five you get to go to the big school!"

Ash grins, kissing the top of her head. "We used to drive past the school on the way to daycare every morning. She was very excited to start going."

"Also, when I turned five, I learned my ABC's. Know what happens then?" She wiggles her brows at me.

I look to Ash for the answer, but she's smiling down at her daughter.

Our daughter.

"What happens when you know your ABC's?" I laugh.

"You get to play piano!"

"That's right. No piano lessons until you know your ABC's, huh?" Ash brushes Maggie's hair back from her face before lifting her gaze to me. "I teach lessons on the side sometimes, and Maggie here was dying for me to teach her. But that's my rule, isn't it?"

Maggie nods. "Another rule, no sticky fingers on the keys."

I quirk a brow. "Oh yeah? How'd you learn that one?"

She rolls her eyes and deep breathes. "On Halloween, I gummed up the keys with sticky fingers. Mommy was big mad!" The way her voice lowers and her brows lift when she says *big mad* cracks me up.

"The sugar monster has a knack for making mommy big mad doesn't she?" I'm about to ask what that is when Ash continues, "Maggie turns into the sugar monster when she's all hopped up on candy."

Maggie flops back on the couch in a fit of giggles. "It's just too good!"

Ash tickles her before brushing her nose against Maggie's.

Maggie brings her knees up, hooks her arms under her knees, and wiggles until she's practically lying down. She looks like a roly-poly bug. "Mommy had to go real far away to clean a messy house before."

"Yeah. I saw her. I live there too."

"You live in the messy house?"

Ash laughs. "I wasn't cleaning it; I was cleaning it out. And Gabriel just lives in a house close to it."

"Do you live in Florida? Disney World is in Florida. One time we went to Disney World, and it was so far away we had to go on an airplane." Every word comes out faster than the last.

"Uh, no. I live here in North Carolina. No airplane needed."

"Have you been on an airplane? I'm not allowed to have gum, but the plane makes your ears pop like Rice Krispies, so Mommy let me have bubble gum that time."

For an hour she rambles about places she's been, movies she's seen, and she even told me about a girl at school named Lydia. I'm still not entirely sure if they're friends or mortal enemies.

She's perfect.

I can't bring myself to get up and leave. I've always been skeptical when people say they loved their kids from the moment they knew they were pregnant, but I get it now. I don't even know her, but God, I love her.

"Gabriel has a pretty far drive, baby. He'll have to get going soon," Ash says in the gentlest voice I've ever heard.

Damn. I've always thought she was beautiful, but watching Ash mother our child is something else, entirely.

It's everything.

"Will you come back?" Maggie asks, bouncing where she sits on the couch.

"Uh, yeah. If your mom says it's okay." I glance up at Ash. If I have to, I'll get down on the floor and beg her to let me.

Luckily, that's not needed because she smiles and says, "Yeah, he can come again."

My racing heart leaps.

"Go play, I'm gonna walk Gabriel out. I'll be right back."

Maggie nods, running back the way she came, and I stand before following Ash out onto the porch.

She shuts the door behind us. "Thanks for coming."

"Thanks for letting me." I offer her a smile, or maybe I've been smiling the entire time, I'm not sure.

As I hit the bottom step, I rest a hand on the railing and say, "Ash, I don't want to make demands when you've been doing this without me all this time, but I would really like to be a part of her life."

I've been trying to decide how exactly to ask her. I get that the club is a scary place. The last thing I want is to put Maggie in a dangerous situation. But I don't care what it takes, I want to know my kid.

She swallows, crossing her arms over her chest before nodding. "We'll work something out."

On the way to the truck, my phone rings.

"Hello?"

"Hey, we found Adam," JT says.

"Where?"

"Florida."

"Good. Make sure the fucker stays there."

40

———

ASH

OCTOBER PRESENT DAY

Gabriel and I have fallen into an easy routine. He comes over once a week for dinner and calls Maggie a couple times a week. It's not much, but it's all I've offered. Things have gotten less awkward, and Maggie adores him. She asks every day when she gets to see him again. I think it's started to heal something I didn't know was wounded.

She's sitting on the couch, waiting for her dad to pick her up with her pink sparkly backpack. He's already twenty minutes late when my phone dings with a text.

> Sorry. Stuck at work. Not gonna make it.
> Kiss Maggie for me.

"Motherfucker," I murmur so she can't hear me.

Looking back at me with sad eyes, she says, "He's not coming, is he?"

"No. He had something come up with work. I'm sorry, Bug." I move to sit beside her and pull her onto my lap.

"He never wants me anymore." A tear rolls down her cheek.

I hate this. I know what that feels like. I spent most of my childhood feeling unwanted, and I hate that I've allowed her to get close to someone who would make her feel that way.

"That's not true. He loves you." I squeeze her. "He's just busy."

She shakes her head. "I wish I had a daddy here all the time."

I run a hand down her back. "I know, baby."

What do you say to that? I wish she had a dad here all the time too. Guilt starts to prick at my heart because I can't help but feel like I'm the reason she doesn't.

"I wish Gabriel was my daddy."

I go completely still.

I've been debating whether I should tell her. I would've already, but I don't want her to get her hopes up if he can't be in her life.

But the thing is, he shows up. He shows up every single time.

He doesn't miss a week, even when I've had to reschedule. He rearranges his life to be here, but I worry he won't always do that. What if the club gets busy? Will he still show up then?

After a few minutes, she crawls off my lap, giving me a sad smile before heading to her room to play.

This might be a bad idea, but I pick up my phone.

He answers on the second ring. "Hello?"

"Hey, I know it's such short notice, but Maggie's having kind of a rough morning. Are you busy?"

It's Saturday. I'm sure Gabriel has shit going on, but I had to try.

"No. I mean, I'm at the shop, but the guys can handle it

without me. Is she okay?" he asks, his voice laced with concern.

"Oh, yeah. She's fine. Her dad—Casey was supposed to take her for the day, but he canceled. She's kind of bummed. You don't have to take the day off. She'll be okay."

"No, really, it's fine. I'll head that way now. I just have to clean up my shit. Do you need me to bring anything?"

"You don't have to do that—"

"I want to. I'll be there in a few hours."

Two hours later, he's standing on my porch in a pair of light jeans, a dark blue hoodie, and the top half of his hair pulled back. *Why is that so hot?*

I let him in, closing the door behind us. "Hey, thank you so much. You really didn't have to do this."

"I told you, I don't mind."

"Maggie!" he sings, walking up the stairs toward her room.

I hear her squeal, and when I round the corner, she's leaping into his arms, laughing. I start to tear up and turn quickly, wiping them away.

"So, what should we do today?"

"Let's go to the park! Daddy always takes me to the park."

Something flickers in his eyes for a moment, but he quickly fixes it. I would've missed it if I hadn't been staring. I catch myself doing that a lot—staring at him while he's talking to our daughter.

Then he flashes her the biggest smile. "I love the park."

He glances back at me.

"I have a ton of stuff to catch up on today. You can take her if you want, though."

His lips part, but he doesn't say anything. I can't quite read his thoughts, so I add, "You don't have to, of course. I can go if you'd rather. I don't want you to think I only called you to be a babysitter."

"No. It's not—I'd love to. I just wasn't expecting you to say that." Then he picks Maggie up as he stands. "You cool with that, Mags?"

She nods, wrapping her arms around his neck. This close, the resemblance is clear. The right side of her mouth lifts a hair more than the left when she smiles, just like his. She also does this thing with her eyebrows when she's mad that's a dead ringer for Gabriel.

"Uh... One problem." He grimaces. "I brought the bike."

Maggie's eyes widen, and she shouts, "Woo-hoo! I'm gonna ride on a motorcycle!"

"Absolutely not." I point at her before turning to Gabriel. "You can take my car."

He leans in and whispers, "We'll talk her into it once I get you a small enough helmet."

When he winks, she giggles, and I roll my eyes because it will be a cold day in hell before I let her on the back of his bike.

After doing the dishes, cleaning out Maggie's room, and about six loads of laundry, I get busy looking at apartments online. Jess doesn't seem to mind us living here, but we're going to have to find our own place at some point.

I'm sitting at the table with a bowl of cereal when Jess strolls through the door.

She drops into the chair beside me. "Maggie with Casey still?"

I shake my head. "He bailed again. Gabriel took her to the park, and then they went to dinner."

"Gabriel? Was he supposed to come today?" She picks up my spoon, taking a bite of my cereal.

"Nope, I called him because Maggie was so bummed. She cried and said she wish Gabriel was her dad."

"Yikes. That's uh... That's kind of sweet actually."

I pull the spoon away from her before grabbing her a bowl and spoon of her own and pouring another bowl.

"So what? He jumped on his bike and came?"

"Yeah, basically."

"Shit. So now what? Are you gonna tell her?"

"I don't know. Should I? I kind of feel like I should. Especially if he keeps bending over backwards for her."

"I mean, yeah." She shrugs. "Maybe. You know I've never been a fan of Gabriel for you, but for Maggie he seems pretty damn good."

"I know."

That makes me so happy and sad at the same time. She deserves a dad who loves her unconditionally, but I wish he could have been good for me, too. The door opens before the room fills with giggles.

Maggie races into the house. "Mommy! Gabie took me to McDonald's!"

Gabriel follows close behind, wincing. "Sorry. I hope that's okay. I should've asked, but I didn't think about it."

"It's fine. *Gabie.*" I laugh, winking at him.

"No." He shakes his head. "Don't start. She called me that at the park and has said it about a million times since. It's very cute." He points at me. "It is not cute when *you* say it."

Maggie flops down on my lap.

"Anyway, I had a great time with you today, Mags." He turns back to me. "I'll head out."

"No! Don't leave!" She runs across the room, launching herself at him, and he catches her like it's second nature.

"Saturday's movie night! It's my turn to pick, but I'll let you 'cause you never had a turn."

"Uh... I don't—" He kneels, putting her down and tucking a stray curl behind her ear. "I mean, that's your special thing with your mom."

My heart cracks wide open. *How am I supposed to feel good about my choices when he acts like that!*

Every opportunity I give him, he takes, while trying not to step on my toes.

"It's fine. If you want to stay and watch a movie, you can"

His eyes meet mine, asking a silent *are you sure.*

I nod with a smile.

"Okay." He claps, beaming. "Movie night."

Jess raises a brow, trying to send me signals telepathically.

When Maggie falls asleep halfway through *Matilda,* like she always does, I slide out from under her to stand.

Gabriel pushes off his knees and heads toward the door. "Thanks for today. It meant a lot to me."

I follow him out onto the porch, letting the screen snap shut behind me. "I wanted to talk to you about something."

He stops at the bottom of the stairs and turns back to me. Crickets chirp around us as the moon drenches him in a soft glow.

"How do you feel about telling her the truth? If you're not ready, it's fine, but she loves you, and I think it might be good for her."

"Like that I'm her dad?"

"Yeah. She's been having a hard time with this Casey shit, and I think it might make her feel better." I move to the top step and lean against the railing, crossing my arms over my chest. "She said something today about wishing you were her dad."

He swallows, blinking a few times. "Uh, yeah. If you're sure, I uh..." Rubbing the back of his neck, he says, "I would love that."

"You can't back out if we tell her. If she knows you're her dad, you have to be sure you're one hundred percent in."

He doesn't hesitate. "I'm in. I've been in from the second I found out about her. Ash, I want to be her dad."

My chest warms. This is the man I knew he was. This is the man I wanted him to be. This is the man I loved.

"Thank you for being there for her."

"Always." His hand drops from the railing, and he starts toward his bike.

I should let him go. There's no reason he shouldn't. So, why do I feel like I'm being shoved off this porch to stop him by a phantom wind?

"You know, it's pretty late. If you wanted to, you could stay. I can sleep with Maggie in her bed." I chuckle, feeling a little silly now that the words are spilling from my lips. "She'll freak out if she thinks she got to have a sleepover with you."

My cheeks heat. *I just asked my ex-boyfriend to have a slumber party. What the fuck is wrong with me?*

He smiles. "Okay."

Maggie's humming to herself while picking flowers to make herself a crown when Gabriel comes out to sit on the swing with me. Mornings are my favorite. I drink coffee and watch her play in the yard. It's almost as if time stops when we're out here with the sun on our faces.

"Morning. Coffee?" I ask.

"Found some." He holds up a cup. "So, what's your plan for the day?"

I shrug, gesturing to our daughter. "This."

"Do you mind if I stay for a little bit? I don't want to overstep if this is your time with her."

"I've had five years with her. If you want to stay, stay."

He's quiet for a beat before saying, "I wish I could take it back. I know I've said it already, but every time I look at her, that's all I can think."

I grab his hand. "Me too."

His eyes are fixed on her. "I think the hardest part is that I know if I'd made a different choice, we could have been really happy. I just wish I could've been there for all of it. To get up with her at night, and help her learn how to ride a bike, and all the other small things. Sitting here watching her, I know there's nowhere I could be that would make me happier."

He flicks his attention to me when he finishes, and tears prick my eyes.

"If it helps, she actually doesn't know how to ride a bike yet. You can do that if you want."

He nods, his mouth spreading to a wide grin. Eventually, Maggie drags him across the yard to push her on the swing. I cross my legs under me and open my book.

One chapter in, footsteps fall on the path that wraps around the house before Casey appears with a scowl.

"What's this?" he asks, nodding toward Gabriel and Maggie.

"What do you mean?" I close the book.

"You didn't tell me *he* was coming today."

I don't particularly care for his tone. "I didn't realize I needed to. Also, you didn't tell me you were coming today either."

"I figured you'd tell me if you were planning on letting a criminal hang out with our daughter." Cocking his head, he leans his forearms on the railing.

Is he kidding right now?

"Hmm, now she's ours? It sure didn't seem that way when you bailed on her yesterday. *Again.*" I roll my eyes. "Also, don't call him that. He's really good to her."

"Oh, yeah? If he's so good, where's he been her whole life?" He sucks his teeth. "You know, I thought you were smarter than this."

"What's that supposed to mean?"

"It means, he suddenly decides to give you the time of day, and you're dumb enough to fall for it."

Something in me snaps. I've been nice. I've tried so hard to get along with him so he'll keep coming around for Maggie, but I can't take this shit anymore.

"Really?" I rear back, snorting a laugh. "You know what? The only dumb thing I ever did was marry *you.* You're such an ass. You flake on her more than you don't, but now you want to act like Father of the Year."

He huffs. "I have a busy work schedule. Now I'm being punished because I have a job?"

"No. You're not being punished at all. Why don't you get it? You're the one who missed out on your time with her yesterday." I point at him. "You did that to yourself."

"Well, thank God the felon was there to swoop in and make everything better, huh?"

"Whatever." I sit back in the swing and cross my arms.

"What do you want? Or did you just come here to be a dick?"

"No, I came to see Maggie because I felt bad about yesterday, but I guess you don't need me anymore."

"Grow up, Casey. He's her dad."

"No!" he shouts. "I'm her fucking dad! I was the one there. Me! Not him!" He points to himself.

"I'm aware of all you've done, but you don't get to let her down and still claim to be her dad. None of it matters if you can't show up for her."

I internally cringe when I see Gabriel heading toward us. It's not that I care that he hears, but I know how bad this could turn. The last thing we need is for Gabriel's temper to make an appearance in front of Maggie.

"You good?" Gabriel asks.

I nod, and Casey huffs.

Gabriel stops, staring briefly before addressing him, "Are *you* good?"

Casey runs his tongue over his top teeth. "I just need to talk to Ashton. That's all."

"Okay, well, don't raise your voice at her again. That's *not* gonna happen."

"Why don't you go spend time with Maggie. That's why you're here, right? So, don't worry about how I talk to my wife."

"Soon to be ex-wife," Gabriel corrects.

"Yeah, well, that's between us."

Gabriel smirks. Then in a mocking tone he says, "Yeah. Well, I think it's actually up to the state of North Carolina."

Casey grinds his teeth. "That also has nothing to do with you or your time with my daughter."

"Look man, I'm not trying to step on your toes here. I appreciate everything you've done for Maggie. With that being said, I will make you choke on your fucking teeth if you raise your voice at her again." He pats the railing, his eyes flicking to me before storming off toward Maggie.

"Hmm, real nice guy."

And I know it's childish, but I have to roll my lips under to hold back a grin.

Gabriel can be a dick too, but something about him sticking up for me even though we aren't together is kind of sweet, and a whole lot hot.

I say, "We can set up a different time for you to come and get her if you want."

He nods before walking away.

The funny thing is, Maggie was right there the whole time. He could have at least said hello to her, but he didn't.

Maggie runs by to go into the bathroom as Gabriel sits on the swing next to me, smirking. "Told you he was a douche."

Rolling my eyes, I pretend I don't still love his jealous streak because I absolutely shouldn't. We're learning to co-parent. That's all. I'm not supposed to want to rip his clothes off when he's just here to get to know his daughter.

"Does he always treat you like that?" he asks.

I half laugh, staring down at my bare feet. "No. He's just pissed you're here."

"You don't deserve to be treated like that." He stares at me until I meet his gaze. "I know it's not my place, but he can't talk to you like that."

I shrug. "It's okay. He'll probably feel bad about it later. He's not normally that much of an ass."

He sighs, looking away for a moment before chuckling. "He doesn't really seem like your type."

"What do you mean?" I grin.

He runs his tongue over his bottom lip before saying, "It looks like he takes longer to get ready than you do."

I burst out laughing and cover my mouth with my hand. "He does."

"Jesus, I'd almost feel bad kicking his ass. That suit probably costs more than everything in my closet combined."

I throw my head back. "Oh, it definitely does."

I finally told Maggie. I was nervous for some reason. I was afraid she'd feel differently if she knew he was her dad, or she'd wonder why he wasn't around before.

None of which happened.

She was thrilled.

She asked if that meant she was supposed to call him Dad instead of Casey. I told her she could call them whatever she preferred and that they would both be okay with what she wanted. She seemed to think about it but has still been calling him Gabie. I don't think he cares at all, though. He seems happy to have her calling him anything.

This time when Casey flaked, it didn't seem to bother her as much. Don't get me wrong, she was bummed, but not quite *as* bummed. I hate it for both of them because they were so close, but I can't force Casey to be the man I believed he was, or the man Maggie deserves. I just pray Gabriel doesn't let her down, too. I don't want her to grow up believing men will always disappoint her, like I did.

41

GABE

OCTOBER PRESENT DAY

Nik and Shane are getting married. That's a sentence I never thought I'd be saying. It took Shane and I some time, but eventually we worked out our shit. I'm not saying there aren't still times I resent him for the years I lost, but I'm learning to let it go.

Ash was worried about letting Maggie come to Ravens Ridge for the wedding. For good reason, but I was dumbfounded when she asked my opinion on it. For the first time, I was a part of the decision.

When she was here before, I was naïve to think I could protect her from everything all by myself. That's not how this works. But I'm no longer blinded to what can happen. There will always be issues with other clubs, but luckily things have been fairly quiet lately. With that being said, we'll have club members keeping an eye on things from the parking lot. Even if someone decides to start shit while she's here, Maggie will be out of here before they get anywhere near the place. I'm not taking any chances with her. It's all mapped out already, and the wedding's not for a few weeks.

I also put extra guys in place for tonight because Ash'll

be at the clubhouse for their bachelor/bachelorette party. Maybe I'm paranoid, but after our fight at the gas station, everyone knows our business.

I'm outside smoking with JT when Nik's car pulls into the lot. The moon shines high above, reflecting off the black paint. Music and chatter erupt from inside when Theo slips out to join our party.

"Fuck, man. How many people did they invite? It's already packed."

Ash steps out of the car, dragging all the air from my lungs. I swear I have no idea how my legs manage to stay under me because she's never looked better. Her pale legs look a mile long in that short black dress that hugs every curve. The strappy black heels she's wearing click against the concrete as she practically glides across the parking lot. But the thing that catches me completely off guard is her hair. It's fucking straight. For the record, I'm a huge fan of the big curls, even more so now that I have a daughter with them. But straight, she has an edge that might actually do me in tonight.

JT takes notice too. He might as well be standing there with his damn mouth open. "Holy shit!"

"Stop gawking, you fucking creep." I smack him on the back of his head.

"Brother, any man with eyes would gawk at her. She gets hotter every time I see her."

"If you don't stop, you'll be a man without eyes." I put out my cigarette on the brick building and go inside. If I have to pretend not to want her all night, I'm going to need a drink.

Or ten.

I weave through the crowd as loud rock music blares overhead. At the bar, I order a beer and find my spot for the night. If I don't put myself in timeout, I'm going to drag her upstairs like a caveman.

"Hey, stud."

I spin around to find Lily standing behind me in a green dress that ties at the back of her neck. Pulling her in for a hug, I say, "Lil."

"I hate to break it to you, but I think you fumbled that one." She nods toward the door just as Ash strolls in.

You have no fucking clue.

She gets a smart-ass grin on her face, and I know I'm not going to like what comes out of her mouth. "You know, it really is a shame you wouldn't share her back then."

"Lily," I warn.

She cackles. "Does she know?"

"What?" I grumble, turning back to my beer just before bringing it to my lips.

Sliding onto the barstool beside me, she flips her hair over her shoulder. "That you're still in love with her, you doofus!"

Closing my eyes, I let out a long exhale. It's almost as if Lily doesn't know when to shut the hell up. "How did you become the world's most annoying human? Was there like an application process or..."

The whole time we're talking, I can practically feel Ash moving around the room behind me. Like I'm just painfully aware of where she is at all times.

"Ha ha. Listen, you can act like you don't care all you want, but you're just as in love with her as the day she left. The question is, what are you going to do about it?"

And this might be the first time Lily's voice of wisdom has ever been wrong. I'm more in love with her than I've ever been. And it's eating me alive.

42

ASH

OCTOBER PRESENT DAY

I have no right to be jealous. He's not mine. Hasn't been in a long time, but the sight of that damn redhead with her hands on him makes me want to scream. She has her arm slung around his shoulders at the bar. It's fucking annoying. Like, *God, it's been six years. Let it go.*

You have a lot of room to talk, Ashton.

She's literally never done anything to me, but I can't help it; I hate her.

And the worst part is, there will probably be other Lily's, and I'm going to have to watch them because we have a child together.

Now that he's present in Maggie's life, I can no longer pretend he doesn't exist. I have to see him. I have to watch as he pulls up in front of my house on that goddamn bike and takes off his helmet, shaking out his hair. I have to watch as he smiles at our daughter like she's the stars and the moon and the whole galaxy. And I may have to watch as he builds a life with someone else one day.

I tip my drink and take a hefty sip.

"Easy, killer. I didn't wear the right shoes to carry you out of here," Jess says from the chair beside me.

I roll my eyes.

Her nose scrunches. "You know, green is not your color. Let's go dance."

She grabs my hand, dragging me behind her.

As we step into the crowd, I decide I'm not going to look over at him again. He's not my business, and I shouldn't give a shit about that redhead. She can have him.

A few songs in, a hand brushes my hip.

"Holy shit, are you trying to get someone killed tonight?" JT leans down to say in my ear.

"What?"

"Gabe's gonna lose his goddamn mind from all the men staring at you in that dress."

I chuckle, swatting him. "Shut up!"

His eyes meet Jess's before he runs them down her body in the most obvious display. Nik said him and Katie split up a few weeks ago again, so maybe he's actually moving on for real this time.

"Careful. She'll eat you alive," I laugh.

Jess is vicious. I don't think any man has ever lasted more than a month with her.

"I must have a type." He laughs, winking at her, but I'm still keeping tabs on what's going on at the bar out of the corner of my eye. "Still not a fan of Lily?"

I glance at him over my shoulder to find him grinning and know I've been caught staring at them.

"I don't know what you're talking about." I flip my hair over my shoulder, smacking him in the face with it.

"Uh-huh, you were glaring for like ten minutes." He laughs. "I think everyone knows how you feel."

"I'm fine."

He chuckles, his chest rumbling against my back. "You're both so full of shit. If you think for one minute, he'd give Lily a second thought with you in the room, you're crazy. You'll always be his first choice even if you don't want him."

My breath catches in my throat. Wanting him is not the problem.

JT takes a step back from me, pulling his eyes away at the last moment to take in my sister. He licks his lips, gliding toward her and wrapping his arms around her waist.

She glares like she's not interested, but then she proceeds to spin around and grind into him.

And that's my cue.

My heels click against the floor as I walk off the dance floor, scanning the crowd. The place where Gabriel was sitting at the bar is now empty. I hate that I even notice, but I can't help wondering if he went somewhere with her. A pang hits my stomach as Nik skips up behind me, grabbing my arm.

"Do you feel those holes Gabe's been glaring into the back of your head all night?" she asks, pulling me with her to the bar.

"What?" *Was he?* "No, I didn't even notice."

She laughs. "I don't know how. He looked like he might spontaneously combust. Shane went over and tried to talk to him, but his eyes never left you."

"Maybe he's just drunk."

She shakes her head. "I don't think so."

I order a drink before turning to face her, holding it in front of me with both hands. "Can I ask you something?"

"Of course."

"Do you think I'll ever stop loving him?"

Her smile turns sad, and she sighs. "I don't know."

Running a hand down my arm, she adds, "Are you sure you want to? I'm not saying you should forgive him, but if it's torture, is it really worth holding a grudge?"

I drop my eyes to my drink, blinking to keep my makeup from running. "I'm afraid." When I return my gaze to her, I say, "I don't wanna get hurt again. Not to mention, this club's…" I shake my head and rub a hand over my brow.

"I get that, but it seems like he's really trying."

I nod before taking my drink and making a beeline for the bathroom. How can one person have such shitty luck? For years, he's all I've wanted, and now that there's a small chance I could have him, I can't allow myself to do it. Love isn't enough to negate everything else. It can't take away the hurt that we've caused each other. It couldn't keep us from imploding six years ago. How can I expect it to now?

The bathroom door swings open before it's fully closed behind me.

"Let's hear it," Lily says, looking at me in the mirror.

I spin to face her. "What?"

She laughs. "You've been glaring daggers at me all night. Go ahead. Say what you need to say, so we can move on."

I open my mouth but before anything comes out she continues, "You don't like me because I slept with Gabe, right? It's a jealousy thing?"

Again, she cuts me off before I can respond. "Look, you have nothing to be jealous of, I'll gladly hand him over to you. He's kind of a pain in my ass if I'm being honest."

My brows pinch.

She takes the few steps to the vanity and slides her butt onto it. "Plus, he's been in love with you from the moment you two met practically. Hell, he quit sleeping with me that summer Max drugged you. Said he just wasn't into it anymore. Man never has been able to separate his heart from his cock. Anyway, you're the one. Have been from the very beginning. I'm not getting in the way of that."

"Uh... okay."

"Okay, great." She nods, hopping off the vanity. "Glad we cleared that up. We good, now?"

I stare, dumbfounded. She lifts her brows like *hello*.

"Oh, uh... yeah."

"Awesome." She trots to the door. "Have a great night."

After wiping my face, and collecting myself, I come out of the bathroom. *No more Gabriel drama.* I'm not going to let this shit get in the way of my good time. I'm going to dance with my friends and enjoy my kid-free night.

That's when I see him sitting at a table and damn near stop breathing. He looks so good. I mean he always does, but he's in black dress pants and a navy dress shirt with the sleeves rolled up. His hair's pulled back from his face at the nape of his neck, and he's leaned back in his chair, staring right at me.

I strut over, plopping down in the seat next to him.

"Stare much?" I tease.

He runs his tongue over his teeth and smirks. My heart dips and a chill shoots down my spine.

That fucking smirk.

"Me?" He glances around. "I was just trying to figure out which body part I'm gonna have to relieve JT of later." He kicks a leg up, resting his ankle on the opposite knee.

"Give it a break. I'm pretty sure it's not me he's after." I laugh, gesturing to him grinding on my sister.

"That might be true. But I've warned him about putting his hands on you, and I just watched him run them all the way down your body."

He quirks a brow, and my mouth goes completely dry.

We've been getting along really well lately, but he's not been flirty like this. I actually was starting to think he must be over me.

But tonight, the old Gabriel is back.

He's smug, and flirtatious, and so fucking sexy.

I narrow my eyes before pretending to scan the room. "I ran into your friend in the bathroom."

His brows pinch. "Who?"

Faking disinterest, I lift my chin. "The sexy redhead."

Scoffing, he says, "You're impossible, you know that?" He pauses, narrowing his eyes. "Lily has never been your competition."

I blink before meeting his stare. Flames rage in his eyes, and my flesh breaks out in goosebumps.

"I don't think I'm in that competition anymore," I say under my breath.

He scrunches his nose, shaking his head. "I guess not. You won a long time ago, didn't you?"

"Gabriel—"

He sucks his teeth. "Don't act like you don't fucking know, Ash. I'm not asking you to forgive me or for anything to change but cut the bullshit for tonight. Don't pretend that you don't know I'm so in love with you I don't see anyone else in this room."

My lips part and my breaths quicken. I can't get words to leave my mouth.

He presses his lips into a tight grin before running his eyes over every inch of my body. It feels like being struck by lightning, and for a moment, I hope he'll never take them off me.

"You look incredible in that dress." He quirks a brow, lifting the vibration around us back to the easy flirtation from before.

"You don't look so bad yourself." Smiling, I tuck a hair behind my ear.

When I reach for my drink, bringing it to my mouth, he pulls it from my hand and slides it across the table. The clear plastic cup falls, splashing pink liquid onto the floor.

"Hey!" I object.

He slams his foot down, leaning forward so his breath splays on the shell of my ear as he whispers, "I have every intention of taking you home later, and you can't consent to that if you're drunk."

Every hair on my body stands up.

I cock my head to the side. "And what exactly makes you think I'd consent anyway?"

He smirks again and leans back in his chair, grabbing his beer from the table.

"We can play this game if you want, but I know you." He brings the bottle to his lips, taking a swig.

I'm not exaggerating when I say, I would give my right limb to be that bottle right now. I sit back in my chair, crossing my arms and legs.

"You're so full of shit."

"No, I'm not." He tips his beer to someone who greets him from behind me.

Kicking his shin, I say, "Dance with me."

He scoffs. "I don't dance."

"I know, but if you think you're taking me upstairs tonight, you better get your ass up." Not waiting for an answer, I stand and start toward the dance floor.

He darts out of his seat, wrapping an arm around my waist; his fingers splayed across my lower abdomen before putting his mouth to my ear. "I know for a fact I'm taking you upstairs with me later."

Then, he brushes past me, grabbing my hand and practically dragging me across the room.

You might know, the second we hit the dance floor, it switches to a slow song. I laugh nervously before I notice Gabriel winking at the DJ.

"What was that?" I glance between them.

He shrugs, smirking. "What's what?"

"You're trouble."

"Yeah. Probably."

He grabs my hand and pulls me to him, wrapping his arm around my waist. His fingers press into the small of my back. My heart does a somersault, my mind not landing on a single thought.

It's always like this with him. When his eyes are on me, everything else ceases to exist. It's just him. No matter how bad I wish it weren't true, there's no way out of the web we've tangled ourselves in.

I want us to be friends, but that's not possible, is it? I found the love of my life at fifteen years old, and now I'll live the rest of it surviving off of nothing but memories.

Even if we have this dance, even if I go upstairs with him, there's too much pain in the rearview for us to make this work.

"You look beautiful."

I can't stare directly at him; if I do, I'll get swept away in his current. That's what he does to me. He'll undoubtedly pull me under if I let my guard down for one second. If my heart's a compass, he's north.

He's always north.

I know I shouldn't, but I want one more night with him. Just one more hit, because make no mistake, I'm addicted to Gabriel Abbott.

43

GABE

OCTOBER PRESENT DAY

I f I were a better man, I'd leave her alone. I'd let her believe we could be nothing. I'd let her have a life that doesn't involve reliving the pain I caused her.

But I'm not.

I've tried, but I'm too selfish not to have her.

She's mine, always has been, and I'm sick of fighting it. I knew the second she strutted over she'd fall into me tonight. I could see it on her face. She's tired too, and I'll always be her soft place to land.

I wouldn't want it any other way.

She looks like she knows where this is headed, and I'd like to say she seems happy about it, but she's scared. I know how much I've hurt her, and I don't know how I'm supposed to fix it, but I have to.

With her arms around my neck, she asks, "Why didn't you move on?"

"You know why."

Her fingers move idly across the nape of my neck. "Yeah, but six years is a long time to be alone. You never thought maybe you could be happy with someone else?"

I shake my head.

"Weren't you lonely?"

"I would have been even if I'd been with someone else. No one gets me like you." I shrug. "It's always been you."

Her eyes drop to my mouth, and holy shit, I think I've been electrocuted. I've kissed her one time in the last six years. It wasn't enough. She stops swaying, lets her hand drop to my chest, and doesn't move. I can't tell if she's trying to decide what she wants or how to tell me she doesn't want this. If I weren't desperate, I might say something to let her off the hook.

"It's still you."

Finally, she sucks in a sharp breath, grips the back of my neck, and pulls me to her. Her berry-colored lips just brush mine at first. Then, something between us snaps. Her mouth presses into mine, and it's like sleeping in your own bed for the first time after a long week away.

With a hand on her back, I press her closer and deepen the kiss. Her lips part, and I dip my tongue into her mouth. She tastes like that fruity drink I threw on the floor. The room around us keeps going, but I can't tell because I'm solely focused on this moment.

She breaks the kiss, and her eyes lift to me. To hide her grin, she bites her bottom lip.

Her breathing quickens, and she stares at me for a beat. I'm about to tell her that she's the only thing that matters to me, and that I'd give up the world for her.

That I have.

But before I can get the words out, she says, "Take me upstairs, Gabriel."

Everything stops. If I could throw her over my shoulder and run up the stairs without drawing attention, I would.

"Yes, ma'am."

I kiss her again, grabbing her hand before leading her to my apartment.

She waltzes into the living room like she belongs here, and I guess that's because she does. The only time this place has ever felt like home was when she was here, and that's probably because she's the only thing I've ever cared to have.

She's all I'd grab in a fire.

She spins to face me and starts to work on the buttons of my shirt. Her eyes meet mine, and her breathing falters. Wrapping my hands around her wrists, I mutter, "You're sure?"

She nods, pausing for only a moment before going back to my buttons.

Then, her mouth is on my chest as she peels my shirt off, tossing it to the floor and wrapping her arms around my neck. I lift her, and she locks her legs around my waist.

With a hand in her hair, I devour her mouth, never letting her up for air as I carry her across the room. Kicking open my bedroom door, my heart pounds so hard I think she can probably feel it against hers. I toss her on my bed, standing over her to take in her heaving breaths through parted lips. When I finally lean over for one more kiss, her hands tangle in my hair like she's desperate to get closer. I yank her dress down and toss it to the floor, leaving her in nothing but a hot-pink thong.

I suck in a sharp breath. She's the most perfect woman I've ever seen, and there's never been a time she didn't take my breath away. She moans into my mouth as I press against her. My hands slide up her thighs to rest on her hips, and my lips brush over her collarbone before trailing down her chest until I reach her stomach.

I stop.

My heart twists.

She did it all alone. I'll never not regret that. There's a tiny sliver of glass lodged in my sternum from what happened. It'll never be removed. It'll slice and gnaw at me for the rest of my life because no matter what I say or do moving forward, I can never take it back.

She runs a hand into my hair, pulling me from my thoughts, and I move to her hip bone before pressing a kiss to the front of her lace panties.

"Please," she whispers.

A smile spreads across my lips.

If she gives me even a moment of her time, she won't ever have to ask for anything again; I'll give her everything. I slide off the tiny piece of lace and throw it across the room before resting her legs on my shoulders. When my breath hits her bare skin, she arches off the bed, gripping the sheets.

I'd gladly get lost in this woman. I thought I could just sleep with other women and it would be enough. But it wasn't like this. It couldn't be because Ash is my perfect match. She's the only person I've ever been drawn to like this. I felt that pull every day for six years, and I felt it again tonight.

She writhes against my hold, whimpering my name. I've missed that sound. I've missed every sound she makes.

Each soft press of my lips has her coming undone a little more. My tongue darts out to make a slow swipe and her legs clench.

I hum into her. "I've missed this, baby."

She starts to say something, but it turns to a gasp when I cover her clit with my mouth. I lick, and suck, and nip. As I slip a finger into her, her legs start to shake. It takes mere minutes for her to tighten around me.

When she finally comes down, I sit up and ditch the rest of my clothes, desperate to be inside her. The bedside lamp is the only light. It shines against the side of her face, leaving her glowing against my sheets.

She smiles up at me with her hair splayed around her like a spiraled halo. With heavy lids, she says, "You're so good at that."

I catch her bottom lip with my teeth, fist the back of her hair, and pull her head back. "Did you forget how much time I spent between your legs?"

She grinds, sliding against my cock.

I grin. "I didn't. I've been dreaming about it for six goddamn years."

Then, I sink into her. She gasps, throwing her head back. Her breathing picks up as I set the pace.

I'm home.

"Fuck, baby. You're so perfect," I groan, unable to stop staring because I've been denied the right to do so for so long, and I never want to look away again.

She is here, and she is mine. Something in me shifts. A desperate need to lay my claim.

I pull her head back again. "I don't know why you thought I was gonna let you blow me off tonight, love."

Defiance shines in her eyes. "You know why. You were paying attention to someone else."

I chuckle and bite her throat just enough to make her gasp before soothing it with my tongue.

When I lift my head again, I say, "You know better. My attention is always yours. You are mine."

She nods.

"Your words."

She pants, her lips parted, and whispers, "I'm yours."

The corner of my mouth lifts. "As much as I love that

jealous streak, it's getting old proving to you who I want in my bed. Who I want to bury my cock in. Who I want to love."

She stares at me with wide, round eyes. "Gabriel—"

"Do not say some bullshit we both know is a fucking lie."

Her lips clamp shut, and I pull away from her to stand at the end of the bed. She was about to tell me all about her doubts, and I don't want to hear it. I'm tired of hearing it. We belong together. She knows it, and I know it.

I yank her to the edge and slide into her again, letting my head fall back as she moans.

She locks her ankles around me, rolling her hips frantically. My thumb finds her clit.

"Oh my god," she groans.

Palming her ass, I slam into her until she flutters around me again, then I flip her over like a rag doll. "Put your hands on the headboard."

As she does, I take her in and go completely still.

"You little fucking liar." I run my thumb over the tattoo on her ass before smacking it with a pop.

She smirks over her shoulder. I suspected she was lying, but knowing that she had my initials on her ass every time that asshole fucked her, does something to me. I push her knees apart before lining up and sliding into her.

"Oh my god, Gabriel," she groans.

"You've missed me too, huh?"

She nods.

I lean forward and whisper, "I want to hear you say it."

"I missed you. God, I fucking missed you."

Gripping her hips, I let go and claim what has always been mine.

"You are so beautiful," I say softly between kissing the

middle of her back. Then I grab her hair with one hand and pull her back to my front.

It takes all of about three thrusts for her to fall over the edge again, panting and writhing. And I follow close behind.

44

ASH

OCTOBER PRESENT DAY

I knew I'd made a terrible mistake the second I woke up. I let myself get wrapped up with this man, again, despite knowing where it leads.

As I stand in his kitchen, trying to talk myself off the ledge, I see the journal sitting on the counter, a picture of the two of us sticking out of it. When I open it, I recognize the photo as one from my corkboard. The page it was marking reads,

Dear Ash,

Today I took Maggie to get ice cream while you worked. It's funny, I should have known she'd ask for a strawberry shake. How did you manage to make a perfect clone of yourself? I couldn't take my eyes off her the entire time. She's perfect. Her laugh sounds just like you too. It's adorable. Do you know what Gabby's Dollhouse is? She spent like twenty minutes telling me all about these cats or something. I wasn't really following. She rambles like you too. I still can't believe we made a human. My whole world flipped upside down, and now she's all I think about. When I see something pink at the store I think, Maggie would like this. I can't even get on my bike without thinking about how careful I need to be now because I have a daughter. Isn't that wild? Anyway, I miss you. I miss us. You're right there all the time, and I feel like I'm drowning. Being close enough to touch you and not being able to royally sucks.

Love,
Gabriel

I frantically flip to the first page, dated the day I left.

Ash,
Today was the worst day of my life.

When the cops showed up, I didn't know if you were even still alive. I'm sorry. I'm so fucking sorry. None of this would have happened if I'd just left you be. I knew we were a bad idea, but I couldn't help falling for you anyway. I showed up at the hospital the second I was bailed out, but your mom wouldn't let me see you. At first, I wanted to tell her to fuck off, but the longer I thought about it, the more I realized she's right. If I let you stay, you'll get hurt. I can't do that. I love you too much to do that. I can't explain to you how hard it was to look at the tears spilling from your eyes and tell you that I don't love you. I lied. I'm fucking miserable without you here. Sending you away was the right thing to do, but it might kill me. I'm not sure I want to live a single day without you. You're the sun. You're everything. I'm going to miss you, but I hope you end up happy. I hope you find someone who can love you as hard as I could. I'd say more, but that's not possible. I hope you move on and you never think about this place. I hope you never shed another tear over the lies I told you. You deserve the world, and if I could guarantee you'd be safe, I'd move heaven and earth to give it to you. I'm yours, always.

    I love you,
    Gabriel

Tears roll down my face as I hang on every word. Flipping a few pages, I stop on one from a few months after I left.

Ash,

    I'm sitting by the lake because I miss you. I want to call you. I want to tell you to come home. Don't tell anyone, but I'm really not okay. I haven't been since the day you left. But now my dad's dead. Things were weird between us after you left and now, I'll never see him again. Between you, Akers, and now my dad, I'm not sure I can handle losing anyone else. And on top of all of that, I'm about to inherit a club I don't even want. They're gonna have Dean take over for a while until I'm ready but to be honest, I don't think that day's coming. I don't think I'll ever be ready. There's no one I can talk to. You were it, and I wish you were here. I need you here. This is the hardest thing I've ever had to do. I keep having to remind myself that I'm doing this for you. If it were for me, I'd drag you home and never let you leave. But I can't be selfish with you. Please be okay right now. I need you to be okay because we can't both be miserable. This choice has to be good for one of us. So, for me, please be happy.

> I love you,
> Gabriel

My heart cracks. There are dozens of entries that span the last six years. I feel like I might throw up.

We're not capable of being a casual hookup; there's too much history. I love him. I never stopped loving him. He wanted me to be happy without him, and maybe I was to a degree, but not really.

I used to think that's how it was. Like, once you fall in love with someone, you're destined to feel that way forever, but now, I've realized that's not actually the case. Don't get me wrong, I care about Casey, but at some point, the pain killed what was left. But the pain could never kill the love I have for Gabriel.

We work well together as co-parents. I don't want to ruin that. It was stupid to think it wasn't a big deal. I was only giving myself an excuse to go through with it last night, because deep down, I knew we'd both be crushed when it was over.

We were too young to make the right choices, and we hurt each other, but the love was there.

Grabbing my things, I leave before Gabriel wakes up.

We can't do this.

Nik and Shane are getting married at the clubhouse. Maggie rode with my mom and Denny so I could come early to set up. I was here all morning before heading to Gran's to get ready. Luckily, none of the guys made an appearance while I was here, but my palms were sweaty the entire time.

I've only seen Gabriel once since the party a couple of weeks ago. He came by to see Maggie. I tried to stay busy and let them have their time together.

I'm sure there's a more mature way to deal with this situation, but I seem to have a problem keeping my wits when Gabriel Abbott's involved, so distance is probably the best answer for us.

When Jess and I pull up in the parking lot, I exit the car and open the door to my stepdad's truck beside us.

"Wow, you look beautiful," I coo, undoing Maggie's

seatbelt. She's staying with Colette for the first time tonight, and she's been talking about it for a week.

"We match," she squeals, gesturing to our mother-daughter blue-and-white sundresses.

After setting her on her feet, we walk into the building holding hands.

I never imagined there would be a day I'd allow my daughter to set foot in this place. It was actually a recurrent nightmare of mine, but before things got awkward, Gabriel assured me that she'd be safe. And I trust him with her.

"Well, if it isn't the two most beautiful girls I've ever seen," Gabriel says, walking over and picking Maggie up as we step into the building.

He looks like a dream in a pair of black jeans and a black T-shirt, except for the shiner on his left eye.

"I've missed you!" he says, hugging her tightly.

She giggles, snuggling into him. It's only been a couple of months, but they've become thick as thieves.

Gabriel's gaze runs lazily over me before he winks.

"Is that my Maggie girl!" Colette shouts from across the room.

Maggie leaps from Gabriel's arms to run to her. "Nana!"

Colette picks her up, and they go over to Shane and Nik.

"I think she likes my mom more than me." He laughs.

"Hell, I'm her mom, and I think she likes her more than me, too." I grin, turning my attention from my daughter to him. "What happened to your face?"

He touches the black eye. "Fight night."

I tilt my head to the side, a half-laugh slipping from my lips. "Isn't that frowned upon?"

He shrugs. "No coping skills."

The rehearsal goes off without a hitch, and we settle in for dinner. It's kind of nice to be here all together. It's like our family's finally come full circle. It's a little awkward between my mom and Shane, but I'm glad she showed up.

"We're gonna head to our hotel. If you need anything later, call," Denny says, leaning down to kiss my head before he walks over to my mom, who's saying goodbye to Shane and Nik.

Not long after, Colette takes Maggie home while we clean up. I'm picking up the centerpieces when I hear shouting from outside the club.

"What the fuck," Gabriel mutters from where he's putting folding chairs on a rack across the room. He takes off toward the door, followed by my brother, then everyone else. As I step out the door, my blood runs cold. My dad stands near the building. Two older members blocking his way.

My heart pounds in my chest, and I can't breathe.

Gabriel charges him. "Do you have a fucking death wish?"

He collides with my dad, shoving him to the wall with an arm to his throat and getting right in his face, his neck turning a deep crimson.

"My kid's getting married! I deserve to be here."

"The only place you deserve to be is in the ground!" His voice sends a chill down my spine.

My dad's false-calm mask slips into place. "You have a lot of nerve to speak to me that way after what you did to my daughter."

"At least I'd never hurt my own kid."

With a malicious grin, my dad says, "Easy for you to say, you abandoned yours."

Gabriel rears back before slamming his forehead into

his nose. Blood sprays. Before my dad can right himself, Gabriel swings, and he goes down.

Gabriel's nostrils flare, and he grinds his teeth. Before he can hit him again, my dad lunges, taking them both to the ground.

My feet move in their direction, but I don't make it far before an arm hooks around my shoulders. JT stands over me. He shakes his head, and I let my eyes fall back to the blood bath in front of me.

Curses and grunts fly but nothing coherent as they twist and struggle.

JT reaches for Shane, but he's already pushed through the crowd. His foot collides with my dad's side.

He cocks his fist, but before he can throw the punch, Nik grabs his arm and throws her full bodyweight back. "Shane! Stop!"

He staggers.

He doesn't hear her.

Pulling a gun from his waistband, he points it at our dad, and my stomach churns.

JT pulls me to his chest, but I can't take my eyes off my brother.

Gabriel jumps to his feet, watching Shane, who's trembling, fury rolling off him in waves.

"Big man," our dad spits from the ground. "Gonna shoot your own dad?"

Shane stiffens.

"He's not worth it!" Nik shouts. "Listen!"

He doesn't move.

"You really are a worthless piece of shit!" my dad spits. "You boys are gonna get what's coming for you. Mark my words."

Shane's nostrils flare, and the gun shakes in his hand.

"Shane!" She places a hand on his bicep, her voice more of a cry than a scream this time. "Please! Stop!"

That's when he hears it.

He takes a deep breath, turning his head to look at her as he lowers the gun. She places her hands on his face.

Something in her eyes has him coming back from the edge of that dark place. His face softens slightly, and his shoulders relax. He stares at her for a moment, sucking his teeth before glancing at our father who's rising from the ground. "Don't come back. You're not welcome."

He spits on the ground before stomping away with Nik on his heels.

One of the older members moves to help my dad the rest of the way up.

"Someone get him the hell out of here," Gabriel shouts over his shoulder as he stomps back toward the clubhouse. When he lifts his eyes to JT, who's on the phone with someone, he shouts, "What the hell!"

JT pulls the phone from his face, shaking his head. "I don't know. My guy isn't answering."

"Fuck!" Gabriel runs his hands over his face as he disappears inside.

Racing inside to grab something from my purse, I come back in time to find my dad stalking toward his car in the parking lot. "Wait!"

They stop. My dad's face softens like he thinks I'm coming to check on him.

I swallow, collecting all the courage I can muster. "Just so you know, I don't hate you."

He stares at me but says nothing.

"I might have even been able to forgive you for how you treated me."

"Ashton—" He steps in my direction, and I take a step back, holding my hand up to stop him.

"But I'll never forgive you for what you did to Shane. All I ever wanted was to be loved." I exhale, biting my top lip. "I don't know what happened to you that you didn't know how to do that, but I don't hate you. I just don't ever want to see you again."

He nods, running his tongue over his top teeth. I think he might say something else, but he doesn't. Instead, he stalks away.

"Here," I say, walking toward him.

As he turns back to me, I hold out the small jewelry box. It's been in my purse since I found it.

His eyes flick to the box and back up at me.

"Take it, and don't contact me or Shane again."

He grabs the box before walking away.

Tears well in my eyes, and I stand in the parking lot, watching him leave.

I mean it. I don't hate him. But I can't forgive him for almost taking my brother from us.

I hadn't noticed but JT stands behind me, watching.

"Sorry, I wasn't trying to eavesdrop, but I couldn't let you come out here with him alone." He holds out his arms.

I crash into his chest, laughing through the tears rolling down my face. "It's okay. You really weren't lying about being a good friend."

"I know my strong suits," he murmurs, a grin spreading across his face. "You alright?"

I pull back. "I always am, aren't I?"

His mouth turns down. When I waltz back into the club, Shane's sitting at a table with his face in his hands while Nik talks in his ear, and Gabriel's nowhere to be found.

I saddle up at the bar and wait for everyone to leave so I can help clean up. There's no way I can get through the rest of this weekend sober.

"Hey, where'd Gabe go?" JT asks, coming up to sit beside me.

I shrug.

"Are you kidding me? You guys are so annoying. Make up already." He laughs.

"I can't. This life—" I let out a long exhale. "I can't do this."

He narrows his eyes at me, opening and closing his mouth before finally saying, "He didn't tell you?"

"Tell me what?"

His brows raise. "Gabe quit the club."

"What?"

"Yeah. Right before the bachelor party. I can't believe he didn't tell you. I mean, it's not official yet, but once the club decides who's taking over, he's done."

"Why would he do that?"

"Are you really asking me that?" He stares at me like I'm dumb.

I shake my head in disbelief.

"If he's president, he can't have you and Maggie. He made his choice."

My hand flies to my mouth. "Oh my god."

"Ash, he loves you."

I sit with my mouth open, trying to process what the fuck is happening. Why didn't he say something? He let me walk away, knowing he'd given up everything for me. God, he's such a fucking asshole. I would have—

Would I have? Quitting the club doesn't fix everything, does it?

Finally, I say, "What if things don't work out again? It's

more than just me that would get hurt this time. I can't do that to her."

"And what if things do work out?"

I scoff. "Well, if history has taught us anything, it's that it won't."

His brows furrow. "No, if history has taught you anything, it should be that you will always find your way back to each other."

I turn in my seat to face him.

"Look, I can't tell you what to do, but I know Gabe. He's learned his lesson. I think you're doing both of you a disservice if you don't at least try."

45

———

GABE

OCTOBER PRESENT DAY

I'd tear off my own damn arm to start over with Ash. When I brought her back to my apartment, I planned to tell her I was leaving the Riders. Then I got wrapped up in the moment. How could I not? She was looking at me like she did before I fucked everything up. I figured I'd tell her the next morning. When I woke up and she was gone, the world came crashing down around me. The whole time I thought we were starting a new chapter, she was closing the book.

After what happened with her dad, I needed to get out of there. I would have killed him, but that feels like it should be up to Shane. He made his choice tonight.

I'm standing in the kitchen when someone knocks. Padding over to the door, I grumble under my breath. I'm not in the fucking mood to deal with anyone.

Swinging open the door, all the air leaves my lungs.

Ash offers me a tight smile. With her hands clasped in front of her, she asks, "Can I come in?"

This would be a great time to say no. To say, *I just need*

some space. Please give me a fucking break because I can't be near you without my chest caving in and my head spinning.

But I love her. So instead, I move to the side and say, "Uh. Sure."

"Listen, Gabriel—"

Yeah, I can't fucking do this again. I need her out of here before I explode.

"Ash—" Pressing my fingers in my eyes, I say, "If you didn't come here to tell me you've changed your mind, please let me be. I can't do this tonight."

We've done enough of this.

I take a step back. The last few months have settled into my bones, and I'm tired. Tired of fighting back how I feel, tired of thinking we might get to the other side only to be disappointed, and tired of pretending I don't love her with every fiber of my being. I don't know who I am without my club, but more than that, I don't know who I am without her.

"I..." She takes a deep breath. "I think I might have been wrong."

I'm not sure where she's going with this, so I just stare at her. Hoping to hear words from her mouth is not the same as actually hearing them, and hoping left me waking up alone last time.

"I'm afraid of what it'll look like if this doesn't work. I'm afraid of what Maggie's life will look like if we explode again."

There it is. The same fucking shit—around we go. I put my hands of my hips and sigh. "Yeah, you've said that."

"No, I know. I just—" She stares at her feet. "I realized tonight that I might also be afraid of what my life looks like without you."

A tear rolls down her cheek as she snaps her eyes back to mine.

My breath catches in my throat and my pulse quickens. I can't take more heartbreak from this girl. She's fucking killing me.

"What are you saying?"

"I'm saying..." She squeezes her eyes shut, covering them with her fingers. "Shit, I don't know what I'm saying. I just don't want to get hurt again." Stepping toward me, she places a hand on my face. "The thing is, being away from you really hurts, too."

Another tear falls, and I can't stop myself from wiping it away with my thumb. Call it self-preservation but I still don't know if I'm sure why she's here.

"Did you quit the Riders?" she asks.

I try to say yes, but it gets caught in my throat, so I nod.

The air between us grows thick as she stares at me like she's trying to decide what to do next.

A steady beat thrums in my ears while I wait for her to choose our fate once again.

Then, as if she can tell that I'm about to implode, her lips crash into mine, and that's it. It's almost palpable the moment we both give up.

Pulling back, I mutter, "Are you sure? Because I can't stand to lose you again. If this isn't for real, you have to go. I love you, but I can't—"

"I'm sure." With tear streaks down her face she nods, a smile gracing her lips. "I'm so fucking sure."

My shoulders relax and I let out a breath, grabbing her face and wiping away the tears. "Thank fucking God. I swear, no matter what happens, you'll never have to do this alone."

She nods.

"I love you, Ash."

Her sobs are broken by a laugh as she says, "I've always loved you."

46

ASH

OCTOBER PRESENT DAY

Gabriel lifts me, his hands splayed across my ribs, and I wrap my legs around him before he walks us through the living room to the kitchen. Setting me on the counter, he pulls away, taking me in. His chest heaves as he creeps closer to me, each step causing my heart to beat just a little harder. As he gets close enough to touch me, he runs his hands up my thighs and under my dress before ripping it up over my head to leave me in nothing but a black thong.

He takes half a step back to run his eyes over my bare skin, and I feel like I can't breathe.

"Fuuuuck, Ash," he practically growls before grabbing my hips.

My heart explodes. I didn't realize just how much I needed to hear him say I'm not less than he remembered.

He closes in, stopping before his lips meet mine to say, "My imagination over the last six years doesn't even come close to the real thing."

Catching my ear between his teeth, he presses himself between my legs and inhales me.

I grin to myself because I know that feeling. I could breathe him in for eternity and it wouldn't be enough. I grip the countertop, and he presses harder, causing my thighs to clench around him.

He pulls back, sliding his hand into my hair. His lips caress mine, gentle and sweet. It's not passion or the heat of the moment. It's like savoring something.

When our mouths part, he drops to the floor between my legs.

Here's the thing, no man has ever compared to him like this. He's the only one who's ever known my body and my mind the way he does. We know parts of each other that no one else can ever know, and that's part of what makes it so hard to stay away.

He kisses the inside of my thigh, wrapping his hand around it. With each inch he travels closer to my core, my skin pebbles in the wake of his path. When he reaches his destination, he slides his fingers under the lace and pulls the thong down my legs, tossing it aside. I tremble in his grip.

When his eyes land on the faded scar on the inside of my leg, he swallows and closes his eyes, letting out a deep breath before his lips brush over the place I was shot. I want to tell him that it's okay, and that I'm fine, when his glistening gaze lifts to me. But nothing that happened was okay, and we both know that.

Eventually, he runs his hands up my bare thighs and swallows down the pain we've both been feeling since that day.

He wraps his other arm around my leg, and his breath lands on my core, causing me to shudder. Pulling me forward until my ass is at the edge of the counter, he places his mouth to my center, his tongue finding my clit. My back arches, my head falling back to rest against the cabinet. I reach down, gripping his hair as his tongue works in long, slow strokes.

Gabriel works me slowly into coming without much effort at all. It sneaks up on me, and I moan, holding onto him for dear life.

He stands, wiping his mouth with his thumb. His eyes darken. "That was my last apology. Now, it's your turn."

I rear back, pinching my brows.

He leans in closer. "You lied about that tattoo on your ass. You're gonna pay for that."

I squeal as he wraps an arm around my waist and picks me up. He explores every inch of my mouth as he carries me to his bedroom and drops me onto the mattress.

Towering over me, he tears his shirt off over his head. He really is a work of art. Especially now. Every muscle is visible under his smooth sun-kissed skin. I'm gawking but I can't help it. He unbuckles his belt so slow, I think I might scream. I squirm, rubbing my legs together, and the corner of his mouth lifts.

He's fucking with me.

"Jesus, Gabriel. Could you hurry the fuck up? If you aren't inside of me in about thirty seconds, I might explode."

He laughs. "I don't know how, but I think you've gotten *more* impatient."

I glare at him. "You're gonna think impatient when I get up and leave."

"You're not leaving." He undoes his pants, and my eyes snag on just how badly he wants me.

"I might."

When I lift them back to his face, he winks, slipping out of his jeans.

He bites his bottom lip. "You're in enough shit right now, I wouldn't test your luck."

I roll my eyes. "Because I lied about the tattoo?"

In one swift move, he grabs my hair and yanks my head back. "Because you've been driving me fucking crazy for six months since you came back. You're all I think about. All I dream about. Just you all the goddamn time."

I smirk up at him. "That sounds like a you problem. I don't know why I'm being blamed."

He huffs. "I do kinda like it when you're mean, though. That's new."

Just as I start to respond he adds, "With that being said, lay down and shut up."

My mouth pops open at his fucking audacity. If I wasn't on the verge of spontaneous combustion, I might actually walk out right now.

"Close your mouth, love." He takes my hand, placing it over the bulge in his briefs. "Unless you'd like me to shove this down your throat instead."

I stare up at him wide-eyed. I'd like to say I don't like it when he talks like that. That this Gabriel doesn't do it for me, but damn it—It's so fucking hot.

I scramble forward, perching on the edge of the bed on my knees. "And what if I *want* you to do that?"

His breath hitches, and his lip's part. I caught him off guard. Good. He should have known I wouldn't back down.

I grin, batting my lashes and flipping over on to my back with my head hanging off the bed.

He's still looking down at me without moving.

"What are you waiting for? An invitation?" I sigh. Dramatically, I say, "Please, Gabriel, put your cock in my mouth."

He narrows his eyes, trying to hold back a smile, but it doesn't work. He slides down his briefs until it springs free, and I lick my lips just before he steps forward and places the tip to my mouth. I open, letting him slide against my tongue. He groans, his head falling back.

He glides back and forth before sliding all the way to the back of my throat. I gag and he pulls back.

"Take a breath." This time, his voice is soft and tender.

I suck air in through my nose.

"Ready?" he asks, and I nod before he slides it back again.

When I swirl my tongue around the tip, he groans. "Fuuuuck, Ash."

Pulling away from me, he slides out of my mouth altogether with a pop. "Turn around."

I nod, flipping around, but when I start to lay back, he shakes his head. "On your belly."

Letting my feet drop to the floor, I spin and feel his hand press between my shoulder blades until I'm bent over the edge of the bed. As he slides into me, his fingers dig into my hips. My legs shake from his long, slow thrusts. Grabbing the back of my thigh, he props one of my knees on the edge of the bed.

"You feel—" A gravelly sound similar to a growl leaves his throat.

"More," I beg.

He doesn't pick up his pace, but slams into me harder. I grip the sheets, whimpering and squirming under him.

His weight presses down on me as he leans forward, gripping under my chin to turn my head before pressing his lips to mine.

Unable to hold back, I break apart again, moaning into his mouth. When he lets go, I go limp on the bed as he swells inside me and lets out a guttural sound, his hold on my hips tightening.

We take our time, soaking up every minute of make-up

sex before heading back downstairs to finish cleaning. Everyone filters out until it's just us, Jess, and JT. She's sitting on a barstool next to him, laughing.

"She's gonna ruin him." I giggle, leaning back into Gabriel's arms.

"Nah, he's a fucking masochist." He chuckles. "He loves a woman who can tear him apart. There's something wrong with him."

"Some could say the same thing about you."

"I'd rather you not ruin me, but if that's the only way I get you, I'll gladly go along."

—

47

ASH

OCTOBER PRESENT DAY

I slip into my black satin bridesmaid's dress. It has an open back and a high slit up one side. Nik and I are getting dressed in my bedroom at Gran's like we used to when we were teenagers about to sneak out.

After I finish lacing up Nik's dress, she spins to face me. I'm not kidding when I say she is the most beautiful bride I've ever seen. She's not girly, so it's kind of shocking to see her in a full gown, but she's stunning. It has a sculpted corset bodice with an A-line skirt and a slit up the side just shy of her hip.

"You look beautiful."

Tears pool in her eyes. "I almost can't believe this is happening. A year ago, I was worried I'd wake up to find him dead, and now I get to spend the rest of my life with the best version of him."

I wipe a tear away before it can ruin her makeup.

"You deserve this. I'm so happy for you."

She fans herself. "Fuck. What are we, a couple of blubbering idiots? I don't know what's wrong with me. Crying's your thing!" I laugh and wrap my arms around her. "Thank you for always being here."

"I love you." I pull back, grabbing her hands.

"I love you, too."

"Now, let's officially make you my sister." I laugh.

"Hell yeah, fuck being his wife. We're about to be sisters!"

All the girls pile into the car to head over to the club. Colette met us at the house so I could get Maggie ready. Colette's been the one solid parent in Shane's life since he moved here. Gran tried, but even she couldn't get through to him like Colette can. Shane asked her if she'd sit in the front with the parents, and she burst into tears.

The girls stow away in one of the rooms to wait for the ceremony to start. The black leather couch sticks to the bare skin of my back. Jess plops down next to me, adjusting the straps on her black heels.

"So, what's your deal with JT?" I ask.

"What? Nothing." She shrugs. "It's casual."

"Oh my god. Jess, do you like him?" I whisper-yell.

"No! Shut up. It's just sex."

Narrowing my eyes, I tease, "Liar."

"You know what, Ash?" She whips her head in my direction, flinging her hair over her shoulder, and pins me with a dirty look. "Worry about your own shit."

"Okay, but don't fuck him over. He's a nice guy and he doesn't deserve your bullshit."

"Yeah, okay. Got it." She stands, stomping away.

I step out into the hall for a second to make sure everything's ready to start, when I run straight into someone.

Gabriel's in an all-black suit with his hair pulled back.

"Holy shit, General," he says with a slow drawl.

I roll my eyes; I did not miss that nickname.

Okay, maybe I did.

"You cannot wear that. You'll never make it down the aisle before I drag you into a dark corner and rip it off."

"Shut up." I swat his arm. "You look pretty good yourself." I reach up on my tiptoes to kiss him. "Want to see Maggie?"

He grins. "More than anything."

Everyone is dancing and drinking at the reception when Maggie races over to us.

"Daddy, did you see that?" She grabs Gabriel's arm.

He goes still, staring at her for a second before swallowing. Then his mouth spreads into a smile and he picks her up.

"Yeah, Mags. That was awesome."

He lets out a warm laugh, hugging her tightly.

I know he said he didn't care if she never called him that, but it's obvious he hoped she would one day.

She hops down, taking off to dance with the other kids.

"Daddy," I say, nudging him as I try to hold back a grin.

He pulls me to his chest, bringing his mouth to the shell of my ear and purrs, "We will be ditching this reception if you start calling me that."

He winks as a blush creeps up my neck, and I giggle.

After kissing me, he jogs out to the dance floor and picks up our daughter. They twirl around with matching smiles.

"He's good with her, huh?"

Glancing over, I find the groom standing next to me.

Taking a few steps back to our table, I sit, gesturing for Shane to do the same.

"Yeah, he is. Getting baby fever already?" I tease.

"No way." He laughs. "No babies for me. I'm barely able to keep myself alive."

My brows pinch in the middle. "I'm so proud of you."

"Thanks." He nudges my shoulder. "We turned out pretty alright, all things considered."

"So, you two are good?" I nod to where Gabriel dips Maggie while she almost hyperventilates from laughter.

"I think so." He looks down at his hands. "I'd do it again if you asked me to." His eyes flick up to mine. "You're my sister. I'll always take your side."

One corner of my mouth lifts and I drop my eyes to the table. "I don't know how he managed to forgive me, honestly."

"He loves you. That's how."

"Are you happy?" I ask, because sometimes it's hard to tell. He seems to be dealing with everything pretty well, but sometimes you can see the storm raging in his stare.

A wide smile spreads across his face. "Yeah. I'm so fucking happy."

I lean forward, throwing my arms around him.

When people start having too much to drink, my mom and Denny leave with Maggie. I'm supposed to help tear everything down, but the reception doesn't seem to be slowing anytime soon. If nothing else, this club loves a good party. I'm standing at the bar waiting for a drink when Gabriel wraps his arms around me. He's ditched the jacket and has his black dress-shirt sleeves rolled up, showing off a brand-new magnolia tattoo on his forearm.

"We should get married," he says into my hair.

I laugh, spinning to face him. "Okay."

"I'm serious. Fuck it. Let's get married."

"We can't. I'm technically still married!"

"Well, not right now obviously." He braces himself on the bar with a hand on either side of me. "But we could probably get a marriage license like, I don't know, the day you're officially divorced."

He grins, and I still can't tell if he's joking.

"You're crazy!" I shove his shoulder.

"Maybe." He shrugs.

"You're serious?"

"Dead fucking serious." He wraps a strong arm around my waist, and I don't know what to say.

"Gabriel, we just decided to give this another shot. That's insane."

"Yeah. I mean, maybe, but I'm certain I won't change my mind, so why not?" He kisses my neck. "Also, I fucking hate Ashton James."

Swatting him on the back, I squeal, "We can't get married because you don't like my last name."

"No?" He pulls back to look into my eyes.

"What about because I love you so fucking much, I can't stand the idea of spending another moment without you."

"We don't even live in the same town! We have a lot to figure out before we get married."

He sucks his teeth. "I've been thinking about that actually. I can't completely leave Ravens Ridge. Not yet at least. Even once I'm done with the club, I still own the shop. And I'll still need a job, so I don't think walking away from it is an option. I think we should move into Gran's. I know you've been trying to sell it, but it feels weird for anyone else to live there. That's our place."

"Don't you worry that someone with a grudge might come after us if we're still here?"

"We'll get security cameras and shit. Plus, everyone knows our business now. They'd find us no matter where we are. At least here, we've got all the guys as back up."

And it is crazy, but why can't I think of a single reason not to? The only thing I want in this world is for all three of us to be together.

I run my thumb over his bottom lip.

"Is that a yes? You'll move here and marry me?" he asks with that cocky smirk.

I glare. "It's a maybe. Let's talk about it tomorrow when you haven't been drinking. How am I supposed to know if this is real or you're just fucked up?"

"Oh, I'm fucked up, baby. I've been fucked up since the day I met you."

48

———

GABE

DECEMBER PRESENT DAY

Waltzing out of our bedroom this morning, I'm stopped dead in my tracks as I reach the kitchen. Bob Dylan's "Mr. Tambourine Man" plays from the CD player on the counter. Ash dances around at the stove in nothing but my shirt with a spatula in one hand. She's fucking adorable. I cross my arms, leaning on a shoulder. It's possible I'd be content to sit and watch her for the rest of my life.

Eventually, she notices me and cracks up. "Excuse me. Creep much?"

"I was just enjoying the show," I chuckle.

I spent the weekend after the wedding installing a security system, and we moved into her Gran's house a couple of weeks later. It was quick, and everyone probably thinks we've lost our damn minds, but I don't want to spend another second without her or Maggie.

She scrunches up her nose and chuckles. "Breakfast's almost ready."

I walk over and wrap my arms around her from

behind. "There's nothing in this kitchen I want for breakfast."

Her eyes bulge, and she rolls her lips under before smacking me with the spatula.

"Gabriel!" she squeals. "Maggie's asleep right down the hall!"

I lean down, grab her thighs, and lift her onto the counter. "Good. Then she won't hear us making her a sibling."

She narrows her eyes, wrapping her arms around my neck. "There will be no siblings for a very long time. And some of us like to eat actual food in the morning."

Smiling, I kiss her lips before stepping back to let her climb down from the counter.

"So, what's the plan for today?"

She pulls plates down from the cabinet, standing on her tiptoes to reach them. "Everyone's coming at noon. I need you to run to the shop and pick up the tables and chairs when you have time."

She planned some sort of Christmas dinner with everyone for tonight. Maggie's thrilled because that means she'll get to play with Ryker and Scarlett, JT's kids. The three of them have been thick as thieves since we moved in.

Ash even invited Lily. She won't admit this, but I think Lily's starting to grow on her. Usually, I just spend the holidays with Mom, but Ash insisted that we do something with everyone, and I'll go along with anything she wants.

"Yes, ma'am." With a grin, I say, "There's a Christmas gift for you out front."

She laughs. "Christmas isn't for two more days."

Wrapping an arm around her, I whisper into her hair, "I know, but it's supposed to snow tonight, and I want you to have it before then."

She narrows her eyes, stepping out of my hold to pad toward the door. When she swings it open, her jaw drops at the sight of her brand-new red Jeep. I don't know when she got rid of her old one, but she's made a few comments over the last month that made me think she misses it. The look on her face tells me I was right.

"Stop!" she squeals. "You did not get me a Jeep!"

She whips her head to me then back to the vehicle before launching out the door, off the porch, and into the driver's seat.

I'd do anything to keep that look on her face.

From the driver's seat she yells, "Go get Maggie! We're going for a drive right now!"

"You should probably put on pants first."

She looks down at her bare legs like she didn't realize she wasn't wearing any despite the temperature.

"Shit! Okay." She jumps out and prances toward me. "Pants, then we go." Wrapping her arms around my neck, she presses her lips to mine. "Thank you, thank you, thank you. I love it!"

"I love you," I say between her flurry of kisses.

She finally stops, pats my chest, and just before rushing to change says, "Now, go wake her up."

I've never seen her get dressed faster in my life. Within ten minutes we're on the road. The radio blares while both of my girls sing along, not missing a word. Ash beams, her hair pulled on top of her head. My daughter in the back seat sports the same messy look. Next to her is Chaos, our rottweiler—well, he's ours now. Dean bought him for my mom when Dad died. He said she needed someone to guard the house. Shortly after we moved in here, Mom brought him to us. Ash said no, but Maggie took all of five minutes to fall in love with him and give her puppy-dog eyes, and Ash caved. Now we have a guard dog.

I can't help but smile because I've honest to god never been happier. This is all I ever wanted. I can survive losing my club, but losing these two would no doubt kill me. A bright laugh leaves Ash's lips. It's still my favorite sound. Even in the dead of winter, it sounds like summer.

EPILOGUE GABRIEL
APRIL PRESENT DAY

Here I am, standing under the magnolia tree behind Gran's house patiently waiting for Ash to come down to me. Shane stands next to me with JT as Nik walks toward us, followed by Jess, and then my perfect daughter.

She's beautiful in the new dress. Ash told her she could pick out anything she wanted, and in true Maggie fashion, she picked something pink.

Then Ash appears, and all of the air evaporates from my lungs. She's in the white sundress she wore the night she came to the clubhouse six years ago. I swallow, trying to hold back a smile, but I can't.

Ash is the sun.

There's an invisible rope tying me to her. She's the one I want to wake up to everyday for the rest of my life.

It took me six years to realize it wasn't the club or my dad standing in my way. It was me. All I had to do was make the decision and let her in. And fuck me, she's in now. She's all over me and under my skin.

Her curls sway in the breeze as she walks toward me, looking every bit like the golden ray of light she is.

When she's finally right in front of me, she says, "Sure you want to do this?"

"I've never been so sure of anything." I lift a brow. "Are you?"

She grins at me, nodding.

Dean's officiating the ceremony. Does he have any qualifications to do so? No. But you can get ordained online, and who else would we pick?

"Welcome! Thank you for joining us to finally watch Gabe and Ash tie the knot. It's about damn time."

There's a soft chuckle from the crowd.

"Gabe made it clear I was to make this short. So, let's get right to the vows." He gestures to me first.

I pull the piece of paper from my pocket and clear my throat. "Fuck, here it goes."

The paper shakes in my grip. "Ash, I don't normally do all of this mushy shit, so you'll have to forgive me if this sucks."

She smiles.

"I've spent my whole life preparing to take over the club. I knew it'd be tough, and I'd face my share of challenges. But nothing could have prepared me for losing you. My darkest nights, and my brightest days are all reserved for you. They always have been. You were the only thing I've never been able to let go of. I knew that long before I knew you'd given me Maggie." I glance over and wink at my daughter. "Even after being torn apart, we still found our way back. For as long as I live, you have my loyalty, my protection, and my love. I'm not promising flowers or a white picket fence, but I promise to be here when things get rough. I promise to take you to the lake when words aren't enough to fix things, and I promise to make you never feel like an obligation to me. I will choose you every single day of my life, even when you're being a complete pain in my ass."

She laughs.

"You are the love of my life, my partner, and my general." The crowd snickers, and Ash shoots me a look. I knew I'd probably get it for that, but I don't care. "From this day forward, you and Maggie have all of me. Forever."

With tears in her eyes, Ash reaches out and squeezes my hand. Dean nods at her next.

She takes a paper from Jess.

"Gabriel, we've never had it easy, have we? Long before we fell apart, everyone told me who they thought you were. I didn't believe it then, and I still don't now, because you spent that time showing me the real you. Nothing could keep me away. I don't need perfect, or easy. Only you. I promise to stand with you through the chaos and be the place you can always come home to. I promise to love you, always. And I promise to kick your ass if you don't stop calling me General." She laughs.

She better get in fighting shape because that's never going to happen. I wink before she finishes by saying, "From this day forward, I am yours."

Dean continues with the exchanging of rings before pronouncing us husband and wife.

It might be six years too late, but I finally kiss my bride. Ashton fucking Abbott.

Continue reading for a sneak peek of what's to come in Book 2

NIK
APRIL

"I'm so glad you came," Ash says, pulling me in for a hug.

"I wouldn't miss it for the world." I feel horrible for being basically MIA for the last month. Especially since she's been in full wedding mode, but I didn't have it in me to pretend I'm not hanging on by a thread.

"Is everything okay?" she asks, a deep crease forming between her brows.

"Yeah." I try to muster a genuine smile, but I'm not sure it's working. "Just busy."

Her shoulders slump just a hair. She's not buying it. "Okay... I'm here if you need me."

Thank God, someone pulls her away to offer their congratulations before she can try to hug me. I'm fairly sure that might do me in at this point.

I make my way to the bar and pour myself a shot. I couldn't miss my best friend's wedding, but I want to be anywhere but here. Not because I don't love her. If my life hadn't completely imploded a month ago, I'd be thrilled to be here.

"Hey, can we talk?" A hand lands on my lower back, and a chill runs up my neck.

I close my eyes and let out a long breath. *Please go away.*

When I finally turn around, Shane's looking down at me. My stomach does a flip, and I want to climb out of my skin. He's devastating in a dark blue button-up and gray dress pants. He's healthier than I've ever seen him.

"No."

"Nik, come on. Just give me five minutes."

I look around to see if anyone is watching. "Today's about Ash. I'm not doing this with you here."

"Here? You won't talk to me anywhere."

Every cell in my body is screaming for me to fall into him. To wrap my arms around his neck and never let go. But I can't, and if we open all of this up here, we won't be able to undo it.

"Take a hint." It comes out sharp enough to slice my own heart right in half. I give him my back, focusing on the shot glass in front of me. "I don't want to talk to you."

He positions himself beside me.

"Nik—" Something hardens in his eyes when they land on my empty ring finger.

His gaze meets mine, and he huffs. It takes all my strength to walk away from him when he looks so sad, but I'm not ready to have this conversation.

I'm not sure I'll ever be.

ACKNOWLEDGMENTS

If you'd told me when I was younger that I'd be writing a book—this book nonetheless—I wouldn't have believed you, but here we are. It has been a journey to say the least, but if you're holding this in your hands, that means we made it. Hell Yeah!

None of this would have been possible though without the incredible support around me. When I say I have the best people in my life, I mean it.

To my readers, writing this book was for me, but publishing it was for you. I genuinely hope you got something out of it. I know I did. Thank you for picking it up. Thank you for taking a chance on me. By doing so, you've given me an outlet to share more of what's in this chaotic brain of mine.

To my husband, thank you for always pushing me to be me. Thank you for talking me off the ledge when I get overwhelmed and picking up the slack when I need it. Thank you for loving me so hard every single day. You are the reason I'm not afraid to do things like WRITE A DAMN BOOK! You believe in me even when I don't, and I love you more than I could ever put into words.

To my children, you are the reason I do anything. You are the sun and the moon and all of the stars. I hope this shows you that you can do anything you want to do. No matter what, your mom will always be in the front row cheering you on. I love you with every ounce of my soul.

To my parents, you are really the reason I am the weirdo I am, I guess. Thank you for allowing me to hide in my room for hours as a child, making up stories in my head. Thank you for always showing me that love matters more than anything else.

To Hannah, I think maybe you deserve the most thanks of all, but we did it! I say we because I feel like you've held my hand every step of the way. What a blessing it has been to have you back in my life. Thank you for being my biggest fan/cheerleader. Thank you for brainstorming with me and encouraging me to fight for my art. I'm so thankful to have a friend like you.

To my beta readers, thank you for all of your kind words and thoughtful feedback.

To Nealey, thank you for reading this book at its absolute worst and loving it anyway.

To Kierra, where do I even begin? Thank you for helping me with branding and marketing, for your encouragement every step of the way. But mostly thank you for being you. You're an inspiration, and you push me to reach my own goals. I love you.

To JJ, thank you for all of your help. This book would not be what it is without you. Thank you for being a mentor and a friend. And mostly, thanks for listening to my crazy ass ramble.

To Haley, without you, I wouldn't have known where to go with this. I had no clue what I was doing when I sat down at my laptop. You took the time to read a very messy early draft and pointed me in the exact right direction. Thank you!

To Peyton, you're my favorite adult on the planet. Thank you for keeping me sane. I don't know what I'd do without you. Thank you for loving me even when I don't love myself and for always telling me what I need to hear.

ABOUT THE AUTHOR

DJ is a midwestern mom and wife who loves books so much she sat down and wrote one. Born with a wild imagination, that lives on through the words and worlds she's created. In her spare time she likes to read, roller-skate, and yap, and can be seen telling anyone who'll listen about her current read. She's messy and chaotic, but life's too short to be bored.

She grew up loving shows like One Tree Hill, Gossip Girl, and Greek. So, to say she loves drama would be an understatement. She loves a book with juicy drama, heart stopping romance, and edge of your seat yearning. That's what she aims to do with her books.

9 798994 563809